VILLAGE BOSS

VILLAGE BOSS

Ronenin Duval

Fresh Ink Group
Guntersville

Village Boss

Fresh Ink Group
An Imprint of:
The Fresh Ink Group, LLC
1021 Blount Avenue #931
Guntersville, AL 35976
Email: info@FreshInkGroup.com
FreshInkGroup.com

Edition 1.0 2023

Covers by Stephen Geez / FIG
Covert Art by Anik / FIG
Book design by Amit Dey / FIG
Associate publisher Beem Weeks / FIG

Cataloging-in-Publication Recommendations:

FIC049070 FICTION / African American & Black / Urban & Street Lit
FIC081000 FICTION / Muslim
FIC031060 FICTION / Thrillers / Political

Library of Congress Control Number: 2023917545

ISBN-13: 978-1-958922-53-8 Paperback
ISBN-13: 978-1-958922-54-5 Hardcover
ISBN-13: 978-1-958922-55-2 Ebook

ACKNOWLEDGEMENTS

I thank the One Almighty God for blessing me with the opportunity to write this novel. This has been an amazing journey of discovery.

I'm grateful to the team at Fresh Ink Group for helping me realize my vision.

Special thanks go to my cousin, Tyron "Juicy" W., for the times you looked out, providing shelter and assistance when I needed it most. And the people who still take my calls and stand by me if I falter: Edna, Marshall, Roy, Gerelane, Tenisha, Maylee, Kaylin, and all who remain from the lines of Wardean, JWL, and JDA. In their memory I deeply appreciate the love, support, and encouragement during my inner battles and victorious realization that the only rational response to any hurdle or adversity is success.

ACKNOWLEDGMENTS

Part One
KINGPIN

CHAPTER ONE

Marcello - 1725

Augustine screwed the top off the whiskey and gulped down half the flask. Afterward, he let out a loud wide-mouthed drunkard's sigh. The quiet Colombian driver who collected him and his two bodyguards at the airport smiled and adjusted the rearview mirror to better see the old Italian in the back seat.

The mafia man beside him extended a box of Italian smokes.

"Cigar, Don Razzoli?"

Augustine's eyes gleamed with alcoholic wetness as he accepted one gladly. Smoking and drinking had become a debilitating habit. He had done both off and on from the moment he boarded his private jet in Naples for a flight to South America. In his mind, he had as many reasons to drink and smoke as to be worried about this meeting in La aldea de Los leones.

Entering the village was a risk. As they grew closer, they spotted men in fatigues roaming up and down the roadside with Kalashnikovs. Others were standing inside the gate to the Kingpin's compound. Every vehicle pulling up to the checkpoint was stopped, inspected, the occupants questioned.

When their limo stopped at the checkpoint, the Colombians stared at them with dark, serious expressions, as if they needed to remind them, they were no longer in Italy.

Two men walked over. One held a thin pole with a mirror he used to look beneath the car's undercarriage, while the second man made his way the back and bent towards the window that rolled down.

"Como te llamas?" he asked, peering into the back seat.

"Augustine Razzoli. I am here to see Mr. Tagola," the old Italian replied.

The man with the pole joined his comrade after his inspection. Augustine stared evenly between the two, until the man who asked for his name walked off about twenty yards chattering into a handheld radio. Then he turned, waving back at the driver as he muttered in Spanish, "Passe! Passe!"

The limousine drove under the raised guardrail into the compound and continued down a stretch of road that took them to the mansion they came to. The woman and two men the Kingpin deployed to show them in were waiting on the walkway. As custom for a don in his country, Augustine didn't exit the vehicle before the bodyguard in the front seat jumped out to get the door. When he did, he staggard up to one of the Colombian men wearing a stylish looking shirt, tie, and sleek shades.

"Bienvenida a Colombian, señor. Welcome to Colombia," he greeted.

"You must be Hector," the old man said, slurring his words.

The Colombian hesitated, held his gaze, wondered how he knew the name when he had no recollection of the two of them ever meeting before today.

He pushed the question down, pretended not to smell the liquor on him, and replied, "Si, I am Hector. Come with me. Carlos will see you right away."

Augustine raised an impressive eyebrow when he gestured in the direction of the steps leading up to the mansion. The sight of it was astonishing. Enormous sculptures were situated between the pillars, chiseled into the replicas of two male maned lions sitting on their hind quarters as if they were there to keep a vigilant watch over the entrance and a fortress compound surrounded by a thirty-foot wall of concrete with built-in watch towers, and cameras that commanded a view of the entire village.

Weighing almost three hundred pounds, Augustine was a big man. His size showed in the way he climbed the steps on the heels of the Colombians. By the time they reached the top of the steps he was exhausted and had to lean against one of the lion sculptures to rest. The young man beckoned them forward when he gathered his wind. After they walked inside, they crossed a marble floor to a pair of glossy white elevator doors. The Latino woman and man accompanying the young Hector broke off in separate directions. They stepped inside and went up to the second level. When the doors pinged open, they followed him down the hallway before they stopped at a door, knocked twice, turned the knob, and led them inside the spacious office.

Carlos looked up from behind his desk the moment they walked in. The bodyguards remained at the door as the young Colombian steered Augustine to the leather armchairs in front of the Kingpin's desk.

"Mucho gusto a conocer te, señor Razzoli. It's a pleasure to meet you," Carlos stated.

"The pleasure is equal," Augustine replied. He settled into the armchair the escort.

"Your presence here is an exception to my rule, Señor Razzoli," Carlos asserted. "No one enters this village unless we have some kind of prior business affiliation. You are only here on the good word of a mutual friend, D'Angelo Cabrini, who tells me that this urgent request of yours to meet with me involves a matter of great importance."

"I can't thank D'Angelo enough for conveying my request to speak with you. His father and I did a lot of business many years ago. I've known Mr. Cabrini since he was just a boy growing up in Calabria . . ."

Carlos watched the old man as he paused to look around the space of his chamber, his eyes settling on the scenic wall paintings, the walled library shelved with hundreds of books and pictures of his family and friends, the two oversized national flags hanging gracefully on opposite sides of the wood burning fireplace.

"Well, that's good to know," said Carlos. "Perhaps you see this as an opportunity for us do business as well."

He opened the top drawer of the desk to take out the thick black folder he slid across the surface of the polished mahogany.

"So, tell me. Is it cocaína or the hardware in the folder that brings you here?"

Augustine picked the folder up and opened it. Inside was a list of top-grade military arsenals: drones, handguns, automatic rifles, RPG's, missiles, torpedo's, tanks, and other armored vehicles. None seemed to strike his interest except the Russian made Black Sting Ray torpedo he noticed among the illustrations.

He slid the folder midway back with his index finger marking the weapon of choice.

"This one," he stated. "After my meeting with you today. There might be a need for me to have some use for it."

Carlos leaned forward to look at the illustrated picture.

"Powerful piece of arsenal," he said with a quizzical grin. "Why would an old man like you be interested in such a weapon of this magnitude? Are you even aware of its capabilities?"

"I'm very aware of its capabilities, Mr. Tagola. The Black Sting Ray was developed in 1998 by the Russians. It can be fired from a sub or ship. And with the kind of accuracy its homing radar has. Once it is fired, it will track down and destroy any targeted vessel moving in the water."

"I see you like torpedoes," Carlos remarked.

"Just this one. Let's just say it holds a special significance for a particular vessel I have in mind to destroy. However, I am not here today to discuss purchasing any of your drugs or weapons. No, the nature of my business today you will find very different."

"If you're not here to discuss the drugs or weapons, Señor Razzoli. What exactly is the nature of your business here today?" Carlos clasped his hands and waited for his reply.

The old man reached into the side pocket of his suit coat for the silver flask he extracted. After a quick sip, he removed the Borsalino he wore and placed it on his lap. As he gently caressed the hat's wide brim, he finally responded. "I came to help you save yourself."

Carlos and the other young Colombian in the chair shot each other an incredulous look and laughed out loud.

"Por su puesto, el viejo esta bromeando con nosotros! Surely, the old man is joking with us!" Carlos uttered.

"Unfortunately, I am not," Augustine retorted. "I came here to give you the opportunity. You see, for years you have indulged in a drug trafficking business that's only made you into a complete fool!"

Carlos frowned. "What did you say?"

"Please, allow me to explain. You are right about one thing. We have never met or had any business before today. But I know who you are, Mr. Tagola. You are just another figure in the long succession of cartel leaders to rise to power out of the notoriously brutal history of the South American narcotics trade. You have amassed this great fortune that's earned you a luxurious lifestyle. But for everything you have done to maintain your empire. The footprints being left in the trails of blood, death, and destruction throughout Colombia and beyond are certainly some of your own . . ."

The young Colombian sitting beside him abruptly scowled. "Que estas hablando? What are you talking about?"

"Mr. Tagola knows exactly what I am talking about," the old Italian answered, without taking his eyes off the Kingpin. "Want specifics? We can start with the turf wars, his payoffs, all the buyouts. I know you probably think you built this empire all by yourself, Mr. Tagola? But you didn't. You had help—lots of it. You just didn't know it. For decades you have only done the dirty work for a hidden agenda that was mapped out for you by people you know absolutely nothing about. But they know everything there is to know about you. Just like I do. And everything you think I don't know; I know!"

The young Colombian beside him catapulted out the chair taking the verbal attack as an insult.

"Cuidarte la boca, viejo! Watch your mouth, old man!" he snapped.

Carlos intervened. "Tranquila té, Hector,"

"Calm down? Miré lo. Look at him. Esta baracho! He's drunk!"

"Basta! Enough!" Carlos retorted.

Hector glared at the old Italian a few seconds longer before he returned to the chair in silence.

"This man says he is here on a matter of great importance," Carlos asserted. "Let's see what else he has to say about these mystery people he claims helped build my empire. You may carry on, Señor Razzoli."

Augustine took another drink, brushed the sleeve of his Versace suit as if he had removed a dust mite. Then he went on.

"The people I refer to are a group of five individuals. They are formed by an international alliance. They belong to a hierarchical society with vast wealth and power. From the day you took over the Medellin cartel they have always been the ones pulling the strings on your drug trafficking business, Mr. Tagola."

The old man stopped talking, signaled to one of his henchmen posted at door. The man on right hurried over to serve him, first with the cigar he requested, then with the gold-plated lighter that flamed it.

"To be quite frank, you are nothing more than a pawn in a game far outside of your league, Mr. Tagola . . ."

Carlos smacked the surface of the desk with his palm and blasted a stern rebuttal. "I am Carlos Alejandro Tagola. You don't know anything about me or my business, nor do the mystery people you speak of. I am the one who built this empire! No one pulls the strings on business in this country, except me! I call the shots!"

The veins in his forehead bulged. The reaction was no surprise. Hearing this had to be unnerving for him, Augustine surmised.

As he sat there, he wondered if the Colombians were studying him as he studied them, from the moment he entered the office. Hector's skin was lighter, nose narrower, lips thinner. He had short black neatly trimmed wavy hair like the Kingpin. Except Carlo's coarser waves, full lips, and dark complexion was the product of a mixed heritage. When he turned to look at the pictures of the cartel leader's family and friends on the shelves of the library again, his eyes fell on a childhood picture of Carlos and

Hector sitting on swings in a park. The one he saw next to it showed them together in adulthood, standing in front of a cargo plane, posing with fully automatic rifles and bundles of cash and dope. The one next to that one was a picture taken of his mother—a smiling Colombian princess, standing beside his proud African father the day after their wedding.

"Your father's name is Hannibal Abaas Ibn Tagola," he said abruptly. "Your mother's name is Mariana Abrigela Tagola. Here's what else I know, Mr. Tagola. The two national banners hanging on the opposite sides of the wood burning fireplace over there are more than office decorations. That's because they mean something to you. You see, the national flag of Colombia on the right represents the country of your mother, where she gave birth to you. The Tanzanian national flag on the left represents the homeland of your east African father. Your mother married twice. Mariana's maiden name was Colón before she married her first husband. He was a Colombian. Your half brother and sister are the two children she bore for him. She was long divorced by the time she met your father. At the time she traveled to Africa as a Catholic missionary, Hannibal was a chieftain living in the Tanzanian village of Taborah. While there, Mariana became educated about the country's people and various religions.

"Even after learning Hannibal was a Muslim, despite differences between the faiths, she became fond of him. They were never permitted to date or be alone together because Islam encourages marriage. Mariana began to seriously study his religion and eventually converted. Two years after she met him, Hannibal conveyed the marriage proposal through a close relative who arranged their wedding ceremony."

"Were did you get this information?" Carlos chimed, but the old man kept talking.

"Your mother didn't like it when you took up with the likes of your three uncles, Federico, Fráncisco, and Ferdinand Colón. Mariana despised her brothers. And she despised Ferdinand the most because she always knew it was him who got you into the drug business. Your uncle was a chief operator for the Medellin cartel led by Escobar. After Escobar was killed by the government's military police in 1993, Ferdinand took over. His reign lasted a good while, until he and his brother Federico

were discovered deceased in the back seat of the bullet-riddled limousine. They were ambushed. No was ever arrested. Some believe it was the
CIA. Once the allegation leaked, top officials inside the agency simply dismissed it as nothing more than a rumor being floated. Many people close
to you thought it was more of a shock when you became his successor. No
one knew about his plans for this. But the day you made the decision to
become the new boss of this village you were just as determined to fulfill
his quest to build an empire from here. Well, you certainly accomplished
that task. On top of that, you have poured millions into this place to give
it a luxurious makeover and a name which has lasted ever since La aldea
de los leonés. The lion village. Only, when you made that decision, you
lost your family. To this very day they refuse to see or speak to you. All of
them—except your father, Hannibal, and a few loyal cousins who remain
close to you. Isn't that right, Mr. Tagola?"

Augustine took a drag off the cigar, exhaling a gray cloud of smoke
into the air before he turned to the Colombian sitting in the chair next
him.

"Young man, your full name is Horacio Hector Colón. Mr. Tagola
is your first cousin. Your mother's name is Natalia Colón. You and
Mr. Tagola grew up together in this very village. It is no wonder why you
and he are the only remaining members of the family who still reside here.
The two of you have always been close since childhood. Your mother
Natalia was just as fearful as her sister Mariana about the activities of
their brothers. She was so desperate to shield you from them, she packed
up and fled with you to the United States . . ."

"Tell me how you know about all of this, right now!" Hector
demanded.

"I understand you find it problematic that I would know such things.
Like all the time you had to served inside that U.S. federal prison after you
and you and your mother moved to America. Yes, I know about that as
well. The sentence you got could have been avoided if the council hadn't
voted to let you fall to protect your cousin Carlos instead . . ."

Bewildered, Carlos inquired, "Espera! Wait! What do you mean by if
the council hadn't voted to protect me?"

"They know all about the connections you have with the corrupt officials working inside the U.S. government and its agencies . . . CIA, FBI, border patrol, Coast Guard, DEA, military, etcetera. What you and Mr. Colón don't know is that the officials you think are helping your cartel, these same officials also work as loyal agents for the council."

Carlos gave him a skeptic's glare. "What kind of council is this?" he asked.

"The kind who has instructed their agents to exploit South American drug traffickers like you."

"Why would they target us?"

"You are very beneficial to their agenda. The fall your cousin took was a mild one—compared to the likes of Escobar, Noriega, Marcos, your uncle Ferdinand, and others. They all had deep connections with various corrupt U.S. officials. Every one of them was considered valuable assets. But once those officials felt there was no longer a need for them. They had to be . . ."

The second he stopped talking, Carlos pressed, "They had to what?"

Augustine pulled on the cigar and replied, "They had to be removed. Silenced."

"Are you telling me . . ."

"What I'm telling you is that men like your uncle Ferdinand and the rest accumulated too much wealth and power for their own good. They got too big, too cocky. Aside from that they had too much detrimental information on certain top level American government officials that made a lot of people in Washington very nervous. Once the council felt there was a need to issue the order. It was only a matter of time before they sent out their agents to pull the plug on them."

"You really expect me to believe it was some council who murdered my uncle?"

"Your uncle was too close to Escobar. They feared the possibility that sooner or later he might decide to retaliate for his demise in some way."

"You refer to these people as the *council*. Who are they?"

Augustine reached inside the inner pocket of his suite coat to remove the photograph he placed on the desk before him.

"The woman you see on the picture is Eleanor Queensberry. The gentleman sitting next to her is Edward Kingstone. Eleanor and Edward are both citizens of Great Britain. The other gentlemen you see are Julian Bisoppontiz of France, Heinrich Rookvaunklaff of Germany, and the American Arthur Knightwood. Together, they are the ranking five members of the CROP. To those closely affiliated with their inner circle they are only known as the CROP."

Carlos's suspicion increased as the question about the old man's motives popped into his head.

"Why have you flown all this way to tell me about people?" he asked.

Augustine's expression changed immediately. He looked riled, not so much by the Kingpin's question, but by the thoughts in relation to the reply he was about to give.

"They betrayed me," he muttered bitterly. "And I think it's high time they know exactly what that feels like!"

"So, it's revenge that brings you here?" Carlos asked.

"Partly, yes," Augustine answered. "Except, I am old. And you are young."

"What does that mean?"

"It means I need someone like you to assist me. Someone young. Someone with enough power and connections outside their inner circle . . ."

"And you really think I would consider such a thing? I know nothing about these people you speak of. But you obviously do. How is that?"

"I was a member on their council at one time. They are former colleagues with whom I am no longer in good standing."

"I must say, you are a brave man, Señor Razzoli. You come to my village, and you discuss the affairs of my family. You tell me it was your friends who killed my uncle. And you make claims against my business for which you produce no proof!"

The old man raised his flask, lowered a second afterwards. "Ah, yes. I thought you would eventually get to that."

He turned and signaled for the other bodyguard posted at the door. He approached with a black briefcase and snapped it open. Augustine said, "If it's proof you want, it's in the case. But as I said, that's only part of the reason I am here. There is more."

Carlos looked at the briefcase and then back at him. "And what might that be?"

"The Russian Black Sting Ray torpedo on the list of arsenals you showed me. The council doesn't know how you acquired it. But they do know it's in your possession. They also know about all the trips you have been making back and forth to Africa . . ."

"I have flown to Africa to see my father since I was a child. What does this have to do with him?"

"The council has fears. It's not your father that raises concern. They fear the Black Sting Ray could end up in the hands of the mujahedeen."

Hector cut in. "Ahi, I see where you're going with this. You're insinuating that because Carlos's father is a Muslim . . ."

Augustine rebutted sternly, "I don't ever *insinuate*. And I am afraid you don't see anything. Otherwise, you would know your cousin Mr. Tagola has big problems. Sure, the council knows about his connections. But he's also building up a military. And his turf war with that rival cartel led by Ortega Diez in Cali has only compounded the situation."

"Wars come with the business," Carlos uttered.

"I know all too well. But Ortega Diez's business is a vested interest for my former colleagues. And many of their top agents now feel the war between you and him is starting to attract too much unwanted attention. As we sit here, there are federal authorities in the U.S. investing Mr. Diez's activities in Cali. He is safe for now only because the CROP has a particular mole in the ranks of the FBI commissioned to make it disappear to protect him."

"Ortega is an insect on the wall to me." Carlos mushed his palms together in mock fashion as if he was squashing an imaginary fly. "That's what I do to insects that get in my way!"

Augustine shook his head; he looked up at the ceiling as he loosened his tie.

"Here's the reality, Mr. Tagola. People are falling sick and dying throughout Colombia and beyond because of your narcotics. My former colleagues couldn't care less about this. They have no empathy whatsoever for those most affected by it. What they do like is the dirty work you do for their agenda. But in their eyes, you are no different than Mr. Diez and the insect you described him as. In fact, you're even smaller, a couple of tiny organisms they view in microscopic proportion."

Augustine sighed, brushed a hand through his hair.

"You know, on my way in I couldn't help but noticed the two amazing male lion sculptures between the pillars. They bear a striking resemblance to the black manes on the Serengeti. I suppose your fondness for big cats must have developed at some point during your travels to Africa. What you said about me being a brave man to come here. I say one of the very reasons I did is because I believed you had the same courage as those lions you admire. Only now I am not so sure. In fact, I wonder if you even know the real story about the black manes and their responsibility to the lion prides on the Serengeti. Do you know their story, Mr. Tagola? It is to protect both his territory and the pride. The females rarely need him around. They are the ones who hunt and raise his cubs when he wanders off to scout and mark the territory with his urine to warn off other male lions. The females have no worries, unless another big male invades and threatens the pride. In that event, they will call out for their leader. The minute he hears their distress call he responds. Because he knows if he fails to defend them the invader will claim his pride and territory and kill off all his offspring to replace them with his own."

Carlos listened attentively when the old Italian added.

"Maybe one day you will see the similarities between a black mane's responsibility to his pride on the Serengeti and the responsibilities men must have toward family and country. Only then will you be able to hear that same distress call coming from the people of Colombia and beyond in their search for a leader bold enough to protect them from the threats they face . . ."

"Interesting story, viejo," Hector chimed. "But the only thing my cousin Carlos is hearing right now is a bunch of basura!"

Augustine rose to feet, collected the picture from desk, placed it inside the briefcase, and snapped it shut.

"Perhaps I have wasted my time coming here, Mr. Tagola. Your cousin has obviously grown as irritated with me as I have with him. With that said, I shall see my way out now."

He turned and headed for the door. The bodyguard on the right twisted the knob that opened it for his quick exit.

But just before he stepped through it, Carlos called out, "Oye, Señor Razzoli. You forgot something!"

Augustine turned around in the doorway to face him. "I can't imagine that. You heard what I came to discuss."

Carlos replied, "Yes. But you said you had proof in that briefcase you're holding. This is a difficult business. Excuse my cousin's sentiments. If you are inclined to stay a while longer and show me. It's the least I can do."

The two held each other's gaze until Augustine tipped his Borsalino at his acceptance of the invitation. Hector held a sneer on his face. But if Tagola wanted the proof, he was willing to ignore it.

He walked back to the chair and sat down. The bodyguards closed the door and resumed their post. It was a pivotal moment.

CHAPTER TWO

Colombia

A little after sunrise the next day, Carlos woke up thinking about the choice he had to make. Continue the lifeline for his drug business, or let it die.

The old Italian left his village, but he was still hearing his words, hearing how he was nothing but a pawn in an advanced game outside his league. It wasn't just the words. There was enough proof he presented to keep him interested until he got the full picture.

The ritual stroll he took out to the third level balcony with his binoculars every morning always gave him time to think and observe the pleasantries of the surrounding vista. For almost a half hour he stood gazing up at a lone hawk in flight, a fox he spotted in search of field mice near the edge of the tree line, the waters of the Rio valley shifting from crystal clear lakes, and bubbling springs, descending hillsides through miles and miles of unforgiving hinterland.

There was never a time he didn't acknowledge the beauty of the landscape. Colombia was a graceful wonder. But as he stood on the balcony, he came to grips with the old Italian's parting words. It wasn't just Colombia and its citizens that stood to be lost, others could be lost too.

Hector knew it was early when he came walking through the sliding glass door. He understood Carlos wanted to be alone. He saw the battle he was fighting within. But there was no way around it. They had to talk. Worst case scenario he was already plotting a course of action to clear his conscious.

"Do you believe he was truthful, Carlos?" he asked.

"What if he was?"

"I know that's what you are hoping. But I personally don't think he was telling us everything."

"He knew too much. And you saw what was in the briefcase."

"Yes. But you also heard what he said about the meeting. That it must stay anonymous. Otherwise, his old friends will not hesitate to come after us."

"Are you concerned about that?" Carlos questioned.

"Concerned? Not at all. I am with you, primo. But you have a big decision to make. So, what are you thinking?"

Carlos lowered the binoculars, and slowly raised his right hand next to his ear to listen. "Can you hear that, Hector?"

Hector heard nothing except the light breeze rustling leaves. "Hear what?"

"The sound of voices coming from the people of Colombia and everywhere else," Carlos replied. "I can hear them calling now. I can hear them calling just like the old man said I would. I can hear them calling out in distress just like the lion prides on the Serengeti."

CHAPTER THREE

Two Months Later
United States District Attorney Office
Washington, DC

Email: 1 Message
Time: 11:45 am

YOU HAVE TWENTY-FOUR HOURS TO TRANSFER FIFTEEN MILLION DOLLARS FROM YOUR SWISS ACCOUNT TO THE BANK ACCOUNT NUMBER THAT WILL ARRIVE INSIDE THE MANILA ENVELOPE. IF YOU FAIL TO COMPLY THE ACTIVITIES YOU CARRIED OUT FOR THE CROP WILL BE DISCLOSED.

District attorney Aron Duffy stared at the message on his computer in confusion. It was a prank, he assumed. But it scared him.

He glanced at the time again. 11:55 am. In five more minutes, he would know there was nothing to worry about. That's what he told himself. But after a few minutes he waited to confirm it. There was a dreadful knock at the office door he wished hadn't come. The moment secretary Norfolk walked into his office at exactly 12:00 pm, the manila envelope she was holding was the first thing he noticed.

"Is that for me, Mrs. Norfolk?" he asked nervously.

"Yes, Mr. Duffy. But . . ."

"What is it?"

"Well, sir, it only has your name on it. There is no return address. I do not recall seeing it on my desk when I went out for a smoke break. But when I returned, I found it lying on my memos. I thought that was odd. So, I called downstairs to the postal clearance department. They said there is no record of it arriving. Shall I call security inspections, sir?"

"No. It's okay. I'll have a look at it myself".

Duffy watched her smile happily when she handed the envelope over. She started to leave, but he stopped her.

"Just a second, Mrs. Norfolk."

She turned. "Something more I can do for you, sir?"

"Yes. If you don't mind. I'd rather you not mention anything about this envelop to anyone else."

"As you wish, Mr. Duffy."

The moment she stepped out, he examined it. The parcel was double-stamped confidential on both sides. He picked up the letter opener on the desk and sliced across the top to free the contents. Inside were two audio disks, snapshots, and a stack of papers containing highly sensitive information. When he began reading the papers the material facts on each page pointed towards corruption and his involvement while serving as the assistant U.S. DA from 2001-2011. The bulk of the information exposed his pilferages of classified information, his concealment of files involving hundreds of top priority extortion and racketeering cases, the favors he traded for finance to help political figures who relied on his guarantee of victories in their election campaigns.

A wave of panic came over him. He began rummaging through his desk in a frantic search for his CD player, flinging out reams of paper, folders, notepads, before locating it in the bottom drawer beneath a box of Kleenex. Seconds after inserting the first disc he heard the voices of two government informants discussing classified documents he gave them while they were still peddling stolen diamonds and artifacts on the black market. After inserting the second audio he heard himself talking to a pair of east coast DEA agents about a shipment of narcotics they allowed to pass through a U.S. customs border patrol with the aid of unnamed CIA agents.

Stunned, he ejected the disk and picked up the snapshots. Some of the stills showed the actual documents stolen in several high profiled cases that involved leaders of motorcycle gangs and the mafia. There were others that caught him in the act of taking under the table payments.

Gripped by fear and overwhelming frustration he reached for the garbage can next to the desk and dumped all the incriminating evidence into it. Then he torched it with the contents and watched them burn while his face reflected the glow of red. Someone out there knew about his activities. Someone out there had all the goods to bring him down. The thoughts crept into his mind so deep he began to picture himself inside an orange jumpsuit with handcuffs on after a federal indictment was issued against him. He would face a trial. And when the grand jury of his peers came out of their deliberations to pronounce the guilty verdict. He would be facing a life sentence.

It was too much to bear. That's exactly what he was thinking when he got up and went to the door to barricade himself in. The smoke billowing out the garbage can seem to have no effect when he sat back down behind the desk. He just stared at the top drawer like he acquired enough x-ray vision to look straight through the wood at the small handgun lying inside side. He could not do prison. He could not face the CROP as a liability. The mere thought of those experiences propelled him to open the drawer and take the one option he felt would help him avoid them all together.

A moment later when the secretary heard the gun go off, she jumped up and ran to the door. It was locked. She didn't know what to think. One shot, muffled by the walls of the office. It was the most awful sound in her ears.

CHAPTER FOUR

Thirty-Seven Hours Later
Washington, DC

It was 1:05 am. Senator Glenn Dyse was standing at the window in his bedroom, his gaze fixed a thousand miles away. There was nothing but silence. Silence and darkness. His son was asleep in the room across the hall. All he could think about was the news he learned about Aron Duffy's apparent suicide and the disturbing email he received thirteen hours ago:

He re-read it in his head a million times. Every single piece of incriminating evidence that came from the envelope he later found in his mailbox drained the color out of his face, leaving his skin dead white, all except for the vivid glow of neon catching angles from the open blind.

It was a warning sign. A wake-up call that let him know the protection of anonymity he relied on for nearly thirty years was no longer there. And for a man in his position options had to be considered in the event the situation couldn't be contained. His call to the emergency contact was made hours ago. Just as he expected, he was told not to worry, no need to cash in, transfer assets, comply with the anonymous emailer's demand, because the situation would be handled. Since then, there had been no word from the contact. He was growing impatient. His hands were trembling. Thoughts of abandonment crept into his mind. He was beginning to question whether the protocol was worth it. If the contact failed to get back. If the CROP failed to enact a swift response. He would be forced to enact his own response. And he was very clear what that response had to be.

Minutes after the thought swept across his mind. The cell phone on the table next to the window began buzzing with an incoming call from the emergency contact.

He answered, "Mr. Bedford, I expected an update from you much sooner."

"Did you get rid of everything in the envelop like I told you, Senator?" the caller asked, in haste.

"Yes. Now, what are you going to do about the problem?"

"I told you I would handle the matter."

"Don't give me that crap. Why am I not detecting a sense of urgency in your tone? You are the CIA's deputy director of operations. You know this is a matter we can't take lightly."

"I said I would handle it," the caller repeated.

"Is that all you can tell me? For namesake, the district attorney killed himself. Did it occur to you he could have gotten the same email? I need more than your empty assurances, Mr. Bedford. In fact, I want you to arrange a meeting for me with the council."

"I can't do that, Senator."

"If I were you, I would think twice about that. Maybe this doesn't register with you. But I could lose my status, my freedom, my family, my money, everything. I will not go down for the CROP!"

"Senator, you are losing sight of the protocol. You need to calm down," the caller advised.

"Forget the protocol! I will not put my family and career on the line for the council anymore. My mind is made up. And it's best you understand that."

"Oh, I do, Senator," the caller uttered. "And you should have listened to me."

"Come again."

"Your services are no longer needed," the caller replied.

"Don't patronize me." the Senator hissed angrily. "You and I both know you are nothing but an errand boy for them. And that's all you'll ever be!"

Then he fell quiet. The light noise he heard behind him made him turn away from the window. There was an intruder standing in the doorway. A man dressed in all black. The outline of his figure was silhouetted by ceiling light cascading into the room from the hallway. And he was staring at him through the slit in the black ski-mask he wore.

Senator Dyse's eyes were wide and staring back as the phone in his hand slowly dropped to his side.

"Who are you? What are you doing here?" he squeaked.

No response came back.

He stared at the intruder, incredulous. Fixed on the gun at the end of his outstretched arm. It was aimed at his face. Suddenly, he was shaking and sweating. The intruder was quietly easing towards him. Senator Dyse's eyes were following the red beam on the gun's laser-sight until a bullet pierced through the glass in the window behind him and struck him in the back. The impact drove him forward. Stumbling, trying to focus on the intruder ducking inside the doorway, he never saw the sniper outside. He never detected the silent round until it smashed into his spine and sent him crashing into the dresser. Seconds after, he hit the ground squirming and gasping and wrenching. The closed door across the hall flew open. And his eighteen-year-old son emerged with his eyes quickly crossing into the room. First, he saw his father lying on the floor heaving and groaning. Then he spotted the man in black back peddling into hallway.

"What are doing to my dad?" the boy shouted.

The moment his voice sailed over the intruder's shoulder. The intruder spun around instantly with his gun aimed, eye-level, straight out. The boy exploded and hurled his hulking body at him like a raging bull.

With the reflex reaction, the intruder flinched against the pressure of his finger on the hair trigger. The gun went off. The single round caught the boy between the eyes and jerked his body back against the wall where he slid to the floor.

Senator Dyse cried out in horror. "You shot him. You shot my son! I'm a U.S. Senator. Why me?"

The man in the mask crouched low and moved towards him. The Senator's phone lay feet away. Through horror and agony, he tried crawling to reach it so that he could call for help. The intruder was quietly inching closer, until another bullet pierced the glass in the window and found the Senator with a head shot that killed him instantly. He immediately jerked back and bounced to his feet, gun aimed at the window now, as he moved back out the room with his breath frozen in his chest. Suddenly isolated in the hallway with the young boy, he stood in front of him staring at his blank face. Wide blue eyes stared back lifeless before he reached down and closed them in anguish and regret. He raced down the steps at the end of the hallway and ran out the front door into the dark night.

Part Two
Ex Con

CHAPTER FIVE

A VIEW OF PHILADELPHIA'S EASTERN STATE PENITENTIARY

I believe very few men are capable of estimating the immense amount of agony which this dreadful punishment, prolonged for years, inflicts upon the sufferers . . . I hold this slow and daily tampering with the mysteries of the brain, to be immeasurably worse than any torture of the body; and because its ghastly signs and tokens are so palpable to the eye and sense of touch as scars upon the flesh; because its wounds are not upon the surface, and it extorts few cries that human ears can hear; therefore, I the more denounce it as a secret punishment which slumbering humanity is not roused up to stay — Dickens 1842

Battle Creek
2011

When Kenny woke up in the middle of the night hearing gunshots go off outside his apartment on Manchester Street. Only two words entered his mind. Summer madness. People in the neighborhood were used to guns going off, including him. But since he couldn't get back to sleep. He stayed awake a little while watching previously taped segments on C-SPAN. When exhaustion kicked, just as it had on other nights, he went back to bed and slept peacefully for a few good hours before dawn.

Normally, he got up early. But that morning he slept soundly right up to noon. He dragged himself out of bed and into the bathroom, tired and slow. After he washed and dressed, he headed out the door for work. Walking down the porch steps he heard more shots. By the time he got to the bottom police sirens were screaming a couple of blocks over from Greenwood Park. He figured the shots rang out somewhere near Oneita could have been closer to Ann, maybe Oaklawn, or Wood Street. He wasn't sure. All he knew was that a group of mundane teenagers hanging at the corner of Kendall and Manchester broke out running towards Holland like they were the subjects of the cop's 911 call.

He walked to his burgundy Marquis in the driveway. When he opened the door to climb in, he heard loud music playing, and peered over the car's hood at the triple-white Cadillac Escalade he saw bending the corner off Hubbard. The giant sub-woofers inside it were banging out a chorus of funky Spanish beats that even commanded the attention from the people on the sidewalk who stopped and stared at the mirrored windows, and the reflection of themselves watching another ghetto dream roll by.

It was a nice ride. Kenny always wanted a Cadillac Suburban like that one. He just didn't have the money. Not now anyway. Barely six months had passed since he walked out the front door of Cotton Correctional Facility in Jackson, Michigan. It felt good to trade in the state issued prison blues and return to his hometown in Battle Creek. But everything thing he told himself he was going to do once he got out the joint—settle down, get married, find a job, save some cash, had become a dream deferred.

Finding a full-time job wasn't easy as he thought it would be. He went in for interviews. But once employers saw the box checked felony on his applications, he heard, "Sorry, we don't hire felons." The formal rejections usually came within three or four minutes of him showing up. Every other week he dropped by the local employment office on Hamblin, to log onto websites for the applications he filled out and sent across the city. No responses ever came back. Faced with the dilemma, he accepted whatever employment that came through temp services. The first was a job at Walmart. He did a stint with factory work in Fort Custard after that. The last temp was the grounds keeping gig at Pine Knoll apartments. His first full-time gig was the current job he was heading to—Main Street Market. The manager who hired him was a tired looking Greek. He wasn't that old. Maybe late forties, pot belly, black oily hair. There was no good side to his face. The guy's attitude kept his face fixed into a permanent frown. A week never passed without him complaining and threatening to fire any worker on the spot he caught stealing the store's merchandise.

Kenny was the only worker employed as a felon. At times he knew the comments were directed at him. He didn't like it. But it was a toss-up: Either work at the market or apply for welfare. The decision wasn't hard to make given that he was already relying on a bridge card for food and not much else. Every day, despite the Greek's petty threats and complaints, he showed up for the weak paychecks. Being an ex-con made for a tough road ahead. Most of his time back on the street was spent trying to write off all the years he was caged up and treated like everything less than a human.

He would go in for work on this day. But just before closing time he drove his Marquis around the back of the store and parked within a few feet of the garbage dumpster. At least once a week he took the trash out along with the cases of wine and beer he stashed inside it. After work he always came back to retrieve them. It was never a mother lode, just a side hustle he tried to flip, but usually ended up wasting it on poker and craps tables out at the Fire Keeper's Casino, like he did this night after he sold off the Greek's merchandise.

When he drove to the casino after work, he thought it might be a good night to flip the grand he made from the sale. Except he walked out with only two hundred. He would drop some of that at the Liberty Beer & Wine on Northeast Capital Avenue. He paid for the bag of Doritos and case of Budweiser at the counter. The cashier was a pretty Indian woman from Bangladesh. She had that tiny red dot on her forehead women wore in India. Kenny took notice of the pleasant smile she displayed when he came to the counter. But the Bangladeshi guy beside her kept watching him—the same way he watched him the whole time he was at the back of the store.

"How are you tonight, sir?" she asked.

"Good," he replied simply. Then he left.

Except he wasn't good. Not after losing eight hundred in one night. He left the store feeling the way he left the casino—in a bad way. Thinking about the money would only drive him crazy, so he shifted his mind away from the lost and started thinking about the plan he comprised to make up for it.

The Sir Pizza between Wabash and Liberty Beer & Wine was closed. But the Marathon gas station across the street normally stayed open late. A lot of fiends and dope dealers who made it their meeting place stayed late as well. So, when he drove out of the Liberty parking lot and parked near the intersection of Wabash and Northeast Capital Avenue. His mind was already set on shaking down the first dealer he saw in the crowd with fat pockets.

With his car parked less than fifty yards away from the intersection. He had a clear view of the gas station. But the plan was risky. There was a police substation a block over. And the area of town he was in was dubbed crack alley. People familiar with the neighborhood knew by day it appeared normal. By nightfall, the place was a circus featuring the main attraction of prostitutes who paraded up and down the avenue showcasing their wares in the bright glare of headlights.

When he retrieved the pistol he kept under the seat, he checked the chamber and placed it beside him. Then he waited almost thirty minutes to see if some unfortunate dealer would show up. The ones who sold twenty-dollar rocks weren't worth the gank. Cats like them pulled up on ten-speed bikes. Real ballers drove up in a Benz or Cadillac. But the fact he knew some of them carried four or five grand was enough for him to hang out a little while longer.

After he cracked open a can of Budweiser and switched on the car's dashboard CD. He tried to relax, letting the Marvin Gaye track trickle into his beer buzz. Ten minutes later, he glanced at the rearview mirror and spotted a vehicle crawling out of a driveway at the other end of the block. Wabash was almost pitch-black. The only light post on the street barely illuminated beyond thirty yards.

The way the vehicle slowly crept up the road at ten miles an hour with the headlights extinguished. It took him only a few seconds to discern that it wasn't a dealer in a whip or some other motorist. It was a cop behind the wheel of a black Dodge that was hardly detectable at night. When the unit's spotlight lit up a moment later, the bright beam washed off the row of houses he passed by. Then it danced into a field across the street searching for any illegal activity that would feed the county jail another body.

Kenny tucked the gun back under the seat and poured the open beer on the floorboard before he tossed the can out the window. Then he suffered a flashback. Maybe it was all an optical illusion. But the cop's nightly patrol with the spotlight ignited his memory bank with a recollection of the nightly rounds he remembered prison guards making with their LED flashlights shining into the cells of the sleeping inmates. The routine rounds made sure no one escaped. That the prisoners were exactly where they were supposed to be.

Prison was such a blank space and a lost memory for much of society. And because so many of the faces inside the penal system were overwhelmingly black, like his, and the neighborhood the cop was patrolling, in the very moment of that distressing flashback, every house on the block that cop's spotlight shined on appeared to him like prison cells, and the black folks inside, like sleeping inmates. It made him think that for the millions of African Americans who thought of themselves as free. The poverty-stricken communities they lived in kept many confined to the same prison-like circumstances. The invisible fences around the redline ghetto districts may have been the only difference. But they were kept under constant observation by the hired authorities whose job it was to make sure they never went beyond the perimeters of the black world. Not unless they had enough green gate passes imprinted with the name and face of Benjamin Franklin.

If it was the1980's, Kenny may have decided to stick around until the cop was done with his nightly round. But this was 2011. And the laws for neighborhoods like his across the nation had changed since he last knew them. Traffic stops for black men these days often involved suspicious intent. Some cops didn't ask for license and registration. They wanted interrogation. They wanted searches without warrants. It was better to abort that plan altogether for tonight, he thought. Then he turned the key over in the ignition for the late-night drive home.

Home for Kenny was the north side of Battle Creek, in the Washington Heights district. Decades ago, during the early years of the Kellogg industrial period, W.K. Kellogg and other rich whites built million-dollar estates in the area. Over time, with the gradual migration of African Americans, Hispanics, Arabs, and poor whites moving in from the east and south sides of town, they fled for the outskirts of town, leaving behind the relics of their old mansions which still stand as testaments to the hard times and despair that followed.

On the second day he was out, Kenny took a stroll through the neighborhood observing the places he hadn't seen in years. Even now, as he drove toward home, his mind quaked thinking about the depressing sights. Houses that once stood vibrant were now condemned or torn down. The tall trees behind the Washington Heights church had been hacked down into a barren field.

Like many African Americans in the city, he didn't see much reason to stick around. Some of the people he grew up with had left to broaden their horizons. Others left to get away from the steady wave of violent shootings. Nevertheless, there was something strange yet mystic about the city that lured people back.

As he drove down Van Buren, the words of his sister Elaine came to mind. "You're going too fast, baby bro. Slow down a bit. You should get on the train and come visit the family."

If only he could break through the aftereffects of prison, perhaps he could slow down enough to be a good brother and a father to the daughter he hadn't seen in decades. But he was back on the street moving like a road runner. And he was back in the hood where life for many of the citizens felt like they were being pulled into a giant whirlpool of failure and confinement.

That's the way Kenny saw things, seemingly unconcerned that he was moving too fast to see himself once again standing at the very edge of it.

CHAPTER SIX

Battle Creek

K enny wasn't expecting a shootout when he stopped by his girlfriend Ditra's place on Frelinghuysen days later. It was sunny and hot. The usual neighborhood scene was out in full bloom, children playing red light, green light, music crooning out of unsealed windows, winos staggering by rambling incoherently.

Ditra lived in a two-story duplex right next door to the parking lot owned by the biggest church on the block. After she missed the overdue payments on her monthly bills, the utility company had her electricity and water shut off. With the heat cranked up the porch was the best spot to chill. He had been on the porch talking with her son Mook and his cousin Doc from Detroit for nearly an hour. Every now and then, whenever a random breeze came through ruffling his muscle shirt, it made him think about how he got through those scorching summer days lying inside a stuffy prison cell. Most of the time he pictured himself on a sailboat being pushed by cool winds and giant waves hurling it towards some tropical Caribbean Island. In the world, a sailboat was the farthest thing from his mind. After he was finally given a parole with only sixty days remaining before he maxed out on a thirty-year sentence, he found himself battling with bouts of anxiety. It was all procedural stuff when his assigned parole agent referred him to Summit Point for a mental health assessment. The therapist he saw told him anxiety and paranoia were common experiences among felons reentering society. Kenny didn't know what to make of the assessment. Prison was a place of oppression and suppression for which one had to develop patience.

He thought he had. Except on this day, Ditra was tripping, and continuously blowing up his cell phone with back-to-back calls. He quit taking them. But the voice mails she left were laced with unfiltered exploits about him and other women. And what she would do if she caught one in her crib when she got back from her discount shopping spree at Save-a-Lot. That was the last voice mail she left less than three minutes ago. On edge, he stepped inside the duplex to grab a bottled water from the deep freezer she had running off a generator down in the basement. Mook came down after him a few minutes later with a hurried look on his face.

"Yo, Kenny. Some dude just pulled up outside in a tan Marquis, asking me and Doc where was the owner of the Marquis parked in the driveway. He looked like he was upset about something. So, I told him we didn't know."

"What he else did he say?"

"That he would be back."

"Who is he?"

"I don't know the guy."

Kenny took a sip of water. That part he didn't believe. It wasn't the first time a guy showed up at Ditra's place announced. Stray characters showed up randomly at her duplex on more occasions than he could remember. According to her, every guy who popped up when he was around was either her cousin or in-law to one of her children. But, of course, he never bought into any of the lies she told. People close to him, friends, family, all started to question why he was even with her. To them, Ditra was trouble. A crazy drama queen he had no business dealing with.

By the time they went back out to the porch, the guy was gone, like Mook said. A few minutes after he sat down on the milk crates he stacked up, another car rolled up in front of the duplex. There was a guy in the driver's seat, a big greasy looking brother, with cornrows and basketball biceps. But Kenny knew him. He was the crackhead who phoned him earlier looking to score some rocks. So, he told him to come by the duplex.

Kenny got up and walked down the steps. When he approached the rusty blue Buick Bonneville he was in, he greeted him, "What up, bro? You said you wanted a twenty. Right?"

The guy replied, "Fo sho. You got me?"

"I got you," Kenny replied.

Then he dug inside the waistline of his pants for the bag of crack he brought out. In the process, he heard loud music, and transferred his gaze to the triple-white Cadillac Escalade he saw driving by with a bassline of Spanish beats rattling the frame. After it bent the corner on Garfield, it drove into the parking lot across the street from the duplex and sat there idling with the sounds blasting.

Kenny thought it looked like the same whip he saw cruising by his apartment in Washington Heights a few days ago. Only this time the windows were rolled down. And when it passed by, he noticed two Hispanic men and a Hispanic woman inside gazing back at him. The guy driving had his left arm draped on the steering wheel. The woman was seated next to him in the passenger seat.

For a moment, Kenny thought the face of the Hispanic fellow in the rear looked familiar to him when their eyes met. But since he didn't think much about them gazing back, he went back to conducting business.

"Here you go, bro."

The guy in the Bonneville stuck his arm out with the money. Kenny grabbed a twenty-dollar bill from his hand and gave him the crack.

The guy looked at it. "Nice size. I got to get back with you."

Kenny replied, "You got the number."

After the guy drove off, Kenny went back to the porch. The Hispanics across the street were still looking at him. For a moment he thought they wanted a beef. But when he sat back down, they drove out of the parking lot. The Escalade made a right turn off Garfield and drove to the end of the block on Frelinghuysen. Then it made another right on North Avenue and disappeared around the corner.

Something about the guy's face in the back seat kept gnawing at Kenny. His features looked a lot like a Latino he went to BC Central High with back in the 80's. The Latino he knew lived in Battle Creek for only a year or two with his mother. But he kept lots of coke and marijuana. And every day after school he drove home in a 1979 brown Monte Carlo with a tricked out electric sunroof and chrome Dayton rims. Since he was not the average teenager in high school, Kenny didn't have to ponder his name. It came to him naturally. Hector Colon! That was it. The dude in the back seat of that white Escalade resembled Hector so much he could have been his identical twin. Except twenty years or more had passed since he last saw Hector. There was no way that was him. But just the thought of Hector gave him a feeling he hadn't felt in a long time.

Most of the student body at Central High School knew Hector. Hector had a lot going on. He was from Colombia. He was popular. He was a fresh face with good looks and a thick Spanish accent that made girls go wild over him. Plus, he had bomb dope. When classes broke for lunch hour, and word spread that Hector was in the little alley across the street from the school selling bud and coke, people stood in lines.

Kenny remembered how Hector formed a close friendship with him and another teen named Ajax. Once the three of them cliqued up, they went just about everywhere together. Sometimes Hector would even take them to his uncle Frank's house in Orchard Park on the weekends. When Uncle Frank saw how close they were, he would let them smoke bud and play pool and video games in his basement anytime they wanted.

Right at the precise moment he started thinking about all the dope he and Ajax sold after Hector plugged them in, Ditra's son Mook interrupted his recollection.

"Here come ol boy now, Kenny!"

The minute he heard tires screech, Kenny turned his head and saw the tan Marquis after it came around the corner off North Avenue. The driver was speeding in the direction of the duplex. Then he slowed up and drove into the church parking lot next door. This didn't alarm him. But the dude jumped out and pointed a long shotgun at him hurling exploits.

"What's up with you and Ditra, nigga!"

The round from his shotgun a half second later glanced off the door frame and shattered the porch light above Kenny's head. Mook and his cousin Doc ran inside the apartment. Kenny jumped up and rolled off the side of the porch banister on a collision course with the concrete in the driveway. His arm and head were the first to meet the pavement. It took less than a second for his brain to process the pain his optic nerve sent through him when the ground cracked open the right side of his face. He was dazed, caught off guard. He saw the car door swing open, he saw the guy swing out, he saw that big ugly gun come first, and then the dude fired. But that was it!

Now he was seeing stars. And he was in a dumb position. That made him hesitate frantically and then get up and run towards his car at the back of the duplex. Inside the trunk was a 12-gauge pump that was sawed off. He grabbed it with his left hand and pulled it into his body and labored back towards the front with every intention to use it.

The guy was still standing at the open door of his car when he reappeared. And he was still wielding that shotgun and shouting like he was on steroids. With the heavy 12 gauge in his left hand, swinging up over the porch and between the banister grate as he leveled it at the guy. Kenny wasn't feeling any more shock, surprise, fear, or panic. Just pure reaction when he let the gauge bark. Boom! Check-check . . . Boom!

The shock wave from the cannons turned the dude's faucet off and carried him back into the sanctuary of the car. Then he took off.

Kenny ran back and jumped in his Marquis and fired out of the driveway after him. When he shot down Garfield and turned left at Calhoun, he was separated by about three car lengths. The two cars both accelerated hard and sped across North Avenue disregarding the red light doing over fifty miles an hour. Then they accelerated past Central High School all the way up Champion Street. Kenny only let up on the gas when he caught a glimpse of blue scrobe lights flickering in the rearview mirror. The police were speeding back in the direction of Ditra's apartment. The dude in the tan Marquise stopped at the corner of Washington for the traffic light. But when he saw Kenny draw up behind him, he lurched forward through the red light, spun his Marquis fiercely to the right, and took off in a blue haze of tire smoke heading southbound.

Kenny coasted to a gentle stop when he got to the corner. He waited for the light to turn green. Assured the guy got the message. He made a quiet left and headed northbound past the Federal Center. Destination unknown.

CHAPTER SEVEN

Battle Creek

Instead of going home, Kenny drove to his friend Kam's place and spent the night in Springfield. Kam had that plush, cozy, two-bedroom apartment with burgundy wall-to-wall carpet, matching sofas, and a queen size bed all to herself. When he woke up at eight o'clock in it that morning. Kam had already taken off in her Kia to report for work. The apartment was quiet. But the flat screen on her nightstand was still on. He slid out of bed and got dressed. Then he walked to the bathroom and stood in front of the mirror above the sink. He peeled the Band-Aid patched on his right cheek back a tad, so that he could examine the injury below his right eye. There was a small abrasion there, a minor scratch at best, but it stung when he touched it.

While he stood in front of the mirror, he overheard a news cast on channel 41 emitting from the television. It had to do with the incident on Frelinghuysen. The police were looking for two Ford Grand Marquis's after a shootout. Last night he thought Kam might have known about the details from the eleven o' clock news. She made some comments about it, probably wondered if it was his car, but she never followed up on it, so he figured it was best not to mention it in the morning. He was pretty sure he wouldn't have to. Kam normally pulled out for work at four or five am. She left breakfast for him in the microwave. He had too much on his mind to contemplate food, so he made do with a cup of coffee and crawled back in bed. He wanted to sleep. Kam didn't care if he hung out there. At times she gave him the keys to go and come as he pleased. Just as he got comfortable, his sister Jenny hit him up with a call asking if he could drive her to the Kroger pharmacy to pick up a script of pain meds for her migraines.

He spent five minutes getting ready to go pick her up. Then he took off in his car and swung to the south side. Jenny stayed in a little house on Harris Street, less than fifteen minutes away. When he turned off South Capital and drove three or four blocks down Meacham, a crew of BCPD police cars filed in behind him—three or four units, overheads and grills flickering like crazy.

One of the officers' voices came over his unit's PA with a harsh, direct, command. "You, driving the red Marquis . . . pull over!"

Kenny wasn't in the mood to pull over. He learned about cops growing up. All he had seen growing up were white men in blue uniforms hauling black men away from their families. Even for minor stuff. He had his own experience. The memory stretched back over a decade when he was pulled over for a traffic citation while on parole in the 90's. He never got that district court minor fine, or probation, or 30 days in the county jail. He got sent back to the penitentiary on a parole violation systematically designed to turn that minor traffic citation into a twelve-year prison sentence.

Only after he recalled the words of his oldest sister Elaine in his head— "Kenny, don't do nothing to go back"—did he comply. As soon as he pulled over, four or five cops leaped out of their squad cars with guns and rifles drawn. A crowd of people quickly gathered across the street like there was a standoff in progress. Some came out of their homes and stood on their porches.

One of the gentlemen standing in the crowd across the street knew Kenny and yelled, "Yo, KD . . . Why they harassing you, man?"

Then a woman from the crowd shouted, "Leave the brother alone! Y'all white cops always in our neighborhood messing with folks!" Except the first cop who appeared outside his window wasn't a white cop. He was an African American cop.

"Put your hands up where I can see them!" he ordered.

Kenny knew some cops nowadays operated outside their ethical procedures of conduct. A wrong twitch could get a guy's front seat painted red with a Glock. He might have taken on some gorilla type dudes back in his heyday, but flesh ain't built to take on bullets. So, he flashed his hands up in full view and played dumb.

"Do you mind telling me why I was pulled over, officer?"

The cop ignored the question. "Sir, I need you to step out of the car!"

"For what?"

"Step out of the car now, sir!" the officer repeated.

Kenny got out.

"Turn around and put your hands on the hood!" the officer ordered.

Kenny complied as three white cops moved in and watched him search his pockets. After finding his wallet he removed his license and state ID and read his name audibly.

"Kenny G. Daws, huh."

"Yeah, that's me," Kenny uttered. "So, what's the reason I was pulled over?"

The cop's eyes darted from the ID to Kenny. "Well, Mr. Daws, we were dispatched to a residence on Frelinghuysen yesterday. The 911 call reported shots being fired around the location. Several people in the area say two Grand Marquis's sped away from the scene. And the Marquis you're driving happens to fit the description of one of the cars."

"Yeah, well. I don't know anything about it," Kenny lied. "Furthermore, my car is burgundy, not red."

The officer bobbed his head lightly up and down as he handed Kenny's driver license to the white officer on his right.

"Run the plates. Make sure they're proper," he said to him.

The cop went back to his patrol unit and came back in less than five minutes.

"The plates check out," he informed. Then he looked at Kenny, sharply. "I see you just got out about six months ago, Mr. Daws."

"Yeah. What else you want to know?"

"Since you asked, we want to search the vehicle," the officer stated.

"Got a warrant?"

The African American officer unsnapped a pair cuffs, dangled them in front of him.

"I got these," he muttered. "If you want, we can a take a ride to the station. And you can wait there until we get the warrant."

Kenny glanced at the handcuffs. Stepped aside. The whole time they combed through the car he said nothing. The K-9 unit showed up with a German Shepard that went sniffing inside the interior and trunk. They found nothing. A Crown Vic drove up and parked behind a patrol unit moments after they were done. Some detective climbed out in a white-collar shirt, blue tie, solid black shoes. He was on his cell phone but cut the call when he approached the uniforms.

"How's it going, Jamison?" He was talking to the African American officer.

"The car's clean," he replied. "None of the witnesses got any identifications or license plate numbers. I would say not good. If I had a penny for every Ford Marquis . . ."

"Yeah, I know. I'd be rich too," the detective interrupted. "Name?"

"Kenny Daws," the officer replied.

All the while the detective was talking, he was looking past the officer's shoulder at Kenny. Kenny was leaning against the front panel of his car when the detective strolled up to him with a few choice words.

"Mr. Daws, I am detective Mackey. I'm not here to waste time. So, here's what I think. I think you were one of the guys on Frelinghuysen yesterday. And I would really like to haul you off to jail right now. But since we have nothing at this point. It's a good day for you. At least for now. However, I will be keeping tabs on you."

Kenny smiled and responded, "Well, if you and your buddies are done here. I got things to do!"

The detective's face crumpled into a fitful frown before he snapped, "Don't get puffy with me! You black . . ."

He paused and cut his eyes at the African American officer. The stunned expression on the officer's face said more than words. The detective backed off.

"Let him go!" he said.

The detective and street cops walked back to their units. The Crown Vic took off first, the first patrol car took off next, then the second car.

Then the third and fourth. Kenny was standing on the side of his Marquis with four doors open when he heard music by the R&B group Maze thumping out of a triple-white Escalade that drove by. It was that same white Escalade again. The one he saw in Washington Heights and yesterday on Frelinghuysen. When it drove past heading towards Fountain Street, it slowed and turned into an alley a few houses from the corner.

It idled a good minute before the rear door opened. The Hispanic man who climbed out waved at him. Then he climbed back in, and the Escalade drove off.

Kenny stared at the guy curiously before he jumped in and drove away. This time he got a good look at him. Could it be him? he asked himself. Then his cell phone thrilled a few seconds later with a short text message that made him smile right after he read it:

Ola, Kenny. I will text you the address later today where I want you to meet me tonight at nine o'clock. It's been a long time, amigo. Hector . . .

CHAPTER EIGHT

Battle Creek

The address Hector texted later that day belonged to a home located in Gull Lake. The driver sat outside of Kenny's district. Gull Lake was an affluent suburban area with magnificent views. Businesspeople stayed in this section. The mansions they lived in sat on beautifully landscaped grounds. Normally traffic in Gull Lake was light. But when he pulled up across the street from the home he was directed to. The curb and driveway were lined with luxury cars. After pressing the doorbell, he stepped back and waited. An elderly Hispanic man answered the door. He had on a velvet robe. The slacks he wore underneath hung over a pair of refined loafers. The cane under his right hand appeared to be supporting him.

"Ola, Kenny," he muttered.

Kenny heard the familiar voice, studied the face behind the scruff beard. "Uncle Frank!"

"Yes, it's me, young man. Please. Come in."

The elderly Colombian held the door open and stepped aside to let him enter. Kenny walked in, heard music playing, and realized there was a party in progress.

"It's been a lot of years, Kenny. How old are you now?"

"You know, I was just going to ask you that very same thing," Kenny said.

Frank returned the humor. "I am so old now. I don't even care to remember!"

The two hackled. Kenny thought about the day Hector introduced him and Ajax to his uncle. It didn't take him long to warm up to them. They were Hector's best friends. And while people knew him as Francisco in Colombia. In the U.S, he was simply Uncle Frank Colón to them.

"Hector told me you would be coming, Kenny. He's down in the basement. I will take you to him," he said.

Kenny trailed him down the length of the hall, checking out the exquisite features inside his baby mansion. Everything about Uncle Frank's home was impressive. When he came to the door that led downstairs. He stopped.

"This is as far as I go, young man." Frank held the door open. "The noise down there is too loud for these old ears now days."

"I understand," said Kenny.

He descended to the basement and gazed around at the large crowd. More than fifty people were down there. The whole place pulsed with loud music pounding out of a half dozen speakers. And there were mirrors everywhere.

Hector was sitting on a plush red sofa talking with a Hispanic woman sandwiched between him and another gentleman. Kenny wandered over and announced his arrival.

"Hector, what's happening, bro?"

Hector heard his name and looked up at him. "Hey, Kenny! I see you came; I was beginning to wonder if you would show up."

"How could I not? It's a surprise to see you."

Kenny turned to glance at the party goers. There were people dancing. Everyone was decked out in a wide array of updated fashion. Hector and the big bulky Hispanic guy to the left of the woman looked like they had on thousand-dollar suits. The Berluti loafers on Hector's feet had that archival B-logo on the vamp. The Hispanic woman winked at Kenny. Then stood up anxiously to a track of reggaetón the DJ put on.

"Bale conmigo," she said to him.

Kenny didn't understand one word.

Hector smiled and diligently translated. "She said, dance with her."

"Me?"

The woman grabbed Kenny's arm, tugging him towards the dance floor before Hector could reply. Without hesitation, she began doing the salsa, cumbia, tango. Kenny didn't know. He hadn't been on a dance floor since the 80's. He thought maybe he could match the woman's sure-footed pace with throwback rusty versions of the Smurf and electric slide with a little gigolo in between. Until he decided to stop embarrassing himself. Instead, he watched her do her thing, along with the party mix of Hispanics, African Americans, Asians, and hip whites who let her take over the dance floor. Energized by the pump and glitter of swirling lights, she danced, enjoyed the attention of the people, until the song died. When the DJ switched tracks. She led Kenny to a quiet corner.

"Can I ask you something?"

"Yeah, sure," he replied.

"What was it like in prison for you?"

He looked at her oddly. "How did you . . ."

She touched his hand. Kenny drew back, suddenly recalling her face. She was in the passenger seat of the Escalade, sitting next to the man on the sofa with Hector, who was driving it.

"It's okay, Poppi. I know you're Hector's friend. Your name is Kenny Daws. Right?"

Her words came out slurred. A little lascivious grin followed. The blend of brandy and coke he smelled coming off her suggested she was tipsy. She was flirting with him so openly, so flagrantly. Hector had been watching from the sofa the whole time. Never said a word. But when he glanced his way this time. Hector was up on his feet walking straight towards them.

"Okay, muchacha. Time's up," he stated, as he approached. "Me and Kenny have a lot to discuss."

The woman looked at him, rolled her eyes. "Ahi, whatever, Hector," she retorted.

Uncle Frank's basement was perfect for large scale entertainment. After she staggered off, Hector escorted Kenny to his bar room. Since it was sealed off with soundproof walls of transparent glass, it allowed them to sit and talk in privacy with a view to the dance floor. Once they sat down at the pearl-smoked Indian countertop in front of the bar, Hector began talking.

"Kenny, I apologize on the young lady's behalf. The way she pulled you onto the dance floor like that was very rude."

"An apology isn't necessary. I was just wondering what her name was?"

"Her name is Gabriela Colón . . ."

"Colón?"

"Yes. She's my first cousin. My uncle Francisco's daughter."

"I never knew Uncle Frank had a daughter."

"Gabriela has been in Colombia all her life. She only came to America a few years ago."

"Hope you don't mind me saying. But she's . . ."

"What . . . beautiful?" Hector cut in. "Many men besides you have reminded her. But tonight, she's drunk!"

Kenny smiled.

Hector peered at their reflections in the wall of mirrors behind the bar, changing his tune. "You know, I wondered what happened to you for a long time after you left all those years back. Eventually, word got back you went to prison."

"Yeah, things weren't quite the same for me after that."

"I heard you got out and went back," said Hector.

"Unfortunately," Kenny replied.

Hector sensed his reluctance to go into details. He didn't have to. He already knew it was a minor traffic violation that sent him back for twelve years. That bitter taste was enough. He saw it. Backed off.

"Well, you're out now. That's all that matters. I know the transition hasn't been easy. Especially with that job at the Main Street Market. I highly doubt that apartment on Manchester is sufficient. I saw it when we drove by."

"Better than a park bench. I mean, I get your concern. But you could have stopped or blew your horn. Why didn't you?"

"I had to see how you were managing out here a few more days before I could determine if you were ready."

"Ready for what?" asked Kenny.

"The offer of a lifetime," Hector answered. "You see, we have that same experience in common."

"Really. How so?" asked Kenny.

Hector replied, "You never knew it, but four years after you went in. I got busted in a federal sting operation in Boston. The feds indicted me on narcotics trafficking."

Kenny looked at him, subdued. Then asked the basic question. "What happened?"

Hector replied, "When you disappeared, I went back to Colombia. Me and my cousin Carlos started working for our uncle Ferdinand. At the time he owned the cartel in South America. But he died. That's when my cousin took over. Carlos kept the farms and manufacturing labs up. Eventually, he put me in charge of the smuggling operations. We were moving a lot of weight in narcotics. And we had lots of ways to move it. Things got a little tense moving weight through Mexico. The cartels in Tijuana and Sinaloa became unhappy with Carlos. They said he was trying to take over their routes. The deal between him and Mexican cartel fell apart. A war broke out. My arrest was tied to it. I was managing a large shipment aboard a freighter destined for the United States. The FBI got a tip from someone the cartel in Mexico had inside the agency. We were put under surveillance. They raided that freighter right after we began unloading it. Some of the farms Carlos had in the U.S. were later raided. Strike teams were sent to Colombia, El Salvador, Costa Rica, and Peru, where they hit several warehouses and labs. I went to trial on eighteen counts of trafficking. Carlos hired some bulldog lawyer out of New York to represent me. It didn't matter. I was found guilty. Got forty years. Did my time at that federal penitentiary in Marion, Illinois. My cousin was a big man in Colombia. The Mexicans just had people with connections to other people that were bigger. The only good thing was that I got out after ten years. Carlos paid off a judge to grant me a sentence reduction."

"Money talks!" said Kenny.

"If that's how you want to put it. But, like I said, I understand the struggle."

Kenny lapsed into a moment of reflective silence. Over the years, he often wondered what happened to Hector, too. He always assumed he would grow up successful. Twenty years was a big leap from high school.

Hector wasn't the same. He was older, radically different. He was being chauffeured around in an Escalade. He was sporting fancy suits and sweet-scented cologne. Right at that moment he could only speculate how it would feel had he known Hector's uncle was a cartel boss back when they were youth. At least now he knew where his supply came from. The reality of him as a kid, twenty years ago, and the man he was now. Kenny thought he knew a little about the Latino kid in school. He knew absolutely nothing about the adult. Except that he appeared to be doing big things these days that added a little more grit to his already polished look.

He pulled back from the short sequence of thoughts running through his mind, and said, "What's up with this offer you mention?"

Hector's eyes darted to the scenic picture of a huge mountain hanging on the back wall of the bar. Then he pointed at it. "You see that mountain?"

Kenny followed his gaze.

"That's the Bolivar Mountain," he continued. "Its height rises an estimated 18,947 feet. It sits near the Rio Valley where I grew up. If you're wondering how I got the number to text you, retrieving information is relatively easy for me. I have been keeping tabs on you since you got out. I know things have been tight for brothers like you out here. It's tight for a lot of brothers everywhere now days. But that mountain." Hector pointed again. "Reaching the top of that mountain is your opportunity of a lifetime!"

Kenny looked away. Stared at Hector. Wondered what game he was on. "I don't get it."

"You see the peak on that mountain, Kenny? It's the highest one in Colombia. Picture in your mind a bunch of rich folks up there at the very top of it where they say success and wealth lies. Then picture in your mind a bunch of poor folks like you at the very bottom of it who have tried to make that climb up because they are told time and time again by the rich folks at the top that when they throw down the ropes of opportunity. The people at the bottom can make the climb up to the top to experience that same success and wealth. In this country they call reaching the top the American dream! Right? But many poor folks at the bottom know the struggle of their failed repeated attempts to climb up. Just like they know the ropes of opportunity the rich folks up there throw down to them are simply not strong enough. They have defects in their designs that allow for only a few to make the climb up from the bottom. So, if too many are climbing up at one time. What happens?"

Kenny answered, "The ropes snap."

"That's right. And most of the poor fall right back down to the bottom."

Kenny glanced through the bar's transparent window at an empty basement. The party goers had left three hours ago. Gabriela had fallen asleep on the red sofa. Hector's driver was cleaning up. Uncle Frank and his wife had turned in hours ago. But here they were, alone, chatting like long lost brothers reunited.

"The offer is a special job my cousin Carlos has," said Hector. "But he wants the right person for it."

Kenny stared at him long enough to register the look Hector gave him. "And you think I'm the person for it."

"I wouldn't be here if I didn't. It all depends on whether you want to reach the top of that mountain, Kenny. From the looks of them rags you got on, you're overdue for a new look."

Kenny glanced into the mirrors behind the bar. He had on a Detroit Lions T-shirt with blue jeans he bought at Max-10's. The discount bubble-Reeboks on his feet came off the rack at K-Mart.

"A lot of years passed between us, amigo. But I never forgot about you, Kenny. This job is one which you will have to prepare for. And there are rules. You cannot move recklessly like that little stunt that happen day before yesterday . . ."

"What stunt?" said Kenny.

Hector held his gaze. "I read about that situation on Frelinghuysen in the Battle Creek Enquire. Uncle Francisco is a faithful subscriber."

Kenny shrugged, said nothing.

Hector took out a pen and wrote on a sheet of paper. "It's late. Here's my number. Give me a call tomorrow . . ."

"You haven't told me any details about the job," said Kenny.

Hector reached inside his pocket and pulled out a thick wad of cash. After peeling off twenty grand, he placed the bills in front of Kenny.

"Take that. Toss out them old Reeboks and buy some real rags. I have planned a trip for us. We can discuss the job then."

CHAPTER NINE

Battle Creek

K enny drove home in amazement. Hector had given him twenty grand. And he followed it up with the announcement of his planned trip. Within a period of twenty-four hours, he felt like his whole world had turned inside out. After he slipped quietly inside his apartment he wanted to relax, to sleep if he could. Instead, he was now lying in bed staring up, eyes fixed on the portion of cracked paint peeling away from the ceiling. Hector was right. The apartment was crappy. It was cramped and stuffy. The floors creaked. The walls were a disappointing shade of gray. The dated couch that made an island in the living room sat in front of a small 13" Clear Tech television with not much else to look at. Lying there on that narrow cot he called a bed, he couldn't stop thinking about the money. He smiled about it, rightfully so, when he was counting it. He had to recount it again just to make sure it was all there. Money. Everybody wanted it. Everybody didn't have it. Hector had it.

The following morning, he fired up the Grand Marquis and drove to Jacob's Men's Wear. He liked the store's montage. It was clean, practical, and offered the latest styles in men's clothing. With Hector's suggestion in mind, he went on a binge. He selected dress shirts off the racks, suits for sure, with ties and casual wear. Not the Versace type. He looked better in Brooks Brothers. Before he left, he even bagged a pair of Stacy Adams and a watch for the wrist. It felt good shopping, he could afford it, plus the generous tip he left with the salesperson on the way out.

After he returned home around 1:30 pm he phoned Hector. Hector wanted him to rendezvous at Battle Creek Airport. Kenny didn't know where they were going nor when he would be back. It didn't matter. He figured he could use a vacation.

He spent thirty minutes packing for the trip, then took off in a yellow cab that drove west on Dickman Road towards the airport. On the way there he passed by a house he once lived in as a child. Memories flooded into his mind, some good, some bad. Like the time he was home alone one night inside that very house. He was only seven or eight. But he remembered sitting on the couch in the living room. It was stormy that night. Some of the windows had spider cracks sealed with duct tape that did little to prevent the fierce wind from blowing in cold air. He was freezing and hungry. There were no lights on. The refrigerator was empty. The front door had no working lock and was barely clinging to the last hinge when a lone figure showed up and walked through it. He was helpless and startled until he heard the voice of his big sister Elaine asking why he was home alone sitting in the dark.

Kenny never forgot the way Elaine found him that night. His sister's rescue was as joyous as the birth of his baby daughter Tia in the summer of 1984. She was asleep in her mother Camilla's arms when he showed up at her bedside. How precious she looked all snugged up in the cotton blanket she was wrapped in. The minute she opened her little eyes he told her how much he loved her.

The memory faded when the cab arrived at the airport. Hector and the woman and the big bulky guy were waiting near the tarmac.

"You're five minutes late," Hector said after he climbed out.

Kenny replied, "Your watch is running five minutes fast."

Hector flashed a smile and said, "Last night I didn't introduce you to my other cousin. This is Toro. My uncle Federico's son."

Kenny looked at the buff Latino driver as he stepped forward with his hand extended.

"Mucho gusto," It's a pleasure, he stated.

Kenny nodded as they exchanged handshakes.

Gabriela was glossing over his attire the moment he exited the cab. "Ola, Kenny," she stated. "Me gusta la ropa nueva," I like the new clothes.

Kenny showed up in a three-button polo shirt with cotton pants and solo pilot sunglasses. He was about to ask Hector to translate. But the quiet hiss of a plane engine made the four of them turn in the direction of the aircraft at the same time.

"Ready for our trip, Kenny?" Hector asked.

Kenny's eyes widened when he saw a jet waiting on the runway. "In that? That's a Gulfstream!"

"A Gulfstream 650, to be exact," Hector said.

Astonished, Kenny asked, "Where are we flying to, bro?"

Hector replied, "Colombia!"

CHAPTER TEN

Battle Creek

The takeoff was swift and smooth. The moment the jet streaked into the cumulus clouds, the city's skyline faded into an afterthought in Kenny's mind. Hector was seated comfortably across from him when a young Latino woman came down the aisle and stopped at their seats.

"Un coffee, señor Colón? she offered.

"Si, gracias," Hector replied.

Hector grabbed the cup of coffee she offered from the tray she was holding. Kenny declined. He was anxious to hear about Hector's opportunity of a lifetime and how his metaphor about getting to the top of that mountain peak could become his own reality.

"So, tell me about this job you mentioned last night," he stated.

Hector sipped his coffee. "First, there is something I must show you."

Hector craned around in the seat and looked at Gabriela. She was sitting with Toro four rows back on the other side of the aisle. As soon as he gestured for her, she rose quickly and walked to their seats with a portable laptop.

"Kenny, what I am about to show you will help you understand the seriousness of this offer," said Hector. He waited until Gabriela settled into the empty seat next to Kenny. Then he gave her a light nod and said, "Show him."

Gabriela pressed the on button to the laptop. When the screen lit up, she held it out for Kenny.

Kenny took the laptop. Transferred his gaze to the screen. There was a video playing. It showed three white men standing at a table inside a warehouse. Five Spanish men were standing on the other side facing them. Big bold yellow FBI letters emblazoned on the jackets and vests of the white men were enough for him to identify them as federal agents. He wasn't sure if the Spanish men were American born Hispanics or Latinos born outside the country. A few seconds into the video two white men wearing dark suits padded into view. One of them had silvery grey hair and looked to be in his mid-fifties. The younger man with him snapped open a briefcase to remove two wrapped kilos of heroin he placed on the table.

"Put these in," said Gabriela.

Kenny took the pair of earbuds she gave him and plugged them into the laptop's audio jack. Then he watched one of the Spanish men with a tribal tattoo inked on his face take out a knife he used to slice into the cellophane. After he extracted a small quantity of the heroin, he dropped it into a bowl. He added a drop of liquid solution and swished it around with the tip of the blade until the mixture changed color.

"Es puro," It's pure, Kenny heard him say.

"There you have it gentlemen," said the silver haired man. "This is grade 4 heroin. I want it on the streets in the U.S. within a few weeks. This is my operation. There will be no questions asked. Get it done!"

"Anytime you guarantee it goes through, no problem. We will ship it," said the Spanish man.

"Who's gonna question the FBI?" the silver haired man replied.

The camera inside the warehouse started to pan around. First it settled on the narcotics stacked up in barrels against the walls. Then it panned on a pair of FBI men who emerged from a back room with two blindfolded Spanish men. The agents and Spanish men at the table watched as they ordered the blindfolded men to sit on wooden chairs. What happened next left Kenny stunned. The FBI man on the right shot and killed the blindfolded guy in front of him with a point-blank head shot. The agent on the left plunged a syringe into the neck of the other blindfolded guy. In less than thirty seconds he started convulsing and foaming at the mouth. Then he fell to the floor and stopped moving.

The screen shimmied and blanked out. Kenny looked up at Gabriela and Hector, astonished. The two of them stared at each other gloomily for several seconds, as if there was something hidden from him that only they knew between themselves.

Baffled, Kenny instantly appealed to Hector. "What was *that*, bro?"

"Take it away," said Hector. He was talking to Gabriela. Kenny gave her back the laptop. Gabriela got up and returned to her seat.

Hector answered, "What you saw happened about two months before you got out, Kenny. One of the men who died on that video was a close relative of ours. The older gentleman in the suit ordered it . . ."

"The guy with the silver hair," Kenny interrupted.

"Yes. He ordered his agents to seize the drugs afterwards. Only they never destroyed them. They sold the drugs to make a profit for themselves. And not all that profit was for cash."

"What about the Spanish men?" asked Kenny.

"They belong to the cartel in Cali, Colombia. These men are at war with my cousin Carlos."

"It's still hard to believe some of them were FBI agents," Kenny exclaimed.

"Corrupt FBI agents," Hector corrected. "The worse kind. My uncle Ferdinand shared stories with me and my cousin Carlos about men like them. He told us that during the 1960's war between the United States and North Vietnam, corrupt military officials and CIA operatives ran secret covert drug trafficking operations. In Cambodia, he said they struck a deal with Hmong guerilla fighters to fly heroin and coke from hidden jungle strips in exchange for the information they were gathering on the communist enemy in the north. The narcotics were being dispensed worldwide on a phony airline service they set up. Much of it ended up in poor neighborhoods in your country."

"I've seen the documentaries about that," Kenny said. "But that went down when Nixon was in office. This ain't the sixties. It's 2011. What's your point?"

"The point is, it didn't matter to them when all that dope poured over into low-income neighborhoods. To them it was a benefit. They got information from the Hmong on the communist. And they used the sales from drugs to fund the war."

"Most wars are funded with drug money," Kenny asserted. "That's old news."

"So are the low-income communities still targeted for the drugs to be poured into. Only now, my cousin Carlos is doing something about it," Hector responded.

"Your cousin," said Kenny. "He's a cartel boss!"

"He was, yes," Hector replied. "But things have changed. I think if he could, he would destroy every manufacturing lab on the face of the planet. What he sees now is an opportunity to rid communities of this destructive poison. To do some good, Kenny. That's what this job is about. And I am offering you that same opportunity."

"It's been a long time, Hector. I am pleased by the offer. But I see you're riding in Cadillacs and flying on jets. So, what exactly have you been up to these days?"

"Oh, just tearing away some of that infrastructure from the biggest drug traffickers. I'm not talking about small time street hustlers either. I'm talking about the real movers and shakers behind the low-level movers and shakers. The ones who really make all the transactions happen."

"That's heavy stuff, Hector."

"Don't worry. If you join us, you will be prepared for the task. And by the time you come back for that daughter of yours, you will be a new man."

"How did you know . . . Never mind. I gather there's real cash to be made in the process."

"Yes, and no," replied Hector. "We've washed our hands of the money made from the narcotics trade. Dirty money only defeats the purpose. Just remember what I told you about that mountain peak, Kenny. Because there's a whole lot of greed and overdue taxes up there."

"I don't understand," said Kenny.

Hector picked up a cellular phone from the empty seat next to him. "You see this?"

Kenny fixed his eyes on it. "Yeah, what about it?"

Hector replied, "This phone will be your first order of business. It has state-of-the-art ciphered email and text messaging. With its untraceable global positioning technology, you can send and receive messages from anywhere in the world that no GPS network can detect. This phone is the job. That's only if you want it. It's that simple."

Hector adjusted the Kufi cap he had on, threw on some coconut-base face oil. "So, what's it going to be?" he asked.

Kenny gave him a straight look and ran the offer through his mind. Thoughts of his daughter, a new job in a foreign country, the unknown ahead. Those three things began swirling inside his head. If he took the job, he would be delving into uncharted waters. He didn't know if he could handle it. But he did know the reality that Hector had acquired some big money, and that was making him lean that way, because suddenly he was wanting some too.

"I'll take it," he muttered. "Beats working at that Main Street Market!"

Part Three
The Soldier's Story

CHAPTER ELEVEN

California
Burmaxx Veteran's Rehab Center
November 2015

D ex Jones's day started out with his same weekly routine. He got up and drove to the rehab center for his therapy session. He parked in his normal slot. He entered the building and strolled across the brass-oak lobby to the elevator he rode up to the second floor. He stepped out and made the short walk down the hallway to the office door of room 213. The door had a gold nameplate on it that read: Therapeutic Psychiatrist, Dr. Rubin Petro.

When he turned the knob and walked in, Dr. Rubin Petro was seated at his desk dressed in one of those elbow-patch jackets he normally wore with rich slacks and heavy Oxford's. The head shrink was a thinnish Cuban American, maybe sixty-three, his hairdo looked like it came off a 1960's Beatle's album cover. But clothes always signified wealth.

"Good morning, Mr. Jones," he greeted. "I see you decided to show up today. Please have a seat."

Dex shut the door and sat down on the couch to his left.

"You missed two consecutive sessions I scheduled. Any particular reason why?"

"Personal matters came up," said Dex. "I couldn't make it."

Rubin Petro scribbled a note on his chart. Then he got up and walked around the desk to take up his position in the chair he pulled up close to the couch so that he could sit comfortably while he delved into Dex's mind.

"I'm concerned about the dreams and flashbacks you shared with me last time you came in. I'm equally concerned that you haven't been taking the prescription I gave you. That's not good when your experiences are directly related to—"

"I know . . . PTSD," Dex cut in. "You've told me a hundred times.".

"Then you should really stick with the meds. The process of therapy is very important. You must take it seriously if you want to get better."

Dex gave his head shrink a frank stare, then replied, "I have been coming here for almost four years. Is that not serious enough?"

The psych just nodded and continued the line of analytic questions. "Have you experienced any recent flashback or dream during the past two weeks?"

"I had a dream last night."

"Care to talk about it?"

"Not really."

"You seem a bit agitated."

"I could be."

"Agitation never helps. You can't keep everything bottled up inside you, Mr. Jones. Especially if you expect to move beyond the past."

"How can I move beyond the past when there are still parts missing that I can't recall?"

Dr. Petro stared at him. He spoke calmly, quietly. "You say these dreams and flashbacks you have at times are difficult to decipher between reality and what isn't reality. Maybe not remembering the missing parts isn't such a bad thing."

"You don't understand what it's like not knowing," Dex replied.

"I suppose you're right. Nevertheless, it's good to get things out. So why don't you lie down on the couch. Try to relax. And if you can I would like for you to take me back through the sequences of the dream you said you experienced last night."

Dex dropped his head and stared at the carpet as if he'd found a spot there to focus on while he pondered for a moment. He didn't want to be inside the office. He didn't want to spend another hour listening to boring conversations. But he stretched out on the couch anyway. He closed his eyes. Measured himself with deep slow breaths until he started to feel himself disconnect from Dr. Rubin Petro to reconnect with the dream he began to narrate.

"I dreamt I was with a platoon of Navy SEALS. There were fourteen of us. It was nighttime. We were on a patrol in the Philippines when we came upon this small town that hardly had any lights. We heard this noise in the darkness. There was a big explosion that erupted afterwards. Everyone evacuated the Humvees with their weapons. The team leader thought we were under attack. He ordered us to start shooting. So, we started firing off rounds. The gunners were ringing off fifty cals. We just kept shooting at everything we saw moving. We just—"

Dex had to stop. He was sweating. His hands balled into fists. He couldn't continue.

"It's okay, Mr. Jones. You can open your eyes now," the psych said. He watched the soldier slowly open his eyes, then inquired, "Was that all you remembered about it?"

"Yeah. I woke up," said Dex.

"And there was nothing whatsoever you recalled about your last mission?"

"Nothing," Dex replied.

Rubin Petro wrote down more notes on his clipboard. When he finished, he pressed the button to the intercom on the table beside the chair.

"Yes, Dr. Petro," a female voice said through the speaker.

He responded, "Page Stephanie. Tell her she can come in now."

Dex stared at him. There was silence in the room. The door opened a moment later, and a tall Caucasian woman strolled in with a petite Asian nurse carrying a metal tray.

"Good morning, Rubin," she said.

Dr. Petro nodded, then looked at Dex. "Mr. Jones, this is Dr. Stephanie Castree. Dr. Castree is our neurol scientist specialist. She's one of the best we have."

She smiled and leaned past him to shake Dex's hand. Dex looked at her long red hair, her slender pale neck, and green eyes. He'd seen her around the rehab center from time to time. She always wore that sterile lab coat she had on over the expensive cloths and high heels she wore.

"Dr. Castree is here to give you the new Hc3 prescription we want you to start," Dr. Petro said. "The Hc3 will be a much more effective treatment than the Hc2 you've been taking."

"We would like to start you off with a little injection today," the neurol scientist added.

Dex glanced at the silver tray the petite Asian nurse was holding. There was a syringe on it. A clear bottle containing the liquid form of Hc3. A brown bottle filled with pills sat beside it. The Asian nurse placed the tray down on the table and rolled up his left sleeve. After she peeled open an alcohol pad and took hold of his arm to clean the injection area. Dex jerked his arm back and sat up.

"Think I will pass on the shot, Doc. Last thing I need is more drugs in my system."

"It's best that you take the shot," Dr. Petro insisted. "You'll get much better."

"I'll pick up a bottle of Bear aspirin on the way home."

"Aspirin won't do anything for your insomnia or paranoia. And they certainly don't help with memory loss," said the psychiatrist.

"I'll add a bottle of sleeping pills to the purchase," Dex retorted.

The psych and neurol scientist cast askance glances.

"Mr. Jones," Dr. Petro continued, "I realize you don't quite understand the seriousness of the head trauma you suffered during your last mission. The coma you were in lasted three whole days. I'm sorry. No over the counter medications will cure the kind of injuries you suffered."

"Doc, you're talking about something that happened four years ago. Right? Well, after four years I still don't remember a thing about it. So, what's the use of continuing a treatment that's not working?"

The neurol scientist flashed her beautiful pearly whites. "Mr. Jones, you should listen to Dr. Petro's advice. Hyorphine Colybezentol-3 is a proven drug in our laboratories. We've seen evidence of recovery in memory lost."

Dex suddenly didn't like the energy emanating in the room. He grew agitated. Annoyed, he stood up and headed for the door.

"Mr. Jones, just a minute," the neurol scientist said. The moment he turned. She snatched the brown pill bottle of Hc3 off the tray the Asian nurse held and approached him. "Look, you're a soldier. I've been treating soldiers for a very long time. I understand how you feel about this treatment stuff. It's not always easy. It takes a long time for veterans like you to recover from traumatic effects. Some never do. We're only trying to help. So, in case you have a change of heart. I only ask that you take these with you."

His soulful brown eyes gazed into hers. He raised his hand, and without looking at the bottle she held up, he grabbed it, and walked out.

The psychiatrist waited for the door to shut behind him before he walked over to the neurol scientist.

"It's the third week he hasn't taken the meds," he said.

His voice seemed to rise with worry. If the soldier's mind was made up, and he wasn't going to change it to take the meds. There was only one option in the neurol scientist's mind to address the immediate problem.

"Better send a report to the higher-ups," she replied. "They will expect the update on his status right away."

She opened the door. The Asian nurse hurried across the room and shouldered passed him on the heels of the neurol scientist when they left.

Rubin Petro sat down at his computer thinking about the day the two CIA officials and the ranked navy men assigned him and Dr. Castree to treat Dexter C. Jones. He was a top priority special case they told him. He and Dr. Castree were specifically chosen to handle his care in a manner they desired. His list of treating men and women being trained to kill by the nation's military forces was a long one. But his treatment of Dexter Jones was by far more different than anyone else he'd come across. Any failure to monitor the capacity of his mental state closely could put them in danger. He understood this clearly when he wrote up the report on his computer and pressed send.

CHAPTER TWELVE

California
Burma's Veteran Rehab Center

Burmaxx Veteran's Rehab Center was ten-stories. When the visitor from Langley walked inside twenty-four hours later. He took the elevator straight up to the fifth floor. The door to the conference room he arrived at was polished mahogany, and it was standing open. Not that too open, but open enough to see Dr. Petro and Dr. Castree seated at the large oval-shaped conference table waiting for him when he walked in and closed it behind him.

"Dr. Petro . . . Dr. Castree," he stated.

They looked at him at the same time. Dr. Petro spoke first.

"Hello, agent Kellerman. Would you like any coffee before we get started?" he asked.

"No, thanks," the agent replied. He padded across the room to one of the soft leathery high-back chairs he settled into. "My superior and I read the status report. I flew out here to get the full assessment in person. I'd like to get started on that right away."

Dr. Castree rose to her feet. The aroma from her perfume was in the air when she padded around the table and stood next to the oversized projector she approached. After she picked up the small remote control, she switched it on. The screen lit up with bright green letters that said: CT SCAN DATA ENTRY REPORT: SUBJECT: Dexter Cornell Jones.

She clicked a button on the remote. Images of the subject's brain appeared on split screen with a report on the far right.

"I will start with the imaging report I did on the subject back in 2011," she stated. "The first exam I performed on him was a non-contrast CT scan, including a bone window technique. A scan of the cervical spine with a sagittal reconstruction image was also performed. The findings on the left subdural hematoma measured 1cm in maximal width. This is seen along the cerebral cavity." She circled the area with a cursor. "It appeared to be mild. But what it showed was an associated depressed left frontal skull fracture with approximately 3 mm of depression. The right side of the subject's brain suffered an adjacent sub arachnoid hemorrhage inside the sulci of the frontal parietal junction. Take a close look at his cerebral cortex highlighted in yellow, agent Kellerman. Do you see it?"

The CIA agent zeroed in on the area where the cursor rested. "Yes."

"That's a small bifrontal contusion measuring up to 1cm bilaterally. The area just below indicated a 1cm right temporal lobe contusion with a small posterior right subdural hematoma along the medial aspect of the temporal lobe measuring 4 mm. An associated sub arachnoid was found along the right Sylvan fissure and right frontal sulci. There was no significant midline shift or hydrocephalus noted."

"What was your final assessment of the subject's coma in 2011?" agent Kellerman asked.

"Mr. Jones's coma was caused by blunt force trauma. We removed bullets from his upper right pectoral and abdomen. We also found one lodged near the spinal region. Images of the cervical spine canal indicated no definite fracture or trauma to the spinal canal stenosis. The CT scan impression showed multiple areas of intra cranial hemorrhage. But the largest bleed was seen in the left subdural space measuring 1 cm in width."

The CIA man waited until she was done talking, and then said, "The status report said the subject hasn't been taking his Hc2. What is the prognosis on the drug's effectiveness if he stops all together?"

Dr. Castree responded, "The drug's is not supposed to wear off . . ."

"But it could," Dr. Petro said, adding his own prognosis.

Kellerman shifted his attention to the psychiatrist. "Explain what you mean by that."

"Well, there's no doubt that the Hyrophine Colybenzentol is the best mind-altering drug developed through our laboratories. I must credit Dr. Castree for the fine job she did manipulating the neurol transmitters in the subject's brain. I mean he hasn't had one recollection of that last mission in four years. To keep a mind erased for that period is beyond outstanding. But the human brain is a very tricky agent Kellerman. There are all sorts of activity going on inside the brain's electrical circuitry. Now, there's a slim chance this will happen with our drug. But the chances the human brain can be triggered by some dramatic event always exist. The good news is our tests patients have not regained their memories in years. But that's because they were still taking the drug. We can't say conclusively what might happen to a subject who refuses to take it over a prolonged period."

"He's right," Dr. Castree corroborated. She switched off the projector and sat back down. "I wish there was something else we could say to ease the concern. But the facts are what they are."

"Let me get this right. You're saying that with him not taking the drug it presents a greater risk we could lose total control over his mind if that ever happened?" the agent said.

Dr. Castree replied, "Correct."

Agent Kellerman looked deflated. After the meeting he stepped back into the outer hallway. He reached for his phone and used his thumb to dial the number to his superior.

A CIA man answered at the other end on the second ring. "How did it go?" he inquired.

Kellerman responded simply, "Not good."

CHAPTER THIRTEEN

California

It was Saturday. Dex was at home sitting on his favorite Lay-Z-Boy recliner, while his cousin Chopper sat on the sofa watching a nationally televised college football game with him. The USC Trojans were playing the UCLA Bruins. The score was tied 27-27 with ten minutes left in the fourth quarter. It was third and five. USC had the ball on their forty-yard line when they came out of their huddle. They were hoping the Trojans would make a major play to untie the score. But after the center hiked the ball, the quarterback faked a hand-off and went across the middle of the field with a short pass that sailed through the hands of his receiver.

"Ahh, he missed it!" Chopper bellowed. "He could have caught that. All he had to do was jump. The ball was right there!"

Dex just shook his head in disappointment. A moment later he was peering out the window at the U.S. postal truck he spotted across the street.

The mailman was already heading across the lawn of a neighbor's house when he got up to go see about the check he was waiting on. When he stepped through the door, he heard his cell phone chiming on the table next to the Lay-Z-Boy.

"Chopper, get that for me. If it's my wife Gina, tell her I'll be back in a minute."

When Chopper got up to answer the phone, Dex walked outside and met up with the mailman.

"How's it going, buddy?" the mailman asked as he approached. Most people in the neighborhood called the mailman Alfred. No one knew his last name. But he was good man. A vet, like himself, with lots of war stories to tell.

"It's my day off. So, I'm watching the game with my cousin," Dex replied. He looked down at the mail bag hanging at his side. "What do you have for me?"

Alfred dug inside it and brought out two paperback books with a couple of magazines.

"What's that?"

"Sorry, that's all I have for you today, soldier."

Alfred gave him the parcels of mail. Dex started to sort through it.

"I don't get subscriptions. Who would send me books and mags?" he asked, bewildered.

"Maybe it's a gift from our government," the mail man stated. Then he started rambling. "You know, they just don't pay military men like us enough. I mean the things we must do. But those pro athletes sure make a lot of money. They go into their sports arenas and make millions. And the only thing they have to worry about is recovering from torn ACL's, concussions, broken bones, and missing teeth. But we go into the worse kind of battles and must worry about the threat of projectiles long as our arms flying at us. Half of the time our injuries don't even involve recovery. We have to worry about avoiding fatalities! Don't you think it's about time they start paying us millions too?"

There was a stony silence when Dex didn't say anything in response. He wasn't listening. He was just standing there. Just standing there gazing at one of the magazines like he was zoned out.

"Hey, Dex. You okay, buddy?" Alfred inquired.

Alfred waved a hand in front of his face. His blank expression didn't change. But when he snapped his fingers, Dex finally flinched and shook his head.

"You say something, Alfred?"

Alfred stared at him analytically aloof. "Yeah. I sure hope you're okay, man. I think you just lost me for a few seconds there. Perhaps you should really take this day off to get a little more rest. Maybe you're putting in too much overtime."

Dex glanced around. "I'm fine, Alfred."

"Well, in that case. Enjoy the rest of your day, my friend."

Alfred parted his lips into a smile and headed back to his postal truck. Dex went back inside. Chopper tore his gaze away from the game as soon as he entered.

"It was your wife Gina who called," he said.

Dex settled back on the thick cushion of his Lay-Z-Boy recliner. "She leave a message?"

"Yep. She said she had to work late. And that she would call you later."

"She say what time?"

"Nope."

Chopper waited until the game went to another commercial. Then he bounced up off the sofa and threw on his Oakland Raider's football cap. Then he went to the door and opened it.

"Whoa, where are you going? The game ain't over," Dex said.

"I got an important errand to run, Dex. I will be back in a couple of hours."

Dex peered at the wall clock above the flat screen.

"Okay, man. Just be careful out there. I don't want to see you on the eleven o'clock news."

"You won't. I'm good, man. Just hold the fort down."

Chopper smiled. He locked the front door behind him when he left. All Dex could do was hope that he would come back in two hours like he said he would. Whatever errand he had to run he hoped it had nothing to do with his old Los Angeles gang banging crew. Chopper was a cool cat to hang with now days. But he was gone now. And he was alone. Alone with too much silence and time to think about his life in the armed forces and the mark it left on him. He was already living with unbidden flashbacks that struck without warning. He was dealing with nightmares that made him talk and weep in his sleep. At times he cried out, punched in the air, and called out people's names Chopper and Gina didn't know every time they heard him.

He wanted to put the whole terrible experience of war behind him. But the scars from war often cut deep for the average soldier. So deep that he was just too frustrated and ashamed to tell Dr. Petro that there was indeed more to the dream than what he shared two days ago.

Even if he told him the morning after they discovered they were never under attack. That it was a twelve-year-old boy playing who caused the explosion when he accidentally stepped on a Claymore mine and blew himself up.

Even if he told him that at the end of the dream, he saw him and his platoon standing over the corpses of men, women, and children mistakenly gunned down that night. What difference would it make now if he told him that it really occurred? There was nothing that could be done to change what happened and make the nightmares go away.

The cheering noise from the game silenced when another commercial came on. He grabbed the remote, channel surfed past TNT, USA, to CNN, and stayed there after he noticed the breaking news alert.

The reporter speaking into the camera was talking about a large multitude of African Americans protesting in the streets of Los Angeles. Hundreds of people were chanting NO JUSTICE! NO PEACE! in support of a young seventeen-year-old black male who was shot and killed by a police officer after a routine traffic stop. Watching it made him think. If he and his wife Gina had a son. it could have been him.

It took a moment to separate the real from the unreal. But this was real. And it was happening. Even though it looked like the nation had progressed forward. At that moment the country appeared to be moving back towards old habits. The scene playing out on his TV looked more like something out of 1960's civil rights march. And there were African American parents who found themselves nervously raising up young black boys and girls with uncertain futures.

He asked himself what was happening across the nation and world. But there were questions about him he hadn't figured out. He was a brave African American soldier who fought valiantly. It was scenes like these that made him question whether fighting for a nation in chaos was worth it. Was it worth the injuries he sustained on that last mission that stole his memory? Because on the day he discovered the small group of navy brass inside his hospital room who told him he had awoken from a coma, he knew he was in trouble.

Suddenly, a sharp pain throbbed in his temples. The prescription of Hc3 was on the table within arm's reach. But he had no intention of taking it. He opened the bottle of Bayer aspirin instead. After swallowing a couple, he scooped up the books and magazines the mailman delivered. He read the titles of the books first. One was titled *The Colombian Cartel*. The other was *Assassin's Creed*. The Time magazine he looked at had the face of a prominent American billionaire on the cover. Then he set it back on the table with the books. He looked at the Luxury Cruz magazine. A picture of a big glistening white yacht graced the cover. The stern was inscribed with the name *Magnificent Jewel*.

The name Magnificent Jewel. The yacht. There was something about it. Because the moment he looked at it he couldn't move. His body was crackling with tension. His eyes were suddenly shimmering in their sockets with REM's. His brain began fluttering between signals. All at once it felt like he was slipping down a steep slope into a mysterious fog without any ability to stop it.

Part Four
Deep State

CHAPTER FOURTEEN

Los Angeles, California

S ometime around midnight, Dex woke up in his bed on maximum alert. He was sweating, breathing heavily, frantically reaching for his .45 semi-automatic. He aimed it at the door of his bedroom like there were enemy combatants about to burst in. It was a chain reaction. They were closing in on him right after he saw himself running across the floor of a jungle choked with undergrowth and dark branches slapping across his face. He stumbled and got bogged down shielding himself under the thick foliage with his eye behind the scope of his sniper rifle. He heard the enemy fire, heard the blood curdling screams of soldiers dying, helicopters flying overhead. He smelled cordite, phosphorus, aviation fuel seeping into his nostrils for the few seconds it took him to realize that none of the phantoms he was seeing and hearing and smelling were outside the bedroom door, but in him, right inside his head.

He placed the gun back on the nightstand. Dreams like this brought on headaches. So, he ate a couple of aspirins and checked for missed calls on his cell phone. There were no missed calls. Just a strange text message that read: We need to have a business chat. Meet me near the basketball courts in Venice Beach.

That was odd. No one knew the number to text his private line except the lawyer. Whenever the counselor called for business, his identification showed on caller ID. Besides, it couldn't have been the lawyer. He hadn't heard from him in months.

When he checked his other cellular, he saw two missed calls from his wife Gina. Why after eight months he hadn't booked the flight to Philadelphia to see her was a mystery. Gina brought it up during their last formal meeting. And she used a subtle approach to figure out why by asking how life was going for him on the west coast. The answer he gave was usually the same. Life in California was great. Being employed at the cable company wasn't exactly his cup of tea. But he was getting by.

The things he told her would have come across as acceptable to her if she didn't know any better. But Gina knew better. She had a strange feeling Dex had been keeping something from her ever since his younger brother passed away. Dex took his death hard. He told her he needed to get away for a while to clear his head. She understood and missed him. But after he flew to California and the trip turned into an extended stay. She became increasingly worried.

Dex knew his love for Gina would never change. Leaving Philly had a lot to do with his brother. But it was also a preemptive move that had much to do with the double life he was living after he took that leave off from his military duties in the navy to attend his brother's funeral. Dex had a second job. Despite her repeated inquiries about why he was acting so strangely, Gina simply could never know about his other life. How would she understand that he was driving around sunny California in a Comcast van installing cables by day, and by night, he transformed into a hit man for hire? For the past eight months he had purposely avoided the flight and kept their phone calls short so she couldn't ask questions.

Gina would never understand that he had become a soldier of fortune. But he did, the day he met up with the lawyer. All the lawyer had to do was call and give him a contract to knock off some big drug trafficker, and the assignment was completed. It was dangerous work. But it paid well. Dex was good at it. The lawyer realized that with the first target. A top cartel trafficker from Mexico. After Dex got the contract, four days later a neighbor of the target who took out his trash one morning discovered him outside his home in Phoenix, Arizona. He was slumped over in the front seat of his Jaguar parked in the driveway.

Dex thought he might feel empathy. But after his brother Marcus was slain on a street corner in Cincinnati by a drug pusher, he didn't feel anything. Marcus battled drug abuse for years. At times he tried to kick the habit unsuccessfully. One day a local drug pusher in the neighborhood approached him. The guy wanted Marcus to pay up on a debt owed. There was a heated exchange of words. But the guy pulled a pistol and shot twice. Marcus didn't stand a chance. Dex figured it didn't matter anymore that he was knocking off drug traffickers. They were flooding inner city neighborhoods with narcotics. He despised drug traffickers, and he despised the corrupt authorities who aided their trade. They were killing more people and dreams than he ever could.

In that sense, there was no empathy to be felt. This had been Dex's thinking ever since the day he got that first contract from the lawyer. But three months ago, it all changed after something went terribly wrong. Two innocent people were killed during one of his assignments. The scene from the night it happened was constantly rewinding in his mind.

In the weeks and months that followed, all he told himself was that he was in the wrong place at the wrong time. Now he told himself only one thing. That he was done being a hit man. That his short-lived career as a soldier of fortune was over. Or was it?

CHAPTER FIFTEEN

Los Angeles, California

Dex was up by nine, but it wasn't just another morning. He shaved and spent thirty minutes of his shower time thinking about that odd text message. After he stepped out and dried off, he threw on a robe, and put on a pot of Maxwell House. He was drinking a lot of coffee. Maxwell House had that rich taste and kick, and he was drinking it black to refuel his brain so that he could stay awake long enough to figure out who sent the text.

The thought that it might have been some adjunct affiliate of the lawyer who sent it was dismissed. Bobby Dossier would never trust a third party to conduct business. Communication between them was always direct and in person. If he wanted to know, he would have to drive to Venice Beach and find out for himself. He finished his coffee, got dressed, and threw on a trendy pair of sunglasses as he slipped out the door. The dolphin-finned 1978 silver Riviera he owned was parked at the curb. The furry white cat he owned was on the windowsill pawing at the glass like he always did when he left. He glanced at Boots one time. Then he jumped into the driver's seat, fired up the Rivera, and was on the road to Venice Beach by eleven twenty-five.

Venice Beach was only a fifteen- to twenty-minute drive away, give or take, depending on the rush hour traffic. When he arrived, he pulled into the parking area and found a vacant lane where he backed the Riviera up to a tire-block. He waited so that he could survey the surroundings a moment before stepping out of the car. Then he made his way to a section of bleachers in front of the basketball courts. Dex didn't go to meetings empty handed. Plus, these were bad times that could turn out to be worse if the person he was coming to meet was a past coming back to haunt him.

He transferred the .45 semi auto from the small of his back to the side pocket of his jacket. There was a small flock of brown sparrows he noticed at the far end of the bleachers. They were fluttering about. So, he sat there waiting and watching the birds for close to ten minutes. At precisely twelve o'clock in the afternoon a blue sedan pulled into the parking area. A tall, pale, big, Caucasian guy with blond hair and blue eyes got out and walked toward him.

"Good afternoon, Mr. Jones," the man said.

Dex assessed his grey suit, black tie, black shoes, and thought he looked government.

"You sent the text."

"Yes," the blond stranger answered.

"For what?"

"Very important people sent me here to speak with you about an assignment they have for you."

"What people? I don't know you. I don't know them."

"That isn't relevant," said the stranger.

There was a sharpness in his tone. Dex didn't like it. He had a European accent that sounded maybe from Bosnia or Russia. He decided he didn't like that either.

"Don't play games with me, mister," he stated. His hand tightened around the pistol grip of his .45. "State your business."

The blond man glanced at the bulge in his right pocket.

"Relax, Mr. Jones. My employers have a problem in South America. There's a man there. A cartel leader in Medellin. They want him taken care of. Complete the assignment and you will no longer have to be concerned about the problem you have in Washington."

Dex's eyes narrowed into a quizzical glare. "I don't have a problem in Washington."

"That's not the way my employers see it. Three months ago, you went to the home of a U.S senator that was shot and killed along with his son . . ."

"The bullet that killed him wasn't mine," Dex interrupted. "It came through his window from someone else!"

"What about the boy?" the blond man asked.

Dex went quiet, thinking the man couldn't be a fed if he knew about what happened in DC. He would have showed up with a tactical fugitive team. And they would have poured out of big black trucks and vans to arrest him.

"I saw someone charging at me when I turned around," he replied. "I tried to pull back, but the gun went off. That senator wasn't my target."

"Doesn't matter to the feds if he was the target," the stranger said. "Doesn't matter if the boy was an accident. You were there. Imagine if the feds found that out. My employers could really make things difficult for you if they wanted. The only reason you are still on the streets right now is because you happened to be an extraordinary soldier of fortune with a very rare set of skills. And they want your services instead. Do yourself a favor. Take the offer. It'll come with a generous price tag."

"How generous?"

"Ten million dollars," the stranger replied.

The number was beyond astronomical, Dex thought. For a moment, he glanced at birds at the end of the bleachers thinking this could be the biggest paycheck ever. Still, could he really do it?

"Your employers expect me fly to South America to take out some cartel leader in his own back yard?"

"For ten million . . . yes," the man replied. "And your lawyer friend has spoken highly of you."

Dex looked at him, surprised that he mentioned the lawyer. "You spoke to the counselor?"

"Yes."

"What did he tell you?"

"That you would be incline to cooperate in order to save both of you from that problem in DC."

"Really," Dex grunted.

"You don't appear to be excited. Ten million is a lot of money. But we both know money isn't the real reason you got into this business. You really got into this business because of what happened to your brother on that street corner in Ohio. You wanted to take down the big drug traffickers because you blamed them for the drugs you felt got him hooked and eventually killed. Well, this is just another . . . opportunity for you to take out another one."

The stranger pulled a business card from the pocket of his suit coat. "Think it over. We expect an answer within forty-eight hours. You can reach me at this number." He raised his arm with the card between his fingers.

Dex didn't take it. "There is nothing to think about. I am not interested."

The stranger placed the card back in his pocket and said, "Perhaps I should make myself clear. Your refusal is not an option. In a matter of weeks, you will carry out the assignment."

Dex stood up irritated. The small sparrows at the end of the bleachers suddenly flew off like they had no worries other than dodging all the discomforts humans brought with their presence. It appears they could sense human tension and wanted no parts of it. He watched them fly off like they understood the orders of the universe and abided in peace with nature more than they did. Then he pulled the .45 halfway out.

"Perhaps I should make myself clear. I am done with the business!"

The stranger glanced at the hand on the pistol grip. "See you later, Mr. Jones. Enjoy the rest of your day," he said. Then walked off.

Dex watched him climb back into the blue sedan and drive away. He heard the sparrows return. A flock flew over him. One of them released a greenish white dropping that landed on the sleeve of his jacket.

"Birds!" he exclaimed. As if the day could not have started out any worse.

CHAPTER SIXTEEN

Los Angeles, California

D ex drove home in silence. The trip was all a waste of time. The entire conversation with the blond-haired stranger left him bewildered. But he couldn't ignore it. Not the part about the DC job. For the past three months he was laying low in South Central, LA. It was a grueling district where matchbox houses sat on dusty lawns and sneakers hung from telephone wires. He didn't have to be there. As a soldier of fortune, he was earning plenty of cash. He could have easily returned to the excellence and luxury of the mansion he owned in Malibu or taken an exquisite retreat to relax on his yacht in Newport Beach. No one knew about that toy except the lawyer. But it was better to play it safe than not.

Living in South Central was a stark contrast. Gangs in South Central didn't take kindly to outsiders. He didn't have to worry about that part when he moved into the house on 61st and Wadsworth. Word spread quickly that he was related to Rodney Chopper Sanders. Practically everybody knew Rodney Chopper Sanders. Mainly because he was built like a miniature tank, had a six-pack abdomen ripped like cobblestone, and earned that nickname *Chopper* by settling his disputes with an AK-47. He was the kind of guy you just didn't mess with. Chopper was trigger crazy. And it didn't matter who was at the other end of his barrel.

One summer, he was on a friend's porch, and they were getting high on weed and cheap pints of Mad Dog 20/20. A squad car from LAPD's finest pulled up. Two uniform officers climbed out with a warrant they announced for the friend's arrest. Chopper dipped into the house to grab a duffle bag with two kilos of coke he'd stashed inside the closet of the friend's bedroom.

Things got ugly after the friend told the cops they had the wrong guy. They went to arrest him. He resisted. So, they pulled their batons and started beating him over the head. Neighbors stood by helplessly witnessing what they thought was the same exact rerun the world stood by watching in 1992, after a group of white police officers were caught on tape beating Rodney King to a pulp. The cops were charged and put on trial. People expected justice. But an all-white jury in Simi Valley delivered a not guilty verdict that outraged millions across the nation.

The city hadn't forgotten it. Neither had Chopper when he glanced through the window and spotted the altercation taking place. He came back out with an AK and started dumping rounds. The cops ran to their patrol car and sped off without looking back. Three days later the LAPD Crime Division arrested him as a prime suspect. But the two cops couldn't identify the shooter. And no one in the hood talked. So, Chopper walked.

Dex used his street cred to his advantage. The gangs respected Chopper so much he put some of his affiliates on the payroll to keep a close watch on his place whenever he was away. But under one condition. They had to stop fighting amongst themselves because he detested the black-on-black violence. Chopper was able to hash out a truce with the other gangs that ended the violence long enough for them to stay alert and keep any strange faces they saw around at bay. Therefore, half the neighborhood had become his security force.

Later that night, he was sitting on his couch watching a news segment about the incident involving the senator and his son three months ago. Midway through it he heard his phone chime with a call from the lawyer and answered it.

"Been awhile since you made contact, counselor. What's with the hold up?"

"I rather not go into details over the phone."

"The lines are secure."

"I can't be certain about that now. We can't be certain about anything anymore," Dossier replied. "It's better we talk in person. Somewhere safe. I will come to you. Where are you?"

"South Central, LA . . . 61st and Wadsworth."

"No way, Dex. I once had a client tell me that's Rollin 60's turf. White man like me might have a problem getting off the first corner I showed up on."

Dex sensed the apprehension; knew he was probably right. "What's your location?" he asked.

Dossier replied, "Chicago. I can be on a jet to California in a half hour."

"Meet me in Newport Beach tomorrow. On the yacht."

"I'll be there," said Dossier.

The lawyer hung up. Dex placed the phone back on the table and mused about the situation in DC for a moment. He just couldn't get a handle on it. If anyone could, the lawyer had to know how the entire thing went awry. He had no doubt about that. Not at all. But for now, he decided he would put off the questions in his head until morning and then go meet Bobby Dossier and try to extract whatever information he could from him.

When he woke up early that morning, he did the usual routine. He jumped in the shower and lathered up. Scrubbed his body all over good, and rinsed off before he dried, and threw on his clothes. He spent five minutes brushing his teeth with a new tube of Colgate. Then he went into the kitchen for something to eat.

Boots was in there. He looked famished, too. He opened the refrigerator and took out a day-old bucket of KFC. Grabbed a cereal bowl to split the few remaining wings with the cat. Then he stepped out the door into the early daylight.

He walked out to the Riviera. Look hard at the corners, scanned left and right and further down the road. Then he bent forward at the waist, unlocked it, and slid into the driver's seat. A sudden movement to his left made him crane his head around. He saw Boots sprinting toward the car. The cat had gotten out of the house. In one leap he hoisted himself through the window and landed on Dex's lap.

"Boots, guess l see I got no choice but to let you come along for the ride this time."

Dex smiled and keyed the engine to life. The car roared off the curb into the sunlight with enthusiasm. Boots settled into the passenger seat, while he switched on the sound box and turned the volume to Bobby Caldwell singing "What You Do for Love."

Gliding down Crenshaw Boulevard, Dex passed Normandy, and continued driving through various rival gang territories. He stopped at one of the corner traffic lights. The light was red when he glanced into the mirror and noticed the BMW and van that had slipped in behind the car on his rear. On a green light, he drove across the intersection wondering if he picked up a tail. Some of the traffic was pouring into right and left lanes and slowing at intervals. Both vehicles were still in his mirror as he headed towards highway 110 for that trip to Venice Beach. It made no sense to guess. If he was being tailed, he was about to find out.

"Hang on tight, Boots!" he told the cat.

Then he slammed the accelerator into the floorboard and spun half circle through the intersection. The Riviera straightened into a beeline and shot up the road going towards the highway. He watched the BMW make a left at the corner. The van continued straight, traveling in a totally different direction. The coast was clear.

CIA FIELD REPORT
FROM: Harry Kellerman
TO: W. B.
EMAIL CLASSIFIED:
SUBJECT: Operations Interference

On August 1st, the value of 300,000 kilos of coke destined for African American populations was intercepted at transport base. August 2nd, the estimated value of 200,000 kilos of coke destined for U.S. Hispanic populations was intercepted at sea. August 17th, shipments of heroin destined for U.S. Asian populations was intercepted at seaport. August 20th, shipments of pharmaceutical opioid fentanyl destined for U.S. Caucasian populations was intercepted at transport base. In connection with the threat and this Agency's operations. It is urgently necessary that I suggest a sooner date for action and your approval that the threat be permanently immobilized to remove this obstacle to the fulfillment of this Agency's projected future operations.

In view of the urgency in this matter, your expedient consideration is warranted.

CENTRAL INTELLIGENCE AGENCY
Washington, DC
Office of the Deputy Director of Operations
FROM: W.B.
TO: Harry Kellerman
EMAIL CLASSIFIED:
SUBJECT: Operations Interference

In line with the suggestion you made in your communication, before the Colombians undertake such actions where the operations cannot recover, I approve and recommend for the Colonel to expedite preparation of the military strike team to act and remove the threat pursuant to the authority granted.

CHAPTER SEVENTEEN

Newport Beach, California

Dex was standing on the deck of his yacht watching the sunset melt the western horizon when the headlights on a cream-colored Lincoln Continental pulled up near the docking area. The lawyer was behind the wheel. He went down into the cabin below to wait for him. When Bobby Dossier walked in a moment later, he looked like he was in awe of the yacht's decor.

"Hello, Dex. I see you added a few fine touches since my last visit. You've got yourself a real beauty here," he muttered.

He peered at the wet bar and vanity countertop, then sat down on the matching Vladimir Kagan sofa across from Dex.

"Cut the small talk, counselor. It's time you bring me up to speed about that DC situation."

Dossier placed his car keys on the table between them. His expression and tone turned serious with his response. "You had a meeting with someone," he said.

Dex replied. "I got a text message from some guy I met with in Venice Beach yesterday. He wanted to talk about a contract hit on a cartel leader in South America . . ."

"Is that all?" Dossier inquired.

"He brought up the senator and his son. Then he attempted to use it to coerce me into taking the assignment. I wasn't interested. But he told me that you said I would. Why?"

There was silence. The lawyer removed a pack of cigarettes from his blazer and lit one before he responded. "Dex, I've spent the last past three months trying to clean up what went wrong in DC."

"That all you have to say?"

"What more can I?"

The lawyer's answer wasn't what Dex expected. He grabbed the .45 from the small of his back and pointed at him.

"Whoa, hold your horses, Dex. What's with the gun?"

"I will say it one more time. Cut through the chase or I might disregard the friendly acquaintance."

"All right, all right. Just put that thing away!"

Dex stuffed the .45 in the beltline of his pants.

"Look, I know the target was supposed to be a trafficker. I really don't know things got fouled up!"

"How can you not? Who gave you the information for the target and location?"

"Dex, you know I can't disclose the names of clients," Dossier replied. "But it appears someone else besides the client wanted the senator gone. All I can say with certainty is that the mix-up happened without my knowledge and control over the situation."

"You didn't think to double check that information on the target?"

Dossier hesitated. "The client's information has always been reliable in the past. I had no reason."

"Well, you should have," Dex asserted.

"I did my best to clean up this mess. But it this is much bigger than what I thought," said Dossier.

Dex stared at him for a moment. "What makes you believe that?"

"The person you spoke with in Venice Beach. I admit, I spoke with him."

"When?"

"Remember the discussion we had inside my office in Chicago three months ago?" Dossier asked the question rhetorically. "I know I told you to lay low for a while until I figured things out. But when you left that day, I worked late. When I got home that night my wife was in bed. I had a link conference in the morning and a trial of a client to prepare for. I was going through the client's case file when I got a text from the same person you spoke with. He said he wanted to meet and talk about that DC job . . ."

"Why didn't you let me know?"

"I couldn't, Dex. He threatened me and Pam. I didn't want anything to happen to my wife. He told me if I attempted to contact you it would be a big mistake neither of us would get to live with."

"So, why'd you call now?"

"He called me. Told me you refused to cooperate on that South America assignment. And that I had this one opportunity to convince you to take it. Otherwise, we would both go down for the senator in DC."

Dex looked at the lawyer with a straight face. "There are too many risks with that. I don't like it."

"Dex, we're talking about our lives on the line if you don't take it," Dossier said.

"Can't do it, counselor. I'm selling a yacht and the mansion in Malibu. It's time to change course. I'm officially done with this business."

"You're getting out? Just like that?" said Dossier.

"It's over."

Dex saw the disappointment in the lawyer's expression. Neither thought working together would materialize into the close acquaintance it had. An ex-soldier turned hit man. A corrupt licensed attorney. It was an odd mix that worked. He had worked with other hit men. But he never got personal with anyone else like he had with him. It wasn't all business with them. Over time, they got to know and trust each other enough to share details about their lives.

While he grew up living in one of the roughest low-income neighborhood districts in the city of Philadelphia. The lawyer grew up as a privileged sheltered white kid living in Des Moines, Iowa. Bobby Dossier didn't know much about African Americans growing up because his parents were segregationists who didn't believe in mingling with African Americans. As a kid, his first impressions of African Americans were tainted by stereo typical misconceptions. His parents told him blacks and whites should never mingle because they had absolutely nothing in common. But little Bobby the kid grew up. And not only had his age and body changed so did the beliefs they drilled into him. He hadn't grown up poor and underprivileged and experienced the prejudices Dex had. But they both agreed that divisions which prevented unity among people were often the result of fears and the things they were taught early on in life.

Dex's eyes were half looking at the lawyer, and the rest of his attention was on the TV monitor above the door of the cabin. A suspicious car had pulled up near the dock and idled there a couple of minutes before it drove off.

"The man within Venice Beach. He told me that he was sent by important people to talk to me. I wonder if they are watching us?"

"They knew how to find us. The gentleman we spoke to sent text messages to secure lines. What do you think?" Dossier replied.

Dex tore his gaze from the monitor to look at him. "I think you need to let me know who gave you that information on the target in DC. This ain't no time for that attorney client privilege crap."

Dex leaned back. The .45 was clearly visible when the lawyer glanced at it resting in his beltline.

"His name is Santiago Riviera," Dossier replied.

CHAPTER EIGHTEEN

Cincinnati, Ohio

Dex usually flew on charted planes. But this time he was traveling on a commercial airliner when he landed at the airport in Cincinnati, a few days after meeting with the lawyer. He checked into a hotel room and stayed there the entire night to rest up.

In the morning, he phoned for a cab that drove him to Clover Hill cemetery. The morning was windy, gray, with a storm front moving in. So, he flipped up the hood on the raincoat he wore and walked through the gate at the entrance. He proceeded along the first trail on the grounds, cut across the grass, and continued around a bend passing by the gravesites. How many were dug there was unknown. There had to be hundreds, a thousand perhaps, but he was only there to view one.

When he approached the site where his brother was buried, he peered at the words on his headstone. It read, *In Loving Memory of Marcus D. Jones (1978-2010).*

Each time he came he would place a flower at the base of it that symbolized the loss of his only brother. Chopper was his only surviving relative now. For a moment he wondered if he had done enough to avenge Marcus. Coming here he thought would bring closure at some point. But it hadn't. It couldn't. There were still too many things going on he needed to sort out.

Even if he half wanted to believe what the lawyer told him. There were parts of his story that just didn't add up. Bobby Dossier tended to stretch the truth at times. He admitted it, laughed about it. Said it was part of his legal profession because lawyers and prosecutors went into court-rooms across the country everyday lying eighty percent of the time to win and broker deals in exchange for tradeoffs between trials and defendants. There was no blind justice when it came to the law for Bobby Dossier. It was all about which defendants had enough money to buy themselves get out of jail free cards. If you had the cash, you walked. If not, the most you could settle for was Cobb's plea bargain agreement.

Bobby was smart, but greedy. Greedy and corrupt to the bone. The phony law firm he and his wife Pamela operated in Chicago, Dossier & Dossier, was nothing but a front. None of his family, friends, and legal associates knew anything about his extracurricular activities. His wife Pamela only knew the general things about him. Once he served as a member of the United States armed forces. He was an accomplished Marine. Before that he was just another law student studying criminal justice and had picked back where he left off studying the profession after he discharged from his military duties.

When it started raining, Dex face was sickened by the down pour. The wind got stronger, buffeting the collar of the raincoat. A thunderclap cracked across the sky, and he glanced up at the bolt of lightning it sent out from the clouds.

Seconds later, there was another thunderous clap. Dex's pulse quickened. The rush of noise jostled him. He flinched like an electric current shot up his tendons. Then he just stood there motionless, stewing in a fog of confusion, eyes widening, fixed, and glazed. His skin prickled with nerves. Something was churning inside him, fragments of mélange images and sensations flickering in his mind. Suddenly, he was inside a fox hole with two wounded members of his Navy SEAL team, then he was standing at the top of the staircase inside the senator's home in Washington, staring down the hallway at a young boy he left slumped on the floor.

He pressed his palms against the sides of his temples trying to shut off the video reel in his head. But the next image that popped up turned real the minute he spotted a couple of Caucasian men cutting between the headstones straight in his direction. The way they were walking in lockstep side by side gave them that matrix look, black shades, long overcoats, guns out!

This alarmed Dex. Paranoid, he took off running. The men began chasing him. Dex sprinted to the nearest tree, ducked behind it, and stayed there girding himself for a shootout after he whipped out the .45.

Then his cellular chimed. He thought the phone might have given up his position. But when peeked his head around the trunk of the tree searching for the two matrix men, they had vanished, right along with all the other mélange images that materialized inside his head.

He glanced at the phone. Saw the missed call from his wife Gina. He was glad she didn't know just how close he was to losing his marbles. He thought for sure he would end up in the crazy house. Then he thought about how much he missed Gina. How much he needed her at that moment. Gina understood more about him than any psych or institution ever could.

When he walked back out through the front gate of the cemetery. The cab was still waiting for him. Sopping wet, he jumped in and closed the door.

"Where to?" the cabbie asked.

Dex responded, "Take me to the airport." Booking a flight to Philadelphia to reunite with Gina was now a top priority on his list that he could no longer postpone.

CHAPTER NINETEEN

Philadelphia, Pennsylvania

The newspaper article Dex was reading during the flight had a picture of Senator Glenn Dyse in it. He didn't know anything about Glenn Dyse. Never heard of him. Never knew he was a Senator until the media put out the big headline.

His target was an Asian trafficker name Chu Jon Sek. How the information Dossier gave him got screwed up between a U.S. Senator and a major triad leader with links to the dragon syndicate societies back in China was something he could not have foreseen. Chu Jon was a producer of raw opium throughout the Golden Triangle. In Shanghai, he processed the drug into morphine, and later into heroin. According to the lawyer he had a good run until he tried to take over areas controlled by other triad societies. He pissed off the big wigs in Hong Kong. Leaders of the White Lotus and Green Gang put out a contract hit on him. Chu Jon was on the run. But he continued doing business in other countries and was operating between Europe and the U.S. when the lawyer thought he found him. Bobby Dossier had a way of finding people. Dex never asked questions about how he tracked down the targets. He just got the calls with a hit list. Except this time the counselor got it wrong.

The flight to Philly was going smoothly until he noticed an elderly white gentleman a few rows back staring at him. He kept feeling the old man's eyes on him off and on. But when he turned to look at him. The old guy averted eye contact and dropped his head into the pages of a magazine he was pretending to read.

A young woman came and slid into the window seat next to him. When she started talking to him. Dex went back to the newspaper. Three minutes hadn't past before a female flight stewardess stopped at his seat.

"Would you like something to drink, sir?" she asked,

Dex glanced at the tray of beverages she was holding. Then he read her name tag. "You got a cup of Maxwell on that tray, Maylee?" he asked.

"I do, sir."

"Then a coffee will do."

She smiled.

The flight captain's voice came over the PA. "Attention, ladies and gentlemen . . . The aircraft will be landing in approximately twenty minutes," he announced.

"Here you go, sir," the stewardess said.

Dex grabbed the coffee.

"Oh, yeah," she said. "The nice gentleman back there told me to give you this." She held a note out for him.

Dex took it, read its words. *Stay alert. They're watching you.* He eyed her. "Who gave you this?"

She turned and pointed at the empty seat where he'd seen the old man staring at him.

"Where'd he go?" she muttered.

"Probably went for a restroom break," said Dex. "I'll go check."

Dex got up in a hurry to look for him. But the flight captain's voice came on the PA again informing the passengers to buckle their seatbelts. The plane was about to land so he stayed put. When it skidded onto the landing strip ten minutes later, Dex glanced over his shoulder looking for the old white guy. The seat was still empty as passengers began filing out of the exit. He waited. But there was no sign of the elderly gentleman among the people he let file out of the plane before him.

Finally, he strolled down the aisle and out through the exit. The moment he got off the plane he started scanning faces. There were hundreds of people at the airport. Anyone could be watching him. No indication materialized that he was being watched until he passed by the airport terminal and noticed the three men he saw climbing out of a Cadillac. They had on suits. He could tell he was on their radar by the look they gave him. He got the same look from the two men he saw exiting the white windowless van that pulled up next to the Cadillac. The moment they began walking in his direction he flagged a taxi and jumped into the back seat.

"Where you headed to, fella?" the driver asked.

"Anywhere! Just get me out of this airport as fast as you can," Dex replied.

He handed the driver a crisp thousand-dollar bill. The taxi shot out of the airport like a rocket. From the rear window he watched the men jump in their vehicles and take off in pursuit.

When the driver headed into the city, Dex spotted an alley near the intersection they were approaching. "Slow down up there," he directed. After the cab slowed and pulled over to the curb, Dex hopped out and ran into the alley. He ducked behind a green Waste Management dumpster, just as the Cadillac came flying around the corner. When the men sped passed it, he didn't wait to see if they would double back once they drove to the other end of the alley. He sprang up from behind the dumpster and ran back out onto the avenue.

He saw the two men from the white van searching for him down the street. As soon as they saw him, they started up the sidewalk. A city transit bus came around the corner behind them with its big heavy frame chugging lazily. Dex glanced up at the block and spotted the transit stop it was heading for on the other side of the street. If he made there before it arrived. There was a chance he could lose the men.

Without hesitating, he swung out into the sea of traffic zigzagging with a bunch of horns blaring, trucks and cars breaking fast, screeching, skidding to a dead stop. But he made it on the other side and raced to the transit where he mingled in with the crowd of commuters waiting for the bus.

He was standing in the crowd watching his pursers cross the street, until he felt something jab him in the back. He spun around and locked eyes with an elderly white gentleman he saw leaning on a cane.

The same elderly man he saw on the plane.

The old man glanced at the men in the suits running towards the transit, just as the bus arrived.

"Take this. I might be able to help you," he said. He slipped a piece of paper into Dex's pocket. "Get on the bus. Hurry!"

Dex got on with the rest of its passengers. Soon as the bus's doors shut, it thundered off the curb. Dex peered back at the men in the suits after they quit chasing it. The old white guy had limped right passed them unnoticed.

He pulled the sheet of paper out. There was an address on it with a short-written message that said. "Meet in The Bottoms at midnight."

Things were getting stranger by the moment, Dex thought.

CHAPTER TWENTY

Philadelphia, Pennsylvania

The cab he took to The Bottoms that night rolled into an old vacant car dealership that went out of business years ago. The windows were boarded up. The rusted-out sign above the office read *Handy Dandy's Auto Mobiles*. Three tireless Ford skeleton frames elevated on blocks of concrete were the only vehicles left behind after the place was abandoned.

After exiting the cab, he started walking down Mantua Avenue. He was very familiar with this part of town. But so much had changed since the time he and his family lived here. The Bottoms used to be a prosperous district that was mostly inhabited by African Americans who carved out a living working inside industrial plants. People worked in top level positions inside the local hospital and police station. They ran a successful fire department and postal service, owned mom-and-pop stores, gas stations, clothing boutiques, salons, and barbershops that kept the district's economy thriving. But after hard times hit people slowly began migrating across the city. The place was a shadow of its former status. It was hard to see how anyone still lived here. Those who remained didn't really have much to live off except whatever money they earned crushing the sheet metal they collected from the old junkyard at the end of Mantua Avenue.

Mantua was a dark desolate street. A lot of the old business's he remembered. Walking by the buildings he felt exposed and vulnerable. A sniper lying in wait on a roof top or doorway had an easy target if it was a set up. When he stopped at the building he was directed to, he paused a beat to make sure he was in the right location. The addressed belonged to a condemned apartment unit. Plywood covered most of the windows. Half its foundation appeared to be sinking into the ground.

Then he went to the door and pushed it open. He looked around cautiously before he made his way down a dark hallway with both hands

securing the .45. He was searching for a stairwell leading to the basement. The one the message in the note instructed him to look for. When
he found it, the steps creaked under his weight so loudly it was virtually
impossible to descend undetected.

There was a dim glow of light at the bottom. The light was illuminating through the opening of the door ahead of him. When he drew
up tight against the wall on the right side. He heard a noise and peeked
around the corner. There was a man sitting at table behind a laptop. He
braced himself, then spun inside the doorway aiming the gun at him.

"Take it easy, Mr. Jones. I told you I might be able to help you. Except
you'll need to take a seat first," the man muttered.

Dex looked at him. He wasn't white and old. The guy looked Hispanic.

"An old white gentleman told me that at the bus stop. He wanted me
to meet him here. You're not him."

"Not at the moment."

"What do you mean?"

The man ignored the question. "Take a seat, Mr. Jones," he repeated.
"If I'm going to help, I must get started."

Dex tucked the gun in the small of his back and sat down at the
table. The man continued tapping on the laptop. Dex studied him. The
guy never flinched a muscle when he came in. Didn't even seem phased
looking down the barrel of his .45 nine-millimeter. He just sat there
tapping on the laptop without looking up at him from the moment he
showed up. When he was finished, he turned it around to show Dex the
screen.

"Have you ever seen or heard of this person before?" he asked.

Dex peered at a photo of the man's face the screen displayed.

"No, I haven't. Why?"

"His name is Winston Bedford. He's the Deputy Director of Operation for the Central Intelligence Agency," the man replied.

He slid his chair closer to Dex's, and pressed a key on the laptop that
started the slide show. The next photo appeared.

"What about this person? He's a CIA field agent named Harry
Kellerman."

"Never seen him before," Dex answered. "Why are you questioning me?"

"No need to get testy, Mr. Jones. Like I said, I might be able to help you."

"Start by telling me who I'm talking to."

"You're talking to the person who took the shot through the window that killed the Senator," the man answered.

Dex was struck. He stared at him speechless. A photo of Senator Glenn Dyse displayed on the laptop right after his admission. He glanced at it. Then the next slide, which left him just as stunned when he saw the face of Bobby Dossier pop up.

"Wait. Go back!" he blurted.

The man touched the back arrow on the laptop and the photo of the lawyer reappeared.

"I know this man," said Dex.

"Of course, you do. Mr. Dossier is the one who provides you with assignments. He also pays you after you complete them," the Hispanic man replied.

"How do you know the counselor?" Dex asked.

The stranger touched the back arrow on the slides. The face of the CIA's Deputy Director of Operations reappeared.

"The lawyer is a middleman for this guy, Winston Bedford," replied the stranger."

Dex's face clouded in disbelief. "What was that situation in DC about. Why the Senator?"

The Hispanic leaned back and responded with a straight face.

"Your target was never a trafficker named Chu Jon Sek. He never existed. The DC job was a ploy. Someone wanted you at the Senator's home that night I carried out the assignment I was given by Bedford. You were set up in case you refused the job in South America. Now it's insurance in case they ever decide to use it. Just like the trips you have been making to that masjid in Oakland to visit that old sheik Abu Saad. If they wanted, they could easily imply that you're connected to terrorism."

Dex looked away again, taken aback by the notion, and the fact that he brought up the name of the old Muslim Sheik. Abu Saad was no terrorist. Obtaining an inner peace was one of the reasons he went to the mosque in Oakland. Every Friday morning, he kept to his routine. He exercised. Then he would shower before noon to prepare for the drive he made from LA to Oakland. He thought going would help get rid of the phantoms and paranoia in his head. He was learning how the Muslims performed their prayers. The first time he showed up, the old Sheik welcomed him. Eventually, he invited him to attend their Taaleem study groups. The two of them developed a genuine mutual respect after he accepted. Whenever he attended the study groups, he would sit and listen for hours as the Sheik spoke about the wisdom in the Qur'an and the Muslim way of life.

It didn't matter what anyone thought about him going to the masjid. The Muslims were always hospitable towards him. Just hearing the prayer call of the muezzin was peaceful. It was like no other sound he'd ever heard before.

"Why are you here telling me all this?" he asked.

"I was the first choice for that assignment in South America before you," the Hispanic man replied. "Then Bedford put me on that DC job for the Senator instead. I think someone higher up than him made the switch. I didn't know the switch had anything to do with you until he asked me to give the lawyer that fake contract he passed on to you.

"You're Santiago Riviera?"

"At the moment I am. Look. Someone wanted you on that job in South America all along. Beyond that, I don't know much else. That's why I asked you to meet me here. I think Bedford is hiding something from me. And I need to know what it is."

Ironically, Dex was feeling the same exact thing about the lawyer listening to the guy. A plan had taken shape without his knowledge. Now, he questioned what more Bobby Dossier might have known about it.

"There was a man the counselor and I met with," said Dex.

"His name is Sebastain Korkov. He's a hired assassin."

"Like you," Dex remarked.

"Sebastain could have easily killed you after you refused the assignment," the man replied.

"Maybe I would have killed him first, if he tried," Dex countered.

"Perhaps. You're an ex-Navy SEAL. A good one at that. I did some checking. Nevertheless, I can assure you the only reason Mr. Korkov didn't try is because there are people more important than him who obviously want you alive. That means you taking that job in South America must hold a great deal of significance. And I advise you to take it. Because it's possibly the only way I can help you."

Dex cut in. "In what way?"

"Don't you want the answer to why you were chosen for the assignment? Well, I do too. I mean, I was replaced by you. But it's a question that neither of us can answer now."

Dex detected a hint that he had a personal objective. "It seems like me taking this job holds a great deal of significance for you as well," he muttered.

A brief silence ensued. The stranger's jaws tightened. His eyes changed deadly.

"There are people I have been searching for over a period. Many years ago, they did something very bad that directly affected my life. I've worked for Bedford for a long time. I must. But I don't trust him."

"Then why continue working for him?"

"He's CIA. They're very good at intelligence gathering. I've always believed that one day this business would lead me to the people I'm looking for. When he took me off that job in South America, I figured there had to be something more to it. Bedford never goes outside the league of assassins for an assignment."

Dex remained quiet. There was an edge in the man's voice that had risen from a deep place in the past. In one sense, he was right. Taking the contract might unveil answers. What happened that night in DC had been on his mind for the past three months. He had no problem taking out a trafficker. But the old Sheik had pointed him in a direction to find that inner peace. And if he didn't get out of the business while he could, he would never get out.

"I hope you find the people you're looking for. But I can't accept the assignment. I don't want any part of it. I'm done!"

The stranger shrugged. "Hey, it's your choice. But I you must be very careful from this point on, Mr. Jones. These people do not easily quit. And they normally don't until they get what they want."

Dex watched him shut off the laptop and flip the cover shut. Then he stood and prepared to leave.

Curious about something he forgot to explain, Dex asked, "What happened to the old white gentleman I was supposed to meet here?"

"Oh, him. Well, he's a man with many faces, Mr. Jones. But he's always around. Probably much closer than you realize."

CHAPTER TWENTY-ONE

Philadelphia, Pennsylvania

G oing to Gina's place now was out of the question. He couldn't risk leading someone to her home. The cheap motel room he booked into the other side of town after leaving The Bottoms would have to do. He was planning to sleep over until morning. But he heard a vehicle outside and went to the window to inspect it. When he parted the curtain and peeked out, a dark colored van drove past. The van traveled halfway down road, before it turned around and headed back in the direction of the motel. He watched it roll into the parking lot of the 7-Eleven store across the street. The headlights went out. A second van pulled up and parked beside it.

When no one got out, he went and grabbed his .45 off the bed, realizing he would have to check out before morning.

He eased the door at the entrance open slowly. Then he walked out, made a left, and headed for the intersection. He started to run, but he walked twenty yards before the lights flared to life on the vans. Two big trucks roared into the motel's parking lot, cutting off his escape. A tactical team from the FBI jumped out in armored vests and helmets, baring down on him with rifle and handguns, all of them shouting, "FBI, get on the ground, get on the ground, get ground!" as they moved in.

Dex went to the ground. He laid there with beam shot laser light marking kill shot points all over his body. One of the vans from the 7-Eleven parking lot pulled up. Three men jumped out donned in suits. When they walked into the bright glare of headlights, Dex looked up. Two of the men had CIA plastic identification pinned to their coats. The man who stepped between them didn't. He just had that smug look on his face, and that blond hair he recognized from their meeting at Venice Beach.

"I told you I would see you later, Mr. Jones," he said.

Dex didn't answer.

The blond man turned to look at the FBI official in charge of the tactical team that swarmed in. "We'll take him from here," he said.

"He's all yours," the FBI official responded.

"You should have cooperated," said the blond man, returning his attention to Dex. "This would have been much easier. Now you're going to do things our way!"

Dex glared at him. "You won't change my decision," he muttered.

"We'll see about that," said the man. He turned to the two CIA men. "Get him in the van."

The men searched him, disarmed him, hauled him into the back of the van. The blond man jumped in after them. One of the CIA men hopped in behind the wheel and took off. After they threw on the ankle and wrist bracelets.

The other CIA man rolled up his sleeve so that the blond man could administer a knockout drug with the syringe he stuck in his arm. Within a few seconds, Dex was suddenly seeing two blond-haired men through impaired double vision. Then his head started lolling left and right and drooped on his chest after he went to sleep.

When they arrived at the Burmaxx Medical Center in Scranton, he was still out. The building was an imposing structure. From the outside it looked ordinary. But there was a secret research and development laboratory beneath it. The van drove around the rear and through the tunnel that leads underground. A couple of female nurses wearing white uniforms stood at the entrance of the research laboratory. The men quickly removed Dex from the van and sat him in the wheelchair one of the nurses rolled up. The electric doors opened and closed at the entrance after they wheeled him inside. The two CIA agents and the blond man followed the nurses down a long corridor. Before they reached the end of it, they made a right and pushed him inside the medical room. There was a clean bed with neurological monitoring machines and other medical equipment within proximity.

The nurses placed Dex in bed. The blond man and CIA agents left. The door opened a moment later. Dr. Rubin Petro walked in with male doctor wearing sterile white lab coats. Dr. Stephanie Castree entered with two more nurses. The male doctor who entered with Rubin Petro opened Dex's eye lids to examine them with a small pen light.

"Administer a dose of the Hydrophine Colybenzentol first," Dr. Castree muttered.

The male doctor nodded to the nurse beside him who immediately rolled up Dex's sleeve. She found a vein to administer the drug into his system. They put a head brace on him with electrical wires attached to a machine designed to monitor the neurol activity inside the human brain. A nurse began flipping switches and pressing buttons on several of them. They unbuttoned Dex's shirt to expose his bare chest to a half dozen electrical pads they placed on it.

"Everything is ready, doctor," a nurse said.

"Good," said Dr. Castree. "Time to get started."

The doctors took over, sending electrical charges into Dex's brain. His body twitched and jerked each time they zapped him. The procedure went on forty or so minutes, before Dr. Castree instructed one of the nurses to wake him with an antidote of amphetamine.

Dex opened his eyes. Doctor Castree stepped closer to examine them. They looked blank, like he was staring out into space when the nurses sat him up on the edge of the bed.

After a quick reflex test, the only test left was his verbal response.

"You can bring the gentlemen in now," she said to the nurse next to her.

The nurse left and returned three minutes later with a trio of high ran king navy officers. The two MP's who walked in behind them shut the door and stood guard.

"Dr. Castree, good to see you," said a Colonel.

"Good to see you too, Colonel Burke," she replied. She looked at the psychiatrist. "I'm sure you know Dr. Rubin Petro."

"Yes, of course. How's everything going here, Dr. Petro?" the Colonel asked.

Dr. Petro responded, "We shall see, Colonel. Stephanie has invited you not as a witness, but to give you the honor of conducting the verbal response test yourself."

Dr. Castree briefed the Colonel. "The subject has been administered a combination of mind-altering drugs, starting with the Hydrophine Colybenzentol. The neurol transmitters in his brain have been manipulated to prepare our subject for a completely new phase of programming."

"What's his current capacity?" asked the Colonel.

Dr. Castree replied, "His vision is fine. He can perhaps even recognize faces. But he will not remember anything about his former self. Once I give you the code word to activate him, he will only respond to the new commands you give him."

The Colonel walked over to Dex, looked at him, and said, "What's the code word?"

Dr. Castree answered, "The code word is new instructions."

Without delay, he began the verbal response test.

"Can you hear me soldier?"

No response.

"Is your name Dexter C. Jones, soldier?"

No response.

The Colonel looked at Dr. Castree and Dr. Rubin Petro, before he stared back at Dex and said, "New instructions."

Dex suddenly responded, "What are the new instructions?"

The Colonel said, "You are Lieutenant Claymore Logan. And you shall accept whatever mission I assign you . . ."

Dex repeated, "I am Lieutenant Claymore Logan. And I shall accept whatever mission you assign me."

NAVY COMMAND CENTER
FROM: Col. J. Burke
TO: W.B.
EMAIL CLASSIFIED:

The subject has been reactivated for duty. I understand the urgency to counter the Colombian's actions is necessary. A strike team has been assembled to leave on schedule to carry out the assignment. But if anything goes wrong, the team must be expendable.

CHAPTER TWENTY-TWO

Chicago, Illinois

"Sorry, the party you have reached is not available . . . Please try your call again later."

Dossier slammed the payphone on the perch, frustrated. Dex hadn't answered his calls in two weeks. He had a bad feeling when he yanked the door to the payphone. His wife Pamela jumped aside as he barged out.

"Bob, what's the matter with you? Tell me what's going on?" she demanded.

Dossier's eyes wandered across the street to a restaurant where he noticed a man sitting in a booth next to the window. Suspicion rose in him. He thought the man might be watching them. He observed the guy when he got up and went to the counter to buy a pack of cigarettes. A woman exiting the bathroom walked to his booth and sat down. After the guy paid the cashier for the pack of smokes, he joined her.

"Pam, let's go," he said.

His wife sensed the urgency from the moment they left home in a hurry and pleaded with him. "Tell me what's going on with you Bob."

He didn't answer. His thoughts were on the phone call he received from Harry Kellerman. The agent figured he wouldn't pick up on the trap when he told him his superior would like to meet with him. Without a word from Dex, he had the feeling that it was time to get out of the country fast as he could.

O'Hare Airport wasn't that far away from the payphone. They would have arrived at their intended destination, had he not stopped to place the call to Dex. When they headed to his wife's car, she grabbed the sleeve of his coat and stopped.

"Tell me what's going on, or I will not be going any further. I have a right to know," she asserted.

Dossier looked mortified. For a moment, he stood there eyeballing the cars passing by on the street in both directions. Then he pulled her closer until their faces were mere inches apart.

"Pam, listen. I don't have time to discuss it. All I can say is that it's not safe for you to be around me right now."

"You're scaring me, Bob."

"I don't mean to. But when we get to the airport, I will put you on a separate flight to Florida. I must leave the country for a while. And I want you to stay at your parents' home in Tampa until I contact you."

"Bob, what have you done?"

She started crying. Dossier wiped away the tears on her cheeks and hugged her.

"There are people who may be watching me right now," he said. "People who may want to do harm to me. I can't risk putting you in harm's way."

As they stood on the sidewalk with their bodies pressed against one another, he peered up at the mercury neon on the buildings and storefronts.

The car was parked a few feet ahead. Pamela dug inside her purse for the keys and a cigarette to calm her nerves. The lawyer glanced up at a camera above a traffic light, realizing the CIA had the capability to surveil people through it. When he glanced back at his wife, she was trying to light up the cancer stick she pulled out.

Anxious to get going, he muttered, "Pam, hurry. Get in"

Right after she lit it, Dossier heard motorcycle engines. Three men on Suzuki's came flying around the corner. The minute he saw black helmets and short barrel assault rifles strapped over their shoulders, he trusted his instincts, and went to the rear door of the car to opened it.

"Bob, what's wrong?" his wife asked.

He shouted, "Get in the car and stay down!"

He grabbed a gun case and a leather bag. When they started shooting, his wife panicked and ran out into the flow of traffic. She was struck by a passing car she never saw coming. The impact hurled her into the air. Her body rolled off the trunk of another vehicle and hit the pavement after she came down.

"Pam! No, no, no!" Dossier cried out. He raced out into the street to help her. But she was gone when he got to her. Enraged, he ran into the doorway of a storefront. Then he opened the case and took out an AR-15. The men on the bikes zoomed passed shooting through the windows of the cars parked at the curbside. The windows of the storefront behind him shattered after he went to the ground.

When the bikes flew down the street he got up and knocked out more chunks of glass with the barrel of his gun before he dove through the window of the store. After the bikes pulled up outside, he heard glass crunching beneath boots moments later. The men in the helmets had come through the window searching for him. Sporadic shots rang out from their weapons. Canned goods and cartons of milk inside the coolers exploded off the shelves as the Dossier made his way down an aisle heading towards the rear of the store. He stopped and hid behind a row of stacked plastic garbage containers.

One of the assailants shouted, "There is no place you can run, counselor. Show yourself!"

The lawyer peeped around the corner of a container and spotted the shooters moving past the aisles with their guns swinging left and right and straight ahead.

"Don't make this hard, Mr. Dossier," the other shooter shouted.

Dossier shouted back through the darkness, "Who set us up . . . Kellerman or Bedford?" Then he eased away from the plastic containers to relocate. There was a door at the back of the store. He opened it and ducked inside. He found himself in a cold room with slabs of meat hanging from the hooks he saw above him. He was standing inside a freezer with no other exit except the way he came in.

Realizing he was cornered, he shouted, "Come and get me, you bastards!"

When he opened the leather bag, he extracted a hand grenade. Then he waited. As soon as he saw the men turn the corner and head down the aisle towards the freezer, all the military skills Dossier learned as a former Marine kicked in. He burst out the door spraying rounds from the AR-15 with his right hand as he launched the grenade at them with his left. The men saw the grenade flying towards them and scrambled before it exploded.

"They set us up. Now they send you clowns to silence me. Is that it?" the lawyer shouted.

He saw the assailant's shadows disappear into the haze of smoke as he crept down the aisle wounded by the thought of his deceased wife. He thought he had nothing to lose when he extracted another grenade from the leather bag.

With the assailants on the move, he started taunting them. "Where are you? That all you got?"

He was moving down another aisle when he spotted the shadows backing up towards the front of the store. The men were trying to escape after they realized he was much more than an attorney who passed the bar exam. The second grenade he let fly found his targets and blew all three men back out the window onto the sidewalk. He ran through the haze of smoke. Once he was back outside, he passed by their bodies and ran back to his wife. He quickly removed his coat and placed it over. Then he planted a kiss on her cheek.

A man suddenly walked up behind him and muttered, "Hello, counselor."

The lawyer turned to look over his shoulder. He saw the face of the blond-haired man staring down at him, saw the gun he was aiming at his head, saw the spark that followed the hollow point through the barrel of the gun after the blond man fired. It was the last thing he saw.

Part Five
Operation Lion's Den

CHAPTER TWENTY-THREE

Colombia

The first light before dawn was less than two hours away when the two Black Hawk helicopters tore into the night sky carrying Lieutenant Claymore Logan and the eleven-man Navy SEAL team he was leading. The choppers were flying at low altitude. The soldiers were braced for action. The mission was a special op. One of the most dangerous they had gone on. They had orders to set up recon and wait for a backup team of Army Rangers before executing the raid on the small village they located two hundred miles south of Medellin. The Lieutenant ignored it. The orders came late. They were already heading straight toward the village with every intent to infiltrate the target's location. The drone they sent out ahead was feeding back real time footage on the area's rugged terrain. Analyzing his handheld monitor, common sense told the Lieutenant that driving on back roads into the foothills was suicidal. The village was a fortress. Mountains stood on every side. Armed guards were on constant foot patrol day and night. The only way in was by air. Three miles away from the drop zone another transmission came on the Lieutenant's head set from the Ranger's Sergeant in charge.

"Come in, Code Gray . . . This is Razor One."

"This is Code Gray. What is it, Sergeant?"

"Lieutenant Logan, I am giving you another direct order not to enter that village with your team until we arrive. Now, you will stand down and wait for us to accompany you. Copy?"

The Lieutenant responded, "Can't do that, Sergeant. We're too close. We're going in."

The Ranger Sergeant was still rattling into the earpiece of the headset when Logan took it off. Two miles out, the team began double checking the gear and communications equipment. One mile out, the Lieutenant had the village in the lens of his night vision glasses. Everyone knew the hazards. They knew things always went wrong. Nevertheless, they flew in determined to carry out the mission anyway.

As they approached the target's compound the Black Hawks flared and hovered thirty feet above the fortified walls encircling the drop zone. The platoon began fast-roping out of the choppers two at a time. They used their hands and feet for breaks to make the optical descent as perfect as they could. The plan evaporated the moment the last man got off the rope and they encountered two dozen or more Colombian guards who popped up through port holes in the grass shooting at them. A projectile shot out of a shoulder-held rocket slammed into one of the Black Hawks. The helicopter burst into a big ball of flames and went down faster after it hit the wall. The one that escaped was nearly blown out of the sky as it flew off leaving the team behind.

Six members on the team were killed within seconds after they breached the compound. The rest scattered, returning fire, moving into safe zones. Lieutenant Logan took off running in the direction of the target's residence with two commandos who kept their M4's popping like overheated fuses. As they ran for cover three more team members were cut down by enemy fire crossing the south lawn. When the shooting suddenly abated, they heard the snick-snack of auto clips snapping shut. The Colombians were reloading. It was a tight window when the Lieutenant broke away and ran to the downed soldiers. He thought he could provide them with aid. The first one he reached had a large hole in his helmet with blood and chunks of brain draining from the wound that killed him. Bullets practically sawed in half the soldier lying beside him. The third man was lying about a hundred yards away. When he heard him groaning loudly, barely clinging to life, he started in his direction, just as a grenade exploded nearby. The blast hurled him to the ground. He got to his feet slowly. Dazed, he stumbled over to the fallen soldier and rolled him over. Half his face and most of his upper torso was blown off.

Sheened in sweat, sucking in smoke, he radioed the last two SEALS. "Code Gray to Dingo . . . Leprechaun. Where are you?"

The voice of Dingo came through his earpiece. "We have eyes on you, Code Gray. We're right behind you."

Logan turned with his night glasses and spotted the two commandos shielding themselves behind a stone barrier. They gave him cover when he ran across the short distance to rejoin them. It looked as though the Colombians were preparing to move in and snuff them out until the Ranger's showed up out of nowhere in three Black Hawks and six Apache helicopters. The choppers dipped in low with spotlights on the combatants. The gunners in charge of shelling the mounted 240-Bravos and .30 millimeters were mowing down every identified target caught in the line of fire.

Logan and his men found themselves heading up a long drive where they ducked down behind a row of luxury cars to shield themselves. They had their night glasses trained on the five armed Colombian guards they saw posted at the entrance of the residence. They were holdouts. Defiantly hardened, they were ready to protect the person inside at all costs.

Logan patted his shoulder three quick times. The two commandos immediately unstrapped M14 sniper rifles and pumped out five precision rounds that left the men at the front entrance lying between the huge pillars.

"Razor One to Code Gray. The rear of the residence is clear. What's your status?"

The Lieutenant heard the transmission from the Ranger's Sergeant in his earpiece and responded.

"Code Gray here, Razor One. The front is clear. We're preparing for entry."

Once the compound was secured, Logan and his men ran up the steps to entrance. Dingo and Leprechaun checked the fallen guards good before they made their entry. The Rangers entered through the back. When they spotted the SEALS moving through rooms on the ground floor searching for the target. They went up the staircase to the second level to begin on their own. Logan led his men into another room to search but found nothing. He feared the worst. The target escaped. Then one of the Rangers upstairs suddenly yelled for his superior.

"Sergeant Havlichek, I think you might want to get a look at this!"

At that moment the Lieutenant pushed past his commandos and ran up the staircase with the two soldiers on his heels. The Rangers were standing inside a large bedroom where they bashed a wall in with a door-buster and several sledgehammers. Behind it was hidden walk-in vault with a mound of American currency stacked up three or four feet high.

"Boys, I'd say we're looking at the range of one hundred or more million dollars here," the Ranger Sergeant stated.

Lieutenant Logan was unimpressed when he walked into the vault. He took one look at the money. Then he ordered his men to continue searching for the target. After they went back downstairs, they headed down the hallway. One of the doors they opened had a stairwell that led into the basement level. Dingo and Leprechaun splintered off and searched rooms on the right side. The Lieutenant searched the ones across the hall on the left when he heard Leprechaun call out for him.

"Lieutenant, better get in here and check this out!"

When he hurried into the room where Dingo and Leprechaun were, he found them standing over the body of a man slumped against the wall next to a huge steel door. His first observations were the black jacket, shirt, and pants the man had on. A black ski mask lay crumpled on his lap like it was snatched off his head and dropped there. The nine-millimeter pistol lying beside him must have fallen from his hand. He bent down to examine him. He had a broken nose. His eyes were swollen. And the scarlet red streak of blood running from the bullet hole in the side of his head looked like it dried some time ago.

"He's a foreigner. I wonder what he was doing here?" Logan observed.

"Looks like he was trying to get past this door, until someone stopped him," Dingo chimed.

Lieutenant Logan started to say something else, but his next words were interrupted by another radio transmission from the Ranger Sergeant.

"Razor One to Code Gray. Where are you?" he asked.

"This is Code Gray, Sergeant. We're in the basement level of the residence. We have a body down here. Possibly an operative. He looks American, could be European. I think we just found some kind of passageway, too."

"Anything else?" asked the Sergeant.

"Negative," replied Logan.

"Okay, we're on our way down, Lieutenant."

Logan and his junior officers eased a little closer to the steel door. It was half open. When they stepped through it, they found a long corridor with more rooms on both sides. Like the ones upstairs, they began searching them. The only thing they found was another stairwell they took down to another level beneath the basement. The rooms they passed by were stocked with munitions. The soldiers realized the third level they were walking through was no basement. It was an underground bunker with a labyrinth of corridors, private rooms, and offices modified into some kind of command center.

Dingo and Leprechaun started searching the munitions rooms. Logan wandered down the corridor checking each room he came to. The doors he approached were closed. But halfway down the corridor there was one door standing open. He held his M4 ready as he spun inside the room aiming at nothing except a swivel chair pulled up to a desk. There was a computer on it. On the back wall above the desk was a panel of camera monitors. For a moment, the Lieutenant stood looking at them. There had to be close to a hundred screens. Some of them were switching to different camera angles of the entire property every sixty seconds. One of the screens showed Dingo and Leprechaun going inside one of the rooms down the hallway to search it. The Rangers were on another screen gazing down at the body of the man they left lying next to the steel door on the floor above them. A camera outside showed the helicopters hovering above the walls of the compound.

There was a half full cup of coffee on the desk that looked like it had been left there by someone leaving in a hurry. By someone who must have seen their full-scale attack coming on the camera monitors when they entered the village. Just as he feared, the target wasn't there. The second attempt at infiltrating the compound got messier than the first time around. It was time to wrap up the search he thought. But when he turned to leave the room, he glanced at the computer on the desk and froze. His eyes were stuck in their sockets the moment he looked at the bright green letters K-Q-B-KNT-R flashing on the screen. Every muscle in his body seized up. He lost all mobility to stop the M4 when it slipped from his hands and clanked on the floor. He just stood fixated, unable to move as people and places and events rushed up in his mind's memory like snippets from a film reel playing back his wife and him, sitting across from each other inside a restaurant, a blond-haired man talking to him in a park, him and a lawyer talking on a yacht, a headstone in a cemetery, an old white guy slipping him a note, a Hispanic man on a laptop, men hauling him into a van,

All at once, he blinked. After regaining his senses, the soldier took a step back looking around confused and lost. The minute he glanced up at the U.S. troops and helicopters he saw on the panel of cameras, questions started rising. Why was he wearing battle fatigues? Why was there an M4 assault rifle lying on the floor at his feet? Where was he? How did he get here?

Below the green flashing letters on the computer were typed written words he thought could be a helpful clue to unraveling his bewilderment. He leaned in close to the screen to read what appeared to be intel with a strange warning that said:

TAGOLA FILE:
ENTRY TYPE MESSAGE:

CROP agents inside the American military and intelligence service have been commissioned to attack my village. They aim to seek out and destroy the file that reveals everything about them and the plan they have to disrupt world peace. They will not find it. Copies have been processed onto microchips and documents. The CROP has risen. The new protocol has begun. And if you are reading this message. Beware! You are now in danger . . .

He immediately glanced down. There were three small microchips lying on the desktop. A stack of documents sat beside them with a heading on the first page that said: Tagola File. A Colombian newspaper sat to the right. No way, he told himself. If he'd been shanghaied, he knew he wouldn't figure out how just standing there. So, he gathered up the microchips and documents and stuffed them into his jacket. Then he reached down and pressed a key on the computer a few seconds before he heard the voice that sailed over his shoulder.

"Any sign of the target, Lieutenant Logan?"

He turned. The unexpected appearance of the three Army Rangers he saw walking into the room made him wary. One of the men wore Sergeant stripes.

"Everything okay, Lieutenant Logan?" the Sergeant inquired.

Dex looked at him with no idea how to answer that now. He didn't know these soldiers. On top of that, the Sergeant addressed him by a name he didn't recognize. Who was Lieutenant Logan? The rank was correct. But his name was Dexter C. Jones.

He didn't know why they were there. But he sensed something wasn't right. The vibe they put out gave him an uneasy feeling. He was in an uncomfortable situation, especially with the message he read off that computer about the U.S. military. It was best to play along and keep his cool for now, he decided.

"Yeah. Everything is okay, Sergeant," he replied finally. "There is no sign of the target."

The Sergeant gave him a suspicious stare. "You sure everything's okay, Lieutenant?"

"I said there has been no sign of the target, Sergeant. What more do you want me to say?" Dex stated.

The Sergeant's face turned red. "I don't like your tone, Lieutenant. And I certainly don't like your attitude."

Dex pretended he didn't notice the subtle movement the Sergeant made behind his back. The K-bar knife on his belt was halfway out the sheath when Dingo and Leprechaun suddenly appeared in the doorway.

"Lieutenant Logan, the rooms clear," Leprechaun stated.

The Ranger Sergeant quietly eased his K-bar back into the sheath when he heard the SEAL'S behind them. Dex's eyes were fixed on the Navy SEALS who showed up. The minute they entered the room he immediately recognized both. He knew them personally. They were former ST-6 platoon members of his. What were they doing dressed up in fatigues like him? And why was Danny addressing him as Lieutenant Logan like the Ranger Sergeant? The entire situation puzzled him. Except his questions would have to wait. That much he knew when he bent down and calmly grabbed the M4 off the floor.

"If the rooms are all clear, we're done here, gentlemen," he stated.

Sergeant Havlihchek walked over to him with a parting statement to make.

"Lieutenant Logan, I gave direct orders to stand down. Those orders came straight from the top. The next time I give you a direct order, soldier, I expect you to follow it. Your preposterous decision got good soldiers killed out there tonight!"

Dex stared at him. The Sergeant was six inches taller and thirty pounds heavier. Dex wasn't intimidated by him nor his snide comments. But he knew he had to get out of there.

"Anything else you got to say, Sergeant?"

The Sergeant retorted loudly. "You heard me, soldier!"

Dex pushed past his shoulder and left the room with the other commandos. The moment they were out of sight. The Rangers walked to the computer and stared into the screen with suspicion that the SEAL Lieutenant was holding something back from them. There were only a few words on the computer left for them to see. File Entry Type Message. And the one that continued flashing. Deleted.

Part Six
Queen's Gambit

CHAPTER TWENTY-FOUR

Atlantic Ocean

B ank director Tom Weinberg glared up at Lady Eleanor and her four male shipmates as they stood by the rail on her yacht, glaring down at him as he sat inside the inflatable rubber life raft he was ordered into.

"Eleanor, I did what I thought was necessary," he yelled to the British woman. "I had no choice!"

"I put you in that position to protect our assets, Mr. Weinberg. Instead, you transferred three hundred million dollars to a known threat to the council."

"It won't happen again, I assure you, Eleanor!"

"Your bloody right it won't. Steps will be taken now to make sure it doesn't."

Tom Weinberg shifted his gaze to her three sons. They were the only crewmen on the yacht. He prided himself as a good banker. Now he found himself in a life raft, floating beside the Queen Jewel after Eleanor instructed her crewmen to put him in a black diving suit and attach the lines on the sides to hooks on the harnesses that were fitted around two black SEALS they released into the water. The SEALS were tugging at the lines. They were agitated, trying to break free, as if they sensed a presence of danger nearby.

"Why am in this life raft? Why am I in a diving suit?"

A menacing grin crossed the British woman's face. "Take a look behind you, Mr. Weinberg?" She pointed to the open water. "Do you like Orcas?"

The banker turned over his shoulder and saw large black dorsal fins slicing through the waves in the far distance. The fins were heading straight toward the life raft. And he knew why. Those dorsal fins belonged to a pod of hungry killer whales who were coming for the SEALS hooked to the lines that prevented them from swimming off.

"Get me out of this thing!" he yelled. "You can't leave me out here!"

Lady Eleanor gave a nod to one of her sons to cut the line that held the raft close to the yacht. Another son went to the navigational controls and started the yacht's engine. The raft was already drifting away when it took off, leaving the banker floating on the waves with the frightened SEALS thrashing below. After the whales moved in on the SEALS, the life raft capsized. Eleanor and the four old men on the yacht had their binoculars out, watching until it disappeared into the depths of the ocean along with the banker.

Satisfied, the whales got rid of the problem, they lowered their binoculars. The event made Lady Eleanor reflect on the words her father Johnathan Queensberry once told her in the summer of 1964. She would never have to worry if he succumbed to the tumor in his brain. She would inherit all the riches of his fortune. A fortune that would make her big and powerful like killer whales in their watery kingdom. He'd reared her to be ruthless like him in business. But not like sharks. He told her she had to be like a killer whale. Because killer whales were bigger and tougher than sharks. He explained the differences between millionaires and billionaires as opposed to men who possessed trillions like him. He said people with money like the Queensberry's were government corporate elite's whose wealth and geopolitical power shaped entire governments. Anyone with access to trillions of dollars was considered whales to him. They were the kind of old men Eleanor surrounded herself with on her yacht. Rich, big, powerful—whales! Big government and corporate industry gave birth to men like them and her father, just as it did with her.

When the five of them retired to the cabin to converse in secret, they sat down at the table with four photographs of the threats raising concern for them.

"How could Sergeant Havlichek allow those Soldiers to walk out of that compound without searching them?" Edward Kingstone stated.

Julian responded, "Maybe he thought it might have blown his cover."

Heinrich butted in, "It was a bad move. Especially, in light of the U.S. naval command assets who say there's been no trace of them since that failed mission. What if they found something? What if it was the Tagola file? I don't like this!"

"Don't draw that conclusion just yet, Heinrich," said Julian.

"But we cannot undermine the possibility," Edward contested. "Those Navy SEALS are not ordinary soldiers. They were prepared through research inside a laboratory for that operation. If they found anything in the village, they were supposed to report back to our people at that command base. It means something may have gone wrong. In that case, they must be found and put down. Otherwise, we've got another problem that could cause this entire matter to get out of hand!"

Arthur Knighthood cut in. "I don't think anyone at the table disagrees with that, Edward. Let's say we go after them assuming they did find something. They will no longer have an army." He paused to display one of the photos before for his next words. "But this man here...Tagola. He still has his."

Lady Eleanor's youngest son interrupted the conversation when he walked into the cabin with a bottle of Billecart champagne. Eleanor was silent. But after the son poured his mother a glass of champagne and left. Julian wanted to know what she was thinking.

"My Lady, is there an opinion you have on this matter?" he asked.

She sipped at her glass of champagne with eyes green as coral reefs. Her face, smooth in youth, was now lined with age. But there was still a remnant of the beauty she once held. "We sent MI-6 agents into that village the day before. The mission result was the same as this time," she replied. "The worth of Mr. Tagola's financial holdings are about as unknown as how widespread his militaries are. He is no doubt the first primary threat."

Edward leaned forward in his chair and stated. "He thinks he can use that file to toy with us. If he releases one word of it . . ."

"He won't," Lady Eleanor interrupted. "He knows he can't. Not now anyway. There's no one he could release it too. We have too many assets in high places all over the world."

"How could he have collected this much bloody information about us?" said Edward. "Everything he knows could only have come from someone among this council, unless . . ." Edward paused with a sudden epiphany and the name of the possible culprit that came to mind. "Unless it was Augustine who did this!" he blurted.

"We should have gotten rid of him a long time ago," Heinrich stated.

"Funny you would say that, Heinrich. You knew about his weakness and his drinking. But you voted to keep him on the council," Julian said.

The comment hardened Heinrich's face. In a low tone, he snapped, "I wasn't the only one to cast that vote!"

Lady Eleanor jumped in. "Stop this bloody childish bickering! That is no longer the issue here gentlemen. The protocol was broken. And I agree with Edward that Augustine Razzoli is more than likely responsible for this situation we're in."

She pulled out a cigarette from the pack in front of her and lit it. The focus of her concern then turned to the American.

"Arthur, you must inform the CIA asset to bring in the knights to deal with our former colleague. There can be no further delay with his matter."

Arthur Knighthood wasted no time. He took out his phone and made the call right then and there.

The conversation between the others continued ebbing around him. Lady Eleanor was the most vocal when the discussion shifted to their financial interests in China and Russia. Julian talked about the sweeping in profits his computer tech companies were bringing in. Edward and Heinrich brought up the implementation of the council's plan to secure world banks in order stifle any attempts by smaller competitors to buy into their ownership.

After a lengthy talk with the CIA man, Arthur hung up. "It's done," he said to Lady Eleanor.

"Good," she responded. Then she brought him up to speed on the current topic of discussion. "Julian just briefed us about the Russian Federation's interest in wanting to meet with your friend Henry Tilkerson in Moscow. But we this man to speak with the Russians unless you are certain that he is the right person for the protocol."

"I am certain Henry will do just fine," Arthur said.

"Then it's time the council invite him aboard," Lady Eleanor replied. "Everyone agree?"

After four men nodded in agreement. Lady Eleanor passed the bottle of Billecart champagne around. When the men were done pouring their fill, she stood up and raised her glass.

"Here's to the renewal of the protocol gentleman," she muttered.

The men stood up in unison and clinked their glasses together with hers in a celebratory toast.

CHAPTER TWENTY-FIVE

Milan, Italy

When Senator Jerry Sabel arrived at the small Italian diner in the taxi he took from the airport he was a little nervous. He normally wore a suit and tie. But when he exited the taxi, he was incognito, dressed down in blue jeans, Timberland boots, a baseball cap, with a hooded sweatshirt beneath a poplin jacket to fit the look the way Lieutenant Dex Jones wanted him to show up.

Not long after receiving that emergency phone call from the Lieutenant, he boarded a plane and left the U.S. without anyone knowing. Dex's urgent request for him to fly thousands of miles to meet with him came out of the blue. His initial response was to decline until he told him how he and a platoon of Navy SEALS mysteriously ended up in South America conducting a covert military operation without knowing how they got there. He sounded like a man in serious trouble. And the fact they were close friends growing up in the same neighborhood in the city of Philadelphia. He caught the earliest available flight.

Mostly all the people inside the diner when he walked in were young Italians in their twenties and thirties. The moment he spotted Dex sitting in a booth alone near the back of the establishment, he headed straight for him.

"Good to see you, Dex," he said, taking a seat across from him. "What's going on?"

"Thank you for coming, Jerry. I'm in a bit of a jam," Dex replied.

"That's what you said on the phone. I'm confused. Tell me more about this situation," the Senator said.

"All I know is that we infiltrated a small village near Medellin looking for a cartel leader name Carlos Alejandro Tagola. I believe I was under some kind of hypnosis or mind control. I must have snapped out of it.

Because I found myself standing inside some room located in a bunker underground."

"A bunker."

"Yeah. And I discovered something."

Dex removed a small box from his coat pocket and opened it. After he took one of the tiny microchips, he held it in the palm of his hand.

"What is it?" the Senator asked.

"It's data chip with a file on it," Dex responded.

Then he told him about the documents he found. Documents, he claimed, were about a hidden order and all the authorities, assassins, politicians, and other officials who were allegedly connected to its existence.

"I need to know what you think about this, Jerry," he stated when he finished.

"I'm not sure what to think," the Senator responded.

The last time he saw his friend Dex was two years ago. Seeing him always brought back old memories of them growing up in the suburbs of Pottsville after his family left The Bottoms district and relocated there. The neighborhood was mostly white. And the high school they attended reflected its population. Dex was only one in the hand full of African Americans who went there. There were times he was subjected to wise cracks and racial slurs levelled by certain students who thought it was okay as long as they did it from a safe enough distance to give themselves a head start to take off running, just in case that black muscled physique of his they feared came charging after them in retaliation. When the two them met, Dex discovered he wasn't like some of the other white kids who harbored biases. He looked up to Dex. And he respected him because his parents always told him and his younger brother to treat all people with respect regardless of their skin color.

Growing up in Philadelphia in the 1990's, they were two teenagers into fast cars, girls, and radio boom boxes thumping out rock, rap, and R&B. Those were the good old days. In the years succeeding, he would go on to become a Senator after college, while Dex pursued his dream of becoming a member of the navy's elite fighting force, ST-6.

Now, here they were, after two long years—a politician and strident Navy Seal, speaking not of the golden days, but of something sinister.

"Don't take this the wrong way, Dex, but all this talk about a hidden order with assassins and agents planted in our military and intelligence agencies is difficult for me to grasp."

"Jerry, you're the current chair to the House Oversight Intelligence Committee. What if there is? What if they have moles planted inside the Hart Building as well?"

"Oh, come on, Dex. These are serious assumptions you're making!"

"Assumptions? Jerry, I have two more duplicates of the file that cartel leader processed onto microchips."

"For namesake, Dex. The man's a drug trafficker! You can't seriously lend your credence to some cartel leader. Do you really expect me to believe this? He's a criminal, Dex!"

"So, you don't believe anything I am saying either. Is that what you're saying?" Dex sat back and waited for him to reply.

The Senator sighed. "Hey, I'm just saying there is a chance the guy could have concocted everything you read in them documents."

"I don't think that's the case," Dex countered.

"Then give me one good reason why I should feel otherwise," said the Senator.

"Here's two. For one, you know I haven't been on active duty since my brother Marcus passed. And two, that cartel leader knew there were U.S. troops coming to raid his compound before we got there."

Dex stopped talking and scribbled down the letters K-Q-B-KNT-R on a napkin then it slid to the Senator.

"If I hadn't seen these letters, we wouldn't be sitting here," he muttered.

"Okay, what are they?"

"I'd like to know *that* myself. All I know is that they were the first thing I found myself looking at when I snapped out of whatever trance I was in. I encountered Rangers who told me I lost nine men. Only two walked out alive with me. I recognized both. They were my old SEAL team members. I didn't understand why they addressed me by Lieutenant Claymore

Logan. After we left, I called them by their names, but neither responded. They didn't know who they were, until I held those letters K-Q-B-KNT-R in front of their eyes. They were given covert code names like me. But the minute they snapped out of their trances at the same time, they called me by my real name, and started asking me questions."

"Who are these soldiers?" asked the Senator.

"Sergio Torres and Danny La Salle."

"Where are they now?"

"Look over your shoulder," said Dex.

The Senator turned to look over his shoulder. There was a Caucasian gentleman with bright red hair sitting in a booth by the entrance. He was gazing out the window at every pedestrian and automobile passing by the diner. The Hispanic in the next booth over gave him a slight nod.

"They saw you arrive in the taxi," said Dex. "We were waiting for you."

The Senator turned his attention back to him. "What is it that you need from me, Dex? I know you didn't ask me to fly all this way just to talk about this matter."

"I can't keep all three duplicates of the file on me, Jerry. I need you to take one back to the U.S. along with a copy of the documents I made. The documents indicate there is information processed on the microchip that reveals each specific threat to the national security of every country across the world."

"What I am to do with this information?"

"I want you to deliver the file personally to the president of the United States. He's a decent man. I think he can help us."

"Why can't you just fly back with me, Dex."

"I can't. Not until we find out what's going on. Furthermore, we haven't reported to the command base since we left Colombia."

"How did the three of you get out of the country?"

"We had help from two Colombian Drug Task Force Intelligence agents."

Senator Sabel took a few seconds to ponder over the whole situation. Two questions came to him. Why would three U.S. soldiers be sitting inside a diner in Milan, Italy? And why was Dex telling him this if he was making this up? Even though he found the tale extreme. He'd never known Dex to lie. That was enough for him.

"I may know just the person who could help me with this request of yours," he said. "He's an ambassador at the U.S. embassy in Rome. His name is Gary Roth. I know him personally. He is a good friend of the president. I will give him a call."

"Thank you, Jerry," Dex muttered.

"Hey, I've known you for a long time. If there's something to this, the matter should be investigated. It's the sensible thing to do."

A couple of Italian patrons who got up from their seats caught Dex's attention. He glanced at them briefly as they walked by heading towards the entrance.

Then he asked, "Has there been any word about the operation back home?"

"I haven't seen or heard a thing about it in the media. Doesn't surprise me. The military is pretty quiet when it comes to covert activities. Although I find it highly unusual that they would not put the word on three MIA's."

"Now you see my point," Dex said.

"I'm starting to. But what are your plans from here?" asked the Senator.

"Not sure at this point. I'll think of something. But going home is not on the table at this point. We got to stay on the move. The Ranger Sergeant I encountered in that room gave me a bad feeling."

"How?"

"The Sergeant's hostile demeanor. I got the feeling he was there looking for something other than the target. What if it was the file? I'm thinking we need to find this guy Tagola."

"What for?"

"Jerry, he is probably the only one who can tell us what's going on."

"Whatever you do, be careful, Dex."

"I will."

Dex shot a glance past the Senator's shoulder, panning around the diner. "We must get going, my friend. We've already stayed here too long."

He radioed the exact message into the transmitter on his collar. The two commandos keeping watch at the entrance heard it in their earpieces and got up and approached his booth.

"Guard this closely, my friend," Dex muttered. He placed the microchip in the Senator's hand. "There's a leather bag beneath the table. Wait until we're outside before you retrieve it."

The Senator nodded. "Okay."

When Danny and Sergio arrived at the booth, Dex slid out and headed for the back entrance of the diner. The senator waited until they walked out, then retrieved the leather bag Dex as instructed.

He started to make the call to the ambassador right then but discovered the charge on his phone had died. After he walked outside the diner, he looked for the nearest payphone.

He spotted one at the end of the block and headed for it. When he stepped inside the shell, he inserted a coin and dialed up the number to the embassy in Rome.

A woman answered on the fourth ring. "You have reached the U.S. How may I direct your call?"

The Senator replied in a hasty tone. "This is Senator Jerry Sabel. I am calling for Ambassador Gary Roth. Tell him I must speak with him at once about a possible threat to the national security of the United States."

Top Secret:

From: L-4Knt-A

To: W.B.

Message: Intercept has been received with the green light to take care of the problem. The intercept is being examined.

PLAY: "You have reached the U.S. embassy. How may I direct your call?"

"This is Senator Jerry Sable. I am calling for Ambassador Gary Roth. Tell him I must speak with him at once about a possible threat to the national security of the United States."

PLAYBACK: "This is Senator Jerry Sabel. I am calling for Ambassador Gary Roth . . ."

Part Seven
League of the
Four Knights Assassins

CHAPTER TWENTY-SIX

Rome, Italy

It was a long drive from the airport. As soon as the taxi pulled into the checkpoint at the American embassy, Senator Sabel jumped out and tried to get past the two MPs at the gates. The soldiers standing guard stepped forward to block his path. Although he informed them that he was there on an emergency basis. Neither soldier appeared to grasp the urgency of his visit. He immediately started squabbling, demanding entry, unaware of the pictures being taken of him by the lone occupant inside the blue Volkswagen parked down the street.

He lowered the 35 mm Kodak camera he was using to take the Senator's picture and placed it on the seat beside him. Then he opened an envelope up and removed a single photograph to compare it to the ones he'd taken. The target's identity was confirmed. The distinguished American Senator fit the exact description of the man he was sent to take out.

Five minutes later, a heavy-set man rushed out the front entrance of the embassy. He held up his binoculars and observed the Ambassador approach the Senator. Then he snatched up the Kodak and snapped a couple more snap shots the U.S. Ambassador. Second target confirmed.

"Let this man through," Ambassador Roth told the MPs. "He's here to see me."

The soldiers immediately stepped aside. After watching the Ambassador escort the Senator inside embassy, the lone figure in the Volkswagen switched on the car's CD player. A loud composition by Oprah blasted into his ears, relaxing the storm in his mind. When the two Americans emerged from the embassy an hour later, they settled into the back seat of a limousine.

He held up the binoculars and wrote down the car's license plate.

Let them go for now, he thought. He would see them again when they least expected him. At the moment, he unveiled himself and the big surprises that always accompanied him.

CHAPTER TWENTY-SEVEN

Rome, Italy

"These are shocking allegations," Roth said. "Eavesdropping equipment and spies at embassies are a constant threat. This hotel room will give us more privacy."

"I understand. I know what I am asking is a lot, Ambassador. But there could be something to this more than we know," said Sabel.

"I agree," Roth responded. "I think it's best for us to fly back to the U.S."

"When do we leave?"

"We're leaving tonight."

Ambassador Roth punched a number into his cell phone to place the first of several calls. The first was to the personal assistant of the president who he instructed to relay the message that he would be returning to the United State to discuss a most urgent matter concerning the country's homeland security. The second call went to the pilot of the government jet to make ready for their flight by the time they arrived at the airport.

"The message has been relayed to the president that we must speak with him," he said after he hung up. "He'll be expecting us when we get back to the states. We leave for the airport as soon as our ride returns."

"Thanks for everything, Gary," said the Senator.

Roth smiled. "It's no problem at all, Jerry. The information you presented is worth investigating. I'd like to see what more the file on that data chip contains."

"I would like to know myself. But my friend says it has a coded password."

"Shouldn't be a problem. We have good intel people who can decode it."

"Perhaps. But my concern is how the president might react to this information. He may not think much of it."

"Trust me, Jerry. When he reads the documents you showed me, he'll be just as inclined to look into this matter."

Senator Sabel poured a glass of Scotch from the bottle on the table in front of him. He wasn't as confident as the Ambassador was about the president's opinion. But they had nothing to lose if they had to convince him to investigate it.

Roth said, "This is more than enough Intel for POTUS, Jerry. Maybe it will be just as helpful to get a copy of the papers to the Department of Justice and petition them to appoint a special counsel."

"Let's not get too hasty with this, Gary. My friend warned me to be careful with this stuff. It's not that simple bringing other people in on this. We can't dismiss what those papers say. Just how many U.S. officials and agencies could be tied to that organization, we don't know. We must deliver to the president personally and no one else. That's what he instructed me."

The Ambassador got up from the chair he was in. He strolled to the window and peered down at the street in front of the hotel, thinking over the Senator's point and everything the documents said about corrupt hand-picked judges, supreme court justices, politicians, law enforcement officials, and world leaders who were being shuffled into specified government positions to maintain certain status quos. He thought about the sections that spoke of a secret league of assassins and government officials directly connected to drug trafficking, espionage, and the laundering of money supposedly stashed in various world banks owned and operated by some obscured hidden fraternity. If the content in documents was true, there was a long list of high crimes being committed. But without any real solid evidence, and just a hand full of names disclosed, the papers were enough to raise suspicion. But they needed more. They needed the microchip chip decoded to collect whatever else Intel the file allegedly contained.

The limousine pulled in front of the Hotel. He muttered, "Our ride is here."

Sabel nodded and said, "I'm ready."

They left the hotel room and walked outside. The chauffeur was standing by the rear door. Ambassador Roth already had the plan mapped out for them in his head. They would fly back to the U.S. And they would drive straight to the White House from D.C. International Airport. There would be no stops. They had to arrive on time to see the president. Everything was going accordingly when they left the hotel. But twenty minutes into the drive to the airport, he noticed the limousine was heading in the wrong direction.

Curious, he tapped the glass partition. "Hey, this isn't the way to the airport. You missed a turn back there!"

"Just taking a quicker route, Mr. Roth," the chauffeur replied.

Roth sat back and resumed the conversation he was having with the Senator. Ten minutes later, they noticed the chauffeur was driving down a dark isolated street with low strung buildings and no traffic. There was a single big Suburban truck sitting in a parking lot. Its headlights blinked as they drove by it. The limo rolled up to a corner at the four-way connecting intersection they came to. The Ambassador and Senator stared out the side window when the truck they saw in the parking lot drove up and stopped parallel to the limo in the wrong lane.

Alarmed, Roth called for the chauffeur once more. "Excuse me. Why are we stopping? There's no traffic light on this street."

No response came back this time. All at once the rear door of the Suburban flew open. The chauffeur suddenly jumped out of the front seat of limo and climbed into the back seat of the truck.

Nervous, Sabel asked, "What is he doing?"

The minute the truck carved through the intersection and left them at the corner, the Ambassador processed the situation unfolding.

"Jerry, get out! get out! We've been set up!" he shouted.

But the Senator had no time to react. And neither did he. The blast from the bomb that exploded beneath the car lifted the entire frame into the air and turned it into a ball of flames and flying debris.

Two blocks away, the limousine driver stripped out of the phony black chauffeur cap and jacket disguise. He took one glance back at the burning limousine, eyes reflecting in the glow of the explosion he set off.

CHAPTER TWENTY-EIGHT

Key Largo, Florida

With the sun shining over the greens, there was a light breeze blowing, palm trees stirring with tropical fragrance. Arthur Knightwood arrived at Henry Tilker's estate thinking it was an ideal day for a round of golf. But the leisure time gave them the opportunity to discuss the business at hand.

Henry had questions about their plans for him. On the phone Arthur had only given him opaque details. But as they rode his golf cart towards the next hole, he gave Henry the news he was waiting for. The council was in the final stages of making him their chosen candidate and a ranking member.

He was excited knowing his life was about to change. But not much was expected to change about him.

Henry was a billionaire CEO owner of Tilkerson Tech Enterprise. He was also a narcissist. A man with an unapologetic ego. He annoyed just about everybody he met. Competitors inside the business world hated him. Even though he craved the lime of attention that boosted his status. He despised anyone who challenged him, including reporters who regularly became the source of disparaging humiliating remarks.

Arthur and the council knew about his antics. They knew about his obsession with money and power and twisting facts on topics brought up in his presence. But they also knew he had that cunning ability to manipulate. And that fit perfectly with the agenda they had in mind.

When he measured up the T-shot on the third hole, Arthur took a couple of mock swings with his knees slightly bent and the club positioned. Then he reared the club over his shoulder and brought it down with a clean sweep that sent the golf ball flying high across the lawn in the direction of the fourth hole.

"What a shot! Except I will do better than that with an eagle, my friend," Henry exclaimed.

"Don't bank on it," Arthur stated. "And watch out for the rough!"

Henry measured his club behind the ball next and swung. They watched it sail wide into the rough. Then they hopped on his golf cart and took off across the grass for the put shots.

Henry's golf course was a playground for him. It was a place where he could unwind while his lavish mansion loomed large in the backdrop. The guests who showed up at his estate saw the Phantom Bentley, Pagani Zonda, and American made Saleen decorating the driveway. Some of them liked Betting, so he had his own racetrack for the Arabian horses he kept in a ten-stall barn. Space and privacy were never a problem. The only neighbors were an NFL running back and movie star who lived five miles away.

Arthur pulled a putter out from the golf bag and prepared for the birdie. But his phone went off, displaying the CIA man's initials W.B. on the caller ID.

"Hello, Winston. Any word yet?" he said after he answered.

"The chameleon took care of the problem in Rome," the CIA man replied.

"Well, done," said Arthur. "What about the Soldiers?"

The CIA man responded. "After the lieutenant's meeting with the Senator, the sources inside the Italian intelligence service sent word they caught up to them in Palermo. The agents attempted to put them down. But the soldiers fired back, wounding several of them before they escaped. They lost them without any lead on where they might have fled to."

"They're probably out of the country by now," said Arthur.

"I doubt it, unless they have help," said the CIA man.

"That's possible. It's been almost a week since they reported to navy command. Contact doctor Castree and doctor Petro. Those soldiers could have possibly been deactivated from their neurol training. If so, we need to know."

"I don't see that happening. They assured us the drugs and training would last the entirety of the mission. The only way that could have happened is if they encountered the code to deactivate. No one has that code except the council. Which means someone on the council would have had to break with protocol and disclose it."

"And that someone could be the person who is no longer with the council," Arthur asserted.

"Augustine Razzoli."

"Precisely! Now, you must do whatever is necessary to hunt down those soldiers and keep things quiet about that mission."

"I will see to it, Mr. Knightwood. No one will know about it. Not even the president, sir."

"Not now. But he might later. Leaks happen, Winston. I think we're going to need a false flag on this one. Something the media will run with right away."

"How about three Navy SEALS turned enemy of the state," said the caller.

"Good place to start," Arthur agreed. "Just make sure Augustine Razzoli remains a top priority to be put down swiftly. Understood?"

"I understand, sir. He's been moving in and out of the Italian peninsula. The last sight of him was in Rome. The chameleon is close by. I can him."

"No!" Arthur lashed. "Don't you ever assign the chameleon to handle the Razzoli job."

"But he's the best we got."

"Winston, just do as I told you. Do not assigned chameleon to Augustine. And don't ever question my decision again!"

"As you wish, Mr. Knightwood," the CIA man replied.

Arthur disconnected. Henry Tilkerson was leaning against his golf cart when he ended the conversation.

"Is everything all right, Arthur?" he inquired curiously.

"Everything is okay, Henry," replied Arthur. Then he positioned the putter behind the golf ball and birdied the fourth hole.

CHAPTER TWENTY-NINE

Washington, DC

The President's emergency intelligence briefing was set for 7:00 am. FBI director Harland McCurry walked through the door of the Oval Office, and found President Ernest D'Kembi in the middle of a phone conversation.

"Harland, I will be right with you. Please have a seat," he stated.

Director McCurry strolled across the thick blue SEAL of the United States carpet and took a seat in front of the executive desk. He peered through the bullet proof glass behind the president at the pair of secret service men making their morning rounds. His focus didn't return to the president until he finished his phone call and looked at him distraught and puzzled.

"Harland, I just got done speaking with the personnel chief at the U.S. embassy in Rome. The Italian authorities say the men in the limousine were Americans."

"That's accurate, Mr. President. The bureau confirmed the identities of both men. Senator Jerry Sabel and Ambassador Gary Roth."

McCurry snapped open the briefcase he brought. The pictures he removed showed the full extent of the damage caused by the bomb.

"What do you make of this Harland?" he asked.

"Could have been the car bomb that was planted. I'm thinking a detonator might have been used. They had a driver. His remains were not recovered at the scene."

"Is he a suspect?"

"Most certainly, Mr. President. We checked out the list of government chauffeurs. The driver that night wasn't among them."

"Was this confirmed by the embassy?" asked D'kembi.

"Yes. The Italian police did too. They discovered the actual chauffeur assigned to Ambassador Roth's limousine floating in a river."

President D'Kembi shook his head in disappointment as he thought about his friend. "Gary relayed an urgent message. He said he was flying back to the United States because he had something important wanted to discuss with me. And that it involved a possible threat to U.S. national security. How could this have happened so suddenly?" he asked.

Harland McCurry started to answer. But the voice of his Chief of Staff came on the intercom to inform him that CIA director Charles Easter was on his way in.

Easter walked moments later. He took one look at the president's face and knew that McCurry must have broken the news to him. Now it was his turn. And the president wasn't going to like what he had to say.

"Thank you for coming Charles," said D'Kembi. "Harland and I were discussing the Rome incident. It appears the only suspect currently is the limousine driver."

"There's a few more now, Mr. President," said Easter. "I know you see this as troubling as I do. But three U.S. Navy SEALS have been added to the list of suspects involved."

"You can't be serious!" the president scoffed.

FBI director McCurry concurred. "I was going to get to that part with you myself, Mr. President. The bureau has taken the same measure."

D'Kembi stared at them in disbelief. "How did your agencies arrived at this decision?" he asked.

Easter answered first. "I got a report on my desk sent by Colonel James Burke, Mr. President. The soldiers went AWOL after a special ops mission and never contacted navy command. He says there are speculations they were taken prisoners."

"Why isn't the Colonel speaking to me directly about this? He should be here," said D'Kembi.

Easter shrugged like he didn't know. McCurry looked aloof. So, the president picked up a bottled water and took a sip to clear the dryness in his throat.

"I expect one of you to contact the Colonel at the conclusion of this briefing. Let him know he owes me a call. In the meantime, what more did he say?"

Easter responded. "Sir, he said the SEALS were deployed to South America to first help train agents working for the Colombian Drug Task Force Intelligence Agency. It was a silent deployment. But according to the Colonel they were there to help capture a major cartel boss in Cali whose name is Ortega Diez."

"I know this name," McCurry said. "The bureau has been investigating Mr. Diez. In fact, four days ago field agent Alex Weiss walked into my office to update me on the narcotic activities in Colombia. Weiss has been stationed for quite some time. I was sure Mr. Diez's name would come up. Except he started talking about a new develop that had to do with a munitions dealer Italy name is D'Angelo Cabrini. There's been talk Mr. Cabrini might be doing business with terrorist groups in the Middle East, so we put him on the radar. He was already sighted doing business with rebel groups in Asia and Latin America as well. According to agent Weiss, in Latin America Cabrini was working closely with an individual name Carlos Tagola. He said this man Tagola has connections to Muslim militia groups in parts of Africa."

D'Kembi cut in. "So, what does any of this have to do with the Navy SEALS who to Colombia to help the drug task force there?"

"While they were in Colombia, agent Weiss said he learned of some shady business activities taking place between the three Navy SEALS and that munitions dealer."

"Harland, how sure can you be that his I formation is reliable?" the president asked.

"Alex Weiss is one of the best field agents we have stationed in South America. He said the information was double checked, sir."

The president gathered his next thought, then looked at the CIA director.

"Charles does your agency have this report?"

"Colonel Burke made mention of in the report he forwarded to my office. Apparently, D'Angelo Cabrini is part the Italian mafia. He was supposedly paying the SEALS to collect weapons and ammunition from military bases stationed inside Colombia. The report says he was selling arsenals through a pipeline operated by the gentleman named Tagola. They were partners in the arms trade. But after the business relationship soured over a deal that went bad, the Colonel indicates in his report that Cabrini paid off Navy SEAL Lieutenant Claymore Logan and his SEAL team to raid Tagola's compound. Army Rangers was called in to stop the action. But they got there too late."

"If you have a file on this SEAL Lieutenant, I'd like to see it," said D'Kembi.

"I brought it with me, Mr. President."

Director Easter removed the Lieutenant's military file from his briefcase and handed it to him. The president read a short synopsis about the Lieutenant that went all the way back to his start up as a trainee at the Naval Amphibious Base in Little Creek, Virginia Beach. Then he flipped through the pages and glossed over the military training and status information in standard notation:

TRAINING AND MISSIONS RECORD

Lieutenant Claymore Logan: ST-6 Commando

Specialist / Scout Sniper Operations
Weapons Specialist
Demolition Specialist
Electronics Specialist
Intelligence Gathering
Underwater Demolition
Urban Warfare Specialist
Jungle Warfare Training completed in Quito, Ecuador
Paratrooper Training completed in Houston, Texas

: Routine work up to ST-6 deployment for special ops

Previous Deployment - U.S. Alabama: Persian Gulf
Previous Deployment - Iraq
Previous Deployment - Kuwait
Previous Deployment - Afghanistan
Previous Deployment - Sudan
Previous Deployment -Peru
Previous Deployment -Guatemala
Current Deployment - Location OTR

Special Black op: (OTR)
Grade: Top Secret High Priority

Operation Code Name: (OTR)

"This man's file is exceptional," D'Kembi said finally. "But I see noth-ing about his family or educational background in it. The status of his current mission's location and the operation's code name are all (OTR) off the record. Why is that? Were either of you aware of this military action to send troops to South America?"

"No, sir," Easter replied.

"Not until agent Weiss walked into my office to brief me, sir," McCurry admitted.

"I can't believe neither of you knew about this. We're talking about U.S. troops who were sent to carry out a course of military action in another country without notice and approval from the executive office or congress. Do you two understand what this means when the FBI and CIA director that I appointed says they have no idea why those soldiers were there in the first place? This will not look good for my administration nor you gentlemen!"

The president rose to his feet and walked to the window exhausted of his duties. Being president didn't allow much for rest. It wasn't easy. Half the night all he thought about was his good friend Gary Roth and the Senator who perished with him. He respected men like them. McCurry and Easter felt the same towards him. It wasn't just that he was elected as the first African American president. Millions of people viewed him as a consummate professional.

They trusted him that he possessed the kind of charisma and political outlook that was good for the future of the country. For a man who started out as a young law student who would later become a prominent democratic Senator, his self-fulfilling presidential campaign run that ended in victory was the ultimate experience of his crowning achievement.

A knock at the door broke into his thoughts. His Chief of Staff entered the office in haste. McCurry and Easter observed him as he walked over to the president and whispered something in his ear. Whatever it was changed the president's demeanor instantly.

"Get the national security adviser and press secretary in here, ASAP!" the President told him.

The Chief of Staff hurried out. President D'kembi walked back to the executive desk. Instead of taking a seat, he stood to address the FBI and CIA director.

"Gentlemen, the Chief of Staff has informed me that a video has surfaced from a terrorist group claiming responsibility for the incident in Rome. The media has it. And they're going to air it."

Five hours later the president and the members of his cabinet were in front of a flat screen television. Because in five minutes, the press secretary was scheduled to release a statement from the White House press room that would be heard by millions of Americans across the country.

While they waited, the National Security Adviser whispered to CIA director Easter, "That (OTR) special op Colonel Burke told you about was absurd. What was he thinking?"

Easter replied, "I have no idea. But someone is going to have a lot of explaining to do."

The men ceased talking when the White House press secretary entered the press room with his brown notebook. Cameras started clicking from eager reporters in the audience. A few late comers scrambled to get the best seats closest to the podium, while the press secretary opened his notebook and got straight to the topic.

"Good afternoon, ladies and gentlemen. Four days ago, the president and his administration were informed that two American government officials might have been passengers inside a car that tragically blew up in Rome. This morning, directors from the FBI and Central Intelligence Agency confirmed the passenger's identities of Senator Jerry Sabel and Ambassador Gary Roth. The Italian prime minister provided a statement that his government will give full support with the investigation and our efforts to apprehend the culprits responsible. The president and his administration express their deepest condolence to everyone affected by this." The press secretary closed the notebook and said to the press core, "I will take a few questions at this time."

Hands in the audience went up simultaneously.

He pointed to a female African American CNN reporter in the first row. "Latavia, we'll start with you."

"Thank you, Carl. Does the White House know why Senator Sabel was at the U.S. embassy in Rome? Was he there as a foreign diplomat?" she asked.

The press secretary replied, "Unfortunately, there's nothing I can share about that at the moment. But we expect to know more about that later through the investigation that's currently in progress."

A male Caucasian journalist from the Post raised his hand right after he answered.

"Yes, Eddie," he said to him.

The journalist stood up. "A video has been released of a terrorist group claiming responsibility. Has the president and his administration received any confirmation from the intelligence community on the authenticity of it?"

"I can't provide you with any comment on that, Eddie. The video is still being closely analyzed by the proper authorities."

"Do you have any information in regard to the identities suspects and their country of origin?" asked the journalist.

"Not currently. The investigation is too early. That's all I have for today people," the press secretary answered.

He cut the briefing short. It was better that way, especially taking questions from the Washington Post journalist. The man was a well-known bloodhound reporter who cut corners to get the story he wanted.

"I have just one more question, Carl," said the journalist.

"I'll take one more, Eddie. But that's it."

"Has there been any progress made on president D'Kembi's quest for a bipartisan solution to denuclearize Iran?" asked the journalist.

"Eddie, on numerous occasions president D'Kembi has repeatedly indicated that he is open to resolving that issue with bipartisanship. Perhaps it's best to ask the party on the other side of the aisle what have they down lately to meet him halfway? But I wouldn't stay up too late waiting for them to answer that one if I were you."

With that, the press secretary stepped away from the podium and left the press room, declining all last-minute questions.

CHAPTER THIRTY

Mexico,
South of the Border

Sometime around midafternoon, agents Adolfo Guzzeta and Carlita Perez pulled into the lot of the motel they arrived at. It was hot outside. The temperature felt like it was above a hundred degrees when they exited their pickup truck. Along with the sweat accumulated on their faces, their shirts were soaked and clinging against their skin when they opened the door to the front office and walked in.

There was an old man standing behind the service counter when they entered. He looked to be in his seventies. Carlos figured the little elderly woman who appeared in the doorway was probably his wife.

"Usted tiene un cuarto abierto, señor? Do you have a room open?" Adolfo asked.

"Si," the old man answered.

"Necesitamos uno parar la noche. We need one for tonight," agent Adolfo said.

The old man nodded. Then he grabbed a key from the rack behind him.

"Cuanto quieres para el cuarto? How much do you want for the room?" Carlita asked.

"Veinte cinco pesos. Twenty-five dollars," he replied.

When Carlita gave him two hundred, the old man's face brightened with gratitude. "Gracias, gracias, Señora."

Adolfo peered at the key to room number eight. It was the last vacancy located at the end of the building. There wasn't much in the space when they stepped inside—just a bed, with three wooden chairs pulled up to the table. Even though there was no television or radio, any room at the Sierra Motel was still a good spot to hide out. The place was practically isolated in the middle of a sunbaked desert surrounded by dry hills. There is hardly any traffic except for tumbleweeds rolling across the roads during the occasional sandstorms or winds blowing into the area from the hillsides.

Carlita rattled in Spanish, "Los soldados necesitarán comida. Voy a la tienda. The soldiers will need food. I'm going to the store."

"Bien. Regresé pronto. Okay, come back soon," Adolfo stated.

He watched her climb back into the truck. Then he closed the door and walked to the table where he set up his portable laptop computer. After he switched on the power, he logged onto a media website and found what he was looking for. Newspaper articles highlighted the newsbreak about three fugitive American soldiers.

Not long after he started reading, three quick raps at the door caused him to jump up from the chair to answer what the Navy SEAL Lieutenant told him would be the signal to let him and Carlita know they arrived at the designated location they all agreed to meet up again. The soldiers watched the door open. They had their weapons out as a precaution but lowered them right away.

"Glad to see you and your men made it here safely," Adolfo said in English.

Dex responded, "Where's Carlita?"

"She went to buy food at the store a few miles up the road. She should be back at any moment. You men to need come inside quickly. There's something I must show you," said Adolfo.

The SEALS trailed him inside. He led them to the small table where the men huddled around him after he sat back down. "Take a look at this," he said. The soldiers leaned in close and were stunned by each of the newspaper headlines they read.

Los Angeles Times
Thursday, October 25

U.S. AMBASSADOR AND SENATOR KILLED IN ROME.
Navy Seal's suspected in terror plot.

New York Times
Thursday, October 25

MISSING NAVY SEALS SUSPECTS IN BOMB ATTACK
Questions swirl around CIA's investigation.

Washington Post
Thursday, October 25

WHITE HOUSE RELEASES STATEMENT ON ATTACK
U.S. Navy SEALS sought in possible link.

Dex erected himself. The warning of danger he read off the cartel leader's computer inside his bunker suddenly came back. His friend Jerry Sabel and the ambassador were killed. Unknown assailants came after them in Palermo, Italy. They barely escaped. But Jerry was gone. They figured the only chance they had to get the file to the president was crossing the southern border into the U.S. themselves. But after seeing their faces on the front headlines of every newspaper across the country. The plan was crushed.

Sergio saw the deep thoughtful look on Danny Boy's face and asked, "What are you thinking, amigo?"

"I think we have no choice but to change course," he answered.

Dex uttered persistently, "There's gotta be a way we can get across the border."

Sergio contested. "LT, even if there was, the subject matter in those documents are merely allegations. Who's going to believe us if we don't have the real evidence and the identities of the very people behind the CROP? I say we stick with our plan to find this Tagola fella. He's the only person who knows the code to access the file on that data chip. And the only person who knows who they are."

There was a knock at the door. Everyone went silent and raised their weapons as they approached it. Danny Boy posted to the right side. Adolfo and Sergio took up the left. Dex placed his eye to the peep hole and saw the beautiful Latina woman outside.

"Lower your weapons," he ordered. "It's only Carlita."

They men did as he said, before he opened the door. Carlita was standing at the door clutching grocery bags.

"Que supresa. What a surprise," she said.

"We made it here," said Dex. "That's about the only good news I have."

She saw the look on the men's faces and stated, "Well, I've got a few more things in the truck. Mind taking this stuff inside?"

Dex grabbed hold of the bags. After they went back in, they searched through the bag of goodies. Carlita had returned with civilian clothes in one bag. Another bag contained bottles of Tequila, canned goods, and sandwiches wrapped in plastic.

Adolfo helped himself to one of the bottles of Tequila right away. Dex appreciated him and Carla for their help getting out of Colombia. They offered their assistance for nothing the moment they detected something amiss. They had problems in Colombia with corrupt evil men overrunning the country. There government officials were afraid of challenging the cartels. Others were paid off to protect them. The cartels were essentially the driving force interlaced within the entire South American economy. Nonetheless, they were dedicated to abolishing their hold over the land.

"I hope this will hold you gentlemen overnight," Carlita said when she came inside.

"We won't be staying overnight," Dex stated. "There's a change of plans we haven't quite worked out yet."

"Why the change?" she inquired.

Dex pointed at the laptop on the table. She read the articles he showed her. There was no talk about medals they earned in combat nor how they put their lives on the line. There was nothing mentioned about the brave soldiers the country's government sent into battle zones across the globe. They were no longer heroes. Instead, they were being branded as traitors wanted in connection with an alleged terror plot they knew nothing

about. Newspapers were fanning their faces across the land under ficti-
tious cover names as if the entire country had turned against them.

"How are you going to get the file across the border, Lieutenant?" she
asked.

"I don't know . . ."

Dex paused. He sat back down in front of the laptop and stared at the
last article he read in the Washington Post. An idea popped into his head.
He wrote down the name of the journalist who ran it. It was a long shot,
he thought, but one that just might work.

Part Eight
The Journalist

CHAPTER THIRTY-ONE

Washington, DC

A t 3:25 in the morning the phone on the stand next to the journalist's bed started buzzing.

He woke up. Foggy, he answered it. "Hello."

"Is this Eddie Flint?" the caller asked.

"Yeah. It's late. Who's calling?"

"I read your article in *The Washington Post* about the three missing U.S. Navy SEALS being sought for the bombing incident in Rome."

"Good for you. So, what is your reason for calling?"

"To inform you that the soldiers had nothing to do with it. This was not the work of any terror group either. I have evidence that strongly suggest this is more than likely a false flag operation meant to frame the men accused of being connected to it."

The journalist interrupted. "Listen, I don't know who you are. But I've seen the video of the terrorist group claiming responsibility. That's clear evidence that speaks for itself!"

"How do you know it wasn't scripted?" said the caller.

"Hey, that's a serious implication. Now, unless you have proof that corroborates this."

"How about the identifications of people who are part of the organization who orchestrated the attack?" the caller replied.

Eddie flung back the covers and sat up on the bed with a sudden interest. "Is this hard evidence you can get to me personally!"

"Yes. But I must meet with you at a safe location."

"No problem at all. Just tell me when and where."

"Get a pen."

Eddie reached for the pen on the bedside stand. Anxious for the information, he asked, "Where do we meet?"

The caller replied, "Mexico."

Eddie echoed, "Mexico!"

"Take the earliest flight possible," the caller instructed. "Don't tell anyone about your planned trip. When you arrive in Mexico, right after getting off the plane, you will call the number I give you. Understand?"

Eddie replied, "Yes." Then he jotted down the number and city airport where he was expected to land.

"After I make the call, for whom shall I ask?"

"No one," the caller replied.

Eddie stared at the phone right after the caller hung up on him. The call in the middle of the night was odd and totally unexpected. But it sounded like a potential headline he wanted.

CHAPTER THIRTY-TWO

Juarez, Mexico

After the plane landed and taxied to a stop at the city's airport, Eddie filed out with the rest of the passengers and walked straight to the payphones outside the terminal. He dropped a coin in the slot and dialed the number as instructed. Someone answered on the third ring.

"This is Eddie Flint. I'm at the airport," he muttered.

The man at the other end muttered back, "I know. Turn around."

After he hung up, Eddie spun around and saw a woman leaning against one of the concrete beams supporting the terminal. Dark sunglasses covered her eyes. She wore plain slacks and a button up shirt.

"Ola, señor Flint."

"Who am I talking to?" he asked.

"Your escort. I'm here to take you to the gentleman with whom you just spoke."

Eddie stared at the attractive face behind the shades and the long black hair flowing past her shoulders.

"Do you mind telling me where we're going?"

"No questions, señor Flint. You will know when you get there," she replied.

Eddie retorted, "Excuse me. I have the right to know where I am going."

The woman walked off heading in the direction of the parking lot. Eddie followed her to a white pickup. The moment she cranked the engine, the truck gave out a loud report. When they drove away from the airport, Eddie picked up where he left off.

"If I can't get an answer, I'll call that number back and find my own way."

"I don't think you want to do that. The gangs and cartels in these parts are plentiful. If you want me to let you out, I can do that. But if they spot a gringo like you walking around in the wrong section of town with big American dollars and a pretty leather bag like that one you brought for your camera. The authorities might end up finding you in an alley somewhere. That's if you are found. Is that what you want, señor?"

Eddie knew all about the cartel and gang problems in Mexico. Juarez was considered one of the most dangerous cities in the country. Gang robberies were common occurrences. The cartels sometimes severed the heads of their rivals and lined them up on sidewalks as a warning to anyone who challenged them. Foreigners could disappear off the streets without a trace at any given time. So, for the question put to him, Eddie settled in and stayed quiet for the remainder of the drive.

Forty-five minutes later they were pulling up to a big red farmhouse in the countryside. On the way there he was gazing out the window at cornfields and the horses he saw grazing on hay on the other side of benign fences. When they drove down the dusty road to the residence there was a white van and a 1956 Ford Ranch wagon parked in the driveway.

"We're here," the woman said.

Eddie nodded. "Thanks for the lift."

The woman got out scanning around the property cautiously for a few moments.

"Señor Flint. I know you only came here to find a big story you can put in your newspapers. But once you get what came for, don't ever forget that you will be at risk for great danger when you leave here."

The warning was eerie. But he took note and followed her around the side of the farmhouse to the back. After they walked up a flight of steps and stood at a door, she rapped on it several times and stepped back. Someone opened it from the inside. The man who appeared in the doorway caused his nerves to flare up. It was the man's face. He wasn't in a military uniform. But the minute he saw the face he knew it was the African American Navy SEAL Lieutenant he ran the article about in *The Post*. The same soldier suspected of being involved with the bomb attack in Rome. He was scared. He started to flee back down the steps, but the woman sensed it, and whipped out a gun she pressed into his mid-section. Eddie froze.

"Don't worry, Mr. Flint," said the SEAL Lieutenant. "No one is going to cause you any harm."

The soldier's words of assurance set him at ease. He relaxed and looked at him.

"Come in. We don't have much time to talk," he said.

When he accompanied them inside. Despite the beards and shoulder-length hair, he recognized the faces of the Latino commando and redheaded Caucasian commando standing in the living room when they entered.

Dex tossed the Latino guy a phone he caught one-handed in midair. "Give Adolfo a call. Tell him to have the plane ready for takeoff in one hour," he told him.

After the soldier strolled into another room to make the call. The two of them sat down on separate couches facing each other.

"Care for a drink?" said Dex, pouring a glass of Tequila. "You'll probably need one after what I have to share with you."

"No, thanks. I don't drink," the journalist replied. "And you can call me Eddie. Everybody calls me Eddie," he added.

"Okay, Eddie." Dex poured the extra glass for him anyway. Then he smiled, and gestured at the shot of Tequila he left him on the table between them. "Just in case you change your mind."

The journalist pursed his lips and said, "I apologize for my reaction outside, Lieutenant. It's just that . . ."

"I understand," Dex interrupted. "My only objective for asking you to come here is to prove that we played no part in what happened in Rome."

"Why did you choose to contact me?" Eddie asked. "Why not another reporter?"

"I went to your website. I checked you out. I like what I learned. You have a lot of followers who support the kind of reporting you do. You've had a long-standing career in investigative journalism. And the credits of your primary focus have centered around investigating big government and private sector corruption."

"That's correct, Lieutenant Logan."

Dex and the woman exchanged looks that created a moment awkward.

"Something wrong?" he inquired.

"My name isn't Lieutenant Claymore Logan," Dex responded. "It's Lieutenant Dexter Jones."

He glanced at the redheaded soldier.

"And my name isn't the guy you identified as Patrick Simms in your news article. It's Danny La Salle."

"The other soldier is not Raul Gonzales either. His real name is Sergio Torres," said Dex.

Dex placed the briefcase beside him on the table and snapped it open so that he could retrieve the documents. Then he opened the metal box and took out one of the microchips to show him.

"There's a file on this tiny data chip. And that file is the very reason my friend Senator Jerry Sabel was assassinated in Rome."

"You knew the Senator personally?" the journalist asked.

"Yes. I gave him a duplicate and a copy of the documents. Jerry was trying to help us after I asked him to get this information into the hands of the president. He asked the ambassador to assistant him only because he was a close friend of the president."

"If you three had nothing to do with this. How can you say it wasn't an act of terrorism?"

"I stumbled across a message with a warning that spoke of an organization much larger. Some sort of secret hidden order."

The journalist's eyebrows arched. "Wait. I need just a few seconds, Lieutenant," he uttered. Eddie quickly unzipped his leather travel bag to retrieve a voice recorder he switched on. "I'd like to get this on tape if you don't mind."

"Not at all," said Dex.

The red power light was on when he began listening to the SEAL Lieutenant's extraordinary tale about a hidden order with planted government officials. He found the story intriguing when he told him they were duped and deployed overseas to carryout out a special ops mission, all while under some kind of hypnotic mind control possibly hatched by the CIA and U.S. military.

It all sounded far-fetched, but the rumors he knew existed around the controversial experiments which has kept the nation's top intelligence agency under a cloud of suspicion for years. Many people suspected decades ago the CIA was trying to develop the ability to read people's thoughts and influence their behavior with mind altering drugs. Scopolamine was exposed as the drug reportedly administered to the Manchurian candidate Sirhan Sirhan before he shot and killed RFK. No one could say with surety that it was a false flag operation. But it was a tactic used by various nations to stage terrorist attacks, shootings, bombings. The blame was always shifted onto a patsy or some other party using the media to push the narrative. The SEAL Lieutenant seemed convinced they were targets of the same kind of set up. Only this one was being orchestrated by some unknown hidden order he called the CROP. Except there was no way to know that himself without proof.

"Lieutenant, I've heard of the Illuminati, Skull and Bones, Rothschild's, and other notable orders. I understand you may have the names of people associated with the CROP. But without the actual identities of the people behind it. And evidence like audio, video, witness statements, or a paper trail that links them. There is not much you can prove."

Dex pointed to the microchip he placed on the table. "This contains the proof." Then he motioned to the documents in the briefcase. "And there's enough information in those papers for the president to consider a probe."

"That's possible," said the journalist.

"Good," said Dex. "I just need someone to get this information across the border to him directly. Someone with a clearance to the White House grounds. And I was thinking . . ."

The moment the Lieutenant paused, Eddie didn't have to ask what he was thinking. The look he gave him said it all.

"So, you're asking me to get it to him?" the journalist asked.

"Eddie, I'm asking you to help us prove we were not involved in that attack. Your media pass gives unimpeded access to be on the grounds."

"Look, you could have told me this before I came. If I do this, I suggest you not leave me in the dark about anything else, including everyone in my presence. So, who is she?"

He looked at the Spanish woman standing beside him. She removed her sunglasses and then answered the question herself.

"My name is Carlita Perez. I was an agent in the Colombian Drug Task Force Intelligence Agency when the Lieutenant and his SEAL team started training with us. My co-worker is agent Adolfo Guzzeta. We were investigating the activities of a Cartel leader named Ortega Diez with the help of the SEALS. At the time, my partner and I didn't know about the separate covert operation the SEALS were in Colombia for. During our investigation into Diez, I went undercover to see what information I could get from one of his smugglers—a pilot named Felix Ortiz. While posing as his girlfriend, I learned he was flying cargoes of cocaine between Colombia and Costa Rica. He flies both small engine Cessna's and big airliners that normally take off from private airstrips owned by Diez. Except I discovered that one of those airstrips was owned by an American CIA agent."

Eddie pulled out a pen and scribbled on a note pad. "You sure about this?"

"Si. One night I went to this pub in Colombia with Felix. A man came and joined us at our table. I overheard them talking about a guy named Hector Colon who was selling arms on the black market. Felix later met up with Hector Colon to discuss the merchandise he was selling. When I relayed this information to the Lieutenant, he and his men were interested in knowing more about Hector Colon. We didn't understand right then why that information was significant to their separate operation . . ."

"Why was it?" Eddie asked, cutting her off.

Dex answered instead. "We were conducting a separate covert paramilitary operation aimed at apprehending a cartel leader named Carlos Tagola. The information she gave us was vital because Hector Colon is Tagola's right hand man. He's also his first cousin. We thought it was too dangerous for Carlita to continue her cover. She'd pulled her out and replaced her with two more task force agents who went undercover. Her brother, agent Carlito Perez, and his partner agent Manuel Vargas. They were posing as brokers to collect information on Hector Colon. They eventually discovered that the weapon he was attempting to sell Felix Ortiz was a Russian made Black-Sting Ray torpedo. Carlita told us she and this guy Felix went back to the pub in Colombia three nights later. While there, Felix was approached by an American FBI agent who offered him one million dollars to keep tabs on everyone Colon met with."

"Why would an American FBI agent offer a smuggler that amount of cash to watch an arms dealer?" Eddie asked.

"We wanted to know the same thing. But once we found out, things turned hazardous. Agents Carlito Perez and his partner Manuel Vargas set up a meeting with two men they thought were liaisons for Hector Colon. They were made. Both men went missing. A week later, their bodies were discovered inside a warehouse."

Eddie glanced up at the Spanish woman as she brushed away the tear that suddenly ran down her cheek.

Dex continued, "Carlita and her partner Adolfo later discovered the two men they were supposed to meet were not liaison arms dealers. They were FBI agents."

Eddie kept the voice recorder rolling when Dex told him all about Operation Lion's Den. And why they infiltrated the village the second time. It had nothing to do with the mission. It was to avenge what happened to the two task force agents. They were aiming to kill Carlos and Hector Colon at the same time because Carlita believed more than anything they were responsible for setting the agents up. Even though they failed to find the pair. Carlita and Adolfo were now committed to helping the soldiers prove their innocence just for their efforts to hunt them down.

There was a knock at the door. Carlita walked over and opened it. A Latino man in a brown aviator jacket strolled in.

Dex introduced him. "Eddie, this is agent Adolfo Guzzeta.

"Nice to meet you," said Eddie.

Adolfo nodded. Then he rattled to Dex in Spanish. "La avion esta listo. The plane is ready."

"Traiga las armas. Bring the weapons," Dex said to Carlita.

Carlita went into another room and returned a few moments later with two assault rifles and a Desert Eagle handgun she handed Dex.

"What's going on, Lieutenant?" asked Eddie.

"Time for us to go. We never stay in one place for too long. If you want this story, the proof is on the table. You have ten seconds to make your mind up!"

Eddie glanced at the briefcase with the documents inside. It was a big story if the chip contained the evidence. With that thought, he grabbed the briefcase and snatched up the microchip.

Dex pulled the slide back on Desert Eagle, hit the release mechanism to check the clip, and snapped it back in place. Then he held it out for Eddie.

"Take this."

"What for?"

"Your safety."

Eddie's hand was trembling when grabbed hold of it. "Is there anything else I need?"

"Just a piece of advice. When you get back to the U.S., be careful where you go and who you talk to. No one must know about this file nor the discussion we had here except the president. Understood?"

"No problem, Lieutenant."

With the journalist's assurance, Dex led everyone out of the farmhouse. Carlita gave Eddie the keys to the Ford Ranch Wagon. She and her partner Adolfo started trailing behind the soldiers in the direction of other woods when he called after them.

"Hey, wait! You expect me to find my own way back to the airport in this old heap?"

Carlita turned around and asked, "Did you bring a cell phone, señor Flint?"

"Well, yes."

"Is it a smart phone?"

"Yes."

"Then Google a map!"

CHAPTER THIRTY-THREE

Moscow

Winters in Russia came early. Julian Bishoppontiz and Henry Tilkerson wore overcoats with scarves tucked inside their collars when they got off their flight. The black ZIL limousine they were waiting on at the VIP debarking area showed up with two Russian officials who got out walking towards them.

"See the man on the right?" Julian asked.

Henry replied. "Yeah. Who is he?"

"Ivan Vlastov. He's the minister of foreign affairs. The man with him is a KGB agent."

Henry studied the men as they approached. They donned those big funny looking wool winter hats Russian men wore with their long black coats covering expensive suits.

"Gentlemen, it's a pleasure to see you," the minister greeted.

Henry replied, "We appreciate the invitation."

"Our president is looking forward to meeting with you, Mr. Tilkerson."

The minster's reception was destined. Strict orders out of the Kremlin called for their visit to be handled quietly. There was no motorcade or extra security sure to attract attention. Just the black ZIL limousine that drove away from the airport with them and the two foreign dignitaries.

Pushing through traffic, the minister commented, "Mr. Tilkerson, I'm sure you're aware of our situation with NATO. The alliance hasn't been so kind to our federation. Your trip here is very important to us."

Despite the trifle grin he gave them, Julian and Henry both knew the Russians had problems. The federation was completely locked out of the NATO alliance. Its business of importing and exporting resources was virtually shut off by many of the world's top leading countries. Food shortages and poor living conditions left the country's citizens with a harsh reminder of prior generations who were forced to endure identical hardships of despair under the rule of corrupt leaders in the era of the old Soviet Union. Top ranking government officials in current times were keeping the bulk of the country's wealth for themselves. Billions were being spent to fund programs that produced weapons of mass destruction. Some of it was used to pay off the mercenaries who silenced the opposition from any reporters and protestors who daringly went up against the ruling authority.

When the limousine rolled into a checkpoint at the destination they arrived at. Vlastoc showed the men and the gat his government ID, and them through. The huge structure they came to for the meeting looked like a palace of some sort. A pair of KGB men walked out to greet them. Julian and Henry and the two Russian officials exited the car and followed them inside.

They were led into a large conference room with chandeliers hanging from the ceiling. There was a huge conference table in the center of the floor with fifteen or more high-back chairs around it.

Julian and Henry took their seats. A group of Russian officials filed into the room behind them. The Russian president was the last person to arrive. He had a security team with him. But the entrance of the doorway was as far as the security men went.

Dominik Petrakov looked shorter than he did on television, Henry thought. Being in the same room with him was a long-awaited moment he'd looked forward to.

"Gentlemen, thank you for coming. We have much to discuss. Let us get started," Petrakov announced.

Julian spoke up. "As you know, Mr. Petrakov, the council has new plans for the west. The person to my right is Henry Tilkerson. The council thinks he is the right person to execute the plans."

"Are you sure Mr. Tilkerson isn't here on another one of his business ventures?" the Russian president asked.

Henry looked at Julian awkwardly and responded. "Mr. Petrakov, I am somewhat confused by the comment. My trip here is solely for a political purpose—if we can reach a deal."

"A deal. Before talking about deals, let me clear up any confusion you might have in reference to your business activities. Do you see the gentleman sitting beside me?"

Petrakov nodded toward the pudgy Russian with brown hair and bushy eye rows. Henry and Julian glared at him as the Russian president carried on.

"Gentleman, this man oversees managing all international loans for the bank of IKA Deutsche. The person to his left is the chief financial officer for Cyprus. Mr. Tilkerson, they have both informed me that you have a few problems which need cleaning up."

Henry responded, "Excuse me . . ."

The manager of Deutsche cut him off. "Mr. Tilkerson, you have several failed business ventures that resulted in the loans you borrowed to bail out some of your companies. Our records show you are very deep in debt dating back years. Surely, you're not confused about that."

Henry had no words. Julian wasn't surprised. The council knew about his financial entanglements. His estimated loans backed up in debts exceeded billions of dollars.

The KGB agent who showed up at the airport with the minister of foreign affairs removed a photograph he held up for him to view. "Do you remember this day, Mr. Tilkerson?"

Henry fixed his eyes on the photograph. It was a picture someone had taken of him and two Russian female escorts exiting a massage parlor.

"There are others where these came from, Mr. Tilkerson," he added.

Henry's gaze slid around the table at the faces of the Russian president and his cabinet of officials. What were they up to? They seemed to have him hemmed him in. Whatever the case, he wasn't going to be out done by them or Petrakov.

He'd seen Russian presidents comes and go. Petrakov was shrewd. An ex-KGB agent stationed in Germany. He returned home and worked his way through the ranks of the government with the objective of changing the entire political landscape of Russia. Considering the turmoil of the nation's famines, World War II, the Cuban middle crisis, an embarrassing defeat in Afghanistan, he believed Gorbachev and Yeltsin had thrown the country's political framework into chaos. Dynamics of Russian political ideology changed when he assumed power. The moment he became president he adapted to the playbook of former president Joseph Stalin over the others, with a personal conquest of dismantling the influence of western democracy to restore the steel curtain of Russia's communist state back to the way it was before the fall of the Berlin wall in 1989.

Julian maintained his silence while he listened to the exchange of chattery. Technically, he didn't really care much for Henry Tilkerson. Besides the character flaws, he knew nothing about politics. However, the council knew all about the growing divide between the two political parties in America. And he saw the perfect opportunity for a compromise that could appease both Henry and the Russians. One that could possibly even bring about future relations between the two countries.

"I think there is a reasonable solution we can discuss here," Julian said finally.

"What is it that you suggest, Mr. Bishoppontiz?" the Russian president asked.

"Let's say the federation provides the help our candidate will need for his campaign run when the time comes. In exchange, the council will see to it that he returns the favor of assisting you with the ambitions you have in mind for your country's progress and problems with the allies. This must include the federation's promise to keep our candidate's problems quiet. And I am certain he would appreciate it very much if you made them go away all together. Gentlemen, keep in mind the interest of the protocol must exceed beyond any obstacles we have here."

When he finished speaking, the Russian president and his cabinet started talking among themselves in their own language.

Five minutes passed.

Suddenly, Dominik Petrakov shifted his attention back to Julian and Henry with a gleam on his face.

"I think there is a benefit for both sides with this as long as the candidate clearly understands the position. We help him. He helps us!"

Part Nine
Battle Lines

CHAPTER THIRTY-FOUR

Brazil

The new job was easier than Kenny thought it would be. His only task was using encrypted cell phones equipped with GSM tri-band roaming global devices. For months he'd sent texts messages and emails with total anonymity. With the clipper chips removed from the phones it was impossible for any GPS network to pick up a signal on him and Hector's location.

Sending messages to the rich was part of Carlos's collection campaign to assure the wealthiest people on the planet shared with the oppressed and those living in improvised third world countries. His sabotage campaign was a self-declared war aimed at destroying as much of their dope and profits as he could.

Kenny's temptation to dive into the action was irresistible. After he'd convinced Hector to let him tag along. The two of them were hopping on jets and flying ultra long distances doing what they felt was right. It was a dangerous act. The thought they could possibly be maimed or killed was never far from his mind. But Hector had kept his word. Neither CROP nor their agents knew anything about his identity. Had they, they would have known those emails and texts were being sent by an ex-con who grew up in a little Michigan town called Cereal City USA.

Kenny was as committed to the campaigns as Hector and Carlos. The dangers they faced were but two ends of the same road to them now. And up to this point the CROP and their agents had been unable to stop the advancement of Carlos's forces.

During his time away from home, Kenny often reflected on the ignorant cowardly things he did to survive on the streets. He realized his mind was nothing but an empty room. He was judged nonstop, branded, and abandoned for mistakes he'd made in life. But Carlos and Hector did none of that. They'd given him another angle on life. And they showed him there was more to it than becoming rich. This was only the desires of men who longed for nothing but the desires of the material world around them. Because they'd lost sight of the scope of modesty, they told him.

Kenny questioned where all the sudden wisdom they were sharing had derived. He got the answer to that when he boarded a plane and flew to east Africa with Hector, Carlos, Gabriella, and Toro. Most of the people in the small village they went to were relatives and friends of Carlos Tagola. They were a strong tribe of Swahili- and Arabic-speaking people. While there, he heard the muezzin making the prayer call every morning, and four more times throughout the day. He heard Carlos's father Hannibal reading verses from the Qur'an, and realized it was the source from which Hannibal was conveying wisdom to his son Carlos, and Carlos was conveying it to Hector, Gabriella, and Toro, and him.

On the last trip they made a trip to the village, Hannibal placed a silver necklace with a crescent around his son's neck and advised him well before they departed.

In the beginning, Kenny could think of nothing else except reaching the top of that mountain peak where the American dream awaited him. Kenny wanted that luxury, that cash! Now they were stoked with the knowledge they learned in Africa. Carlos and his band of crusaders had a much better plan in mind.

CHAPTER THIRTY-FIVE

Ecuador

When word spread to the cartels that it was Carlos Tagola shaking up the business transactions of the underworld's narcotic trade, many huddled in talks to unite against him. His foot soldiers were burning up cocoa and poppy crops, intercepting shipments aboard freighters and planes, blowing up manufacturing labs, turning back smugglers from borders and coastlines. Many backed down because Carlos was internationally well connected with his armies stationed around the world. Many simply backed down fearing he'd gotten too powerful to be stopped!

No one understood this more than his archrival, Ortega Diez. Even with the help he was getting from corrupt U.S. officials. He was losing the turf war. He'd expanded his business to neighboring Ecuador. And instructed his chief operator Enrique Vasquez to set up a headquarters in the seaport city of Guayaquil.

The busy Gauyas river was his obvious attraction. The coastline of its west bank was the agri-exporting site for some of the biggest ocean vessels coming into Ecuador from the Pacific through the gulf of Guayaquil. Enrique was moving illegal drug shipments down the river's drainage for the entire three years he'd been in control operating Ortega's business inside the country. The valleys of its Sierra stretched through the chain of the Andes mountains to the transversal foothills populated and farmed by local indigenous Indians. The people who lived along the coastal region of Esmeralda were Spanish speaking indigenous Indians infused with the blood of African descendants brought to South America in slave ships by Spanish conquistadors who'd invaded the country centuries before and forced them into labor on plantation long side the enslaved Indians.

Enrique saw this as an attractive location as well. After he moved into the area he intimidated and forced many of the indigenous Indians from their lands. Ortega was able to take over their oil, timber, textile, and agriculture. Much of the region's amazon rain forest were cut away so that he could grow cocoa plants. New roads were laid to ship tons of narcotics to the primary shipping ports of the swift flowing rivers. The Indians who remained were offered jobs to harvest coca plants from the fields to survive on, while Enrique lived comfortably in city limits of Guayaquil. Ecuador wasn't a major hub for drug trafficking. But with Enrique's help Ortega Diez established a strangle hold.

Carlos sent Hector as his emissary to relay the message that he must shut down all operations in Cali and elsewhere and join them. Ortega refused outright. Hector returned to Ecuador once more hoping he could establish the truce that would set aside the war between the two major factions in Colombia. But with Ortega it was all about business as usual.

Angry Ecuadorians fed up with his chief operator's ill treatment of the land and its inhabitants felt otherwise. A group of fishermen sent word to Colombia that they knew when and where Enrique was preparing his next shipment of drugs. Hector was dispatched this time with an army of foot soldiers looking to close Enrique and his boss's operations the hard way. The load of cocaine he was supervising was on board a docked freighter that was preparing to leave in route for the U.S. Hector and his men had been surveilling the ship. He instructed several to go underwater in diving suits. The men swam up stream behind draggers to plant limpet minds around the ship and its cargo bay.

Hector waited for the men to swim back before he hit the switch on the detonator. A series of blasts went off instantly. Gunfire was exchanged on both sides as they moved in. The Cali men standing near the cargo bay took the brunt of the explosion. The freighter was on fire with men jumping overboard as Hector moved down the currents of the Guayas River in speed boats carrying several assault teams who quickly went aboard the ship. Within minutes they'd gained control of it and the entire shipping port.

Hector and Kenny went aboard looking for Enrique Vasquez with the assault teams. Most of Ortega's men abandoned ship. After searching the upper levels of the freighter, they made their way down to the lower and found four members of the Cali cartel and Ortega's chief operator Enrique Vasquez cowering in a corner of the mechanical room.

CHAPTER THIRTY-SIX

Washington, DC

N ews reports about the protests and riots erupting across the country were as problematic as the incident in Rome for President D'Kembi. The stability of the nation wasn't what he envisioned coming to the White House as the newly elected commander-in-chief. And now that he was in his second term he was still being tested. What could be done to ease the racial tensions and eradicate incidents of excessive force involving policemen were the thoughts going through his mind until an aid barged in.

"Sorry to disturb you, Mr. President. A reporter from the Post called with an urgent request to see you in person. He said would talk to no one else but you."

"It's nine o'clock at night. If he's requesting an interview . . ."

"It's not an interview he wants, sir. He says he possesses information regarding the situation in Rome. And that some of it pertains to a possible threat to national security. He left a number for me to call before he hung up."

"What reporter?"

"Eddie Flint, sir."

"Get him back on the line. I'll authorize the clearance myself," D'Kembi said.

He took a seat behind his desk after the aid left. Then he glanced at the briefing report he got that morning about the incident in Rome. He didn't know what the reporter had to offer. But he was familiar with Eddie Flint. The day of his inauguration he sat down with him for an interview. At the time he'd asked what his administration was going to do to help the nation rebound from the struggling financial crisis he'd inherited. The country was suffering a recession. Healthcare was a major issue. And almost every bill he sent to the floor for a vote was shot down by disgruntled opponents. The representatives who played down their no votes to the public claimed it was merely a difference of political ideas. But many people felt it had to do more with his race than anything else.

The first time entered the political spectrum in the nation's capital, he faced hurdles. None of it surprised him. In youth, he'd seen more than his share of the books, magazines, movies, and newspapers portraying young male African Americans as the unlikeliest of heroes. They were often criminalized. But he overcame the stereotypes to achieve a dream he hoped would be the model for those who inspired his success.

In one article, Eddie Flint wrote, Ernest D'kembi represents progress for our nation. He stated in another article, D'Kembi believes in a diverse America. People support his ideas of equal opportunity.

As he sat there contemplating the circumstances, D'Kembi thought about the millions of American citizens who voted him into office. He realized something had to be done. Otherwise, the growth of the nation and the legacy he left behind would be at stake.

CHAPTER THIRTY-SEVEN

Washington, DC

Eddie was stepping out of the shower when he heard his phone chiming in the living room. He wrapped a towel around his waist and went to answer it. By the time he got to the phone he had missed the call. But there was a message left for him on the voice mail that said he was a granted a clearance to enter the grounds of the White House to meet with the president.

Five minutes later, he was dressed and walking out the front door of his home to his Durango sitting in the driveway. Even though he was back in the U.S. he had become increasingly nervous. He'd read the documents for himself. Nothing in them unveiled the identities of people behind the CROP. But there was still enough information in them to run a potential story that was as explosive as Nixon's Watergate, the NSA wiretaps, or the CIA's Iran-Contra affair.

It was a good lead to a story he intended to keep quiet. But against the SEAL Lieutenant's advice he didn't see any harm it would do to ask his friend William Mead how he felt about running a headline on the information he'd collected. William Mead was the chief editor at the Post. A man he knew he could trust. When he told him, Mead pushed back stating no one would believe it. When he expressed that he possessed documents and a data chip that could prove it. He said he wanted to review the evidence. That he would call back to let him know when and the place they would meet up. But nearly eight hours had passed since they talked.

As he drove over the Frederick Douglas freeway heading towards Anacostia, he wondered why William hadn't called back like he said he would. Impatient, he dialed his number back. The editor's voice recording came on; "Sorry I'm not available to take your call . . . Please leave your name and message at the sound of the beep."

Beep.

The journalist left his voice message. "Will, it's me . . . Eddie. I've been waiting for your call. Contact me soon as you get this."

Eddie glanced at the Desert Eagle lying on the seat beside him. He didn't like guns. He hoped there would be a reason for him to need one. But when he looked into his rearview mirror, he spotted a sleek black Audi weaving between cars and cutting lanes. He noticed that the car was pushing over the speed limit. Then his cell phone chimed. Thinking it was the editor returning his call, he answered it quickly.

"Will, it's about time you called back. What took you so long?'

"Mr. Flint, you've been snooping around in places you shouldn't," a man's voice replied.

Eddie shuddered. The man's voice on the phone sounded harsh, angry. And it wasn't William Mead's.

"You've got two options Mr. Flint. Hand the file over and live . . . Or die," the man said.

Eddie replied in shock, "Who is this? I don't have any files. I suggest you do not call this number again. Understand?"

The caller's reply came to him swiftly. Automatic gunfire ignited from the black Audi behind him. All he heard was SPARAAT . . . A TAT TAT . . . SPARAAAAAT. Frightened, he ducked toward the floorboard in his Durango. It was pure instinct that made him reach for the Desert Eagle on the seat as the Audi came up on the truck's rear. The shooter's arm was sticking out the car's passenger side window with a ring of fire around the barrel of a machine gun. When the car sped up to the side, Eddie closed his eyes and let off two rounds that sailed high over the car's hood. He sped up enough to put the car behind him. But a moment later the back window of the Durango shattered. Shards of glass sprinkled on the back of his head and the front seat. Another flurry of bullets caused him to lose control of the steering wheel. The Durango fishtailed off the road and slammed into the guardrails spewing sparks and rubber and metal across blacktop. Things got worse when his head popped up over the dash in horror at the sight of an eighteen-wheeler semi-truck that had stalled on the side of the road with its yellow hazard light flashing.

The Durango was heading for a straight on collision with it. Eyes wide with panic, Eddie punched the breaks into the floorboard. The Durango skidded into a sharp turn and flipped with a series of summersaults before it bounced up and sailed over the side of guardrail.

CHAPTER THIRTY-EIGHT

Atlantic Ocean

A rthur was sitting inside the yacht's cabin with Lady Eleanor, Edward, and Heinrich, when he got a call from the deputy director of CIA operations.

"Yes, Winston," he answered.

"There's a news report airing right now you need to see," the deputy director muttered.

Arthur grabbed the remote to Lady Eleanor's television. When he hit the on button and flipped it to a news program, the four of them tuned in to listen to the report coming from a female reporter talking into the camera.

"Authorities said the identity of the victim, stemming from the shooting that occurred on the Anacostia freeway, is that of Washington Post investigative journalist, Edward Flint. We spoke to several witnesses who said the journalist was driving his Durango southbound when another vehicle came up behind him. After shots were fired, the journalist's vehicle crashed over the side of the guardrail directly behind me." The reporter turned and pointed to the general area as she carried on. "First responders say they discovered him strapped into the front seat. He was unconscious. But they managed to pull him from the burning vehicle before it exploded. EMT's say they were able to revive Mr. Flint before they airlifted him to DC General Hospital in critical condition."

"What about the file?" Arthur inquired.

"They think it perished in the explosion," the CIA man replied.

"If they don't know this for a fact, you know what has to be done."

Arthur disconnected.

Edward stated, "That journalist is one more problem we'll have to add to the list if he leaves that hospital alive."

"Who might the solders try to pass the file off to next is the question," said Heinrich. "I warned you this might happen. Your people inside MI-6 and MI-5 haven't produced a thing on their whereabouts nor the Colombian's."

"Well, they could be hiding right under your nose in Germany," Edward countered sarcastically. "What have your people in the Stasi secret service done lately?"

Lady Eleanor cut in. "Babbling like children again, eh."

Then Edward's phone alerted him with an incoming call. "Yes, Edward Speaking."

"Ola, señor Kingstone," the caller said. "I hear you've been searching for me. Looks like I've found you first. I knew it was only a matter of time before you and your friends found out about the file I have on you."

Edward heard the Spanish voice of the male caller. When he mentioned the file, it was enough for him to connect with the caller's identity.

"You're quite a clever lad, Mr. Tagola," he responded. "But it appears you've contacted me with the help of a former colleague of mine."

The minute the others heard him say the name Tagola, no one uttered another word.

"What is it that you are trying to achieve by your actions, Mr. Tagola?" Edward asked.

"Glad you asked. Let's start with you transferring five billion dollars from the banks you own in Britain. The funds must be wired to Bridgeport International in the Netherlands," said Carlos.

"That's outrageous!" Edward cried.

"There's a worse word I could use for the kind of information I have on you and every one of your friends on that yacht. Imagine if all this information about the CROP was exposed to the rest of the world?"

Edward stayed mute. Augustine had weakened them. The Italian had put a crack in their wall of secrecy to such extent he had no choice but to choose his next move for the Colombian very carefully.

"All right! I'll arrange the transfer."

"You got twenty-four hours," said Carlos.

Edward sat the phone on the table after he hung up.

"What did he say?" Heinrich inquired.

"He's asking for five billion dollars." Edward replied.

"The man's gone mad! Who does he think he is?" Heinrich barked.

Lady Eleanor responded, "He thinks he's a man Heinrich. A man who doesn't yet know that he's no match for us. That's all, ol chap."

CHAPTER THIRTY-NINE

DC General Hospital
Washington, DC

When Eddie slowly opened his eyes, he was wearing a neck brace and bandage around his head. His left arm was in a sling. He woke up lethargic, remembering that he'd been shot at, that he'd crashed into the guardrail with his truck. Then he suddenly heard a voice.

"Mr. Flint, if you can hear me. My name is Dr. Anderson."

The journalist looked up at the blurry image of the doctor standing over him with a stethoscope. There were blurry images of the other people standing around him as well.

"Where am I?" he asked.

The doctor replied, "You're at DC General Hospital. You experienced a terrible accident yesterday. But you're fine now. The injuries you sustained when EMTs brought you in were not as life threatening as we originally thought. In fact, we have downgraded your status from critical to stable condition."

"I . . ."

"Please don't try to push yourself, Mr. Flint."

"But the briefcase. It was inside my truck. Where is it?"

"Briefcase?"

"Yes. I need that briefcase!"

"Mr. Flint, you came into the emergency room with nothing except the cloths on you back."

"The briefcase was in the truck, I'm telling you!"

"Mr. Flint, the EMT's who brought you in said your truck exploded moments after they pulled you out. There was nothing left of it."

Eddie went silent. The file and documents were lost. Everything happened so fast. Someone tried to kill him. The realization set in. So did the pain that suddenly shot up his arm. He moaned aloud.

"You were shot in the left arm. Your shoulder was also dislocated. You'll experience some periodic discomfort there and with neck and back strains. The good news is the ex-rays showed no broken bones," the doctor informed him.

The nurse next to him placed a pad under Eddie's back. Another nurse checked his blood pressure. Then she injected him with a pain killer sedative that made him drowsy. Within a few minutes he'd drifted back to sleep.

Chello Fransis walked inside DC General and looked around. There was the family of a patient sitting inside the waiting room on the right as he made his way down the hall, unnoticed by the three nurses he passed. The young female African American receptionist he spotted behind the information desk was chewing on a wad of gum and reading a magazine when he walked up.

She glanced up at the shiny DC Police Department badge on his shirt and said, "Something I can help you with, officer?"

"Yes. Could you give me the room number for the journalist admitted yesterday. I know it's late. But this is official police business. I'd like to ask him a few questions."

He had a foreign accent. His smile was disarming. The nurse couldn't resist smiling back.

"No problem, officer. First and last name of patient?" she uttered.

"Edward Flint," Chello replied.

She slid her chair up to the computer and punched in the information. "Ah, yes. Mr. Flint is in room 228."

"Thank you, ma'am."

She pointed. "Take the red strip down the hall. Make a right. And follow the room numbers."

Chello tipped his police cap then walked off thinking his hit on the journalist would go as smooth as the ones he'd carried out Bulgaria and Rome. The receptionist saw the badge on his shirt, but not the weapon he brought for the job. The ink pen in his top pocket above the badge contained a needle for a tip that was laced with venom from a slap-jack ant. The insect was one of the deadliest in the world. One light prick and the journalist would succumb to its poisonous effect within seconds the same way the Consulate did in Bulgaria, when he bumped into him on the crowded dance floor at a black-tie party.

The Consulate never felt the prick of the needle that pierced the fabric of his shirt. But after broke skin and he dropped to the floor with the crowd rushing to his aid. The black suit and tie he wore to blend in with the other male guests allowed him to escape easily unnoticed.

It was ten minutes past midnight. For almost three and a half hours, Eddie was drifting in and out of sleep. The doctors and nurses were gone after he woke up from the sedative. He was alone with the sound of beeps from medical monitors in his ears. Then he heard the doorknob click and the hinge slowly creak open. He thought it might be the sedative that had him hearing things. But when he heard feet shuffling into the room, he realized he wasn't.

Someone entered the room. He lifted his head up and peered through the seam in the curtain around the bed. The dim light in the bathroom furnished a silhouette of the figure who snapped the door shut.

"That you, nurse?" he asked.

There was no answer. The figure walked towards the hospital bed and flung the curtains open. All he saw was the long barrel of gun. The person clutching it moved up to the bedside with agile speed. Startled, he tried to call out for help, but the black glove the intruder placed over his mouth prevented him.

"Shhhh," the intruder whispered low. "Quiet! I'm not here to hurt you. I'm going to remove my hand now."

The intruder eased back. Eddie felt relief and confusion when he looked up and saw agent Carlita Perez standing over him in the green glow of the monitor lights.

Stunned, he blurted, "What the are you doing in here in the U.S.? What . . .?"

Carlita responded, "You must leave here now. Come with me and you will be safe!"

Eddie glanced at the gun she was holding. "What's the gun for?"

"To protect you with. Someone has a hit out on you. They tried to kill you on the freeway. You must get up and get dressed. We must hurry!"

Carlita helped him sit up. His clothes were beside the bed. She helped him into his pants and shoes. Then she took the chair and wedged under the doorknob to secure the entrance.

"I don't think I can walk. I can't do this!" the journalist exclaimed.

"You can do it, or you can wait around until they come for you again," Carlita explained.

Eddie got the point. With the help of this Colombian task force agent, he got up off the bed grimacing in pain. Carlita wrapped his right arm around her waist then guided him to the window. She opened it. When she helped him onto the windowsill, they heard the doorknob rattle. They froze. A second later they heard a thump from a shoulder and the several more that followed. Someone was trying to get inside the room.

Carlita hissed at the journalist, "Hurry. Go!"

Soon Eddie saw a hand come to the door to move the chair away. He lowered himself out the first-floor window. Carlita climbed out after him. Two rounds from a silencer whizzed passed over her head, peeling bark off a tree in front of her when she hit the ground.

"See the white Dodge in the parking lot?" she said, turning to the journalist. Eddie shook his head affirmatively. "Go to it. I'll be right there. Stay inside!"

Eddie took off limping. Carlita ran around the corner of the hospital. When she peeked around it and saw the shooter's arm out the window aiming the gun at the journalist, the gun in her hand barked. The armed recoiled back inside.

Eddie made it to the car and got in. Carlita jumped in behind the wheel a few moments later and fired up the engine. As they sped out of the parking lot a bullet pierced the rear window and lodged in the dashboard.

Eddie glanced back at the cop he saw running after the car until he stopped, realizing they'd gotten away.

"That was a police officer shooting at us back there," he blurted. "Why was he trying to kill us?"

"That man back there was no police officer. He was a sicario."

CHAPTER FORTY

Costa Rica

"What did she say?" Dex asked when Adolfo hung up on Carla's urgent phone call.

Adolfo wasn't sure how the Lieutenant and his men would react. But he had to break the bad news.

"The journalist had a meeting at the White House. He was on his way there to see the president when he was shot and ran off the road. After he was taken to the hospital, a hit man showed up to finish him off. She got there in time to help him escape."

"Does he have the file and documents?"

"They were in his truck. It blew up after they pulled him out. The information was destroyed."

Sergio approached Dex. "What now, LT?"

Dex answered, "Carlita thinks Ortega Diez's pilot Felix Ortiz can lead us to Tagola and his cousin Hector Colon. She is certain we'll find him here."

"What if he's not in Costa Rica? Then we've wasted our time," said Danny Boy.

"What if she's right?" Dex retorted. "If that FBI agent offered Felix Ortiz a million dollars to keep tabs on Tagola's cousin Colon, he'll have info that can help us find Tagola."

"The last time we followed up on information Felix Ortiz reportedly had on Colon, agent Perez's brother Carlito and his partner Manuel lost their lives. And then we almost lost our entire team going back into that village because of it."

"I think the Lieutenant has a good point," Adolfo chimed in.

"What do you know?" Danny Boy barked.

"I know much more than you know about this man Ortiz," Adolfo replied. "Ortiz was on our agency's watch list for quite a while. He's also in the data banks of the American DEA. He's been busted smuggling drugs so many times I lost count."

"Then how is he still flying and not in jail?" Sergio inquired.

"That question was just as puzzling to me and Carlita. We didn't know why, but our agency forbade us from asking questions about charging him. Ortiz was obviously off limits. There was information pertaining to him strictly classified at times."

"Maybe it was because of his boss Ortega's connections," said Sergio.

"It had nothing to do with Ortega's connections. Carlita believed Felix Ortiz had connections with the American FBI agent before the night the two of them discussed keeping an eye on Colon's activities."

"So, you're saying that conversation was no coincidence," said Danny Boy."

"Carlita believes Ortiz was a double agent," Adolfo replied.

The SEALS looked at each other. Dex said, "It would be a logical explanation why he was never charged with smuggling. What if that offer the FBI agent made for him to watch Colon never existed? It could mean they both had motives to keep an eye on Colon. Carlita's brother Carlito and his partner Manuel were on to something. If their investigation was closing in on Tagola, there's no telling what kind of information the FBI agent had on Tagola. He had to know something."

"Sounds to me like that FBI agent is as good a source as Ortiz. And we got one chance at clearing our names. It's your call, LT," said Sergio.

Dex looked at agent Guzzeta. "Adolfo, you are sure your Costa Rican friend can assist us?"

"He knows a lot of people with contacts," Adolfo responded.

"Then let's pay him a visit," said Dex.

The SEALS and agent Adolfo took off heading south through a field. The ranch of the Colombian agent's friend wasn't too far from where they left the plane they flew into the country. The entire trek on foot was about forty minutes. It was late at night when they arrived. The residence he lived in had a fence around it. When they opened the front gate and walked up the steps to the front porch, they found only one light illuminating the front door. Adolfo knocked four or five times then waited.

Quietness.

"Who is it?" a voice asked from the other side.

"It's me, Rico—Adolfo Guzzeta," the Colombian agent answered.

A man with curly black hair and tired eyes opened the door a second later. "Adolfo, is that really you?" Rico smiled. "Entre. Hace mucho tiempo desde que te he visito. Come in. It been a long time since I've seen you," he said. Adolfo and the SEALS walked in behind him.

"These soldados are the ones I called and told you about. We need your help," said Adolfo.

"Primero, hablamos en privado. First, we talk in private," the Costa Rican said.

The SEALS waited in the living area while Adolfo walked into the kitchen to chat with him.

When they sat down, Rico spoke in Spanish. "Quienes estas buscando? Who are you looking for?"

Adolfo replied. "Estamos buscando un umbre se llama Félix Ortiz. We're looking for a man name Felix Ortiz."

"El es un pilota de Ortega Diez. He's Ortega Diez's pilot," said Rico.

"Si. Tu puedes ayudamos? Yes. Can you help us?"

"Por su puesto, que necesitas mas? Of course, what else do you need?" Rico uttered.

Adolfo responded, "Comida, ropa, armas, Food, clothes, weapons."

The Costa Rican smiled. "No problema."

After they returned to the living area, Rico looked at the American soldiers and said, "Come with us."

He led them to a trap door built into the floor of a room at the back of the residence. After he removed the lock and opened it, he descended to the basement with them. The basement contained multiple rooms. The first room was a miniature quartermaster stocked with bedrolls and neatly folded clothing. The second room had cabinets full of canned goods and other provisions. There was a camera mounted on a tripod in the third room. The printer against the far wall was used to produce fake identification cards and passports.

Rico took their pictures. After they picked out their bed rolls, food, and clothing, he led them to a door where he pressed a red button to deactivate the locking mechanism. The wide electric door opened from the bottom up to expose a small warehouse.

The SEALS walked inside. For a moment they stood looking around in awe at the stockpile of weapons they saw before them. The shelves and racks were filled with small arms pistols, fully automatic rifles. One of the shelves held digital encrypted satellite phones and gadget devices.

"This place looks like a miniature Fort Knox!" Danny Boy exclaimed.

While the SEALS glanced around in amazement, Adolfo wasn't surprised. He knew Rico was an ex-agent with the Costa Rican secret service. And he'd stolen most of his stockpile from the agency before he retired.

Danny Boy grabbed up a .556 cal. belt fed (SAW) Squad Automatic Weapon. "Now *this* is a real beauty!"

Dex picked up a M9 9mm. He toyed with it for a minute. Then glossed over the racks that held a collection of American made M16 .556 mm's, short barrel M4's equipped with M-dot quick accusation sights, .762 M14 sniper rifles. On the table in front of him lay a Spanish 9mm Pk pistol. Sergio grabbed a Sterling L-2 submachine that cycled five hundred rounds a minute. The Jewish Uzi next it cycled nine hundred and fifty rounds a minute.

When Dex noticed the Costa Rican even had collected British demolition charges and military equipment, he blurted, "We'll need some of those explosives, NV's, fatigues, radios, and grease paint."

Rico responded, "Take whatever you need, soldados. Any friend of Adolfo Guzzeta is a friend of mine."

CHAPTER FORTY-ONE

Costa Rica

Staying at the ranch overnight allowed the SEALS to recharge. By sunrise the next morning they were up and ready for their next journey. Rico spent half the night preparing the fake ID's and passports for them. When he emerged from his bedroom, he handed Adolfo a duffle bag containing a hundred thousand dollars.

Dex shook his hand. "Thanks for everything, Rico," he said.

"De nada," the Costa Rican replied.

He tossed Adolfo the keys to the beat-up van outside. It was an ancient piece of metal, but perfect for a low cover. After they loaded it, they left the ranch and headed to the next town over with the first lead Rico gave them in their search for the pilot.

Driving through the flat land in the Morten region was the fastest route. They arrived an hour later. The first sign of the city limits was the train tracks they crossed. There was a sign on the other side that said *Welcome to the City of G* and that was it. The feast of words identifying the town was missing, probably smeared by vandals or tropical rains.

The city they arrived at was Guirola, Costa Rica. The people standing on street corners in some of the neighborhoods they drove through didn't look particularly happy watching foreigners pass by.

As they neared their destination, Adolfo glanced at the paper with the address Rico wrote out for him. He pointed through the windshield at a four-story apartment building up ahead. The structure sat in a housing complex. There were lots of addicts in this part of town. Car thefts occur frequently. So, when they pulled into the parking space, Dex got out with Adolfo. Danny and Sergio volunteered to keep watch over the hardware inside the van.

Adolfo headed up the sidewalk with the duffle bag of cash strapped over his shoulder. Dex trailed behind him with his eyes darting around as they approached the entrance. When they entered through the door, the people stared at them like they didn't belong there. Some of them ducked inside the tenement thinking they might be from the local police department. But the two women nodding off from heroin as they passed by on the way up the steps didn't seem to care. One of them gave Dex a toothless smile as he slid along the banister.

They were walking down the hall on the second floor when Adolfo stopped at the apartment they were looking for. He knocked and stepped back.

"Que quieres? What do you want?" a man asked from the inside.

Adolfo responded back in Spanish. "Somos amigos a Rico. Nos mando aki que hablar contigo. We are friends of Rico. He sent us here to talk with you."

The chain on the lock rattled loose. A moment later the gentleman Rico referred them to for information stood in front of them looking sickly thin. The muscle shirt he had on sagged off his shoulders exposing his ribs. And from the dark rings under his eyes. His hair was disheveled. Dex assumed he'd been up for at least a couple of days with no sleep.

"Passe. Come in," he uttered.

Dex and Adolfo walked into his apartment. It was filthy. There was a tray on the end table with hashish and cocaine on it. The man was addict. But they still needed the information he possessed.

"Trajiste el dinero?" he asked Adolfo.

Adolfo unzipped the duffle bag and took a stack of bills he held up. "You requested thirty thousand for the info. It's all here." The junkie reached for it. "Not so fast. Give us the information. Then you get the money."

The junkie shook his head. "Okay," he muttered.

He guided them into the small dining room where they sat down at a table across from him.

"So, you're looking for the pilot of Ortega Diez," he stated.

"Yes. Rico says you know him," Adolfo replied.

"Of course, I know Felix Ortiz. But I want five grand more for the information," said the junkie.

Adolfo hesitated. He wanted to break the man's jaw just for asking. And he would have had they not needed every word that came out of his mouth to be legible enough for them to understand. So, he reluctantly reached inside the duffle bag for the five grand he placed on the table.

The junkie smiled. Then he jumped up and went to the kitchen. He stood with his back to them while he measured out the crystal meth that swelled in his chest after the quick hit he took from a pipe.

"I made a few calls after Rico phoned me up last night," he said, returning to his chair at the table. "The pilot you're looking for is scheduled to fly to Costa Rica tomorrow night to pick up a load of coke that is destined to be transported to El Salvador."

"Where will he be landing?" Adolfo asked.

"At an air base in Lloponga."

"Estas seguro? Are you sure?"

"Yes, I'm sure. I know his flight schedules, just like I know his routes and every single location of the landing strip he takes off and lands at. The one in Llopongo is a hub for El Salvador. His shipments are transported to Panama and then onto Mexico. After they are offloaded there, they are destined for the air base in the U.S . . ."

"What air base?" asked Dex.

"They use one in Houston, Texas. The smugglers always utilize various sites to ship the dope. Much of it gets in through shipping ports along the east and west coast. I know all about Ortega's smuggling operations as well as the American official's helping him."

The junkie seemed matter of fact. Curiosity rose in Dex the moment he brought up the participation and aid of American officials in the drug trade. "Do you know if Ortega's pilot was working with an American FBI agent?"

"You're talking about Alexis Weiss. He's a major player in Ortega's operations."

"How do you know so much about Ortega?" Dex asked.

"Because I was his main pilot before Felix Ortiz. In fact, I was the best smuggler he had until he fired me."

Dex and Adolfo exchanged a quick glance at each other as he continued talking.

"Ortega said I wasn't fit to fly anymore. That he couldn't trust me. I mean, I did sample some of his product here and there. But when profits started coming up short. He had a couple of his men hold my arm on a table while another one took off my thumb with a pair wire cutters. I thought maybe I could recover it and have it reattached. Except he made sure that didn't happen. He mixed it in with a bowl of dog food. Then he fed his Cane Corso right in front of me! It didn't matter that I was his brother-in-law. Ortega is no good!"

"How long were you married to his sister?" asked Dex.

"Diez años, Ten years. She pleaded with him to spare my life. He did only when she agreed to his demand for her to divorced me."

For a moment, Dex studied the man's appearance rising from his drug addiction. The thought crossed his mind that maybe Ortega spared him because he figured it was just a matter of time before he eventually fell victim to an expected overdose.

Adolfo said, "Tell us how to get to the precise location of the airstrip he's flying to."

The junkie pulled a map out of Llopopango, Costa Rica he placed on the table.

"This is the entire layout of the landing strip." He pointed to a location on the map. "Felix is scheduled to arrive sometime around midnight." Then he pointed to another location. "If you take this route here, it will cut your travel time by three or four hours at most. Felix will be bringing in a big load of cocaine on an airliner. There will be loaders on the ground waiting to haul the shipment onto a couple of American C-130's. The planes will stay grounded for a day before they take off for Panama the following night."

"Okay, we'll use this map," said Adolfo. He reached for it.

The junkie snatched it up. "No so fast."

"What's the problem?" asked Adolfo.

The junkie smirked. "That'll be five thousand more for the map."

His request angered Adolfo, once he realized the junkie was hustling him. "I just gave you five thousand . . ."

The junkie snapped, "So what! Pay me, or no map."

"If you insist," Adolfo responded. "Then he pulled silencer out under the table and put two rounds into his stomach. The junkie's eyes widened with shock as Adolfo brought the gun up over the table and put one more round between his eyes. The junkie's head jerked back. Then he drooped forward, and his face slammed onto the table's surface.

Dex leaped out of his chair, stunned. "Adolfo, are you crazy, man? He was our source!"

Adolfo gathered the money back into the duffle bag and responded, "We couldn't take a risk of him calling up Ortega and Felix Ortiz to let them know we were on our way to that airstrip. Do you think he wouldn't if they gave him another five grand? He was greedy. And you can never trust an addict, Lieutenant. Now, let's go find the pilot!"

CHAPTER FORTY-TWO

Washington, DC

Eddie lived just a few blocks from the campus of Georgetown. He figured it would be safe for him and the Colombian woman to hide out there. But when she turned onto his street, there was a truck that didn't belong to him sitting in his driveway. Two ominous looking Sedans were parked at the curb out front. And the men walking around his property he didn't know either. Carlita turned the car around and headed back to the same motel they checked into overnight. The next day they checked out and drove straight to the airport to fly out of the country.

It was close to four o'clock when they arrived at Washington National. A jetliner had just landed. Eddie watched the passengers walk down the steps of the exit ramp smiling and chatting happily to be returning home. He could neither do, nor feel, the same because there were people after him. With no other alternatives, he had to leave his family and friends and his life in the U.S behind. They didn't know nor could they imagine him flying off to another country with a Colombian woman he only met days ago. But once they discovered his disappearance, he knew it would be headline news.

Carlita was scanning the crowd when they walked inside the airport's terminal. Eddie guided her to the service counter. Then he took out his ID card and passport for the woman standing behind it.

"I'd like two tickets to Medellin, Colombia, please," he informed her.

The woman took his passport and glanced at Carlita briefly as she stood behind him.

"She's with me," Eddie muttered.

Carlita handed her the fake ID and passport she used to into the country.

The ticket woman smiled at Eddie and said, "Hey, you're Eddie Flint! You're the journalist from the Washington Post. I read your news columns all the time. I couldn't believe what happened to you on the freeway. I saw it on TV. I'm so happy to see you're out of the hospital."

Eddie figured the Washington Nationals baseball cap and dark shades was good enough to hide his identity. But it wasn't. The ticket woman not only recognized him, but she also smiled and stared at him like a starstruck teenager in the front row of a Justin Bieber concert.

"Thank you for your concern. But if you don't mind. I'd like those tickets now," he said.

"Oh, sure. No problem. I'll be right back."

The woman walked away examining their identification and passports. Then she got on a cell phone and glanced over her shoulder at Eddie.

Carlita spotted a couple of custom agents in the crowd who were looking in their direction. One of them was on his phone at the same time woman behind the counter shot him a quick look and hung up. The two custom agents started walking towards them.

"Vomonos! Let's go!" Carlita said, grabbing Eddie's arm.

"What about the tickets?"

"Forget 'em. We got company."

Eddie peered over his shoulder at the two custom agents he saw parting through the crowd of people with their eyes zeroing in on them. The men had guns inside shoulder holsters. Eddie flew on enough flights to know customs agents in airports normally wore side holsters. They went for the nearest exit. As soon as they were outside Carlita flagged down a cab they jumped into. Eddie directed the cabbie to back to the motel. Once they were safely inside, she tried calling Adolfo and Lieutenant Jones. But neither of them answered.

Two hours went by. Eddie was standing by the window keeping watch when Carlita opened her travel bag on the bed and took out two handguns with extra clips. He observed her for a few moments as he tried to hold back the thought going through his mind. But it came out.

"No one told me I would actually be shot at!" he stated.

Carlita looked at him and retorted, "We warned you. You didn't listen."

"Just tell me why you came all this way," he said.

"The Lieutenant asked me to."

"So, you've been following me . . ."

"I've been keeping an eye out for your safety!"

"You sure it wasn't for the file?"

Carlita jammed a clip in one of the guns and said, "Both. You heard what the Lieutenant said happened to his Senator friend after the CROP discovered it was in his possession. I'm just wondering how they knew it was in your possession. Did you say anything to anyone about it, señor Flint?"

Eddie turned away from her and peered through the crack in the curtain with a guilty conscience. He wanted to avoid answering. But the woman was a Colombian drug task force agent and probably a trained interrogator who'd detect a lie the minute she heard it. So, he came clean.

"All right, look. I called a friend of mine I work with. He's the top editor. But I only discussed the possibility of running a story in the future on this if we got all the evidence. That was it!"

Carlita shook her head. "That was very foolish! That police officer at the hospital and those two custom agents at the airport were hit men, señor. They were agents of the CROP, just like the woman at the ticket counter who called them on us. You cannot trust anyone now. Not even this editor friend of yours."

Eddie walked to the chair next to the bed and sat down.

"Okay, I messed up. But there's no way my friend William is a part of some hidden order!"

Carlita jammed the second clip into the gun and muttered, "Don't be so sure about that." Irritated by the reporter's naivety, she stuffed the guns back into the bag and went to the window to keep watch.

Eddie sensed her discomfort. "I was sorry to hear about what happened to your brother and his partner during their undercover investigation," he said, changing the subject.

Carlita remained silent as she gazed through the small opening in the curtain.

"Carlito was only thirty-eight when he was murdered," she said finally. "There was talk inside the agency that he was being considers for a promotion before he died. He and Manuel were both good men.

She paused briefly and reflected on she and her brother's past lives.

"I remember the first day me and Carlito signed up to work for the task force. We were eager to do something we felt was good for the people of Colombia. It was a bad time. It is now. The cartel's drugs and violence associated with the narcotics trade still affects many of the country's citizens. Me and Carlito started working tirelessly with various anti-drug agencies and our military to stop the spread of violence and drugs. But the fear among government leaders is so prevalent. The cartels continue to act with impunity and often remain unchallenged."

Eddie thought about the predicament they were in after she finished talking to them. It was his fault. He'd broken his word to the Lieutenant. Now the file was gone and perhaps his only chance at landing a big story. But joining her and the soldiers in their effort to prove their innocence and uncover whatever truth was out there to be discovered about the hidden order of the CROP could present another opportunity. Only he didn't know what danger they faced next. And that still scared him.

CHAPTER FORTY-THREE

Costa Rica

D ex studied the map when they arrived near the location of the airstrip in Llopopango. At nightfall they hid the van and set out walking through the surrounding woods, hacking away undergrowth with machetes with a light breeze blowing, crickets chirping, twigs snapping beneath their feet, until they saw a sprinkle of lights in the distance.

Dex held his NVs up and spotted barbwire at the top of fence as they neared a clearing in the woods. On the other side was the airstrip. He estimated it had to be about fifteen thousand feet of runway. All they had to do was get through the fence and wait for the pilot to show up. The tall grass gave them cover as they moved up close to see if it had motion detectors or cameras. There weren't any. The security was poor. The only obstacle was the fence itself. Two airplane hangars sat on the right side of the airstrip. A small concentration of loaders was milling around the cargo compartment of a C-130.

Sergio saw headlights and alerted the others. "Get down!"

A jeep making rounds around the perimeter drove by them. The driver flashed a searchlight as he continued along the stretch of asphalt next to the fence.

"Start cutting through this fence," said Dex. "We don't know how long it'll be before he come around again."

Danny Boy pulled out his wire-cutters and made a large enough incision in the fence so they could fit through. He led the way. When they made it to the other side of the road, they ran behind the closest hangar. There had to be forty or more Costa Ricans working the forklifts and other heavy machinery they heard out front. If the men detected them, the SEALS and Adolfo knew they could not hesitate to start shooting even though they were outnumbered.

"What if that pilot doesn't show up?" asked Danny Boy.

Dex peered into the night sky and replied, "He will."

Adolfo followed the SEAL Lieutenant and his men as they made their way along the back of the hangar until they came to a window they located. Dex raised his head up and peeped inside the hangar. The lights were out. But through his infra-red NV's he saw hundreds of barrels stacked near the walls. He figured they were filled with dope. The pad lock he checked on the door next to the window was so skimpy, it took only a few seconds for Sergio to take it off with a pair of bow-cutters.

They entered the dark space of the hangar and found two Range Rovers parked inside it. Dex blamed the time on his watch and saw that it was ten minutes past midnight. He ordered Adolfo and Danny Boy to take up positions on one side of the hangar, while he and Sergio took the other side nearest the door.

After a half hour went by, maybe Danny Boy was right. The pilot might not show up. He was beginning to think they were hoodwinked. But under the noise outside the hangar, he suddenly heard the faint sound of the plane's engine in the air.

"You hear that?" he asked Sergio.

"I hear a plane," the commando replied. "Think it's the pilot?"

"It's got to be him," said Dex.

"I hope you're right, LT," Sergio stated.

"Sergio, do me a favor," said Dex.

"What is it?"

"I know it's been a long time. I haven't seen you and Danny Boy since our last mission together. You are both like brothers to me. So, if you don't mind, I would appreciate it if you just called me Dex. Copy?"

"You got it, Dex!"

Even though it was dark in the hangar, Dex saw the whiteness of Sergio's teeth when he smiled.

"All right. Check out the movement outside before that plane lands," he said.

Sergio moved up next to the garage door and peered out the window. The airliner was coming in for a landing. He whispered into the transmitter on his collar to alert the others. The plane bounced onto the airstrip and stopped moments later. Felix Ortiz emerged through the exit ramp with a duffle bag and briefcase.

Three men walked over to him in overalls. As he headed in the direction of the hangar, they were talking to him. The four of them stopped when he got to the garage door. Sergio heard them speaking to the pilot in Spanish before they walked away. Felix Ortiz buzzed up the garage door high enough for him to duck under it. Once, inside he buzzed it down. Then he went for the light switch.

Sergio eased up slowly behind him with his M4 and said, "No prende la luz! Don't turn on the light! Y no te mueve! And don't move!"

Ortiz felt the gun's barrel against his back and slowly moved his hand away from the light switch. Dex, Adolfo, and Danny Boy emerged from their positions and quickly colonized the area around him.

"Que Quieres? What do you want?" he asked.

"We're going to have a little talk. But right now, we're going for a little ride in one of those Range Rovers."

Adolfo stepped forward. "Donde esta las llaves? Where are the keys?" he demanded.

Ortiz replied, "En mi bolsillo derecha. In my right pocket."

Adolfo collected his keys. Danny Boy grabbed his duffle bag and briefcase. They ushered him to the Range Rover on the left. The dark tinted windows on it made it impossible for anyone outside to see its occupants inside. Adolfo and Dex climbed into the front seat. Danny Boy and Sergio sat to the left and right side of Ortiz in the rear.

When the garage door buzzed up, they drove out of the hangar heading away from the airstrip. The Costa Rican's were too busy loading the cargo onto the C-130's. None of them paid any attention to the truck as it rolled past. No one even looked their way.

CHAPTER FORTY-FOUR

Costa Rica

Twenty miles into the countryside, Adolfo turned off the main road and headed down a trail of gravel and dirt. Ortiz knew any chance of the men at the airstrip coming to his rescue was slim. Adolfo found a clearing in the woods and stopped. Danny Boy pulled in behind them inside the van they retrieved after leaving the airstrip. When they got out with the pilot, Dex walked over to him.

"Take a seat. It's time to talk," he said to him.

Ortiz looked around, then at the ground. "You expect me to sit on the ground."

"You will only be asked once!" Adolfo snapped.

Ortiz watched Danny Boy hand a baseball bat to Sergio. Ortiz complied when he saw how eager they were to encourage each other physically.

He went to his knees and sat on his heels. "So, what is it you want to talk about?" he asked.

Dex responded, "I know you work for Ortega Diez. But I'm not here to discuss your boss. I want you to tell us where we can find Hector Colon or the American FBI agent you've been working with."

Ortiz looked at him contempt.

Danny Boy stepped towards him with his bat. "You hear him?"

The pilot frowned and spit on his boot. Danny Boy put the bat on his chest and pushed him to the ground. Then he whacked him across the leg. Ortiz cried out in pain and rolled onto his belly. Sergio's bat landed a hard blow on the back of his hamstring. When the pilot turned back over, Danny Boy and Sergio took turns smashing their fists into his face.

"Tell us where they are!" Sergio demanded, but the pilot wasn't talking.

Adolfo walked over to the soldiers. He pulled his gun and said, "Move back!" He took a lock of Ortiz's hair in hand and pulled his head up. Then pressed the barrel to his head.

"Adolfo!" Dex called out. "Take it easy. We need his information!"

Adolfo lowered his weapon, but kept his eyes glued to the pilot. "I wonder how Ortega Diez would react if he knew you were working with that American FBI agent behind his back," he stated to him.

Ortiz finally responded to the implication. "I don't know any FBI agent."

"What about the pretty Colombian Latina you were dating, Silvia Cruz. I'm certain you know who she is. What you didn't know is that she was my partner working undercover for the Colombian Drug Task Intelligence Agency . . ."

"Oh, I know more about her than you realize," the pilot replied. "I knew she was an agent three weeks after I met her. I also found out her real name is Carlita Perez and not Silvia Cruz. And your name is agent Adolfo Guzzeta. Right?"

Ortiz let out a chuckle.

Adolfo pushed his face into the ground and started walking away.

"Eres muy debil, Guzzeta! You are very weak, Guzzeta," Ortiz said to him in Spanish. Then he spoke in English. "Do these men you're with know how foul you are!"

The last words that rolled off the pilot's lips made Adolfo stop. He turned around and walked right back to him. Then he aimed his gun at the pilot's right kneecap and fired before Dex could react this time.

Ortiz cringed and balled up into a fetal position wailing from the excruciating pain that engulfed him.

Adolfo shouted. "Diga nos donde encontraremos el agente Americano y Colon, ahora mismo! Tell us where we will find the American FBI agent and Colon, right now!"

Ortiz glanced down the barrel of his gun, then conceded. "Okay! I know where you can find FBI agent Alex Weiss. But I don't know where Hector Colon is. Eso es la verdad! That is the truth!"

Adolfo waved the gun. "Donde esta? Where is he?"

"There is a big shipment being prepared to leave the Colombian shipping port in Medellin a few days from now," Ortiz replied. "Señor Weiss is overseeing the operation with an American military official. That's all I know!"

Dex walked over and said, "Why did this FBI agent offer you a million dollars to keep an eye on Hector Colon's activities? Did it have anything to do with the Russian torpedo he was selling?"

"It wasn't just about the torpedo," answered Ortiz. "Hector Colon is Carlos Tagola's front man. Keeping an eye on Hector meant trying to help him find his cousin. Carlos cut off all agreements with him and other people he's been causing a lot of big problems for. There were people upset that Hector was trying to sale that torpedo because he's been doing business on the black market without their approval. But after I met with him, he never surfaced again."

Pressed for more information, Dex asked, "How can we find his cousin, Tagola?"

"I seriously doubt you can find him. He's like a phantom. He's always moving in and out of those villages. One minute he's there. The next minute he's gone."

"I think this guy is giving us the run-around," Danny Boy interrupted.

Dex replied, "We don't know that. Not until we see for ourselves. Let him go!"

Adolfo blurted, "Let him go? Now *that* would be a major mistake! He'll tip off the Americans!"

Dex gave him a hard look. "You said the same thing about the addict before you killed him. We need to avoid that here. We have a military code of conduct with prisoners in the U.S."

Sergio removed a small brown pill bottle from his jacket, and stated, "Maybe this will help."

"What's that?" asked Adolfo, eyes fixed on the bottle he was holding.

"They're pills . . . Hc1. These are the only things I can remember getting from my doctor before I was deployed. I stopped taking them because I experienced memory loss afterwards."

Dex rushed over to him. "Let me see that." Sergio gave him the prescription. Dex looked at the label. The label read BMX Hc1. "Where did you get these, Sergio?"

"The navy medical center called me in for a checkup. They did a cat scan. They said I had a little swelling on my brain. The doctor gave me these pills and then sent me to some psych for therapy."

"I get it. You're thinking if this pilot takes that stuff, he'll forget all about what happened here," Adolfo said to Sergio.

Dex answered for him. "That's exactly what he's saying!" Then he dug inside his own pocket and pulled out an identical of the Hc1 to show him. "I have one too. He's right. I experienced the same thing before I stopped taking them."

"Guess we're all in the same club," chimed Danny Boy. The others watched as he pulled out the same pills from his pocket. "Never knew you guys had this stuff on you all this time. I got mine from a shrink at a Burmaxx medical center in Boston. That's all I remember."

"Yeah, I got mine from a shrink too. It's very possible might have seen the same shrinks and doctors," said Dex. Then he took Danny Boy and Sergio's Hc1 and tossed them on the ground before he walked over to Adolfo.

"I agree with Sergio. If this stuff works, this man will walk out of here and not remember a single thing. So, let's try it out."

Dex emptied two of the little blue pills into Adolfo's hand. Then gave him a canteen of water. "Give it to him."

"Lieutenant, do you seriously think these pills are going to work on this man?" Adolfo retorted.

"Give it to him," Dex repeated.

Adolfo bent down close to the pilot. Then he barked, "Abra la boca tuyo! Open your mouth!"

Ortiz glared at him. The minute the Colombian task force agent aimed the gun at the other kneecap, he complied. After Adolfo pushed the pills down his throat and made sure he swallowed them. He stood back up and waited with the soldiers.

Dex finally called the pilot by name fifteen minutes later. "Mr. Ortiz, after you leave here you won't remember a thing what happened. Understand?"

They waited a half minute. The pilot suddenly stated.

"If you think I am going to forget what your men and that payoso Guzzeta did to me, think again! Ortega will hear of this. And he'll come after all of you!"

Adolfo immediately aimed the gun at his skull with SEALS looking on. Dex thought he was using it as a scare-tactic again. Then he fired.

He turned and looked at the soldiers. "I told you it wouldn't work, Lieutenant. No need to worry though. He definitely won't remember a thing now."

CHAPTER FORTY-FIVE

Atlantic Ocean

After Edward Kingstone typed in the code that gave him direct access to the bank's mainframe. The process to clear the funds took less than a minute. Just like that, the electronic transfer of fifteen billion dollars was sent to the Netherlands to meet Tagola's demand. It was the only way to protect the autonomy of the CROP's identities. But he gave strict orders to their agents inside MI-6 to get a trace for the account number Colombian gave him. At some point he thought it might lead them to the Colombian. But reports he was getting back weren't good. Each one was saying the same thing. They couldn't get a trace on the number. And the funds being transferred were mysteriously rerouted to various unknown accounts and places minutes after being deposited.

Edward still didn't want to believe this was happening to them. They were rich and powerful. Lady Eleanor possessed the entire fortune from her father's banks and pharmaceutical companies. Arthur's banks and companies were bigger than Exon Mobile. Julian's French mother was a diamond contractor. His Russian father left him enough banks in Russia to influence the entire securities exchange throughout the eastern and western hemispheres of Europe. Heinrich was the prodigal son of parents who'd controlled all the major banks in Germany before he took over. They were too much powerful to be toyed with by the Colombian. He tried not thinking about it any longer by shifting his thoughts back to the business the council was about to address with the candidate they invited aboard the Queen Jewel for the final initiation.

"Mr. Tilkerson, we are among us for this moment," he said. "I must inform you that a few days from now a group of Senators we placed inside the U.S. congress will meet to discuss matters very important to us. Some of those matters will concern the legislative action we expect them to push through the House and Senate after you are sworn into office. The bills we want passed and amended have already been decided by the council. You will align yourself with the party of these representatives. As a candidate, they will back your campaign. And once you are president you will then back them and keep them in positions of power. You must propagate the protocol and always adhere to the principles of the agenda. Do you understand how vital this is to the council, Mr. Tilkerson?"

Henry glanced at his friend Arthur Knighthood, then at the others. "Yes."

His run reply sealed the agreement between him and the CROP's hidden plan for America. People were feeling the early stages of the protocol already. Once he came into office with the administration he planned to put in place. They were going to read about it even more in newspapers, hear it on their radios, see it on on their televisions, with no idea whatsoever about the bigger agenda the CROP had in store for them.

"The meeting I and Julian had with President Dominik Petrakov went excellent! I found it very interesting," Tilkerson went on. "Petrakov is a tough negotiator. But I am starting to like the guy."

"Glad you feel that way," said Edward. "However, the team you planned to send to negotiate the talks with the Russians will be replaced with the team the council chooses."

"But I told Petrakov I would send my own. Why should I not?" Henry retorted.

The council members exchange glances, except Lady Eleanor. While they were talking, she was gazing through the lenses of her binoculars at a pod of Orca's slicing through the waves. Until she chimed in to respond to his question.

"Mr. Tilkerson, you're a new face on this council. We'll be making the decisions for you currently. It will be wise to listen to Edward's words."

She paused to brush back the strands of hair blowing in the wind before continuing. "The seat of the man you are replacing on this council did not understand the protocol like we thought. He disappointed us, Mr. Tilkerson. He became an old drunk. And then he betrayed our trust in him. This must never happen again."

"I won't betray this council," Henry muttered.

Eleanor lowered the binoculars and looked him in the eye. Then she gave him her looking glasses. "Take a look out there," she told him.

Henry raised the binoculars and gazed out across the open water.

"What do you see?" she asked.

"Orcas," he replied.

"Precisely," Eleanor remarked. Then she called to her son on the upper level. The young man descended the steps and walked over to her.

"Yes, mother."

"Dear boy, I would appreciate if you and your brothers prepared the meal for the whales."

"As you wish, Mother," the young man responded.

He went below deck immediately. A few minutes later he came back up with his two brothers Stanley and Phillip Queensberry. The men went the cage sitting near the yacht's port side rail. Henry not only noticed it when he came aboard, he noticed that it was sitting on a hydraulic lift, and wondered why there were SEALS inside it with harnesses around them. The crewmen raise the hydraulic then opened the cage. The four mammals inside dove into the water one by one. The crewmen went back down the below deck and reappeared with two blindfold men wearing black rubber diving suits. The two men were removed of their blindfolds and lowered into the orange inflatable life raft Henry also noticed when he came aboard.

"What's are they doing?" he asked curiously.

Eleanor stood up. "Come to the rail with me. I'll show you."

Henry, with the other men, got up and accompanied her to the side of the yacht.

"I didn't know there were other guests on board. Who are those men in the life raft?" Henry inquired.

"Those me are not guests of ours, Mr. Tilkerson," Lady Eleanor replied. "They are the sons of our former colleague Augustine Razzoli. The man you have replaced. Our enemy!"

Henry heard the loathsome tone in her voice when she said the name.

One of his sons glared up at her coldly and shouted. "You picked the wrong family to mess with old woman. You will not get away with this!"

"What's he talking about?" asked Henry.

"His father broke the principle of the protocol's code of silence," Eleanor responded. "Now I am going to show you the end results for it. So that you don't make the same bloody mistake. Phillip!" she yelled. "Release the raft's anchor line my dear boy."

Henry watched him cut the anchor line that kept the life raft bobbing beside the yacht. The SEALS were splashing around it frantically when Augustine's other son shouted.

"My father will hunt every one of you down! You can count on it!"

Eleanor smiled menacingly as she held up the binoculars again. "It will all be over soon for you lads," she mumbled under her breath.

Henry stood at the Port side rail watching the raft drift away. The pod of Orcas started streaking towards the raft the moment they detected the SEALS presence in the water. The raft had drifted a mile and a half away before the entire pod moved in on the SEALS. Henry watched the raft capsize. The two men inside vanished into the depths of the ocean within seconds after the whales attacked.

Lady Eleanor lowered her binoculars. "Arthur says you're the right candidate, Mr. Tilkerson. Do not disappoint us."

Henry investigated the pupils of her eyes and saw a coldness there, a ruthlessness deeper than his own.

"You could have easily expressed this to me," he retorted.

"There are things I rather not explain in words. So, I explain them with action."

"I . . . I assure you I will not disappoint you, my Lady."

Lady Eleanor didn't show any sign that she was satisfied by his assurance. She studied him for a minute or two. Then she walked back and sat down under the canopy. The men settled back into their seats. Her son Stanley brought bottles of brandy and poured them drinks. They made a toast and drank their fills.

Then they got back to the discussion of the protocol.

Midway through it, Arthur's phone trilled at 4:00 pm with a text message demanding he transfer five hundred billion in funds from his banks to AGI International in Hong Kong within twenty fours. He thought it was a joke. But Julian's phone trilled with a text at 4:02 pm demanding the transfer of five hundred billion from his banks to the Bank of International Interest in Thailand within twenty-four hours. Lady Eleanor's phone thrilled at 4:04 pm with a text demanding she transfer five hundred billion from her banks in the United Kingdom to specified accounts in Uzbekistan and Spain within twenty-four hours. Heinrich's phone trilled at 4:06 pm with a text demanding he transfer five hundred billion from his banks to a bank in Bahrain. Edward thought he'd escaped this time. But at 4:08 his phone trilled with a text message demanding he transfer five hundred billion from his banks too.

"This is ludicrous!" Julian exclaimed.

Edward added to his sentiments. "It's that Colombian Tagola. He's up to his bloody antics again!"

CHAPTER FORTY-SIX

Washington, DC

arlita stayed up half the night keeping watch. Eddie was asleep. He'd been out for hours after she gave him a couple of pain pills and a teaspoon of NyQuil she purchased from the store across the street. She wasn't sure if she felt anger or pity for him. The past few days had taken a toll on him. He looked nothing like the journalist she met at the airport in Mexico.

It was six in the morning. The first thread of dawn appeared. The small TV on the dresser had been on all night. She hadn't paid it any attention. Not until she glanced at the news reports scrolling across the bottom line on a segment of CNN's New Day. The moment she realized some of it had to do with events happening in her country, she jumped up from the chair and hurried over to get a closer look. She was stunned by what she read.

DRUG LABS THROUGHOUT SOUTH AMERICA MYS-TERIOUSLY BLOWN UP . . . FARM FIELDS USED TO GROW COCOA PLANTS IN COLOMBIA SET ON FIRE . . . PLANES CARRYING DRUGS SHOT DOWN OVER PANAMA AND PERU . . . U.S. NAVY SEAL LIUTENANT CLAYMORE LOGAN SOUGHT IN DEATH OF SENATOR AND HIS SON IN WASH-INGTON . . . NAVY SEAL'S LIEUTENANT CLAYMORE LOGAN, JUNIOR OFFICERS PATRICK SIMMS AND RAUL GONZALEZ, WANTED IN CONNECTION TO TERROR ATTACK . . . WASH-INGTON POST JOURNALIST EDWARD FLINT MISSING GOES MISSING FROM DC GENERAL HOSPITAL . . .

"So, what's the latest?" Eddie asked.

Carlita glanced at the journalist's the minute she heard his voice. He'd woken up.

"They know you're missing from the hospital," she replied.

Eddie sat up and yawned. "I figured it wouldn't take long. What do we do now? We can't stay in this motel room forever."

"We leave at nightfall," she answered.

"Why wait?" he asked.

"The sun will be up in another ten minutes. It's too early. Since taking a commercial flight is now out of the question. We need another plan. I'll think of something. But right now, you'll need to shave and dye your hair another color."

"Shave . . . dye my hair."

"Yes. Your first disguise didn't work too well. The ticket woman at the airport recognized you immediately." She grabbed the paper bag on the dresser and tossed it to him.

"What's in it?" he asked.

Carlita responded. "Your disguise kit. Take it."

Eddie took the bag. Inside was a Bic razor, a tube of after shave, a box of Just for Men hair dye. He looked at Carlita.

She responded, "The new look will be good for you. Right now, you look awful. Plus, you stink. A shower wouldn't hurt when you're done.

Eddie shook his head. But given the situation they were in, he got up from the bed and lumbered into the bathroom.

Carlita's phone went off moments later. When she saw that it was from Adolfo, she answered in haste.

"Adolfo, donde esta? Where are you?"

"We're on our way back to Colombia. How's things with you and the reporter?" he asked.

"Not good. We'll have to find another way out of the country. Agents of the CROP spotted the reporter at the airport. They came after us."

"Give me a minute." Adolfo relayed the news to Dex then put him on the phone with her.

"Carlita, this is Lieutenant Jones. Where you are? Tell me the exact location."

Carlita didn't know many of the streets in Washington off the top of her head, so she called for the journalist. Eddie rushed out of the bathroom and looked at her.

"The Lieutenant's on the phone. He wants our location," she said to him.

Eddie grabbed the phone. "Lieutenant Jones we're at a motel on Canal Road. We have a real problem!" he muttered.

"You'll be okay, Eddie. Do you know how to get to Garfield Park?"

"Yes. It's near New Jersey Avenue, just off the southeast freeway."

"Okay, make sure you and agent Perez will be there by 2300 hours. Put her back on the phone," said Dex.

Eddie gave her back the phone. "Did you find Felix Ortiz?" Carlita asked.

Dex replied, "We caught up to him in Costa Rica just like you said we would. He told us where to find the FBI agent in Colombia."

"We need a way out. We . . ."

"Don't worry. I've got a plan. Eddie has the information where you and he must be by 2300 hour tonight. We'll meet you in Colombia. You'll have the address before you get there," Dex stated. Then he hung up.

They waited until it was dark again. When it got close to the time for them to leave, they exited the motel room looking for transportation. Carlita found a Pontiac Trans Am sitting in an isolated corner of the parking lot. In all, Eddie estimated it took less than 3 minutes for her jimmy the door open and hot wire the engine to life. He didn't know if the woman had a mechanic license to compliment her credentials as a task force agent. But after two attempts by assassins to snuff him out and two near escapes, he'd taken off in a stolen car with her.

Carlita followed the directions he gave her to get to Garfield Park. On the way there they encountered the protest they heard was supposed to take place on the news this morning. The news mentioned nothing about the mission of Operation Lion's Den the SEALS carried out. But the protests and riots breaking out was a hot topic. Driving by, Eddie saw large multitudes of African American's and Hispanic's marching down the streets. People came out by the thousands. The protests began earlier in the day on 23rd and spread across the Potomac all the way to the mall on Constitutional Avenue. Another group skirted down Logan Circle and continued to 12th, 13th, 14th streets to meet up with other protestors at Franklin Park. Their anger had boiled over about the rash of excessive force being used by police officers over the past two months.

Eddie glanced at the signs that signified the issues they wanted addressed - RESIST RACIAL DISCRIMINATION! END POLICE BRUTALITY! HOLD BAD COPS ACCOUNTABLE! He heard them chanting - NO JUSTICE! NO PEACE! NO JUSTICE! NO PEACE!

Raising public awareness of such incidents was his life's work. He understood their grievances. Weeks before his trip to Mexico he covered a rally that was organized by Native American Indians in North Dakota protesting the U.S. government's intention to give big oil corporations the green light to set up Dakota Keystone XL pipelines so they could begin fracking operations. Native Americans saw it as another intrusion on their sacred lands. So, they were fighting to put an end to what they felt would eventually result in environmental hazardous effects on the region's wildlife and people living on nearby reservations.

While the oil industries showed little concern, the government hadn't done much to deplete the other concerns he was reporting around the country. There were universities experiencing a spike in student protests against supporters sympathetic to the views of hardened white supremist walking into campus classrooms and auditoriums spewing hate speech. Hard-line conservative lobbyists were striking out against supporters of Plan Parenthood. Women were taking up the issue of being shunned and criticized over their petitions for equal pay and the passage of tougher laws to protect them from sexual harassment. Thousands of inner-city youths were failing every year inside schools, deemed inadequate, because many local and state governments were showing only minimal interest in providing funds for supplies adequate to meet their educational needs. EPA scientists were stuck in a constant battle with skeptics dismissing the seriousness of global warming. Anti-gun violence protestors were lobbying for more support from the government to take on the NRA.

As a journalist, he put out facts told through the lives of people exercising the right to free speech with the hope of seeing real changes in the kind of laws that would provide them equal protection. But in an era where people were being maimed and killed because their race or religious beliefs.

Some of the crucial decisions made by many of the country's leaders inside their tribunals suggested they were giving little consideration to the implementation of new policies on the issues put before them.

When they arrived at Garfield Park it was 10:40 pm. Dex's phone call back let them know he was sending a helicopter to pick them up. Twenty minutes later they heard it coming. The chopper dropped in low and fast with the propellers throwing of wind gust as they ran to it.

The pilot opened the door for them. "Carlita and Eddie. Right?" he said.

Carlita replied, "That's us."

She helped Eddie into the rear seat before she climbed into the front seat beside the to the pilot.

"The name's Soaring Hawk. Most people call me Hawk," he said.

"Pleasure to meet you," Eddie muttered.

He saw a dream catcher hanging over the man's vest and collared shirt he had on when they entered the chopper. The guy was buff. He had long black hair tied back in a long braid. His dark complexion and features resembled Native American Indians. With a name like Soaring Hawk, he had to be Native American, Eddie concluded.

"Buckle up!" he told them. A few seconds later they took off in the chopper.

CHAPTER FORTY-SEVEN

Miami, Florida

H ours after their flight from Washington, Soaring Hawk landed the chopper at a private airfield in Miami. Two men ran under the propellers as he cracked the door open.

"I need a plane fueled up for a flight to South America," he yelled as they approached.

"We got a four-seater jet, Hawk. I called for the tanker. Will that do?" one of the men yelled back.

"Get it ready!" Hawk replied.

The men darted off in the direction of the jet they saw sitting on the runway. As soon as Hawk cut the engine to the chopper, Eddie had a question for him.

"How do you know Lieutenant Jones?" he asked.

Hawk hesitated, peering out the window at the big tanker pulling onto the runway to fuel the jet, before he replied.

"I was in Panama when I met him. I was deployed there with a SEAL team to capture General Manuel Noriega so we could bring him back to the United States. It was a typical platoon, two junior officers, the field chief commander, and eleven other enlisted members. The night of our mission we had inside information that Noriega and a couple of cartel leaders were going to have a meeting on his yacht to hash out a deal out that would allow the drug smuggling operations easy passage through the General's country. We set up reconnaissance on the site of the meeting. Then we waited for them to show up. But they didn't. So, we packed up and skirted the shoreline of the lake hoping to detect a sign of his yacht. We must have walked a mile and a half and saw was no sign of it. As we continued down the shoreline, I suddenly heard noises in the nearby woods. No one else on the team seemed to hear it.

By the time they did it was too late. Our mission was compromised. The General knew we were coming. And we found ourselves under attack by the Panamanian defense forces who started shooting at us."

Hawk paused and signed as he shook his head. "We lost four good men that night. And we were fortunate to get out with the remaining members of the team. We got out because of the covert back up team. At the time we had no idea they were deployed to capture Noriega as well. Dex was the field commander of the team that came to our aid that night. He and his team spotted the zodiac we beached three miles down the shoreline of the lake. He and his men were watching movements. But when they detected the presence of the Panamanians, he and his men climbed into the trees to set up into elevated sniper positions. The minute the firefight broke out, they began picking off the Panamanians. With their help we drove Noriega's forces back into the woods. We went home after that. But we failed to bring back the target. The mission was a total disaster."

Eddie cut in, "I wouldn't say it was a total disaster. Noriega was later arrested and indicted on international drug trafficking charges. After he extradited to the U.S., two federal juries deliberated over his trials right here in Miami and in Tampa. They issued guilty verdicts in both trials."

"True. But this was total disaster if the mission wasn't."

Hawk rolled up his pants to expose his amputated right leg and the titanium prosthetic attachment replacing it from the knee down.

Eddie leaned forward to look at it.

"The doctors removed the bullets. But there was nothing they could do to save it. When they amputated it, that was pretty much the end of my career as a Navy Seal. It took a lot of rehab. I had to learn how to walk with this thing. What happened that night was very difficult for me to talk about for a long time. But one day I got this call out of the blue from Dex. He said he was calling to see how I was coming along. He started visiting me. We started talking. Eventually he brought up what happened. But he got me to talk about it. It was the first time we discussed it. So, we ended up talking many more times after that and became close friends. He encouraged me to get past it.

"Of course, the trauma remained, and I could never go into the field of combat again. But he suggested that I consider taking up aviation training. So, I tried it. I fell in love with it! I've been flying ever since I got my pilot license. I also own my own private aviation company now."

Carlita thought the story around the circumstances that led to his aviation career was bittersweet, as she continued listening to him.

"I remember when I returned home to the reservation. My tribe asked me, 'Soaring Hawk, why do you go fight for the white-eye when they continue to take more of our lands?'"

Hawk paused. Eddie assumed he was pondering the question his tribe put to him and maybe the plight of his people as well. He was right.

"My people reminded me of what our tribe the Sioux had to endure, and what the Apache, Chippewa, Seminole and others endured after losing their lands." Hawk pointed to a group of men standing in front of on the hangars. "You see those men over there? All of them are Native Americans. Each one of them grew up on reservations like me. I was three years old when my mother moved me from the city to go live with my grandparents on the reservations. I didn't understand why until I was a teenager. That's when she explained how she wanted me to learn the ways and customs of our people so that I would know their true history. My mother was a woman who adamantly wanted to preserve the culture and traditions of the Sioux just as much as my grandparents. But growing up on the reservation I often felt like many of the youth now days.

"The reservations are boring. Employment numbers are very low. Many people are disenchanted by their living conditions which make each day a struggle to survive. People on the outside think we Indians have it so made because we call the reservations our lands. It's not that rosy. Yes, we say we live as an independent indigenous nation on sovereign plains. But the reservations suffer from many other problems. Discrimination against the tribes remains prevalent. Hard times linger with increased crime rates, drug and alcohol addiction, internal strife, corruption by tribal officials who pretend they are preserving Indian heritage while the American government persist in their disregard in upholding the former treaties made with our ancestors."

"So why did you enlist to go fight for the American arm forces?" Eddie asked.

"At the time I enlisted I was married," Hawk answered. "My wife and I had two children to provide for. I knew I wasn't going to make enough of money I needed to raise them on the reservation. So, I left with the intention of never going back to Paha Sapa (Black Hills). But after I discharged, I did go back."

"What made you change your mind?" Eddie asked.

"I returned to the reservations because I always remembered what my mother told me as a boy. My mother wanted me to learn about the historical heritages of the Indian people. I felt it was just as important to pass this on to my own children as well. It was my responsibility as a father to teach and encourage them to join other Sioux in the struggle to preserve the rights of our culture and sacred lands. Unfortunately, the truth is that some white-eye today still embrace the past practices of their forefathers. Many years ago, those white men created secret adoption agencies. Indian families were being tricked into turning over their children because they had little or nothing to survive on. And because the white-eye made promises, they told them that their children would grow up being taught a good education. That they would learn trades and other skills to help them obtain work and make enough money to provide food and shelter for them and their families when they returned to the reservations. But none ever returned. It took decades before the adoption agencies were exposed as nothing more than institutions created to experiment on the minds of the Indian children they enrolled into the schools."

Carlita suddenly broke her silence and asked, "How were the children experimented on?"

"The experiments were designed to teach the children how to think, dress, and worship in the way of the white-eye. They stayed inside those institutional schools until they were young adults. By the time they graduated they knew absolutely nothing about the history and customs of Indian life. After Crazy Horse, Black Foot, Geronimo, and the others who made their stances to protect our lands. The invader's primary objective for the secret adoption agencies was to break the last resistance of the brave

Indian warrior fighters. They figured the only way they could do that was by stripping the children of their identity generation after generation so that they would assimilate into the ways and customs of the white-eye."

Hawk went quiet for a moment, then said, "The fortunate thing is that there were good white-eye men and women back then who discovered those secret adoption agencies. Once they exposed them to the public the institutions were shut down. They were sympathetic to the treatment and struggles of the Indian people, like many whites are today."

Eddie listened in silence. He considered himself to be among the white men and women who understood their struggles. He was familiar with the Indian removal bill that was signed into law. The law made it legal to have Indians removed from their own lands by force. Its horrible effect set in motion the infamous trail of tears. Some of the events even took place near Paha Sapa (Black Hills) where Soaring Hawk grew up.

History books inside classrooms and libraries across the U.S. describe the story of the Black Hills as a place that brought white prospectors into the area looking to cash in on the reports of gold discoveries. In 1847, General Armstrong Custer led his calvary into the Black Hills with intentions for gold, but then seized their entire territory.

Soaring Hawk was right. There was no getting around the fact that the struggle against discrimination was ongoing. Native American Indians.

Eddie thought back an article he'd written in relation to the organizations Native American Indian tribes began establishing in the 1960's to address the long battle against discrimination and encroachment on their lands. Even though they retained the right to reside on the sovereign lands, many people didn't know that they were not free to construct whatever businesses they wanted for their economy. Because there were certain building permits that still required them to seek special permission from the U.S. government to utilize the lands.

The Indian Hawk spoke with when they arrived walked back to the chopper.

"Hawk, the plane is fueled. You're all set," he informed him.

They exited quickly and walked to the waiting jet. Hawk started flipping switches when he entered the cockpit. Carlita and Eddie fastened their seatbelts. The plane's engine roared to life. Hawk gunned the jet down the runway. Seconds later they were back in the air.

Part Ten
The Sicilian Defense

CHAPTER FORTY-EIGHT

Rome, Italy

M arcantonio Capola muttered, "Pawn to king four!"

Augustine Razzoli replied with the Sicilian defense. "Black queen pawn to bishop four!"

It was the standard reply to Marcantonio's opening move. The two men had been inside Augustine's private study playing chess and sipping glasses of Dom Perignon for hours, while they discussed business affairs.

Marcantonio was a shrewd businessman. He'd spent his whole life in Sicily. Augustine Razzoli spent the better part of his life in America. Nevertheless, they had become allies in the underworld of the mafia with a bond shared from their Sicilian blood line.

In Italy, Marcantonio and the other bosses he did business with called him by his birth name Augostino Razzoli. He was son of the Italian Salvatore Vincent Razzoli. Born in New York. Life for Augustine and his family began when his grandparents Augosto and Catherina Razzoli immigrated from Italy. At the time country was experiencing an economic crisis and widespread internal strife between Italy's northern peninsula and southern Sicily. The conflict got so bad his grandparent's Augusto and Catherina defected from Naples Italy to America with their only son Salvatore.

Augustine's father Salvatore was four years old when they arrived at New York's Ellis Island. Ellis Island was the principal port of entry and chief receiving station. Augusto brought his family to America in search of a better life. But he also brought with him a title he'd earned back in Italy. Mafia don. He always kept his business dealings back in the old country. While his wife Catherina cared for little Salvatore, Augusto Razzoli boomeranged back and forth from America to Naples to stay off the radar of U.S. authorities.

Augustine never got the chance to meet either of his grandparents. Everything he knew about them came from stories his father Salvatore told him about himself when Augustine was growing up in Manhattan's Little Italy. He told him how he and his Sicilian mother met and married before she gave birth to him and his two older brothers Bruno and Angelo Razzoli. When they grew older, he taught them everything there was for them to know about the family business he'd taken over after his father Augusto died.

Salvatore made a promise to himself that he would follow the trend of his father Augusto by passing on the family business to his three sons. With his age starting in, he sent Bruno and Angelo to Naples to handle the day-to-day operations before he passed. He put Augustine in charge of the family. Which meant that his youngest son made all the major decisions concerning the family's business in America.

It was the way Salvatore wanted it. Augustine had to be protected for two reasons. He had to be protected from any threat of harm that may arise from his old enemies in Italy. Plus, he had bigger plans for him when he paid for his enrollment at the University of Yale as a full-time student so that he could pursue the kind of political career he aspired for him. Between his three sons he knew Augustine would be the one most capable of fulfilling his personal ambitions. The observation was clear. Augustine spent more time with his books and getting good grades in school while Bruno and Angelo played hooky and got into the trouble that ruined any chance for them.

After the federal strike force team made up of the New York State Organized Crime Task Force, FBI, NYPD detectives, investigators from the U.S. District Attorney Office lunched a full-scale operation that took down the five families of the American mafia with R.I.C.O indictments, Salvatore Razzoli saw an opportunity, an opportunity at a power grab that would expand the power of his empire in Italy to the U.S. and the rest of the world.

Augustine completed the first part of his plan when he graduated from Yale with a degree in political science. Eventually, he became a talented politician who ran for the governorship of New York and won decisively over his opponent in his first campaign bid.

Salvatore would fall ill years later from old age. Eventually, he revealed to Augustine that all his success as a politician and his path to becoming elected governor had been paved by the hidden order of which he was part. He told him of his brothers Bruno and Angelo in Italy, too. They were also secretly initiated into the order.

His father told him he would have been initiated as well if were to remain a don. Augustine was flown to Naples so that his brothers could prepare him for the ugly side of the order. It wasn't until they sailed across the channel of the Mediterranean to the small island of Corsica off the mainland of France did he realize the roles his brothers Bruno and Angelo played within the order.

He wished he could forget the day they pulled up outside the home of the target Bruno and Angelo were sent there to assassinate. They told him to wait out in the Cadillac parked at the curb out front. Augustine waited like he was told. But not long after his brothers entered the residence a Sedan pulled up on the opposite of the street. Four men got out quickly and walked inside. Five minutes later, Bruno and Angelo ran out and jumped into the car. He had no idea what was going on, until Bruno and Angelo sped off ranting furiously how the CROP and the four men he saw entering behind them had broken a principal code of the family by killing the target and everyone else in the home.

There was nothing good about that day, except the young boy he stopped on the sidewalk. Had he allowed him to enter the home like he intended, he might have been slaughtered too. Hearing his brothers mention the CROP meant nothing to him until he became part of the order like them.

He discovered that it was them who sent the four men. But their father Salvatore would not live to confront the CROP about the principal code of the mafia they'd broken. He passed away the next day. A cloud hung over the family ever since. The way they saw it, the CROP owed the Razzoli family a debt that would be paid or the Mafia would declare war. So, they worked out a deal on the table. The thought of going to war with the Mafia was something the council didn't want. The Mafia was a formidable force, and the possible exposer was an even bigger threat. They agreed to sit down and negotiate any deal they put forth.

Augustine only had one in mind that would help him fulfill what his father Salvatore envisioned for him. As head of the family, he put forth his remedy. He demanded they allow him to replace his father as a ranking member on the council. He also demanded that they back him as a candidate and pull whatever strings were necessary for him to get elected as the president of the United States after he stepped down as governor to put in his campaign bid.

When the council agreed, Augustine looked forward to walking into the White House as the newly elected commander-in-chief of a super-power nation. He also looked forward to reestablishing the rise and power of the American Mafia and across the globe. He would then make the Mafia untouchable like his father planned. Because he would be president. And at the same time, he would be the boss of all bosses!

Marcantonio made his next move. "Knight takes queen!" he stated.

Augustine countered with a reply Marcantonio missed. "Rook takes bishop . . . Check mate!" said Augustine, ending the match with his queen sacrifice.

Marcantonio threw his hands up with the defeat. Then he poured himself a drink. Not that it would make his game better. He could never beat Augustine. Although it was simply a pastime for him now. He'd learned the game a long time ago. And so did his former colleagues on the council. It was perhaps the only thing he had left in common with Eleanor, Arthur, Edward, Julian, and Heinrich. In youth, their parents enrolled them in the private Academy of Physics and Psychology in England. They were instructed to take up the science and art of studying the human mind. They were also instructed to sign up for the chess club. As a result of their parents' association the five of them became close friends. They liked playing so much, each time they got a break from the academy's arduous studies they would chat and play chess. Unbeatable, they were considered the best among their peers in their league.

Except Augustine knew those close ties of friendship had been broken and could never be mended now. He and his brothers had no longer had any illusion about the callousness of the council and the protocol they stood by.

All at once the door flew open. The bodyguard sitting to the right side reached for his weapon in his shoulder strap. He relaxed when he saw it was only the house made. But the way she barged in, announced with a look of worry on her face, raised Augustine's concern.

"Something wrong, Flora?" he inquired.

His wife Claudia appeared in the doorway a few seconds later. She was sniffling back tears, expression fallen.

"I asked you a question Flora!" he said.

His wife responded, "It's Mikey and Dino . . . Our sons are gone, Augostino. They're talking about them on the news right now!"

Augustine grabbed the remote off the table and flicked his television on. He went straight to the news channel and saw the faces of his two sons Michael and Dino on the screen. Every muscle in his body seized up. He couldn't move. He just stood there listening to the report detailing how South Atlantic coastguards discovered their remains after they washed ashore with a shredded life raft.

Rage seeped into him instantly. Just as he got up to console his wife a muffled round pierced through the window and missed his head by inches. He ducked as another round split the glass. Marcantonio suddenly jerked back gurgling and clutching his throat after the sniper's bullet struck him in the neck.

"Get down!" Augustine shouted.

The maid pulled his wife to the floor with her. The bodyguard had pulled his gun out. But he had no time to react before the sniper outside the window took him out.

"Claudia!" Augustine shouted. "Get inside the safe room with Flora. Go now! I will meet you there!"

The two women crawled through the open door into the hallway. Augustine belly crawled a crossed the floor to the fallen bodyguard. He took the gun the bodyguard was still clutching in his hand and shot every light in the study. Next thing he heard was machine gun projectiles coming through the window with more than one shooter. Soon as they paused, he started firing back through the shattered window, shooting indiscriminately into the night until the gun emptied its last round.

With no bullets left he crawled out into the hallway. He was sweating and breathing heavily. His shirt was damp suddenly. He thought it was sweat that he felt with the pain he felt. But then he saw where one of the rounds had found its mark. He placed his hand over the wound bleeding through his shirt just above his hip. The gun closet across the hall from the study was just a few feet away. He went to it and snatched an American made AR-15 off the rack.

"Don, Razzoli, get inside the safe room!" a voice at the far end of the hall shouted to him.

He turned and spotted two of his bodyguards. "Find the shooters!" he shouted back.

Augustine staggered down the hallway toward the first. Their security camera monitors he had installed there. When he peered at the panel of angles, he saw that the bodies of the twenty mafia men guarding the residence outside were sprawled across various areas of the property where they were stationed to keep a watch out for intruders. Right at that moment he knew the only persons capable of mowing down that many men at one time undetected were the four Knight's assassins.

One of the bodyguards yelled from the living room, "Don Razzoli, they're coming! You must go inside the safe room!"

Augustine's suspicion was confirmed when he glanced at the camera angle above the entrance. The faces of the four knights, Alexi Stacheko, Borloff Kashovich, Sasha Kishliak, and Sebastain Korkov appeared on the monitor as soon as they ran up the to the front door with altered AK-47's for extra rounds.

Augustine heaved his big frame towards the basement. When he got to the bottom of the steps he descended, he heard the high-voltage pops of gunfire being exchanged between the Knight's and the security men in this living room. He made his way to the safe room. His wife Claudia and the maid saw him show up outside the door on the camera monitor in the safe room. They pushed the door open then pulled him inside. After they shut it, Augustine heard the gunfire upstairs go silent. He peered at a camera angle upstairs. The four assassins were inside the living room standing over the bodies of his last two security men after they gunned them down.

He watched the assassins moving stealth like down the hallway. Alexi Stacheko spotted the trail of blood leading from the study to the gun closet. They followed it to the empty room that held the panel of camera monitors.

Sebastain Korkov led them inside when he noticed the monitors. He glanced at the king size bed. There was a suit draped over the chair that sat at the foot of it. A woman's makeup kit sat on the dresser. His eyes quickly swayed back to the monitors. He peered at the cameras scanning various angles of the property outside. The interior angles on the upper level of residence showed no sign of the target. But he spotted Augustine and the woman in one of the angles showing the lower level and then safe room they were hiding in.

"He's in the basement," Sebastain Korkov said to the others.

Down in the basement, Augustine and the women had their eyes on them inside the room at same time. Augustine knew they were heading for the safe room by the way they ran from the room. The four assassins showed up at the entrance of the safe room a few minutes later.

Sebastain clanged the butt of his altered AK-47 against the huge impenetrable steel door and shouted as he stared into the eye of the camera above it.

"We know you're in there, Mr. Razzoli. Come out now, and the women will live!" he shouted.

Augustine's voice blistered out a speaker on the ceiling above them seconds after.

"I know who you are Sebastain Korkov! And I learned about the protocol of the people who sent you before you were born. Leaving witnesses isn't one of them. I might be old, but I'm no fool!"

"Ah, so you know my name old man. But you don't know me . . ." Sebastain shouted back.

"Oh, I know you, including the others with you!" Augustine interrupted. "So, go back to the American CIA man. Tell him to give my former colleagues the message not to send puppies to fight with old bears next time!"

Sebastain face transformed into fury after he heard the insult. The old man was taunting them. Infuriated, he aimed his AK at the camera and shot out the lens.

Augustine and the women lost sight of them the after camera exploded. While Claudia Razzoli and the maid treated the wound on Augustine's side to stop the bleeding, they could hear were the four assassins speaking in Russian as they shuffled back and forth through the basement for almost ten minutes.

All at once they smelled gasoline. "What are they doing?" Claudia asked.

Augustine pulled himself up with the AR-15 and staggered to the firebox encased in the wall in the other side of the safe room. The smell was getting stronger.

When smoke started coming through the cracks his instincts kicked in. He shattered the glass on the firebox with the butt of the rifle and grabbed oxygen masks inside.

"Put these on. Hurry!" he told the women.

Then he staggered across the room to oxygen tanks in the corner. The women helped him turn up the air on the tanks in a matter of seconds. Since they couldn't get to them, it was clear to Augustine the assassins had no intention of leaving the house and had improvised another means to eliminate him. There was no doubt about it now. He knew it the moment he got a whiff of the gasoline and realized they were setting the entire house ablaze.

CHAPTER FORTY-NINE

Washington, DC

S ebastain Korkov's electronic coded message sent to Winston Bedford was good news for the deputy director of operations: Augustine Razzoli was no longer a problem for his employers, he informed him.

Elated, he flicked the channel of his television to an Italian news program detailing the event in the aftermath before reporters showed up at the Razzoli residence with their camera crews. TV footage playing back video at the scene showed the Razzoli home engulfed in flames. Roman police and fire crews were scattered across the property.

As he watched the home burn, billows of smoke swirled skyward. Then he saw a team of firefighters coming out the front door of the home with two women wearing oxygen masks. More firemen came out seconds behind them. Just by the way they were struggling to hold up the stretcher under the weight of the huge body lying on it, he knew it was the old Italian. Augustine Razzoli's face was covered with a breathing apparatus like the women. But it didn't matter, he thought. There was nothing they could do to save him. The four knights did their job. Sebastain assured him. He believed him until the camera zoomed in with a closeup shot of the old man's massive body on the stretcher. His eyes narrowed as soon as he saw his arm move.

Bedford hissed in disappointment to himself as he slammed his palm on the table. "He's still alive!"

The old Italian raised his arm slowly. Then his middle finger flicked up for the camera, as if he knew he and the CROP would be watching, to get the message he sent back in reply.

CHAPTER FIFTY

Key Largo, Florida

Henry Tilkerson's country club was punctuated with a resort style swimming pool and sport court accented by palm trees beautifully situated over many acres of his property.

He named it the Paradise Valley Country Club right after architect's completed its construction. It was a convenient meeting venue. And today it would be the center for the private murmurings between himself, Arthur Knightwood, Lieutenant Colonel James Burke, fourteen republican senators, and two democrats.

"I got a call from Japan and from Su chi Lu in China," said Colonel Burke. "The Chinese are very upset about the freighter that went down in the black sea."

"Do you believe the Colombian's were behind this too?" Arthur muttered.

"Yes, I do. The freighter was struck by a missile fired from a fighter jet! How Tagola is obtaining fighter jets is beyond me."

"He's using his international contacts. That's how! His raid campaigns have expanded because of them," Arthur responded.

"We must bring more troops on this. It's the only way we can stop the guy," the Colonel asserted.

Henry broke in, "Don't you think that would be a bad move, JB?"

"Not at all!" answered the Colonel.

"I think Henry is right," said Arthur. "Calling in more American troops after Operation Lion's Den could make things even worse than they are. We must weigh the risk of possible exposer. Keep in mind we do not have every single congressional representative on Capitol Hill in our pockets. The council has also received a report that President D'kembi is asking a lot of questions about that mission in Colombia now."

"He's going to be asking even more about that freighter lost in the Black Sea," Burke retorted. "In a matter of hours, the navy expects the event will be receiving worldwide attention."

"I suggest you prepare another story for the media to put out about the missile attack," said Arthur.

"We have one already prepared. The Chinese were conducting war games when the freighter was mistakenly struck by the missile."

"I like it. Go with that one," Arthur muttered.

"What about president D'kembi? Winston informed me that he's seriously considering a request for a probe into Operation Lion's Den."

"Let him do whatever he wants. Nothing will come of it beyond the preliminary stages. These senators we have here and others on inside the Capitol Building will see to that!"

Arthur glanced around the table at the faces of the representatives who'd been placed into positions of authority to back the council and the agenda of the protocol. His phone went off with a call from Edward Kingstone right after the congressmen and congresswoman nodded in agreement.

"Hello, Edward."

"Did you hear about the freighter in the Black Sea?" asked Edward.

"The Colonel informed a few minutes ago."

"Eleanor is furious. The bloody bulk of the drugs on that ship were produced by Burmaxx pharmaceuticals!"

"Her disappointment is totally understandable. Colonel Burke says Su Chi Lu has received the news. Who briefed you?"

"The people at MI-6. The freighter wasn't the only loss. The Colombians launched several simultaneously. Four cargo planes were blown up before they got off the ground in Liverpool. Five planes loaded with cargo in Venezuela were shot down. Some of the pilots bailed before they were struck with anti-aircraft missiles."

Arthur took a moment to let the startling information sink in. Then shared his thoughts.

"Maybe Colonel Burke's suggestion might not be so bad after all," he commented.

"What does he have in mind?" asked Edward.

"He thinks we ought to bring in more troops. It would be a risk if we gave that order."

"As long as they are handpicked. I see no other option we have at this point. Any word from Winston about Augustine yet?"

"Not yet. I'm starting to get concerned about him."

"You should be. That bloody trader Augustine is still alive after the four knights were sent to take care of him. The report came in with the others from MI-6."

"I guess that accounts for why Winston hasn't contacted me."

"They set his home on fire! And that bloody Italian! That . . ."

"Easy, Edward. I'll contact you when the meeting is over. We'll discuss Augustine then."

Arthur disconnected with Winston Bedford still on his mind. The man was probably embarrassed because he failed to get the job done again, he assumed. But for the moment the meeting had to carry on.

Colonel Burke and the senators were discussing the huge shipment of narcotics being prepared to set sail from Colombia when he tuned back in. The Colonel was also telling them about other shipments that would be loaded on cargo planes by triads before they took off from China. Some of the senators started stressing the concerns they had.

"Colonel, I have no problem with our troops overseeing the drugs leaving the Colombian shipping port. That deal you struck with Ortega Diez to allow him easy smuggling passage across our borders for the next five years, I find that very reasonable given the profits we'll make from it. But I am not so sold on the idea of trusting Chinese triads to handle the cargo on those planes. The Chinese are clever. They always want something extra besides money in return. So, what is it they want, Colonel?"

"They want the usual," the Colonel answered." They want a little classified information on our secret corporate computer technology, and a little classified information from our military files. It's nothing we haven't stolen from them. Right? You see, the Chinese need us. And we need their business. Therefore, we can't afford to cut off ties with the Chinese."

"What is Ortega Diez getting, Colonel?"

"Well, seeing how Carlos Tagola is on a rampage, Ortega wants our protection and aid against his campaigns. Which will include providing more weapons and manpower to for his cartel."

"That triad leader Su Chi Lu has a lot of investments in U.S. markets. But his company Silo Tech is losing stock. It's one of the biggest he has. But there's a competitive company crashing its stocks now. They're pushing him out. If they succeed, they will bust up his company. That could start war between the syndicate societies. If that happens it the names of American officials invested with Silo Tech and other Chinese companies could be exposed."

The rest of the Senators present murmured in agreement as they thought about the possibility of their own business dealings with Silo Tech being revealed.

"There is no reason for any of you to be concerned about that," Arthur interrupted. "The council has reached a deal with Silo Tech."

"What kind of deal?"

Arthur responded, "The Chinese have always been interested in western medicines for years. Eleanor agreed to help Su Chi Lu. The council will keep his company from being pushed out by allowing him to expand her pharmaceutical companies there. Burmaxx pharmaceuticals will be manufactured in China, so they will be available in Hong Kong and other cities . . ."

"I see where you're going with this. Su Chi Lu will get cheaper rates buying from Burmaxx. But what if other Chinese companies start buying these drugs? The triads are known for breaking down their products and selling them beyond their sell-date. Many of those outdated supplies could end up on export ships heading right back to the United States. Those outdated drugs could wind up in neighborhoods across America, including our own!"

"I can't dispute the possibility of that, Senator. China does export many of its pharmaceuticals under western brand names. However, the bulk of the drugs they break down and sall beyond their dates are sold to the poorest countries. So, who's going to worry about old medicine winding up in poor countries with little or no medical supplies?"

"Mr. Knightwood, studies show there's a steady increase with opioid epidemics in middle class white America. The topic is being discussed a lot now days in chambers on Capitol Hill. It's raising concern."

Henry Tilkerson responded, "Senator, of course there will be a lot of white Americans affected by the increase in opioid use. But the focus of you and your colleagues on the Hill will be the same as my administration once I'm in office. To shift the focus of their concerns about the opioid crisis to that of the protocol agenda."

"I don't know if that will sell easily, Mr. Tilkerson."

"Trust me Senator. When my base of supporters is established by my promises to bring back their jobs from overseas. They will believe it because that's what they want to hear. They want their coal mining jobs, an increase in minimum wages, tax cuts. Now, will I keep all those promises? No way!"

Speaker of the House said, "Mr. Tilkerson, we certainly look forward to getting you elected. I'm sure one promise you do plan to keep is that big tax cut for corporate America!"

"Mr. Speaker, that tax cut for big business is priority for you and me both! Therefore, I want to thank each Senator present here for your support."

The Senators applauded in unison as Arthur observed them. He was proud that it was him and the rest of his associates on the council who sent them and many others to Washington to carry out their handy work. Each time they got one elected to office, they took their oaths, gave their public interviews before reporters, radio hosts, and TV cameras. Afterwards, they quietly blended into their committees unnoticed and separated from others as members of a secret protocol.

CHAPTER FIFTY-ONE

Buenos Aires

After the flight to Argentina, Chello Fransis checked into the Faena Hotel. He could have explored the pleasantries of the spa nurtures, holistic therapies, and drinks served from a four thousand bottle wine list. He could have dined on the hotel's finest cuisines or hung out inside the lounge and pool bar that brought in the fashionable crowds who enjoyed the rojo tango shows that captivated the audiences daily and nightly. Instead, he settled for the comforts of a private suit with ceiling windows that brought in the sky. Chello didn't do crowds. Seclusion was more to his liking. Alone, he could meditate like he was now, sitting cross-legged on a rug in the middle floor with the tenors of an opera singer flowing into his ears. It was the only remedy that quelled the rage inside him each time the memory of what happened to his family in their homeland of Corsica tormented his thoughts.

Life was so pleasant there. His parents were Corsican wine growers who gave him and his two older brothers anything they wanted. But the life he knew growing up as a boy changed one day after he came home from a neighborhood soccer game and discovered the door of their home cracked open. He remembered he called out to his parents and brothers as he entered. But no one answered.

When he walked into the dining room, he found out why. He discovered them sitting around the dining room table, each one shot in the head at point blank range. The killers left a note he found in the collar of his father's shirt. There were only two words written in crimson blood on it, Mafioso Italiano. Italian Mafia.

Many years have passed since that day. Nonetheless, the memory was still fresh in his mind. In fact, hunting down the men responsible was going through his head the moment the phone in his shirt pocket started vibrating. When he saw the CIA man's initials W.B. on his caller ID, he answered.

"I gather you're calling to inform me that you've located the reporter that got away," he said, taking the call.

Bedford replied, "He hasn't been seen since Washington International Airport. His location is unknown now. I'm calling because I have another target that's a bit more problematic for my employers. I want you to take care of this. The target's name is Augustine Razzoli."

"What country?"

"Italy. You have two days to get this done. That includes travel time. But I must warn you . . ."

"Warn *me*! Are starting to doubt my work, Mr. Bedford?"

"It's not that, Chello. It's just that the knight's already attempted to put this old man down. But he survived."

"Have you pinpointed the city of the target?"

"The knights tracked him to Rome. After their failed attempt, I suspect he's probably left by now. I have a gut feeling he'll return to his father's homeland in Naples. Most of his family is there so he'll feel secure. But you're the best we got with the business."

Chello retorted, "If his family is around him as you say, I suggest you send someone else. You know my rules. No women, no children. His family is off limits!"

"You misunderstood. Let me be clear. It's not his relatives I speak of. Mr. Razzoli is a mob boss. He's the head honcho of one the most powerful Italian Mafia factions in Europe. I mean that family."

The words Italian Mafia put Chello in deep state of silence instantly. That's because he'd flashed back to Corsica recalling the day how he was walking past the big black car, when the man he saw inside it called out to him.

"Kid, come here . . . See that ice cream truck down the street? Take this money. Go buy yourself an ice cream," the man told him.

What if he hadn't taken the money and ran off down the street to go that ice cream? he wondered. What if he had just gone inside his home that day instead? He might have been able to save his family.

"Chello, you didn't answer the question," said Bedford. "Will you take the assignment?"

The CIA man's words brought him back from the recollection.

"Have the additional information on target ready by the time I arrive in Naples. I'm leaving the airport right now!"

Winston set his phone down on the desk in front of him after Chello disconnected. Then he stared at the last coded email message sent to his computer by Arthur Kightwood. He ignored it, just as he had ignored the phone calls. The council would only demand answers on why the journalist, Navy SEALS, and Colombian's had not been dealt with. For him, the biggest threat to the order had to fall before he made contact. Delivering no news to the boat people was better than delivering more bad news. But there was one thing that puzzled him. Arthur Knightwood was so adamant against allowing the chameleon to handle the Razzoli job. He didn't understand it. But he was going with his own intuition this time. Suddenly his phone chimed.

He started to answer it. But when he saw it was from Arthur Knightwood, he grabbed the cup of coffee he had on the desk and strolled to the window. The phone continued to chime on the desk as he stood there staring out at the city skyline.

CHAPTER FIFTY-TWO

Naples

There was a motorcade of luxury cars waiting at the airport for Augustine and his wife when they got off the plane that flew them from Rome. They were met by his brothers Bruno and Angelo, who climbed out of the limousine that pulled up in front of the aircraft. The two men walked up and took turns embracing him as a sign of respect. Almost a year went by since he last saw them. Bruno and Angelo had aged considerably from their youth but even now they were as dangerous as they were when they were young men.

"The council will pay for what they did to Mikey and Dino," Bruno told him.

Augustine replied simply, "Soon."

With his wife at his side, he scanned the faces of the fifty plus Mafia men who exited the vehicles. The men stood guard with their backs to them as they surveyed the surroundings of the airport with automatic rifles in plain view.

Augustine and his wife entered the limousine with his brothers. Claudia was scared. Even though she knew the danger she feared existed from the day his father Salvatore made him head of the Razzoli family, she never doubted his promise at their wedding that he would protect her at all costs. She immersed herself in the silence of her own thoughts.

Augustine was thinking about how naive he and his brothers were for all the years they relied on council's word that they would fulfill their end of the deal by helping a Razzoli son become the president of the United States. But the three of them had fallen for the lie. And the biggest mistake they made was becoming an ally.

With their father's permission, Angelo and Bruno had become trained assassins who carried out their contract hits. He wished he'd known about his brothers' trade before that day they traveled to Corsica with him. The two regretted the thought of it, they avoided the subject altogether. The CROP made fools of them. And the decisions they made they would forever live with.

When they arrived at the family home their father made the headquarters in Naples, there were more heavily armed Mafia men waiting outside to make sure the family was safely escorted inside.

Augustine waited until his wife Claudia and the house maid went up the staircase with her luggage. Then he turned to his brothers.

"I need to spend a little time alone," he told them.

Bruno and Angelo reluctantly dispersed. The men strolled into the great room.

Augustine went up the staircase to the office on the second floor. When he plopped down in the leather chair behind the desk, he experienced a bout of light headedness. He figured it was his blood pressure flaring up. Years of overeating coupled with binge drinking had caught up to him. The weight he gained as he got older didn't help.

He took a couple of blood pressure pills and tried to clear his mind. But as he sat alone in the office he wondered about the young Colombian. It had been some time since their last contact. The was no doubt about his plan to strike back at the CROP. Tagola's assistance was more vital now than it was when he first met him. If he wanted, he could have easily requested the help of Mafia factions across Europe and beyond. It only took one phone call to inform them of the war he was about to declare against his former colleagues for the actions they took against his family. But that would result in more innocent lives being lost. A war between the order and the Mafia would amount to catastrophic losses. And the council would still be shielded, nonetheless.

He would stand for this. Despite the favors owed to him by other Mafia leaders around the globe, he knew there were CROP agents even among the factions of Mafia organized crime families. He had a better plan devised. But he could trust no one else to assist him. No one except the black Colombian. To this date, Tagola had proven what he felt all along about him. He was a man with courage. And with his power and connections, he could provide the aid he would need to take down the CROP all together.

When a knock at the door fifteen minutes later. His brothers Angelo and Bruno walked in and sat down in the chairs situated in front of the desk he was seated behind.

"I told both of you I needed some time alone, to think!" he said.

"Augostino, soon as I heard what happened to Mikey and Dino and you in Rome, I came here the minute I heard you were returning to Naples!" said Bruno.

"This is no time for you to be alone," Angelo muttered. "The council attacked this family. They crossed the line. We're at war now!"

Augustine looked at them. He understood the rift between himself and the council could not be fixed. He knew it before he saw the news report describing how his sons were discovered with their limbs chewed off by marine mammals. He knew it before the Knight's assassins showed up and burned his home to the ground in Rome.

"We've come to aid you, Augostino. Anything you want. Just let us know!" Bruno stated.

He looked at them a minute or two longer after a long moment in thought. Then he broke his silence.

"You are my brothers. I understand how you both feel. But this is personal. And this is something that I must handle myself."

"Augostino, what you're saying is too dangerous. And it's crazy! You can't be serious about taking on the CROP by yourself. We cannot allow you to do that!" Bruno railed.

Augustine responded, voice in maximum effect. "Listen to me! If we go to war in the way you want, that war will continue between this family and the CROP until they are sure we are no longer a threat. This time it was my sons. It would be you, your sons, daughters, and wives next. Is that what you want? For me to put this entire family at risk?"

Angelo and Bruno exchanged looks when the point set in.

Augustine said, "You said you would give me anything I want. What I want is for the both of you to leave Italy immediately. You will take your families and my wife and go somewhere where it's safe.

"You have my word," Angelo replied.

"We'll go, Augostino. But what about you? You can't stay here," Bruno stated.

"I'll be fine. I've got a plan. And I'll keep a few is security men around."

"A few! I don't like the way that sounds. You should come with us!" Angelo insisted.

"Angelo, you will go without me. I'm not asking you." Augustine snapped.

"You have become a stubborn old man now!" Angelo retorted.

"Well, I learned it from you two when we were young. Perhaps it was that day we went to Corsica! Our father must have groomed you and prepared you well before you became part of the CROP as their mercenaries. But he did nothing but use you. After what happened on that island, your lives have never been the same."

Bruno sighed as he shook his head. "Corsica was a long time ago. Why must you insist on bringing it up time after time? It's over, Augostino!"

"Not for me!" Augustine snapped. He reached into the side pocket of his suit coat and removed his flask of Marcello.

"We came here to assist you, Augostino. That is what we're here for. Not to talk about the past. Now, surely there must be some other assistance we can provide," Angelo stated.

Augustine took a long swig. "There is one other thing you can do for me."

"Anything, Augostino. Just name it," said Bruno.

"I have a phone number to a certain man I want you to contact should anything go wrong."

"What shall we say?"

"You will simply say that you are my brother calling on my behalf. And that you want to collect on what he gave his word about."

"What do we do then?" asked Bruno.

"Well, now. Let's talk about that."

CHAPTER FIFTY-THREE

Naples

After Chello debarked off the plane he took to Naples, he made his way through the crowded terminal to the parking lot. The contact blinked the headlights on a BMW twice when he spotted him coming.

Chello arrived at the car a few moments later. There was another gentleman sitting in the passenger seat when he climbed into the back and closed the door.

"You're late," said the contact sitting behind the wheel.

Chello locked eyes with him when they peered at each other in the rearview mirror. He was the same CIA contact he'd met in Rome before he carried out the job on the Senator and Ambassador. The CIA man in the passenger seat he didn't know.

"There was a delay due to bad weather," he replied. "Do you have the rest of the information on the target?"

The man in the driver doing the talking held up an oversized manilla envelop. "Everything is in there. The assignment must be completed by morning. Bedford's orders."

"I move on my time, not Bedford's," Chello responded.

The contact locked eyes with him again but stayed quiet. The wrong spark and the assassin in the back seat could easily leave them for Italian authorities deceased inside the car by morning instead.

"Okay, it's your assignment," he replied softly.

Chello stuffed the envelope inside his duffle bag and jumped out. After the contact drove off, he walked out of the parking lot. The sidewalks were glistening from a light rainfall as he made way his towards the first intersection. Halfway down the block a car rolled up to the curb and stopped beside him. The driver beeped the horn once as he powered down the passenger side window.

"Hello, there old comrade," he said.

Chello saw the face and the blonde hair of the assassin he recognized instantly. "Sebastain, why are you in Italy?" he inquired with suspicion.

Sebastain answered in Russian, "Come in out of the rain. I'll tell you why."

He was grinning when Chello opened the passenger side door and jumped in. The car pulled off. Chello glanced out the windshield at vehicles, at the Italian pedestrians, and neon lights flashing on signs above the buildings they passed.

"I got a call from Bedford past night," Sebastain muttered. "He said he wanted to tag along on this Razzoli job with you. The old man will probably have extra security on post. He just wants a little added insurance the assignment will be done right this time."

"You wasted your time traveling here. Bedford never mentioned that to me. Secondly, he knows I work solo. And so do you!"

"Sorry, comrade. Not this time. You're a knight, remember? Just like me, Alexi, Borloff, and Sasha. If Bedford calls for joint action. You can't just separate from me."

Sebastain paused.

"He also wanted you to know the price on Razzoli's head will be an extra ten million for the both of us once we complete the job. I can give him a call if you want confirmation."

"I can do that myself," said Chello. He took out his cellular and made the call.

Bedford answered, "Hello, Chello the contact said you have the information on the target."

"I have the info. But you mentioned nothing about Sebastain Korkov?"

"Look. I know you work alone. It was a last-minute decision I had to make. I figured it wouldn't hurt to have Sebastian's talents as well. We need Mr. Razzoli gone. You could use some backup. This is a special case, Chello."

"He says the price is at ten million now!"

"That's twenty million for you when the job is over."

Chello peered through the car's rain splattered windshield thinking about the risks involved in taking down a Mafia don. It required skills. There was no denying the capabilities of the man beside him. Sebastain was a skilled assassin. He knew it first-hand. They both went through the Ceeber Training camp together in Siberia.

He remembered the first day they entered the camp together with the small group of men and women who joined them. Every prospect who went there was trained to become assassins. Only a selected few were chosen to be part of the elite groups. The recruits who came from various countries were mostly trained by non-active military officers and ex-intelligence agents. Five days each week they were required to follow a rigorous workout routine from sunup to sundown. They studied everything from academics to foreign languages, martial arts, intelligent gathering, handling various firearms, explosives, chemicals, poisonous venom, disguises, and other methods used to carry out their deadly trade.

The only word that defined the Ceeber training camp was torture. Nevertheless, they became elite recruits that stood out among their counterparts and honored by their inception into the highly coveted league of the four knights assassins.

As soon as Chello ended the call with the American CIA deputy director of operations, he looked the blond-haired Russian assassin.

"Let's get this straight right now. I make the plans. The target is mine to take him out. So don't get in my way. Understand?"

Sebastain stated. "No problem, Chello. No problem at all."

CHAPTER FIFTY-FOUR

Colombia

While Ortega's foot soldiers were loading the last of the drugs into the at the Colombian shipping port, agent Alex Weiss and Sergeant Havlichek stood by watching them move in and out of the freighter's cargo bay.

Weiss flicked the cigarette he was smoking on the ground and muttered, "With the troop's presence, everything is going according to plan."

Sergeant Havlichek gave him a conspirator's smile and replied, "Colonel Burke wanted me to convey his gratitude to you. You've done an exceptional job at organizing these operations for years. But he's still a bit upset over the cargo lost after that freighter went down in the Black Sea."

"I understand. The operation was just as big as this one. I doubt any of us will get over that one soon. Billions of dollars were lost in profits because of it. And it happened because we underestimated Tagola."

"I agree. Su Chi Lu's men were not prepared for the attack he launched. Neither were the Brits. But that's not going to happen here tonight!" the Sergeant stated.

They didn't know it, but the Navy SEALS and Adolfo Guzzeta were on the roof of a nearby building surveilling them and the freighter being loaded. They wanted to get their hands on Weiss. They just hadn't figured out how they were going to accomplish it with the presence of U.S. troops.

While Dex observed the activity below, thoughts of his wife Gina swelled inside his head. How was she coping? Did she know it was him in the papers under that fake name? he wondered. He wanted to see her. He missed her.

The only thing he had now was his trusted commandos. The fact Danny Boy LA Salle was Irish American, that Sergio Torres was a Cuban American, and he was African American. The differences in the race and backgrounds had no bearing on them. They'd always considered themselves a band of military brothers as much as they did human brothers.

Growing up, Dex understood the difficulties for African Americans. He could have ended up like so many of his friends from The Bottoms in Philly who fell victim to the cycle of drugs and crime that often resulted in them getting caught up in the criminal justice system. But he promised himself two things. That he would not end up in jail or prison. And that he would never add to the destruction of his own people by selling them drugs and committing crime against them."

He thought his enlistment into the armed forces was the best thing that happened to him. He'd dreamed of becoming a Navy Seal. Danny Boy and Sergio said they had too. They had what it took to live up to the duties of the elite fighting force. That required them to operate in hostile environments while abiding the articles of the U.S. military (COD) code of conduct. They were soldiers trained to kill by a government as heroes to the public. Only now they were on the run being portrayed as unappreciated enemies-of-the-state.

That was the last thing going through Dex's mind when the explosion at the shipping port went off.

Dex aimed his NVs at the freighter. The cargo bay was on fire. Machine gun fire followed the blast. Weiss and Sergeant Havilcheck were scrambling for cover. The ship was suddenly under attack. The SEALS trained their glasses at the building right across from their position. There were men moving on the rooftop. The bullet sparks and hot flashes they saw were coming from their automatic weapons and what they knew were shoulder-held rocket launchers. The men in Ortega's cartel and the U.S. troops on the ground started returning fire. Within seconds there was an intense gun battle.

"Who are the men up there shooting at them?" Danny Boy asked.

Another explosion slammed into the freighter. Adolfo zoomed his lens just in time to see some of the men on the roof pop their heads up. Then he blurted under the noise of gunfire, "They're Colombians! I got a visual on Hector Colon. He's up there!"

"Are you sure it was him?" Dex asked.

"Yes. I saw him. It was Hector!" Adolfo replied.

Dex had his glasses searching the rooftop when another projectile from a rocket launcher ripped into the freighter. He swung the NVs back in that direction. The vessel was titled sideways in the water, slowly sinking.

"Anyone got a visual on the FBI and the Sergeant?" he asked, peering at the billowing smoke and flames around the shipping port.

"I can't see a thing down there!" Danny Boy said.

"There's too much smoke!" said Sergio. "We lost them."

Dex trained the NVs back on the roof of the building across from them.

"If Hector Colon is on that roof, we don't need him!" he said.

Adolfo grabbed his shoulder. "Lieutenant, are you sure about this? You know what happened to Carlito and Manuel. If we go down this trail after Hector Colon, it could be our last."

Dex responded, "It's a chance we have to take. This may be our only opportunity to get out of this mess. We're going after him!"

Danny Boy shouted, "They're on the move!"

"We must keep 'em in sight. Let's go!" Dex barked.

The SEALS broke out running across the rooftop. Adolfo fell in behind them. They hurried to the fire escape and scaled down the ladder. Back on the street, they spotted Hector Colon and his men fleeing away from the building next door. One his men yelled for Hector to hurry as he fled towards the four big suburban trucks ahead of them. The men waiting inside opened the doors for him.

"Hector, we need your help!" Dex yelled out. "I have the Tagola file!"

Hector paused at the door of the truck. He craned his head around. In the unexpected twist of fate of crossing paths, the two of the locked eyes. The Colombian smiled before he jumped in and sped off with his convoy.

"He was smiling like he was toying with us!" Danny Boy muttered.

"He's clever," said Dex. "He was letting us know he knew we were on that roof surveilling agent Weiss and the Ranger Sergeant. They were up there watching us the whole time. Let's move out! We can't lose him!"

They ran to the Hummer H2 Adolfo made available. Dex jumped into the passenger seat. Sergio and Danny Boy jumped inside a Land

Cruiser and followed them when they took off flying after Hector. They trailed the four trucks through streets, speeding down each block, bending around corners until they reached a four-way connecting intersection.

All at once, the trucks split up and went down separate roads. Adolfo made a sharp right and stayed with the truck they thought Hector climb into. Dex radioed Danny Boy. And told him and Sergio to keep with the one straight ahead in case they got it wrong.

When the truck they were following turned off the access road they were on. Adolfo continued trailing from a distance. When the truck reached its destination at an old, abandoned airfield, he got off the road and cut through a tree line where he found a good spot to park the Hummer out of sight.

After he cut the engine, they held up their NVs and peered through thick overhanging branches shielding their location. They observed the truck as it rolled up and stopped outside a building. There were eight other big suburbans and a half dozen jeeps parked.

"How many do you think is inside?" Adolfo asked.

With the NVs trained on the building and truck, Dex answered, "Could be over two dozen, maybe more."

They kept their watch on the building for almost five minutes. A big Dodge Ram 2500 HD rolled up with a Range Rover. Hector Colon jumped out the suburban with three men carrying assault rifles. The huge garage door on the building powered up. Armed men swarmed out with weapons and splintered in different directions. Hector and the three men he jumped out with rushed to the back of the Dodge Ram. As soon as they opened the door to the bed of the truck, they started pulling tripods, American made M16s, and belts of ammunition.

Adolfo muttered, "What are they doing?"

Dex replied, "It looks like they're preparing for something."

More men came out of the building with RPG's. There were close to a hundred Colombians organizing into tactical-like battle positions.

"Whatever it is they're preparing for, it must be big!" Adolfo stated.

"Shhhhh. You hear that?" Dex uttered.

Adolfo tuned his ears in to identify the faint sound. "Sounds like helicopters. What do you think?" he asked.

Dex listened to the sound growing closer, then he recognized the sound of the rotors, and replied, "That's a fleet of American Black Hawks and Apache helicopters heading this way!"

CHAPTER FIFTY-FIVE

Colombia

Sergeant Havlichek sent out a last-minute radio transmission.

"Bristol Two, this is Razor One. Backup is on the way. Prepare to strike the targets on sight. Hit them hard! Copy?"

The Ranger in the cockpit of the Black Hawk ahead of him crackled back, "Affirmative. We're two miles out."

Dex and Adolfo still had their eyes on the Colombians moving into their strategic positions around the airfield. Some of them were stationing themselves on the roof of the building with electronic remotes they intended to use to raise up steel barriers through slits constructed in the ground. Fifty caliber ACOGs were mounted on tripods. SRAW weapons capable of knocking out tanks and other light armored vehicles were brought out.

"This isn't going to be good," Dex stated to Adolfo.

Four Apaches flew over their heads right after the words rolled off his lips. A squadron of Black Hawks flew over behind them. The choppers were heading straight for the airfield. As soon as they cleared the tree line at low altitude, the gunners got behind the 240-BRAVOS on the swingers and started shooting high powered velocity caliber projectiles at the same time the Apaches let loose a barrage of missiles that ripped into the building and hangars.

Hector and the men on the ground were firing up at them with the .50 cals and the projectiles ejecting from the rocket launchers. Two of the Black Hawks were struck. The pilots lost control. Both choppers went into tail spins and spiraled into a fast decent before they hit the ground and blew up.

The battle went on for nearly fifteen minutes before Hector started pulling his men out the moment he spotted American Chinook helicopters arriving with a backup team. Soon as the choppers touched down in a field near the battle zone, U.S. soldiers started pouring out of them, eighty or more men, as three more Chinooks arrived.

Hector Colon ran and jumped inside the big suburban with a crew of men and took off heading away from the airfield. More of his men climbed into three trucks and pulled out after him.

Hector's convoy flew right past the Hummer in which Dex and Adolfo were riding. Danny Boy and Sergio spotted the convoy of trucks speeding across the trail up ahead of them. Then they saw Dex and Adolfo fly past following them. Danny Boy made a right turn onto the trail behind the Hummer and got in on the chase. Hector and his men were driving deeper into the countryside. The terrain started looking familiar to Dex and Adolfo. All at once they realized where they were heading. The trucks were heading straight towards LA aldea de los Leonés.

"Lieutenant, I don't think it's wise if we follow them into the village," Adolfo muttered.

"Keep driving!" Dex barked. "We have no choice!"

The Apache and Black Hawk helicopters reappeared a few seconds later, sending tracer rounds through the treetops. Fireball flashes lit up ahead of them when several trucks from Hector's were blown up as they sped into the village.

Dex and Adolfo skidded to a stop to keep from crashing into the flaming vehicles. Adolfo made a quick turn and drove down another trail. Danny Boy and Sergio continued trailing them in the Land Cruiser. They were searching for a different route into the village. But when they got within a mile of it, the mountains around the village suddenly came alive. Bright red flashes started spitting out of them like a galaxy arcade game. The choppers were being shot out of the sky with shrapnel flying in every direction. Adolfo punched the brakes on the Hummer and looked at Dex.

"You still want to follow Hector Colon into that village?"

Dex's eyes were wide as silver dollars when Adolfo looked at him. The mountains around the village had opened with hidden built-in anti-aircraft weapons shooting missiles out of the hillsides. There were probably a lot more surprises inside those hills Dex conceded silently. Adolfo was right. If they went in, they might not come out alive this time.

"Pull back!" he barked. "Get us as far away from this village as fast as you can!"

CHAPTER FIFTY-SIX

Colombia

The safehouse Adolfo drove to in Medellin would have to do until they came up with another plan.

They had been there for nearly four hours. Dex pulled out the microchip and studied it. All he could think about was how another opportunity to find the man who could help them unravel the mystery behind it had slipped by.

He was sipping from a cup of coffee when he heard a vehicle pull up outside the residence. Adolfo, Danny Boy, and Sergio heard it too. They collected their weapons and went to the door. Dex peeked through the seam of the window's curtain. There were figures walking towards the front door of the residence after the taxi let them out and drove away from the curb. After checking the load in his .45, he joined the others.

Someone started knocking.

Gripping his sidearm, Adolfo asked, "Quienes?" Who is it?

A woman responded, "Abra la puerta! Open the door! It's Carlita."

They were anticipating Carlita's arrival, since she called a half hour earlier. The moment they identified her voice, they lowered their guns and opened the door.

Dex smiled, relieved to see her standing in front of them with Soaring Hawk and the journalist.

"It's good to see you people," he muttered. "Hawk, I can't thank you enough for flying Carlita and Eddie to Medellin."

"Ah, it's nothing Dex. I know when I saw that guy Lieutenant Claymore Logan on the news, I said to myself, the resemblance was too striking. Your call only confirmed my suspicion that it was a cover name for a special ops mission you were on. I wasn't at all worried about the headlines. I was prepared to assist you anyway I could."

"It's been a long time since I've seen you, my friend. Come in. There's a lot more I must tell you," said Dex.

Hawk entered behind Carlita and Eddie. When Adolfo shook his hand, Hawk towered over him by a good two of three inches. He was the biggest Indian he'd ever seen.

"Hawk, remember Sergio Torres and Danny LaSalle?" Dex asked.

Hawk answered when they shook hands with him as well. "How could I forget. They were with your platoon the night you helped us fend off Noriega's defense forces after we were ambushed by them in Panama."

"Maybe we'll get around to celebrating this little reunion of ours later. But right now, there is much I must discuss with you," said Dex.

Dex led them to the far side of the living area. Everyone sat down at the table there. Dex told him the entire circumstances surrounding their deployment and Operation Lion's Den. He brought him up to par on the file he discovered. He told him about their quest to find Carlos Tagola. And how they missed the window of opportunity to catch up with his cousin Hector Colon when him and a crew of men fled into the village of La aldea de los leonés after attacking and destroying a freighter packed with a shipment of drugs the Cali cartel was planning to smuggle out of the shipping port in Medellin with the help of military officials.

After he was done talking, Eddie said, "You're telling us you actually *saw* members of a cartel faction destroying the crop of their trade? That's impractical, Lieutenant."

"We thought the same thing," Dex replied. "But what I saw pretty much added up to what Ortega Diez's pilot told us. He said Carlos Tagola was causing problems for a lot of important people in high places now days. I believe what we saw go down at that shipping port tonight could be the very reason why the pilot said those very same people were angry with Tagola. If Hector's destroying shipments of drugs, I don't doubt they think Tagola is behind it. The question is, why would he be doing it?"

Carlita shook her head as she listened attentively. She hung on to every word the Lieutenant said. Not only did she not want to believe that traffickers like Carlos Tagola and Hector Colon were destroying the very crop they profited from. In her eyes, they were the culprits who had her brother Carlito and his partner Manuel killed. Hector did whatever Carlos ordered. He was the right hand that kept him shielded. The Colombian Drug Task Force had known that for years. But as she stood there listening to the details the Lieutenant told them about the event. She couldn't help but wonder if it was truly them who sparked the attention of the media's news report, she saw on the television in the motel room back in the U.S. about drug farms and manufacturing labs being burned and blown up in South America?

Dex set up a laptop computer. Then he looked at Soaring Hawk and kept talking.

"Hawk, I don't have a clue for what purpose our platoon was chosen to carryout Operation Lion's Den. But we know there were American health officials who also played a role.

"Dex, what you said about that Hc1 pills being prescribed to you and your men is pretty heavy man. You're also talking about officials at the highest levels of government!"

"The matter is much deeper that, Hawk."

"What do you mean?"

Dex removed the microchip file from the metal box he extracted from his pocket.

"This is the data chip that holds the Tagola file I mentioned earlier. Tagola left a message on his computer that points to the C.R.O. P. It's some kind of secret order. They want this file very badly. It's the sum of all their fears."

"Why?"

"Because it contains information that can expose everyone connected to it. I believe that information can help us. Now, we've tried numerous times to hack through its entry. But each time we were unsuccessful. I figured the alternative was to have someone more experienced at code breaking work hack into it. Someone like you, Hawk."

Hawk's eyebrows rose. *"Me?"*

"Word spreads, man," Dex said. "I know it was a long time ago since that night in Panama. But after you got back to the states, while you were in the hospital to being treated for your injuries, your members said a lot of good things about you. They said you were a genius at computers too. Some of the navy big wigs I spoke to said you trained with experts. They said you became so good they enrolled you into a government course study program for codebreaking. But they politely declined to discuss the classified intelligence gathering projects you did for the Pentagon. Nevertheless, I found out later about your hacking abilities were far more advanced than mine."

Hawk smiled. "Let me have a look at that data chip."

After Dex dropped it into his palm. Hawk held it close to his face to examine it. Then he turned the screen on the laptop towards him. He unzipped the backpack he brought with him.

"I never go anywhere unprepared for the unexpected," he muttered.

He took out a transmitter device. Then he took a smaller laptop computer he flipped opened. After inserting the microchip into the transmitter's receptor. He pulled out a second transmitter and plugged into circuit receiver Dex's laptop, and the other into his laptop, so that the information he typed in would feed into the microchip to access the file. Everyone huddled around him when he started tapping on the keyboard of his laptop. He kept at it for ten minutes before he went back inside his backpack and dug out another device.

"What's that?" Adolfo inquired.

"It's a bug penetrator device I am going to use to infiltrate the chip's authorized sensory coded program. With its file magnet I can neutralizes the chip's security sensory, and manipulate that coded program, to replace it with a new program after I type in the new coded messages I will create to defeat and override any existing high-grade encrypted Barrie's blocking access to open the file."

Hawk plugged in the device. Everyone watched with tense expressions as he started typing again. Twenty minutes later he stopped and looked around at everyone.

"That's it!" he muttered finally. "Now we wait to see what comes up."

Danny Boy stated excitedly, as he gave him a fist bump, "I knew you could do it, Hawk!"

The words they read a moment later after they popped on the laptop's screen said: TAGOLA FILE: ACCESS GRANTED: New Protocol Enlightenment . . . Global Politics . . . Populism in France, Germany, Hungry, Poland, Sweden, New Zealand, United Kingdom . . . Brexit Agreement . . . European Spring . . . Social students of the far-right . . . Western and eastern social Institutional order . . . Anti Europe centric resulting in mass global protests with the objective of creating destabilization . . . Beware of Russian oligarchs screening for new assets.

All at once they disappeared, replaced by the emoji smiley face screen savers rotating in circles.

"What the heck was that?" Danny Boy blurted.

"A bunch of gibberish!" Sergio exclaimed.

Dex turned his head from the screen to look at Hawk. "What happened to the file? You gotta get it back up!"

"I'll try, Dex."

Hawk got back on his keyboard and started tapping. He would have to repeat the process of bypassing the file's security sensory detectors with his coded messages to gain access again. The maneuver was a complicated one. Only this time he attempted to use a sheath to mask the hack. After he repeated transmission using his coded messages to override the file's security program, he punched the main key to bring up the file. Except the only thing that came on the screens were the yellow rotating emoji smiley faces.

"Sorry, Dex. The program wouldn't let me back in."

The news hit hard. Dex railed in disappointment. "There's gotta be something else you can try."

"There isn't. The anti-theft sensor on the microchip is extra sensitive. I have never seen this kind of security except at the Pentagon. The minute that sensory discovered my foreign coded message to access the file, it released a virus that immediately cloned the unauthorized entry detected. The file automatically closed itself. I could repeat the process a hundred times over and that virus automatically recognizes my cloned codes. On top of that, when this program detects a breach, it will block any future newly created coded messages. I don't how this Tagola fella could have gotten hold of computer software used by government homeland security. But he sure knew what he was doing!"

Dex stated rhetorically, "So, you're saying he programmed the data chip to shut down the file's information at the precise time he wanted it too?"

Hawk replied, "You got it."

Eddie shook his head, frustrated by the result. "Isn't that just dandy! Lieutenant, you said there was evidence on that microchip. Instead, we get nothing but a bunch of blah blah blah about global populism and Russian oligarchs. I almost lost my life over it. And from what you told us, it doesn't look like you'll find that Tagola fella either!"

"Hey, no one pushed you to show up in Mexico," said Adolfo. "That was your decision."

"Well, I wish I hadn't. I don't want to be here either!" Eddie bellowed.

Adolfo pulled his sidearm and aimed at the journalist's head. "I don't like you, Señor Flint. You talk too much!"

Dex saw the crazed look in Adolfo's eyes. The same look he saw before he took out the junkie and the pilot. "Adolfo, put the gun away!" he snapped.

Dex sent him an intense message with his eyes that suggested there would be no repeat of the previous actions he displayed in Costa Rica. So, he put the gun away and fell silent.

Dex looked at the trembling journalist. "You'll be fine, Eddie. Just because we didn't get a lead on Tagola like we wanted tonight doesn't mean we stop we stop looking for him. The search must continue."

"I know how to find him!" Carlita uttered, abruptly cutting in.

Everyone turned their eyes on her. Dex got up from the table facing her. "What do you mean you can find him? How?" he asked.

"I would like to discuss that with you privately, if you don't mind, Lieutenant."

Dex excused himself from the others and walked into the kitchen with her.

When they were alone, Carlita started talking. "Lieutenant, I was thinking about what you told us about Carlos Tagola and Hector

Colon. When you said you witnessed Colon destroying the drugs on that freighter bound for your country, it was truly hard for me to believe it."

Then she paused, avoiding eye contact with him. Dex knew then there was something on her mind.

"Carlita, what's bothering you?"

Carlita replied, "You said before that you really believed it was that FBI agent Weiss who set up my brother Carlito and his partner Manuel, instead of Tagola and Colon. Do you still think that?"

"I do. Those they met up with were FBI agents. It makes sense to me. I think agent Weiss was threatened by the fact their investigation was getting close. And he set them up before they uncovered something he felt would expose his ties to the CROP. Weiss wants that file just as much as the people he works for. Tagola has price on his head. He is as much a hunted man as we are now."

"Then I suppose . . ." Carlita paused again.

"You suppose what?" he muttered.

Carlita's demeanor changed immediately with her response. "I suppose you were right, Lieutenant. And I've been wrong all this time. I need to go to La aldea de leonés right now!"

She went to leave.

Dex grabbed her hand and stopped her. "Whoa! Wait a minute. What's gotten into you?"

"Didn't you say you and your men followed Hector Colon to the edge of village?"

"Well, yes. I did. But . . ."

"Okay, if Hector Colon is still there, I can find him. Then I'll have him take me to Carlos Tagola."

"Carlita, you cannot go into that village. A battalion of U.S. soldiers were turned back tonight after they tried to infiltrate it. Besides, Hector is probably long gone by now."

"What if he isn't? What if he's still there? If he is, it might be the only chance you'll have to find Tagola."

Dex released her hand and took a step back with mixed emotions as he stared into her eyes. She was right. And she was determined. Realizing there was nothing he could do to stop her, he offered his only logical response.

"We're going with you."

"No! I must go alone, Lieutenant. I know this village well. I know the people. I can get information you and your men won't be able to acquire."

"How can you be so confident about that? I know something has gotten into you. Now, what is it?"

Carlita didn't answer. She looked away for a moment, attempting to obey her impulse to withhold what she could no longer hide from him.

"I used to live in that village when I was a little girl. Don't ask me why I didn't tell you because I didn't think it mattered. It was a long time ago. But now you know. Now, if you'll excuse me. I must get going if you want me to find Hector Colon."

Carlita went to leave.

"Wait!" He walked over to her. "Take the Land Cruiser," he said. "Danny Boy has the keys."

"Thank you, Lieutenant."

Dex nodded. "Be careful."

"I will."

Dex watched her walk out to the living room to collect the keys from Danny Boy. He knew it was against his better judgement to let her go to the village alone. The others thought the same when she walked out and shut the door behind her. But they let her leave anyway.

CHAPTER FIFTY-SEVEN

Colombia

Carlita knew all the short cuts into the village. And she knew the safest route to get in undetected. On the way there she passed the pond where she and her brother Carlito often went to play when they were children. They liked skipping rocks across the pond, just to watch the water break with splashes. Most of the kids from the village came there. While Carlito and the other kids swam and played in it, she watched from the dry shoreline because she was always too afraid enter it. The pond was cold and murky looking at her. The water's edge was the closest she ever went. No matter how much the other kids teased her.

After adjusting the rearview mirror inside the Land Cruiser, she peered through the front windshield at a small cluster of people cross the intersection. An elderly man exited a store he was locking up for tonight. There was hardly any traffic. At that late hour many of the homes she drove by were unlit. It was surprisingly strange to see the village this ghostly quiet given the details the SEAL Lieutenant said went down here hours earlier.

She drove the Land Cruiser into the parking lot of a restaurant and killed the engine. The plan she had in mind was to call her friend Julia Benítez. She was the one person she knew would tell her anything she wanted to know.

She was about to place the call to Julia on her cell phone, but she saw a Range Rover pass by the restaurant moving at a slow rate of speed. This put her on alert, so kept her eyes on it as it drove to the end of the block and made a U-turn heading back towards the restaurant. The truck crawled into the parking lot and stopped directly behind the Land Cruiser with the engine idling.

With her concern heightened, she answered her phone the moment it started chiming. "Ola."

"Carlita, this is Dex. I had to check and make sure you're okay. Where are you now?"

Carlita kept her eyes on the Range Rover as she replied to the SEAL Lieutenant. "I made into the village. But I got company. I'm sitting in a parking lot right now, with a Range Rover that just pulled up behind me."

Dex bellowed through the line. "Get out of there now. Abort the plan!" he barked.

She didn't want to. But when the Range Rover suddenly rammed into the back of the Land Cruiser, she keyed the engine on and shot out of the parking lot. The truck took off after her. She heard gunfire seconds later. She knew the bullets were meant for her when the back window of the Land Cruiser shattered. At the end of the block, she made a sharp left turn. She missed colliding with a fire hydrant rounding the corner, but she managed to straighten the vehicle out as headed back down the same shortcut to get out of the village the same way she came in. As she sped up more bullets tore into the vehicle and blew out the right rear tire. The Land Cruiser swerved off the main road with rubber spinning off the rim. Next thing she knew, she was heading down an embankment straight towards the murky cold pond she dreaded going into as a child. Seeing the water rise to meet her with only seconds to act. She flung the driver door of truck open and leaped out onto the sandy shoreline right before it drove itself into the water.

Dazed, sprawled out on the sandy beach with her head turned towards the Land Rover she saw floating belly up in the pond. Carlita found herself groaning from the hard landing she felt when she hit the dirt that left her entire face smudged.

A pair of Range Rovers appeared at the top of the shallow embankment. She knew she had another problem when the men inside jumped out and approached with fully automatic rifles pointing at the stranger they cornered.

One of them started shouting, "Es una mujer! Es una mujer! It's a woman! It's a woman!"

Another gentleman screamed in her ear, "Que haces aki muchacha? What are you doing here, woman?"

Carlita spit out the sand in her mouth as the men surrounded her. With the men standing around her a big suburban rolled down the embankment a moments after they tried to get her to talk. Three men jumped out. One of them parted through the men as they stepped aside. Carlita slowly raised herself up and sat on the ground. When he walked, she lifted her head to look at him. She recognized him.

Hector recognized her as well. So much that he frowned before he unleashed his discord.

"Por que has regasado a la aldea? Tu no tienes negocio aquí? Why have you come back to the village? You have no business here!" he argued.

Carlita responded, "Hector, necesito hablar contigo. Hector, I need to talk to you. Yo estaba buscando té. I was looking for you."

Hector bent towards her. "Eso una broma. No? That's a joke. Right?" Hector stood as he addressed men around her in English. "Did you hear this woman, caballeros? She says she wants to talk to me!"

One of them bellowed from behind them, "She said your name, Hector. Who is she?"

"Just someone we knew from a long time ago. But she forgot where she came from. So, it's good you can't remember her either, Recardo," he replied.

The men started talking in low tones. She knew it was about her. And she knew what she would hear next.

One of them blurted, "That's Carlita Perez!"

Carlita gazed up at the man who said her name, then back at Hector. "Hector, you must take me to Carlos. There are men I know who need his help."

Hector rebuked her. "You never wanted to see him before. In fact, you said you never wanted to see or speak to either of us again. Did you think I would forget how much you said you despised us? Why after all these years have you come here to tell me this?"

Carlita stared up at him, unable to deny the validity of his words. But she was determined to get through to him.

I didn't come here to fight, Hector. I know about the drugs you have been destroying. I saw news reports myself about drug farms being set on fire and manufacturing labs blown up. I know there are people looking for you and Carlos because they want to put a stop to it."

Hector grabbed hold of her arm. "You don't know anything. Get up!" Carlita stood up. "Some of my men will drive you back to the city. Don't ever come back here. This is your only warning."

"Hector, listen to me. It's bad enough Carlito is dead. He didn't deserve what happened to him. I want to find the people responsible. I know you're upset because of what I said in the past. Yes, I admit. I was angry back then. And you know why. But I was wrong to think you and Carlos had something to do with Carlito's death. People change, Hector. I came here because I thought maybe I could make things right!"

Carlita started crying.

Hector saw the tears streaming down her face.

One of the men behind them shouted, "Don't listen to her, Hector. She'll only turn on us again. We can't trust her. We must get rid of her!"

Hector spun around and glared at him. "No one will touch her. Understand!"

"Carlita works for the Colombian Drug Task Force Intelligence Agency, Hector. He's right!" another man bellowed.

"I can't dismiss that. But it doesn't matter. Carlos will never allow any harm to come to her," Hector rebutted.

"Take me to see him. I just want to talk to him," Carlita repeated.

"My men will take you back to the city so that you can go back to your job at the drug task force agency. I'm sure they will be waiting for you to fill out your report for them in the morning."

Despite Carlita's plan to enter the village alone. After she took off from the safehouse in the Land Cruiser, Dex and the others piled into the Hummer and followed her anyway. They trailed her as close as they could, following her and the men chasing her in the trucks. The moment she bailed out the Land Cruiser, they took cover in the woods, watching her and the men through their night glasses the entire time before Hector Colon walked her back up the shallow embankment to the Range Rovers.

"You shouldn't have let come here alone, Lieutenant," Adolfo said.

"It was her call," Dex replied. "That's the way she wanted it."

Dex saw a man handing Hector a walkie-talkie radio he started talking into. A moment later he and his men shifted their attention from Carlita and stared towards the area of woods where they were hiding. It seemed like Hector was looking right at them. And then they heard bushes rustling. This put them on immediate alert. Everyone spun around with their eyes and weapons darting in every direction. Dex gave a quiet signal to retreat. But as they began to leave to take up a different position. A voice shouted through the darkness.

"Bajan las armas. Están rodeado! Lower your weapons. You're surrounded!"

As they stood motionless, Danny Boy yelled loudly, "Lower yours!"

Someone fired a sniper round that came out of the treetops. Danny Boy jumped back from the bullet that disturbed the dirt around his feet. They cocked their heads skyward looking for a solo sniper. But the red laser beam dots that lit up their center mass, legs, arms, and heads a second later to let them know there were a lot more up there. At least ten or fifteen, Dex thought, sitting up there in camouflaged coats of leaves among the branches. Just like the bushes they heard rustling before Danny Boy nearly got his foot blew off. Except when they rustled this time, they got up and started moving towards them with human legs beneath them. Then they discovered some of the giant trees around them were watch towers. They were made of fake bark and camouflaged with built-in doors that opened for men who came out of them four at time. They surrounded them just as a man's voice in canopy repeated the first command. "Bajan las armas!"

Dex glanced up in the trees, then at Adolfo, and his men. "Stay calm. And put the guns on the ground," he ordered.

"You sure want to do this, Dex? What if they start shooting?" Danny Boy muttered.

"If they wanted to shoot, they would have done it already. We're in a bad way here, Danny Boy. Just lower your gun and toss it," Dex replied.

Everyone laid down their weapons. After snipers up in the trees fast roped it to the ground, they marched the four Navy SEALS and Adolfo from the woods and took them to Hector Colon.

Hector looked at Carlita as they approached. "You brought these intruders into this village!" he shouted.

He walked up to the four Navy SEALS and glared at Danny Boy. "What are you looking at, gringo?

Danny Boy retorted sharply, "Nothing at all!"

Hector's eyes narrowed as he raised the barrel of his assault rifle and pressed it against the soldier's forehead hard enough to leave a red circle when he lowered it.

"Be thankful Carlita knows you, gringo."

When Carlita approached, she walked over and stood next to him. Dex was surprised they didn't stop her.

"Lieutenant, Hector knows about e-file you found in the bunker," she said. "I told him everything. He knows the people looking for you are the same ones looking for him and Carlos. They know it was the American FBI agent who set up Carlito and Manuel. They were looking for him. Agent Weiss is one of the reasons they were at the shipping port in Medellin when you showed up.

"Carlita, why don't you tell this Americano that if you had not got Carlito to sign up to work for that phony task agency, he would still be alive!" Hector scolded.

"Hector, Por favor. No mas!"

"Don't interrupt me when I'm talking, Carlita. What you told me is a very dangerous matter you should not have involved yourself with. And now you expect Carlos to talk to you. Well, I doubt if he will."

"You're the one person who can convince him to, Hector. If you won't ask him for me, do it for Carlito. I don't know why you and Carlos are doing these things. But I know people change. What you're doing for Colombia is an amazing thing. I forgive you, Hector. I forgive both of you."

Hector stared at her and thought about her brother Carlito. Then he imagined how inconsolable, forlorn, and broken hearted she must have been when news of his death got back to her. Each time she mentioned him, he saw the hurt in her face, heard it in her voice, and felt the fury of her determination to hunt down the people who caused his untimely demise.

Hector pulled out his cell phone and walked off with his back to them. Then he made a call. Carlita waited with the others. He turned to look at them for a moment as he continued talking to the party he had on the line. Then he put his phone away and walked back to Carlita.

"Carlos says he'll speak to you. I will take you to him," he stated.

Carlita smiled and replied, "Thank you so much Hector. What about the soldiers who need his help?"

Hector looked at the Navy SEALS and Adolfo. "They're coming too. We leave on a plane in one hour."

Another Range Rover drove up a few minutes after he made the announcement. Everyone turned, only to see two Colombian men jumping out with the trembling journalist they escorted to Hector.

"We found this gringo hiding in the back of a Hummer," one of the men informed him.

Hector looked at Carlita. "Who is this man?" he asked.

Carlita replied, "He's with us."

Part Eleven
Minority Report

CHAPTER FIFTY-EIGHT

Philadelphia,
City of Brotherly Love

On this day the sun was cresting the tops of the buildings, casting off its sweltering rays. Brody Jenkins's and his girlfriend started arguing outside a local neighborhood convenient store after she keyed scratches on his Lexus. The owner called in a 911 report of domestic violence. Within minutes three PPD patrol cars pulled into the store's parking lot. Four cops got out and started walking towards them. Brody spotted them. The warrants he had for child support and unpaid tickets rushed up, so he took off running across the avenue.

The cops gave chase. Back in high school, Brody was a track star who never lost a race. The officers couldn't keep up. When they began losing ground, he heard one yell, *"Gun! Gun! Gun!"* Then he heard the air ignite with gunshots behind him. He his legs went limp in mid stride. Seconds after he fell and hit the pavement face first.

When the cops got to him, he was lying in the middle of the street gurgling death throes. The supervisor on scene was Sergeant Livingston. He knelt to check his pulse, but it wasn't there. He glanced up at the officer who first shouted and fired his gun at Brody. Then he cut his eyes at the second officer who fired at the same time.

"Davison, Polenski . . . We all saw the gun. Right?" he muttered to them. The question was more of a statement.

Officer Davidson quickly comprehended and replied, "Yeah, he had a gun!"

"He definitely had a gun!" Officer Polenski answered.

Sergeant Livingston gave them a curt nod and said, "Okay. You two know the drill . . . Polenski, get the extra. Hurry!"

Officer Polenski ran back to his squad car. Sergeant Livingston then cut his eyes at Officer Peterson, the fourth officer on the scene. He was a rookie in his twenties. He completed his training at the police academy last month. This was only his third week on the beat. He was pacing about like he was about to piss his pants when the Sergeant called his name.

"Officer Peterson, get over here!" the Sergeant bellowed.

Peterson walked up and stared down at the young African American he saw lying in the street with a pool of blood around d him.

"We all saw this guy with a gun, including you. Okay!"

Peterson replied, "Where's the gun, Sergeant? I never saw any gun on him."

He looked confused and shocked. The Sergeant and officer Davidson glanced at each other.

"Sure you did, Peterson. You saw him with a gun," Livingston muttered.

"I didn't see a gun, Sergeant," the rookie repeated.

Officer Davison was glancing around at the onlookers when officer Polenski drove back to the scene with the overheads flickering on his squad car. The curious crowd of spectators that gathered quickly started to edge closer thinking they were witnessing another unjustified police shooting.

Polenski leaped out of the front seat of the squad car he parked sideways to block the view of the spectators. Realizing they had to act fast, he threw on a police windbreaker, and concealed the prop gun inside a plastic zip-lock bag. When he arrived back at the scene, Officer Davidson was searching through the pockets of Brody Jenkins's clothes. He found nothing on him except a cell phone in his hand and a can of Mountain Dew that had fallen out of the pocket of his jacket when he hit the ground.

"You got the prop?" the Sergeant asked.

Polenski unsealed the zip-lock plastic bag and removed a .380. The dispatcher's voice squawked over the radio in his squad car as Sergeant Livingston bent down and replaced the cell phone with the prop gun.

Peterson stood behind his three coworkers thinking that cell phone was the only thing he'd seen Brody Jenkins with, besides that can of pop.

"He's got dope on him too," Polenski said. The officer gave his Sergeant a plastic bag containing nuggets of crack cocaine. Livingston placed the dope near Brody's jacket.

Officer Peterson argued in protest of the contrived plan he saw unfolding. "Serg, what are we doing here? This is not what I signed up for. It isn't right!"

Livingstone removed the purple latex gloves he had on. Then he stood up and glared at the young officer.

"What did you just say?"

Peterson repeated, "I said, I didn't sign up for this kind of thing. What you're doing is not right!"

The Sergeant grabbed the collar of his uniform, pushed fabric against his neck, and slammed him against the side of officer Polenski's squad car.

"Listen to me, you young punk! You're but a two-bit rookie on these streets. You're on my watch. And today is your training day. Therefore, I advise you to learn quickly about the blue line of silence out here. When we submit that report to headquarters, your statement better be the same as ours. You got that?"

Livingston released him and stepped back with a crazed look in his eyes.

Shaken, Officer Peterson straightened out his collar. "Yeah, yeah. Whatever you say, Serg," he mumbled, placid, but he got the picture.

CHAPTER FIFTY-NINE

Philadelphia

Gina Jones was glued to the eleven o'clock news. Another young African American male was shot by police. How could it have happened again when the nation was still in turmoil over the other senseless shootings? she asked herself.

She couldn't help but to think of her husband Dex a how much she feared for them both. Like millions of people of color, she hoped to see the day when her people would experience the real equality and protection ratified in the constitution.

Direct action politics was needed to combat those who resisted changes and the inclusions that expressed the lives of minorities mattered too. How else will the country move forward in finding the solutions to peel back the uneven scales of justice and treatment between citizens?

As a college professor and community activist, Gina knew the nation's history. Questions like these often flood into her mind. Every man and woman who stood in the interest of minorities recognized the vitality of the struggle for equal rights.

Disgusted by the news broadcast, she was about to click off the television until the man's face she thought eerily resembled her husband Dex popped on the screen with the breaking news report. He looked so much like Dex it was scary. But the reporters said this man was Navy SEAL commander name Claymore Logan. And that he was wanted for questioning in the death of a U.S. Senator and two other officials who died in Rome after their car exploded. Dex would never do such a thing. No one could have ever been convinced otherwise. Besides, Dex wasn't in either of those places. He was in Los Angeles working that nine-to-five at the cable company. No way that was him, she told herself.

After she dismissed the notion, she was about to click off the television again, until another segment about Brody caught her attention as well. Except this time, it was about the protest that rose out of the shooting in the aftermath. The news video showed people firing rocks and bottles at a barricade of police officer lined up behind their blue shields.

An officer got on his PA system and bellowed at the sea of angry black and brown faces marching through the streets. "Everyone, stay back and calm down. It's time for you to return home to keep the peace."

Gina knew the crowd had heard that plea many times over. It showed. Because they continued marching down the main avenue in solidarity as they pushed upon the police barricade of riot shields. Some of the squad cars were tipped over, set on fire, the windows were shattered.

Bothered by the whole scene she clicked off the tube and prepared for bed so she would be ready for the lecture she was planning to give her students at the college in the morning. She crawled beneath the covers thinking about Brody Jenkins and the millions of minorities across the nation looking for the fix to the nation's problems. It seemed there were no answers in close sight for the foreseeable future. Not even in the city of brotherly love.

CHAPTER SIXTY

Philadelphia

It was close to 8:30 am when Gina arrived on campus to teach her political science course the next morning. She looked forward to seeing the students. When she strolled into the classroom, she placed her book bag on the desk and took a roll call of the students present. Six of them were absent, but she got started anyway.

"All right, everybody, I have some good news and bad news to give you. The bad news is that at the end of class hour today you will have another homework assignment to keep you busy."

The students booed.

"The good news is that I am canceling today's exam. That means you will have an extra time this week to study for the final."

The class applauded, cheered, and whistled. Gina unsnapped her leather book bag and took out a CD she inserted into the video player beneath the flat screen sitting on the stand next to her desk. After pressing the *on* button, she collected a piece of chalk on the ledge of the blackboard and scribbled out the day's course study on the History of the Bill of Rights.

"Students, we're going to pick up where we left off yesterday. Yesterday we were talking about the original draft of United States Constitution proposed right here in the city of Philadelphia at Independence Hall. We know the delegates who first gathered there on May 25, 1787, were focused on the main topic of putting forth components for a constitution with a fundamental system and principals by which the government would function under the oversight of a continental congress. In the early stages of development, this country we call the U.S. existed only in the form of a small confederation of states. The articles drafted by the delegates who gathered at Independence Hall were the first political constitution to codify the powers and practices of the continental congress's responsibility of governing."

The door of the classroom opened. Gina paused as she watched the six students she marked absent file into the classroom. After she wrote the names of Tenisha Leonard, Yolanda Underwood, Roy Stacks, Omani Tate, Nathaniel Eastbrook, and Edna Royce, she promptly addressed them.

"It's good to see everyone is here now," she said to them. "But all of you missed the opening discussion about the course study from yesterday. Therefore, I'd like you to help me refresh the rest of the class on this topic of the History of the Bill of rights.

"How about we start with you, Tenisha Leonard. Can you explain to us why the articles of the confederation continental congress in the early stages of the country's development were not sufficient?"

"Do I have to?"

Gina glared at her, realizing these six were some of the brightest students in her class. But they were late. And lateness was something she didn't tolerate.

"Yes, you do. This is the third day in a row you've been late to class this week."

The bright-eyed pupil gave a curt frown and replied, "The establishment for the government at the time was a congress. There was no president or judiciary to preside over the disputes between the few states back then. And without a president to enforce the laws. The first constitution ever proposed contained very little guarantees to protect individual equal rights."

"That's correct," said Gina. She pointed to the next student. "Mr. Roy Stacks, what were the concerns that early drafters like James Madison and Alexander Hamilton have about the constitution and the issues around majority rule?"

The student replied, "James Madison and Alexander Hamilton were concerned about the potentiality of the nation's majority rule abusing its power to oppress the minority. They felt it was necessary to establish executive and legislative branches of government in order to prevent possible threats of tyranny. Madison emphasized this subject in great detail through his writings, when he said it was of great importance for the republic to not only guard the society against the oppression exhibited by its rulers. But it must also guard one part of society against the injustices of the other part."

"Very good," said Gina, moving on to another students. "Omani Tate, I'd like to elaborate on the perspectives of Alexis de Tocqueville in regarded to this matter."

The student replied, "De Tocqueville expressed that if it be admitted that a man possessing absolute power may abuse that power by wronging his adversaries, then why should not the majority be liable to the same reproach?"

"You did very good," said Gina, as she shifted her attention to the next one. "It's your turn Nathaniel Eastbrook. Tell the class the reasoning behind Alexis de Tocqueville's perspective on this matter?"

The student answered, "De Tocqueville believed that a nation founded on the principles of democracy required the rights of the minority of its citizens to be equal to the rights afforded to the majority of its citizens."

"That's correct," said Gina, peering at the next student. "Ms. Edna Royce. You're the last one to be quizzed. So, here's the question. In the post-civil war era, what was Alexis de Tocqueville referring to when he said those most in need of being protected under the amendments of the Bill of Rights restructuring within the United States constitution?"

The student replied, "He was referring to the treaties established with Native American Indians, the rights of freed slaves, and other non-white."

"Excellent," said Gina. Then she addressed everyone present. "You see, class. The document of the U.S. constitution sits inside the National Archives in Washington, DC. But it has not always been sufficient. It had to be carefully crafted into what it is today . . ."

"Pardon me, Mrs. Jones. But it still isn't sufficient," interrupted Tenisha. "I'd like to elaborate what I mean, if you don't mind."

"Not at all, Tenisha. Everybody has a voice in this class. Go right ahead."

"Well, I was thinking about the answer Edna gave you in regard to Alexis de Tocqueville's reference about equal protection for the treaties of Native American Indians, former slaves, and other non-whites. Yesterday we spoke about the 14th Amendment's added to the Bill of Rights in 1886. And we talked about its three clauses."

"Yes, we did. And do you recall what those clauses are?" asked Gina.

"I do," the student replied. "The first clause stipulates that any person born in the U.S. is a citizen of the United States. And that any person who resides in one of its states is a citizen of that state. The second stipulates that states are prohibited from depriving any citizen of their life, liberty, and property without due process. The third stipulates that due process under the law is a requirement for every single state in the country."

"You aced every clause of the 14th Amendment," said Gina. "So, what's your point in relation to your statement about the constitution's imperfections?"

The student answered, "Well, those police officers shot and killed that young man Brody Jenkins yesterday. So, I was just wondering why he wasn't afforded his right to due process before they pulled their triggers?"

Everyone fell silence in the classroom, except for a few white students who gasped aloud. Gina knew a debate was about to come next as it had on other occasions in her class.

It started when an African American male student broke through the silence and said, "He never got due process because they gunned him down in cold blood!"

"That's not what happened," a white student quickly contested. "The officers said they were on patrol in a neighborhood known for its high crime rate. They said they feared for their lives."

"That's the same old excuse we hear every time this happens," another African American male exclaimed.

"Maybe the cops were wrong," said a white female near the back row. "But what about the blacks and Hispanics shooting at each other?"

"Watch how you're talk, damita!" a Puerto Rican female stated in the front row.

The African American female sitting beside her said, "No, let her talk. We do have way too many problems with this. Look at the gangs. What is it going to take for them to wake up and realize they're on the same team? Does it always have to take white supremist groups to remind them what team they're on? Of course not. We must be the ones to stop the violence in our communities."

A Mexican student cut in, "I think Alexis de Tocqueville was ahead of his time when he offered his perspective on the possible threats of tyranny by the majority over the country's political system and minorities a half a century before the United States was formed."

"Give us an example of what you mean," an Asian American student requested from the second row.

The Mexican student responded, "Well, he summarized it plainly. The majority make the laws but can break them!"

The class went silent again. Gina could have stepped in to stop the debate. But she didn't. Why would she? The class was made up of students from various races discussing real issues. And while they debated socially political topics to find common ground. There were politicians and leaders today merely using the issues as talking points.

Gina didn't worry about debates taking place among the young people in her class. Studying political science and black history gave them the opportunity to learn about the African American experience. It was the young people outside the classroom she was most worried about. She couldn't help but wonder how many of them among their generation today understood history? She couldn't help but wonder how many knew about a man name Dred Scott who declared himself a citizen and free man in the South, only to be disgraced by a U.S. Supreme Court's ruling in 1857 which said he could not be a U.S. citizen because former slaves were considered only three-fifths of a human being.

Did they know it took the 13th Amendment to outlaw slavery in America, the 14th Amendment to overturn the supreme court's Dred Scott decision in order in order to grant former slaves' citizenship, the 15th Amendment to bar federal and state governments from preventing a citizen's right to vote because of their race, ethnicity, or former servitude?

Gina saw how essential it was for them to learn about their descendants and other minorities who endured the experience of living through the dark period of Jim Crow laws designed to keep the races separated. They had to learn about the 1896 high court ruling in Plessy vs Ferguson which permitted a separate but equal policy in the use of facilities. Even though the ruling was also overturned in the 1950's, there was still the issue of segregated schools which had to be challenged and overturned in the case of Brown vs Board of Education in 1954?

Many of them weren't born when the riots ignited in Little Rock Arkansas over the first black student's enrollment in Central High.

With a steady increase in the dropout rate among the youth now days, what did they know about the 16,000 U.S. national guard troops former president John F. Kennedy deployed to march James Madison onto the campus of Mississippi State University for his enrollment as the first black student there? Had they watched the entire documentary Eyes on the Prize? Had they saw the part showing video footage of then-Governor George Wallace barricading the doorway of the University of Alabama with his body to stop African American students from entering.

The 1965 civil rights act was passed to protect minorities from discrimination whenever they entered establishments of businesses and employment. The voting rights act ended poll taxes and literacy tests leveled against the minority populations. But with so many millions of young people today having not witnessed the struggles and loss of freedom fighters like Malcolm, Martin, Mega, Rosa Parks, Gina could only question how many knew and appreciated being the recipients of the struggles they put forth?

CHAPTER SIXTY-ONE

Washington, DC

President Ernest D'kembi stood at the window inside his office watching protest outside the White House. The demonstrators were marching down Pennsylvania Avenue chanting slogans with waving banners and signs that read: END POLICE EXCESSIVE FORCE, RESIST DISCRIMINATION, END RACISM, SUPPORT WOMEN'S EQUAL PAY, WE SUPPORT POLICE REFORM, PROTECT VOTING RIGHTS. Twenty-four other cities were holding simultaneous rallies when he turned to face his national security adviser.

"We have to find a solution to this. People are fed up," he asserted.

"I agree, Mr. President," said the adviser. "We have been closely monitoring the protests in LA and Philadelphia. The demonstrators seem more agitated there. The governor in Missouri has issued a curfew and declared a state of emergency in wake of the riot."

"How many casualties?" asked D'kembi.

"Unfortunately, seven in Missouri, eight in Cleveland. The most recent uprising was sparked in Cincinnati."

"This isn't good," D'kembi commented.

"Looks even worse after that group of white supremacists that showed up at the rally in Cleveland to lend support for the officer who allegedly shot an unarmed suspect on the fourth of July. I don't think any of the mayors were prepared for those riots," said the adviser.

"Neither were we!" D'kembi stated. "Thank you for your briefing. Now, if you'll excuse me. I have an important call to make."

The adviser nodded. Then he left the office. D'kembi immediately called up the CIA and FBI directors on a conference call.

"Hello, Mr. President," said East Lake when he answered.

"Good afternoon, Mr. President," McCurry muttered when he took the call.

D'kembi replied, "Gentlemen, I just finished speaking with the national security adviser about our domestic problem. But it's time I speak to Colonel Burke about that situation in Colombia. Has anyone reached him?"

Eastlake said, "Your call could not have come at a better time, Mr. President. I have the Colonel in my office right now."

"He should be in this one. Put him on!" said D'kembi.

Colonel Burke's voice came on the connection. "Hey there, Mr. President. Sorry I didn't get in touch with you sooner. But . . ."

"You should have," the president interrupted. "We've got a messy situation at home. And I have a lot of questions I want answered about that covert op mission in South America."

"I'm sure you do, Mr. President," Burke stated.

"Word got back to me you authorized this action without informing me or congress . . ."

"If I may explain, Mr. President."

"No, you may not. I am still talking. This was a reckless action you took. Do you realize how many calls are coming into this office from the Senators? They want a probe into that affair. And if that probe includes committee hearings. I will lend my support for the inquiry. You can count on it. So, whatever you have to say in defense. It had better be good. Eastlake and McCurry informed me they received reports from you about the soldiers and some cartel leader with possible ties to the group claiming responsibility for the incident in Rome. What are the chances of us apprehending this cartel boss?"

"We tracked him to Bolivia after an aircraft blew up on the runway. We know he was behind it, sir. He's on the run now. But we're close to pinpointing his location."

"How come I didn't get the report on Bolivia. Harland, Charles . . . Did either of you get that report?"

Eastlake answered, "I got a call from the deputy director of operations Winston Bedford a half hour ago about it. I was going to brief you after you called. Colonel Burke confirmed the attack when he showed up."

"Mr. President, Agent Alex Weiss sent the bureau the report from Colombia five minutes ago. His report indicated the three Navy SEALS were there."

"When did this incident in Bolivia take place?" D'kembi asked.

"Night before last," McCurry answered.

"And you're just now telling me?"

"I wanted to cross check this information, sir. Weiss said the report came to him by other agents in the field."

"So, how certain can you be the SEALS were there?

McCurry replied, "Sir, the agents said they intercepted communications Weiss forwarded with his report. I was reviewing the audio when you called. I heard the name Lieutenant Claymore Logan mentioned on it. That's all I can say."

D'kembi shook his head as he kept his eyes fixed on the protestors passing by the White House.

Then he muttered, "Why would those soldiers want to involve themselves in something like this?"

He turned from the window when another member of his staff abruptly walked into the office with a secret service escort.

"It'll have to wait. I'm in the middle of a very important conference call!" he informed.

"The journalist, Eddie Flint . . . He called back. I have him on hold, sir. He wants to speak to you."

D'kembi's demeanor changed. "Patch him through!" The young lady walked out. "Harland, Charles, Colonel Burke . . . I have a call I must take. I will contact you later."

D'kembi disconnected the conference call and pressed the button on the intercom phone.

"Mr. Flint. I was sorry to hear what happened. Where are you? You said you had proof that the soldiers were innocent . . ."

Eddie interrupted in a rushed whisper, "I can't talk long, Mr. President. The proof I had was lost inside my truck. There are people looking for me. They tried to kill me. I'm in serious trouble. We need help."

"Tell me where are you? I can send someone to pick you up," said D'kembi.

"It's not that simple. You don't take the risk. I can't tell you where I am right now. And I can't talk any longer. I must go . . ."

"Wait. Don't hang up Mr. Flint!" D'kembi said, but the journalist hung up.

D'kembi found himself stuck in the moment, weighing the reporter's claim to the information the intelligence directors were relaying back to him.

The minute he switched on the flat screen and flipped to the news channel, his mind was dueling with the domestic protests and riots taking place as well. The country already had a long history of divisions and conflict. How much longer it was going to take to mend those divisions, he didn't know. Key police and prison reform proposals debated between the Senators on the Hill were often ending in stalemate filibusters, which translated into the same roadblocks that had delayed real changes in the laws for decades.

D'kembi knew the constitution from beginning to end. While studying law in college he spent hours researching lower and federal court rulings. Many he agreed with, others he vehemently opposed. The case in point was the surprising number of judges now days who were putting the right to free speech into question. Minorities felt targeted by predominately white Judges who seemingly had a problem with the manners in which they were protesting injustices. Millions of white people who supported civil rights saw themselves as much a target by other whites who called them democratic liberals and troublemakers marching beside a rainbow coalition of people, they felt had no right to complain about incidents of injustices in ways not to their liking.

While the protests of minorities were being labeled as violent mobs whose demonstrations were disruptive to the rule of law. Their opposer's were quick to overlook the history and reality when it came to the manners of protests in America. Surely, they hadn't forgotten about the first white colonists in the country who began staging disruptive demonstrations against their white English oppressors as far back 1776. How disenchanted could they be by the protests of minorities when they knew from the era of those opposing the 1960's war in Vietnam, to the complaints of coal miners, united auto workers, weather underground, students of the democratic society, public housing commission, public housing tenants, mothers on welfare, anti-nuclear power groups, Klan rallies, bombings of Plan Parenthood offices. America has seen more than its share of peaceful protests turn into violent disruptive demonstrations at both ends of the political spectrum.

Gazing at the protestors marching down Pennsylvania Avenue, D'kembi felt he couldn't just sit back if the country was on the verge of peril. He had to act. If he didn't, he might appear insensitive, soft. He had to act. But how?

Part Twelve
Motherland

CHAPTER SIXTY-TWO

Africa

Carlos was hopping between countries because it allowed him to stay one step ahead of his enemies. Now he was back in east Africa. Kenny was with him. Whenever word spread the son of Hannibal Abaas Ibn Tagola was back on Tanzanian soil, clan leaders came from the neighboring villages as far away as Mozambique, Angola, Chad, Sudan, Uganda, Kenya, Morocco, Zaire, Egypt, Ghana, South Africa, and other countries in Africa, to provide their support.

"Much has changed for me here," said Kenny. "I'm not sure if I want to return to America. The knowledge we have acquired here is very endearing and valuable. This land feels more like home to me now."

Carlos responded, "What you feel is natural, Kenny. That's what happens when you pass through that dark corridor of ignorance and emerge into the bright light of wisdom. But our task is far from over. And you agreed that at some point you would go back to finish what we started. Remember?"

Kenny stared at the crescent moon Hannibal Abaas gave Carlos as a present. "Of course, I remember. But when Hector returns, I'm going on one more run with him!"

Carlos gave him a light grin. Kenny had been with them for a short while. In that time, he had done well.

"We shall see," he replied.

Inwardly, Kenny was still basking from the success after they destroyed that cargo plane filled with narcotics before it got off the ground in Bolivia. What Carlos conveyed to Hector after he stopped him from taking out Ortega's chief operator Enrique Vasquez rang true. Fill Enrique in on the same truth the old Italian shared with them back Colombia, and he might turn. Enrique not only turned on his former boss's activities, he joined Carlos's crusade and provided them with whatever information they needed on Ortega to help them carry out their raids.

Kenny recalled how calm Hector was when he pressed the button on that detonator that blew Ortega's cargo plane on the runway in Bolivia. The next day they found themselves walking out the doors of the Vista Hotel in Venezuela. But the experience was something he could never forget when he, Hector, and Enrique were passing by the lurid signs advertising the food products being sold by street vendors.

He noticed an old Venezuelan woman with a little girl who was staring hungrily at the fruits and vegetables on one of the vendor's carts. It was obvious they had no money to buy any of it. They looked poor. He knew growing up what poor looked like. The old woman wore merely rags for cloths. A soiled scarf covered her long grey hair. The little girl standing next to her was no more than twelve years old. She was frail, like she hadn't eaten in days. Seeing her small limbs made Kenny think back to his childhood in Battle Creek, when he was home alone on that cold stormy night, until his big sister Elaine unexpectedly showed up and rescued him. All the nights he stayed up at the foot of unmade beds, empty refrigerators, unheated homes, were too many for him to recall. But who was going to rescue the old woman and little girl was the only question that rushed up in his mind when he saw time in despair. It was the reason he stopped and pulled out fifty thousand dollars in cash he walked up to them with. It was the reason he didn't hesitate to put the Spanish Gabriela and Hector was teaching him into words.

"Señora, este dinero es para ti y la niña. Ma'am, this is money is for you and the little girl," he told the old woman.

She looked at him, overwhelmed. Her eyes welled up with tears of joy. Hector and Enrique waited while he helped them collect the bags of food he had purchased from the vendor for them.

"Tangan cuidado. Take care," he told them.

The old woman muttered back excitedly, "Gracias jovenito . . . Gracias muchísimo! Thank you, young man . . . Thank you very much!"

He gave her courteous nod as Hector and Enrique watched the little girl bite hungrily into an apple retrieved from one of the bags. Then the three of them got into a car sitting at the curb across the street and drove off.

CHAPTER SIXTY-THREE

Africa

The plane was still in the air when Carlita woke up with Hector sitting beside her.

"Where are we?"

Hector replied, "Africa. Right now, we're flying over Uganda. We will be landing about four miles from Ugogo soon, somewhere between Zungomero and Lake Tanganyika."

"Where do we go from there?"

"When we arrive, we'll fly to Tanzania on the helicopters that will be waiting for us."

"Why can't we just fly straight to Tanzania?"

"Flying straight to our destinations wouldn't be safe now. This is strictly a security measure."

The low chatter between Carlita and Hector woke Dex from his power nap. When he saw them talking, he eyed Danny Boy, Sergio, Hawk, and Eddie sitting in the other rows. He didn't notice until Adolfo stepped out of the bathroom with his cell phone. Whoever he was talking to he hung up when they made eye contact. Eddie stood up. After he came down the aisle, he settled into a seat on the other side of them.

"Lieutenant Jones, I spoke to president D'kembi . . ."

Dex looked at him. "You what?"

"I called and talked to him . . ."

"How long did you talk to him?"

"No more than thirty seconds, I'd say. I had to let him know why I never showed up to meet with him. Plus, I told him again that you and your men were being framed."

"I just wish you would have said something."

"I thought maybe you would stop me."

"He would have been right to do so, señor," Hector interrupted. "Thirty seconds is a long time. That's all the time the people looking for you need to trace a call."

"Eddie, where's the phone you made that call with?" Dex inquired.

"I tossed it just before we got on the plane," Eddie answered.

"All right. But no more calls, Eddie."

Dex wondered about the call Adolfo made as well. He figured it had to be important. There was no need for him to be worried about his phone being traced. Adolfo's cellular was a private security line that could never be tapped or pinged by any GPS network.

After the plane landed an hour later, Carlita got off with everyone else and headed for the helicopters.

As they were walking towards them, Hector stopped and stared with suspicion at the choppers and the buildings in front of them. Everyone started looking around.

Carlita noticed he was acting strangely and asked, "Hector, what's wrong?"

"Something's not right," he replied. He quickly turned to one of the Colombians who got off the plane with them. "Where are the pilots?"

The man he was talking peered at the choppers and noticed there were no pilots inside.

"Yo no se. I don't know," he stated.

Carlita pointed to Hawk and Adolfo. "These two men know how to fly. They can fly us to Tanzania."

Hector was about to respond, when three of the choppers exploded in front of them. Everyone started scrambling for cover. Right after the blasts went off, men ran from the buildings firing at them. Dex pushed Carlita to the ground to shield her with his body. He glanced around, saw nothing but jungle around them.

"Get into the trees. Find a hiding place. Take the reporter with you," he told her. "Adolfo, you go with them."

The Navy SEALS were returning fire when Adolfo and Eddie grabbed Carlita up and fled towards the thick jungle. Hector and his men started shooting back at the men the minute they realized they were being attacked. The firefight was fierce. Hector was struck.

Dex saw him fall and ran towards him with his gun blazing at the attackers. Hector was on the ground holding his right leg when he got to him.

"How bad is it?" Hector asked.

Dex checked the wound. He got a bullet in his thigh. "Be still, you'll be fine," he said.

Dex took out his knife and cut a strip of fabric from his shirt he used to wrap the area of the wound.

Hector blurted, "They ambushed us!"

"Who are they?" Dex asked.

"CROP agents!"

Dex tied the knot that stopped the blood draining out. Danny Boy and Sergio threw smoke bombs to obscure the view of the attackers. When he saw that Carlita and the others made it into the jungle, he grabbed Hector up and fled into thick trees, with Danny Boy, Sergio, and Hawk giving them cover.

Meanwhile, Carlita was looking over her shoulders every few seconds in search of soldiers. She hoped they would be right behind them. Because the deeper they ran into the jungle, they were lost and didn't know how to get out. Eddie began to slow down. He couldn't keep up. He was breathing heavily. He felt a sharp pain in his side like he'd been hit by a brick. Carlita stopped and aided him while Adolfo stood watch. Eddie touched the side of his shirt and found it damp in the same area as the pain he felt. When he moved his hand back and looked at it, there was blood on it.

"I've been shot! They shot me!" he cried.

Carlita ripped his shirt open to examine it. "It's just a flesh wound, señor Flint. It only looks worse than it is. Come on. We must keep moving!"

Eddie moaned, "I . . . I can't."

"You can. I know you can. Now, on the count of three, okay. Uno, dos, tree . . . Vámonos!"

Eddie haggled up to his feet with his arm around Carlita's shoulder. He stumbled forward. Carlita held onto him as they navigated through the tangle web of trees and foliage. Adolfo was leading them around a ridge on a hill when the journalist suddenly lost his footing and fell off the side of it. Eddie was clinging to the grass and dirt and twigs. Carlita grabbed one of his hands. She tried to pull him back up.

When she lost her grip, Eddie went tumbling down the slope and ended up going down to the bottom.

She heard him cry out for help, and yelled back, "Señor Flint, we're coming. Just hold on!"

"Carlita, let me go down after him," Adolfo said abruptly. "Go find the soldiers."

"You will need my help, Adolfo."

"We'll be fine. Just find Hector and the soldiers. They're probably looking for us."

"Okay, I'll go look for them. But take care."

"We will. Now go!"

"All right. I'm going."

Carlita ran off. Adolfo took off down the hill. When he got to the bottom, the journalist was lying on his back bawling in excruciating pain. But he was conscious.

Eddie groaned as he approached. "Agent Guzzeta, I can't move my leg. I think it's broken. I need your help."

Instead of rendering aid to him, Adolfo took out his cell phone and made a call. A man answered, and he barked angrily. "You sent your people," he said. "That wasn't our deal. I told you we need Hector Colon alive right now. I told you to wait until he leads me to his cousin Carlos. Then I would let you know, so you can kill them and the soldier's all together. That was our deal. Now keep your end of the bargain!"

Adolfo hung up. When he looked at Eddie, the journalist was staring at him in disbelief.

Stunned by his words, Eddie muttered, "What are you doing, Agent Guzzeta?"

Adolfo crouched beside him. "It's going to be all right, señor Flint." He stuffed the phone in his pocket. "Sorry you heard that, señor," he said, extending his hands towards him.

Eddie growled, "Get away from me! You stay away from me!"

Adolfo's face turned grim. He grabbed his wrists and held them like a vice grip. "Let me help you."

Eddie started struggling. Adolfo let go of one of his hands and covered his mouth.

"You're a reporter, señor Flint?" he growled. "And you got a big mouth. So, I'm going to shut you up so you don't report this!"

Eddie was squirming to get free beneath the pressure of his hand. Adolfo's was too strong. But he jerked his face to the side, dislodged his hand enough to bite into it.

Adolfo howled out as teeth sunk into his flesh. Eddie didn't let go until he wrestled the gun away with his other hand and aimed at his head. "Wait, no, no, no! You don't have to do this!" the journalist pleaded. Adolfo pulled the trigger anyway.

"That's it, Hector. Keep moving!" said Dex.

Hector had his arm around Dex's shoulder as they ran through the jungle. But then he fell to the ground. He was breathing heavily, sweating. Dex bent over him. When he started to get to his feet, he felt blood on the back of his shirt and examined the area. Hector had taken a bullet in his lower back. He hadn't felt its effect or pain until now.

Dex cradled him. Carlita saw them through the trees and ran towards them. Her eyes went straight to Hector as approached.

"Lieutenant, what's happened to Hector?" she inquired.

"He's got a couple of rounds in him."

Carlita rushed to his side. Dex moved away as she knelt over him. "Hector, we must get you to a doctor. Do you hear me?"

Hector replied weakly, "No. You have to leave without me."

"That's not going to happen. You're coming with us. We're going to get you to a doctor," Carlita insisted.

Hector contested, "No, Carlita. I will be okay. But you must leave me with my men."

"Hector, we need you. Without you, we will never find Carlos!"

Hector motioned her towards him with his hand. Carlita leaned in closer. He whispered in her ear.

"The island of Zanzibar. You'll find him there. But you must tell no one."

"Are sure, Hector?"

Hector pointed. "On the other side of that river there's a village. It's not that far away. When go there you must tell the people I sent you with information for the chieftain."

Carlita turned. She glanced at the river over her shoulder. The men Carlos put under Hector's control came out of the jungle towards them with their weapons after patrolling the area.

Carlita hesitated.

Hector placed a hand on her shoulder. "Those men will tend to me. I will be okay. Now, go quickly."

Carlita stood up when his men rushed to his aid. Dex pulled to the side.

"Hector whispered something to you. What was it?" he asked.

"We must cross the river. The village is three miles away. He said we'll find help there from the chieftain. But we must hurry!"

Dex looked around. "Where are Adolfo and Eddie? We can't leave without them."

Carlita was about to answer, just as they spotted Adolfo walking down a trail towards them. She went to meet him. He was alone. He was sweating. His hand was wrapped up.

"Where's señor Flint?" she inquired. She could tell by his expression the news wasn't going to be good.

Adolfo replied. "He didn't make it, Carlita. When I got to the bottom of that hill he was gone. He took a hard fall. There was nothing I could do for him."

CHAPTER SIXTY-FOUR

Africa

Crossing the river didn't take much time. It was shallow, brown, not much more than a stream flowing eastward into Lake Victoria. But when they set out on their journey they were on their own. All of Africa with its majestic mysteries lay ahead. They stayed near the river, skirting its shoreline like Hector instructed. Carlita couldn't stop thinking about the fate of him and what happened to the American journalist without feeling empathy. But she knew they had to keep moving.

It took a little two hours for them to find the village. When they arrived, the people came out to meet them. There was a man there who spoke English sufficiently for him to communicate and translate their words. Once Carlita told him about her conversation with Hector, the man took her straight to their chieftain. The man conveyed her words to him. They were more than receptive. He gave her a map and wrote down the quickest and safest routes to take on their journey to the island of Zanzibar. The only thing he didn't provide was transportation. But he made sure they had provisions of food and clothing before they set out on foot again.

The he said the Ugandan capital of Kampala would have to be their first destination. They could find transportation there. Hours passed after they left the village. They were more than halfway through their journey when Hawk spotted paw prints in the dirt and signaled for everyone to stop and be quiet. A moment later a leopard ran out of the bush onto the trail in front of them. When Hawk whipped out his handgun and pointed it at the wild cat. It scowled, displayed its fangs, then ran back into the bush and disappeared.

Hawk put the weapon back into his holster then pointed towards a family of baboons he saw feeding on a banana plantation in the far distance.

"Looks like that leopard was on a hunt we interrupted," he muttered.

Everyone turned in the direction of the baboons. Baboons on a banana plantation told them they were close to human settlements as well as their destination. It wasn't uncommon to see baboons and other primates feeding this close to African cities. Local villagers and townspeople see them more frequently now days. Because corporate capitalism and industrialization were forcing much of the land's wildlife out of their natural habitats to search for food elsewhere.

After walking another hour and a half, they saw the skyline of the city of Kampala looming on the horizon.

Dex thought the view of the horizon looked like a picture-perfect photo. Seeing the skyline of this African city made him think back to the history class he attended in high school. He remembered the first picture he'd seen of the city after the teacher passed out references of encyclopedias. He read the entire summary of it. It was the first time he became aware that Kampala was the Ugandan capital once besieged by turmoil under the ruthless dictatorship of the country's former president Idi Amin in 1979. Wanton rebels from Tanzania stormed into the city, nearly crumbling in their struggle to remove its tyrant leader from office.

As they continued walking, Dex watched more of the pictures he'd seen inside the encyclopedia come to life. Most of the churches, monasteries, and covenants they passed on the dry bed of road they were taking towards Kampala were built by Europeans who introduced Christianity to the continent after their incursions of Africa in the nineteenth century. Parts of the land were colonized. Christian missionaries increased the number of Coptic churches they built with the aim of replacing the mosques that rose out of the Islamic faith. The millions of Africans affected by those incursions saw much of their culture washed away or reshaped to conform with the customs and beliefs of their invaders. But things were changing in modern times. The inhabitants of Africa were reclaiming their cultures and pride. There was an increased rate of new Muslim converts with the influence of Islam and its mosques once again expanding rapidly throughout the continent.

While they were walking, they came upon an old truck with a dusty canvas covering the bed. Dex popped the hood on it. The only thing he saw was the earth beneath it. There was no engine. Not a single wire in sight.

"We won't be getting any transportation out of this old heap. But I supposed we could leave the weapons under the canvas while we head into town," he muttered.

"What if someone comes along and discovers them. You sure that's a good idea, Dex?" said Hawk.

"Hawk, we entered the country illegally. We can carry our sidearms. But if we walk into the city toting these rifles all eyes will be on us. We're leaving the rifles. Danny Boy, it's probably best you stay here to keep an eye on them."

"Why me?" Danny Boy blurted.

"What, you got a problem staying back?" Dex retorted.

"Yeah, I got a big problem with that. I say we go as brothers because we're in this mess together. There's no reason for us to split up now!" Danny Boy replied.

Hawk volunteered, "I'll stay behind. Let him go Dex. He's right."

Dex turned and looked at Carlita. "Stay behind with Hawk. That ambush was a close call. I won't risk putting you in harm's way again," he said.

"If Carlita stays, I stay," Adolfo stated.

"Okay, the three of you will wait until we get back."

Dex glanced skyward and figured they only had a good twenty minutes of sunlight left. After he and his men placed the rifles under the canvas, they took off walking in the direction of the Ugandan capital. It was nighttime by the time they got there. But even though the sun faded, Dex saw how much Kampala had bounced back from its old days of violence and revolt against the dictatorship of the country's former leader Idi Amin. Many of its buildings were revitalized. The roads were clean and crowded with scooters, buses, trucks, cars, and people strolling through its epicenter.

Dex knew he made the correct choice by leaving the assault rifles with the others, the moment they spotted a couple of uniformed

Ugandan police officers walking the block on the other side other side of the street. But that wasn't all. A truck load of Ugandan soldiers drove by them.

Dex got an uneasy feeling the way they were eye them with suspicion as they drive by. He watched the truck with the soldier slow down when it reached the corner of the block. For a minute or two it sat there idling, before the driver put it in reverse and started backing up straight towards them.

When some of the men jumped off the back of it with AK-47's, the Navy SEALS quickened their steps and ducked into an alley. There, they encountered a couple of men who came walking towards them.

One of them yelled at Danny Boy, "Hey, you . . . English man with red hair. Do you want buy shilling for American dollar?"

He spoke English, but a had deep Ugandan accent. Dex knew Danny Boy's skin stuck out like sore thumb in Africa. But he realized the two men in front of them were only money exchangers trying to upgrade their currency with the U.S. dollar.

Dex saw an opportunity to get what they came looking for and answered the question himself. "Help us find transportation. I will gladly pay you extra!" He pulled out his wallet and waved it.

The taller Ugandan with the long dreadlocks replied, "Where do you want a ride to, English speaking man?"

"To the border of Uganda and Kenya. Get us transportation, I will make it worth your time."

The two men looked at each other. The shorter one grinned and said, "Follow us."

Dex glanced up at a Coke-a-Cola sign illuminating red neon as they trailed them down the length of the alley until they saw a dead end ahead. The two Ugandan men stopped and turned around to face them.

"What is this?" Danny Boy muttered. "Is this a joke?"

They didn't respond. But the clips they heard snapping into rifles around them let them know the two men had lured them into a trap. Everyone spun around searching, eyes darting into the dark crevices of the buildings.

A man's voice yelled from the shadows of a doorway. "Do not be alarmed. We know you are the American soldiers. You have nothing to worry about. We have been sent here to assist you!"

"How do we know that?" Dex yelled back. "How do you know us?"

"The chieftain from the village you left told us you were coming to Kampala."

Dex, Sergio, and Danny Boy didn't move when a group of Ugandan men came out from the shadows to reveal themselves. The men walked over to them with weapons down by their sides. They were dressed in Ugandan battle fatigues just like the men they saw on the truck that passed by them.

The young-looking man who stood in front of the other men like he was in charge spoke.

"I was told there were six of you who came to the chieftain's village. Where are the other three?" he asked.

Dex answered, "They're waiting for us on the outskirts of the city."

"And the Colombian woman is among them?" the man asked rhetorically.

"Yes. How did you know about her?" Dex inquired quizzically.

"Men close to Mr. Colon contacted us first, told us where you were going."

"Had to be the men we left with him. Then you must know of Hector Colon?"

"Of course, all the men you see here know him," the young Ugandan replied.

"Hector's still alive then!" Dex said.

"He was at the time his men contacted it us. But after we heard them coming under heavy fire. We haven't received any word from them since."

Dex stepped closer to him. "I have no doubt the people who ambushed Hector Colon are still looking for us here. Which means we must get out of the country as quickly as possible. But we'll need transportation and licenses to get through the checkpoints at the borders. Can you help us with that?"

The young Ugandan turned to his right and pointed in the direction where they saw three Humvees parked. Then he said, "I told you that's what we're here for. You're with us now. And we have orders to take you wherever you wish to go."

CHAPTER SIXTY-FIVE

Africa

Carlos answered his phone this time. It came as a bit of relief for Augustine to hear him pick up after months of no contact. But when he did, he bellowed into the phone, "Mr. Tagola, I've tried repeatedly to contact you. I thought maybe the council found you."

Carlos responded, "You thought wrong, señor Razzoli. It's quite the contrary that has kept me busy. How have things been for you?"

The old Italian answered quickly, "Assassins showed up at my home in Rome. It was urgent that I reached you. So let me get straight to the point. These men will come for me again. What I want from you is the arsenal I told you I might have use for in the future. The one we discussed during our meeting in Colombia. Remember?"

"You mean the torpedo?"

"Yes. If I were to give you a specific location where I wanted it shipped. How fast could you deliver it?"

"I would say three, maybe four days . . ."

"That's too long. It would have to be delivered within twenty-four hours whenever you get the call. No later than that."

"That might be difficult."

"You said might be, which means it's very possible. I know you could make it happen. You gave me your word that arsenal would be delivered anywhere I wanted it delivered whenever I needed it. Now, are you a man of your word, Mr. Tagola?

Carlos answered, "Consider it done."

"Excellent," said Augustine.

"So where shall it be delivered to?"

"That will have to be determined. But when you get the call, you will be provided with the precise location. Have a good day, Mr. Tagola."

"Hold on a moment, señor Razzoli. Before you hang up. You said something during our meeting in the village that I've been curious about. You said revenge for their betrayal was partly the reason you shared those things with me. But you never told me what that betrayal was. I see no reason for you to keep me in the blind about anything about the CROP now."

"I didn't think it was relevant to go into specifics about that at that time, Mr. Tagola. But if you must know, the story goes back decades and even centuries. You would have to know something about the history of Italians and Sicilians and the experiences they were exposed to at the height of World War II. It's the only way you will understand their betrayal."

"Then tell me now," said Carlos.

"Well, to begin with. Benito Mussolini was the leader of Italy during World War II. And while he was the country's prime minister, he formed an alliance and relationship with the leader of Germany's Third Reich. Hitler. Now that alliance pulled Italy into the war that the German dictator declared against Jewish populations and other country's they invaded. Hitler's aim was to take over Europe and later the rest of the world, except he was eventually defeated. After his defeat, the people of Italy staged a successful revolt against Mussolini and removed him from his position as prime minister. You see, he was blinded by his partnership with the Nazi regime, so much so that he didn't stop to think that after they were done using him, they would have saw to his demise just the same, had not the Italians got to him first."

"What does that have to do with you? I mean, I don't understand," Carlos cut in.

"Of course, you don't Mr. Tagola. You see, there's another story in the history of the Italian people not often told. One that goes further back. Back to a time when the war expeditions of an African general name Hannibal the conqueror was very well known in Europe. During the second Punic war he set out from Africa with a powerful force of forty thousand warriors and thirty-seven elephants to launch a full-scale invasion on the Italian peninsula. Sicily, Sardinia, Milan, and other cities he conquered were brought under African rule. When left Italy he crossed the Alps into Spain. When he left Spain, he returned to Italy with his elephants and warriors, and marched towards the gates of the world's most powerful empire at the time, Rome. The reigning emperor was Luscious Amemilius. Hannibal's warriors encircled his army at Cannes, in southern Sicily. After a series of battles that took place there, the Romans lost eighty thousand soldiers along with three major defeats. Nothing would have stopped this African general from taking Rome, were it not for the bone freezing elements of the Alps they encountered crossing the mountains to reach the city. The heavy loss of his army, equipment, and elephants was too much. The bone chilling temperatures dwindled the strength of his military and forced what remained of his warriors back home to Africa."

"I know about this man," said Carlos. "My father said my grandparents named him after this African general. He told me all these stories when I was a boy. Hannibal the conqueror was born in Carthage, what is known today as Tunis. When he left Italy, he was aged and weak. The Romans were so shaken by his presence in Italy. They were desperate to regroup under the new emperor Scipio who crossed the Mediterranean with his army to deliver this African general a final blow because they feared he might return. My father said this occurred during the last part of other Punic wars. And that Hannibal was never the same after he returned to Carthage. Rumors spread that the support for his military and war campaigns waned. There are some who say Scipio did defeat Hannibal in Africa. They say his defeat came at the hands of the Carthaginian people themselves after he became moody and erratic in old age and was ultimately forced into exile."

"Perhaps no one will ever know how the general's reign really ended," said Augustine. "But the fact remains that Hannibal and his warriors remained in Italy fourteen long years. And even though they went back to Africa there was something they left behind."

"What?" Carlos asked.

"Their African bloodline, Mr. Tagola. It should come as no surprise for you to know that our mixed DNA is something we both have in common. Traces of the African bloodline are still seen in many Italians to this very day. My mother was Sicilian. The council was very aware of the story of this African general and his expeditions in southern Sicily when they assured my family, they would put a Razzoli in the White House. It just took me all these years to realize why they never intended to."

"Are you saying they betrayed you because of Hannibal . . . Because he was an African?"

"Here's what you need to know about my former colleagues, Mr. Tagola. You need to know they are greedy and hoarders of wealth. But they didn't create the CROP. The hidden order has been around for quite some time. They are only a generation who inherited the beliefs and practices established by their forefathers who consigned themselves to the beliefs and practices associated with Arianism. These beliefs and practices included a fascist totalitarian style of governing at the exclusion of other races of people they considered socially impure in comparison to what they perceived as purity belonging to none other than the white Anglo Saxon race. Hitler later embraced this same ideology. The difference between my former colleagues and their predecessors is that wealth and greed became the driving force for them more than anything else."

"If what you say about race and them placing people into positions of power who they prefer. How did president D'kembi manage to become the first African American ever to win his election in the U.S.?"

"They underestimated his campaign run. The council has a long history of interfering with the electoral process of governments around the world. However, given the history of elections and voting rights in America, they didn't think they had to interfere. They figured they could let the people vote freely because in their minds an African American would never be able to pull off enough votes to win. Except they were wrong. Not once, but twice. D'kembi's victory infuriated them. His second victory infuriated them even more. They miscalculated. They didn't realize how much the country had evolved. That it was moving progressively in a more unified direction. Only as I explained to you before. They have a new plan to make sure that miscalculation doesn't happen again. They aim to replace D'kembi with their own candidate. And the man they have in mind to replace him will be given the instructions to carry out whatever they want.

Carlos fell quiet. The old man had driven him into another deep turbulence of contemplation, just as he'd done back in Colombia. Augustine was no longer a part of their madness, he thought. He had denounced their activities. And for that the old Italian had earned his respect even more.

CHAPTER SIXTY-SIX

Africa

It was raining. Carlita, Adolfo, and Hawk were keeping dry inside the hollow truck when the SEALS and Ugandan soldiers showed in the Humvees.

When they jumped out to meet them, Adolfo immediately addressed Dex. "Lieutenant, who are the men you brought back?"

The young Ugandan leader introduced himself before Dex answered. "My name is Idris. We are soldiers from the African union regional task force. Most of the time we work as national park rangers to protect our elephants from poachers."

Dex chimed in, "Idris and his men found us in Kampala. He says they were sent to provide us with assistance."

Carlita brushed the droplets of rain from her face. "Lieutenant, we have to get across the border into Kenya," she stated.

"They're taking us to the border," Dex replied. "But I say we wait until morning." Dex looked at the young Ugandan. "Idris, is there a place you know we can stay for the night in Kampala?"

He answered, "I think the Imperial Hotel will suffice for you, Lieutenant. The accommodation will be made before you arrive."

The young Ugandan did just that. When they drove back to Kampala and entered the lobby of the hotel, the gentleman standing at the reception counter had the keys to their rooms waiting for them. Dex, Sergio, Danny Boy, and Hawk checked into the room directly across the hall from the one Carlita and Adolfo were accommodated with. After they showered and ate, Danny Boy dozed off on the couch, Sergio and Hawk fell asleep in the armchairs. Dex couldn't get to sleep. He was thinking back to the conversation between Carlita and Hector in the village and what she told him before she went there alone. The questions in his head had been there since they left Colombia. And the only person he knew could answer them was her.

The others were still sleeping when he quietly slipped out and knocked on the door across the hall. He didn't know if Carlita was awake. But he knocked three times and waited. When nobody answered after a couple of minutes he started to wait. But as he turned to leave, he heard the lock click. A moment later, the door opened, and Carlita was standing in front of him.

"Everything okay, Lieutenant?" she asked. She looked surprised by his late-night visit.

Dex answered, "I know it's a bit late. But if you don't mind, I would like to have a word with you in private."

She gave him a puzzled look for a moment, then replied, "Okay, sure. Adolfo's asleep. But we can talk on the balcony if you like."

Dex nodded. "That's fine."

Carlita shut the door lightly behind him after he walked in. Dex followed her out to the second-story balcony. They went to the rail and stood there. Carlita sensed there was something heavy on his mind by the serious look on his face.

"What is it you want to talk about Lieutenant?" she asked.

Dex replied without hesitation. "I want you to tell me about the feeling I got when I heard you and Hector Colon talking back in Colombia. It appears you were no stranger to him."

Carlita did what most people did when they wanted to avoid talking about a subject. She quietly turned away and gazed out at the lights sparkling across the city of Kampala.

"I'm not sure what you mean," she replied.

"I heard what Hector told Danny Boy. My ears didn't deceive me. He told him that had it not been for you, things would have turned out differently for us. Those words were not the words of a stranger. Words like those come from people familiar. What is it you're keeping from me?"

He took a step closer to her. "Look at me, Carlita. We have traveled a long way. There are already plenty of secrets we have yet to uncover. Given the situation me and my men are in, I think I deserve to know?"

Carlita turned to face him, unsure of how the Lieutenant was going react when the answer to his suspicion suddenly spilled from her mouth.

"Hector Colon is my cousin."

Stunned by her revelation, Dex looked at her like he hadn't heard her correctly. "I asked you a very serious question. If this is some joke . . ."

"He's my first cousin," Carlita repeated.

"If Hector is your cousin. That means . . ."

"I already know what you're about to say. So, there's no sense in me stopping there. I might as well get it out now. Yes, Carlos Tagola is family too. In fact, he's my brother, Lieutenant!"

Dex's expression slowly morphed into a frown. "How could you keep something like this from us?"

"I had my reasons," Carlita answered.

"What were you thinking? You could have helped us find Hector and Carlos sooner."

"It was never going to be that easy to find them, like you believe. And quite frankly, Lieutenant, I didn't want anybody to know that Carlos Alejandro Tagola was my brother."

"Why?"

"Because I was too ashamed. You had your reasons to look for him. And I had mine. You needed his help. And I wanted to kill him. Because I hated him and Hector both. I hadn't spoken a word to Hector in over twenty years before he found me inside the village that night. My mother Mariana parted ways with my brother Carlos years ago, just like her sister parted ways with her son Hector. Mostly all our family parted ways with them when they got wrapped up in the narcotics trade. No one expected that. My mother always blamed her brother Ferdinand."

Dex stared at her for a long moment. "Why didn't your family try to convince them to get out?"

Carlita shook her head dismissively to the question. "You didn't know my uncle Ferdinand. We tried. But after they chose the drug business there was nothing we could do. My uncle Ferdinand was a dangerous man. No one dared interfere with his affairs, not even family. The people of Colombia feared Uncle Ferdinand the same way they feared Carlos when he took over as his successor. Carlos became his mirror image. But me and our brother Carlito chose different paths. We went to work for the Colombian drug task force intelligence agency with the intent of removing like people off the street like him and Hector It didn't matter that he was our brother."

"You said you didn't want anyone to know Carlos was your brother. What about the agency?" Dex asked.

"We couldn't afford to divulge that information. Our mother warned us not to. It would have jeopardized our careers. She encouraged us to stay away from Carlos and Hector to protect us. And we did. But that night you said it was them destroying the drugs I started feeling differently. I felt the same when I came to the realization that you were right about Carlos having nothing to do with Carlito and Manuel being set up."

Carlita put her hands up to her face. The tears that began streaming down her cheeks erased Dex's frustration. The minute he heard her sadness, he drew her close and embraced her.

"I'm so sorry I kept this from you, Lieutenant," she said. "You're the bravest caring man I've met," Carlita said.

"It's okay. But no more secrets. We still must find your brother."

"I understand, Lieutenant."

Dex released his embrace then stepped back. "Good. Now, is there anything else I need to know?"

Carlita looked at him, eager to redeem herself. "Hector told me where I could find my brother Carlos, in case he didn't make it. That's why I told you we had to make it to Kenya. The chieftain in the village advised of the routes through Kenya and the DRC to Tanzania. He said they were the fastest. But because of the violent clashes between park rangers and elephant poachers we must be careful. I thought it was logical when he said we must go to Tanzania. Carlos is my half-brother. His father is Tanzanian. But he's not in Tanzania."

"Then where is he?" Dex asked.

Carlita answered, "The chieftain said it's best that we take a plane over Mount Kilimanjaro to Arusha and from there to Bagamoyo."

"Where then?" asked Dex.

Carlita replied, "We will have to find a boat that will take us from the mainland across the short span of water to the island of Zanzibar."

"He's on the island of Zanzibar?" Dex asked.

"Yes."

Dex felt satisfied by her answer. There was no point in even continuing the conversation. It was the news he had been waiting for.

"Better get back to sleep. You'll need the energy when we get back on the road. I will see you in the morning," he stated. He turned from to make his exit.

"Lieutenant, just one more thing," said Carlita.

"What?"

"Hector told me not to mention this to anyone. Besides me, you're the only one who knows. The directions to my brother's location must remain between us."

Dex nodded. "You have my word."

The night was long, quiet. But the private chat they wanted to have had another set of ears close by. Adolfo had woken up and crept out of the bedroom. He'd eased up by the sliding glass door that opened to the balcony. And from there he stood listing to the tidbits of their conversation until he went back inside the bedroom and left the door partially cracked. Right after he watched Carlita escort the SEAL Lieutenant out and shut the door behind him. He immediately pulled out his phone to make another call.

The next morning the SEALS were up early. Dex peered out the window and saw the Ugandan soldiers outside leaning against the Humvees. They were waiting on them. When they left the room and knocked on the door to Carlita and Adolfo's room across the hall, no one answered. After knocking a few more times with no response. They left through the doors of the hotel to meet up with the Ugandans.

"Good morning, Lieutenant," Idris greeted. "Is everyone ready to go?"

"Not quite. Have you seen the Colombian and the other gentleman who came to the hotel with us?"

Idris translated the question in Swahili to the other Ugandans. Then he responded. "None of men have seen them, Lieutenant."

Dex got a funny feeling something was amiss. "We must split up. We'll search the room. Idris, I would appreciate if you and your men check around the hotel grounds."

The SEALS went back to the hotel room. They kicked in the door and searched the room thoroughly. There was no one inside. When they met back up with the Ugandans outside, the soldiers still hadn't detected either of them. Everyone climbed into the Humvees and drove around the city of Kampala looking for them. They passed by the fruit markets and hardware stores with billboards displaying the face of a newly elected Ugandan president. Dex thought it couldn't be that hard to spot Carlita. Mostly all the Ugandan women were dressed in their traditional busuutis. They were strolling down the streets with small babies on their backs, toting bags of beans, maize, and charcoal. After they still saw no sign of them, they found themselves tossing around the decision to journey on without them. Dex and his men were reluctant to do it. But after coming up empty. There was no other alternative.

The Ugandans left Kampala with the SEALS and drove the back roads where there was less traffic. They Humvees were traveling into the bush lands. On the way, Idris started talking about their work to protect elephants from illegal poaching. Central and eastern Africa was ground zero for the insatiable thirst for ivory in Africa. That desire through the black market was steadily increasing. With many African cities stricken by poverty, the elephants were under siege. Armed militant poachers were cashing in, spreading fear through village after village. Dozens of elephants were found massacred, their tusks taken off with chain saws. Whether they were Sudanese rebel militants crossing the continental on horseback or hunters from Chad. Idris told them that African soldiers like them working as park rangers knew there were an estimated thirty thousand elephants being slain each year. But they were determined to continue their brave efforts in the fight to protect them.

Long hours passed for them on the road. They had driven to within a hundred miles of Lake Victoria. land they had crossed the Kazinga

Channel on a bridge just barely wide enough for the Humvees to drive on. The next bridge they came to was just as narrow. But after they crossed it, they drove to a small fishing village three miles from Lake Victoria. Dex was surprised how easy it was for them to get through the checkpoints. Idris spoke to the guards in Swahili when they stopped. Each time he heard him say the name Carlos Tagola, they were allowed to drive past them.

How had he attained this much influence through the land, Dex wondered. When he asked the young Ugandan about it, Idris explained it in full. He went into detail how Carlos Tagola was revitalizing the infrastructure of African cities, how he was refurbishing the villages and towns, how some of the poorest countries in the east, west, south, and north were suddenly experiencing an up swell in economic growth and development because of him.

When they finally reached the Ugandan-Kenyan border checkpoint it was the same routine. They stopped, Idris told the guards in Swahili they were passing on the orders of Carlos Tagola, and the guards on border patrol allowed them an unrestricted into the country of Kenya. They kept the Humvees chugging to the capital of Nairobi. There, they found a place to lay over for the night. The next morning, they set off driving through the small peninsula towns of Kismu and Kisiki and didn't stop until they arrived in Isebania. Isebania was only a short drive to the border between Kenya and Tanzania. And Dex and his men were anxious to cross it.

CHAPTER SIXTY-SEVEN

Great Britain

Carlita awoke from another drug induced sleep. Isolated, still sealed inside the same cold room, a man sitting a white round table in the center of the floor. The white walls and white floor reflecting the blinding lights on the ceiling made it difficult to recognize him.

But then he spoke. "At last, the princess has awoken."

Carlita knew it was Adolfo soon as she heard his voice. "Where am I. Why have you brought me here?" she asked, bringing him into focus.

"I wouldn't worry about that. The only thing you should worry about is telling me where Carlos is. You're very good at keeping secrets. All these years you worked for the task force agency. Not one single person ever knew that agent Carlita Perez was the sister of the biggest king pin in South America. But someone knows now—me!"

"You're confused. What's happened to you, Adolfo?"

"Don't play dumb with me, Carlita. Either your brother Carlos hands over that file, or this is not going to end so well for you."

Carlita lashed out defiantly. "Bastared . . . Nos traicionaste! You betrayed us!"

Standing on the other side of the observation room's two-way mirror, Winston Bedford and Lieutenant Colonel James Burke could hear and see every interaction taking place between Carlita and Adolfo.

"She's feisty," said Bedford.

Colonel Burke muttered, "I'm sure the council will be more than excited to know we have the sister of Carlos Tagola in custody. But will it be enough to bring him out in the open. That's the question?"

"We shall see," Bedford stated. He glanced at Adolfo through the window. "Tell me about this person who brought her to us."

"His name is Adolfo Guzzeta. He and the woman are agents of the Colombian drug task force agency. He knows Weiss."

"I can see that. Agent Weiss has been stationed in Colombian for quite some time now. Did you talk to him about the guy. What's his motive for bringing her in?"

"Weiss said he's in it strictly for the money. He wants to become a wealthy man. He thinks this woman is his ticket."

"How much is he asking for?" Bedford asked.

The Colonel replied, "He was on a plane flight to Africa with the three soldiers when he phoned agent Weiss and told him he wanted five million for information on the Navy SEALS and Carlos Tagola. They landed in Uganda. He told us the soldiers were heading towards the border between Uganda and Kenya. If we can pick up their trail . . ."

"More than likely they're in Kenya by now," Bedford interrupted. "We'll have to put out an update of international alerts with GPS tracking surveillance on this information. Maybe then we can pinpoint where they're going from there if can't get anything out of the woman."

Bedford let out a series of hard coughs as he buried his face in a handkerchief.

"You should get that checked out," the Colonel stated.

"It's just a little cold."

The Colonel watched Bedford clean off a drizzle of dampness from his nostrils. He'd known the deputy director of operation a long time. He knew when he was bothered by something. He saw it in his demeanor when they met at the airport, right after he got off the emergency flight that took him to Britain. And he thought he had a good idea what it was.

"I spoke to Arthur Knightwood."

Bedford looked at him briefly, then back through the two-way glass window. "Really, when?"

"A couple of days ago. He mentioned told me you assigned the chameleon to the Razzoi job. He didn't sound pleased about it."

"I'm aware, Colonel. The man has a hang up about the chameleon I've never seen before now. None of this is going as we expected. And Eleanor has been a real thorn in my side. She's a crazy woman. I believe she had the nerve to ask if I liked Orcas!"

Colonel Burke chuckled. "That, I find humorous."

"Well, I don't!" Bedford retorted. "She threatened me, Colonel."

"Ah, I think you're being a little paranoid director. That's all. Perhaps we should talk about the president's and his suspicion around Operation Lion's Den."

"You're right, Colonel. Because has gotten back to me that President D'kembi, the National Security Advisor, and Secretary of Defense are scheduled to meet with a committee of Senators about soon."

"We'll have to notify our people on the inside to be prepared," the Colonel muttered.

"They better be. The gang of eight committee is calling for an independent outside counsel to investigate what role the navy played in the operation."

Colonel Burke went quiet. The White House was tight lipped as of late. But there were rumors getting back to him as well. Rumors suggested there were congressmen in the House and Senate discussing the possibility of public hearings. The whole affair being aired before a nationally televised audience was the last thing he wanted to think about. So, he changed the subject.

"What are we going to do about agent Guzzeta?" he asked.

"See what else he knows. I'll have someone bring him the money," said Bedford.

"So, you're really going to pay this guy five million?"

Bedford tore his gaze away from the two Colombians in the observation room.

"Our people will meet with him. They'll bring fake bills and duffle bags of coke. The local peace officers will discover him and the coke later. See where this is going?"

The Colonel grinned, then replied. "Yeah, a corrupt Colombian task force agent killed in a drug deal gone bad."

Bedford nodded. "Exactly!"

CHAPTER SIXTY-EIGHT

Naples

The old man was a trespasser, staggering pass the front gate to Augustine's home. Three guards standing out front spotted him, and immediately started walking towards him.

One of them barked in Italian, "Hey, you! Stop there. This is private property. You have no business here."

The old man was rambling incoherently when the security men approached. They detected the smell of liquor on his clothes as they stood scrutinizing his demeanor and the bottle of whiskey in his hand.

Another guard muttered, "He's drunk! Probably one of the peasants from the hills. You lost, old man?"

The trespasser lowered himself to the ground. His knees were on the pavement of the driveway. He was sitting on the back of his heels waving the whiskey bottle at them like it was a peace offering.

Then he muttered in Italian. "Care for drink?" he offered.

The third guard said, "We don't want your filthy whiskey, peasant! We want you off the property. Now, up on your feet!"

The minute he grabbed the old man's shoulder, Sebastain Korkov fired a round from a sniper rifle that shattered his skull. Soon after, the other two guards turned towards the woods in search of the shooter. Chello freed the gun from the strap on his ankle holster and put down both men instantly. The security wasn't as heavy as they expected. This allowed him to run the length of the drive before he cut across the front lawn and proceeded to the rear of the target's residence. From there he ran along the back wall to a sliding glass door. He was taking a few seconds to look around him when the door unexpectedly opened. Another guard walked out. Chello was standing only a few feet away. The guy lunged at him the moment he turned and saw him. Chello blocked the blow thrown and put a round in his chest. When he dropped to the ground, Chello stepped over him and quietly let himself inside.

Augustine was upstairs sitting inside his second-floor office secluded. He was chugging down glasses of Marcello -1725. Returning home to the mansion his father Salvatore left to him and his brothers in Naples left him contemplating. He was thinking about how the home hadn't changed much from when Bruno and Angelo first made it their headquarters to carry out their father's wishes.

The knock heard at the door interrupted his thoughts. A pair of his bodyguards entered.

The bear-chested mafioso wearing a contemporary stylish shark suit muttered, "Is everything okay with you, don Razzoli? We're just checking to make sure."

"Leave me! I'm fine!" Augustine snapped.

The men shut the door back when they stepped out. He had left the office all day. It was way past nightfall. If he hadn't been drunk earlier, they were certain he was now.

Augustine peered at the panel of his security monitors built into the wall to his right. Then he reclined his head back into the cushion of his leather chair and closed his eyes peacefully. His head slumped to one side. Five minutes later the doorknob rattled with a twist. The door opened. His eyes opened to find an intruder in his office. The man was approaching his desk with a silencer pointed at his head. He could have yelled to alert the other bodyguards or tried to escape the threat in front of him. But he made no attempt to move. Instead, he gestured a hand towards his panel of monitors and spoke calmly.

"I've been sitting in this office watching those security cameras over there for the past days and nights. I finally saw something interesting. I saw this drunk old man staggering up my drive. Then I saw him gun down three men with accurate precision. Know what I said to myself? I said, this is no old man. No old man moves with such agility. This could only be the fifth element of the four nights assassins. The man of many disguises. The chameleon. I am not at all surprised you would be the one Bedford sent next to finish me off after the others failed. Well, here you are in the flesh, Chello. I have no doubt you have waited for this day ever since you were a little boy. It's been so long since we last met. Perhaps you don't remember this face. But at last, we meet again."

Chello's eyes narrowed.

"Yes, you're starting to remember now. I didn't think you could forget the face of the man who saved your life. I never forgot about what happened to your family in Corsica all those years ago.

Chello eased closer to the desk with the beam dot laser sighted silencer. Something about the man's face made him hesitate with his finger on the trigger. His words made him reflect to the days of him and his brothers playing in their parent's vineyard, running between grape vines clinging to wooden trellises, hiding behind the trees in the orchards, bushes and brightly colored flowers blooming everywhere. Then he pictured the robust old man sitting behind the desk with a slug in his head.

"It was you!" he said finally. "You were the man I saw inside that car parked outside my parents' home that day. You sat there while the men inside murdered my family!

"I sent you away so you wouldn't go inside. Otherwise, they would have done the same to you," Augustine said.

"You're right. I've been waiting for this day a long time, just to see you pay!" Chello's hand tightened on the pistol grip.

Augustine opened his robe to display the bomb vest he had on underneath. "Go ahead, shoot. We both die! One flinch on the pressure point of this detonator I'm holding is all it will take. I've got enough C4 packed on this thing to blow up a whole city block. No one in this house will survive the blast."

Chello's eyes fell on the vest and the right thumb he suddenly saw resting on the pressure point.

"I knew I couldn't expect to make it through the night once the council sent the knights again. So, I have been here waiting. But taking you out with this old man isn't what I want, Chello. What I want is to tell you the truth of what really happened. You see, me and the men who went to your home that day didn't kill your family. The men inside were my own brothers. Your father Salvatore had information on a particular group of people who felt threatened by what he knew. They put a contract hit on him. Yes, my brothers were sent to Corsica to recover the information. I won't deny they were there to carry out the contract. I was there at the request of my father. But I didn't know your father was the target. My brothers told me to wait in the car while they went in. A car pulled up with four men minutes later. Those four men went inside too. When you came along, I sent you away because I figured something fishy was up when I saw the men armed with guns. After you ran off to that ice cream truck, I heard shots inside the home. My brothers came running out. They jumped in the car and sped off angry. They were cursing and complaining about the men they said came in and killed your father as well as everyone else inside . . ."

"You're lying!" Chello interrupted.

"It's the truth," Augustine rebutted. "The same people who sent my brothers also sent those four men. They even pinned a note on your father's shirt to make it look like it was the work of the mafia. But hurting women and children is against the principal code of our people. Not so for the ones who sent them. They have no boundaries."

"You really expect me to believe this!"

"You don't have to. Take the envelope in front you." Augustine directed his attention to the large envelope sitting on top of the desk.

Chello cut his eyes down at it.

Augustine added, "Everything you want to know about the people who sent those four men is inside it. How did I know it was Winston Bedford who sent you here to kill me, if I was lying? There's information in there about the CIA as well. He's one of their agents, Chello."

"How do you know my name?" Chello barked.

Augustine replied, "How did I know you are part of the Four Knights assassins is a better question. Don't you think? I'll tell you how. I know because I made it possible for you to enter the Ceeber training camp in Siberia. Think back to twenty years ago when that gentleman approached you inside that pub. You were there by yourself having a drink. He began talking to you about this hit league he called the Four Knights assassins. He told you about the millions you could earn. You eventually became part of the program. The day you met him was not by chance. You were recruited by him because I told him to. I know you thought you were working for Winston Bedford all these years. But you weren't. You were working for me and the secret council of which I was a part. When they found out you survived, they wanted to come after you. But once I recruited you and you became a top elite assassin, I convinced them that your skills as a Knight would be a very valuable asset to them if you stayed alive. From the day you became an orphan, I put you under my protection, Chello. You went to live with your grand-parents. They raised you dutifully. I made sure they became wealthy so that you could have everything you wanted."

Chello stood quietly, reflecting on the times he would hear his grand-parents chattering excitedly between themselves about all the gifts and cash deposits they were receiving out of nowhere from some anonymous source.

"You're all grown up now. What a young man you've become," Augustine muttered.

"These are tales you got from Bedford. I'm not convinced, old man. You're only saying this to save your life!"

Augustine gestured to the shelf that held pictures of his family.

"See the pictures of my two sons Mikey and Dino on that shelf? Days ago, their remains washed up on a beach shore. Their limbs were chewed off by killer whales. They were left in the middle of the Atlantic Ocean by the very same people who sent those four men to your home in Corsica. And those men were not ordinary hit men, Chello. They were Knights assas-sins. My former colleagues had my sons killed like they did your family. Rest assured I share the same rage you felt all those years ago. That's the one thing we share now. That, and desire to track down the people responsible."

Chello glanced at the faces of his two sons. Then he cut his back to the old Italian realizing the gun in his hand was no match for the bomb vest around his torso.

"If I let you live, then what?" he muttered finally.

"You will walk out of this house alive. And you will vindicate both of our families. Isn't that what you wanted?"

Augustine slid the envelope across the desk to him. "This information will lead you to them. Find Bedford. He's their main asset in the west. I'm sure he'll have useful information. He knows their movements."

Augustine glanced at one of the camera angles when saw a man on the ground floor walking across the living room.

"You didn't come alone, I see." He sat up and leaned forward, gaze fixed on the face that came into view. "Sebastian! He came back after all. Looks like Bedford's employers were thinking ahead. They want to make sure neither of us leaves alive."

When Chello cut his eyes at the camera angle, Sebastain was standing over the bodyguard's he'd taken out downstairs.

"What are you talking about?"

"My former colleagues. They figured if we cross paths, you might discover the truth about what they did to your family in Corsica. Bedford knows you work alone. Sending Sebastain can only mean they consider you a threat now."

Chello's eyes were suddenly glued to Sebastain Korkov as started up the staircase.

"He's coming, Chello," Augustine warned. "You don't have much time to decide. Take the envelope and leave while you can. I saved you once. I'm trying to save you now!"

Sebastain Korkov was moving in and out the rooms he was searching as he proceeded down second floor hallway. He stopped midway down the hall the moment heard music and followed the crooning violins of an Italian symphony to the target's office. He waited a second or two. When he swung inside the door with his assault rifle aiming, Augustine was still sitting behind his desk with both hands resting on his huge belly.

He smiled at the assassin. "Hello, Sebastain. Back again, eh."

"Yes, I'm back old man. And you won't escape this time," Sebastain replied.

"Too bad your companion couldn't stick around. Seems Mr. Fransis had to leave in a hurry for a bit of business."

Sebastain glanced at the curtains fluttering on the open doors behind the target's desk. There was cool air blowing into the office from the balcony. He turned and peered at the panel of camera monitors. One of the screen angles outside the old man's office should a long rope hanging off the railing of the balcony. Another showed the chameleon running across the lawn after he'd used it to scale down the side of the wall.

Augustine moved his thumb to the pressure point on the detonator. "No need to worry about him. It's just you and me now. So, what are you waiting for? Get it over with, you mad brute!"

Sebastain glared at with eyes of razors that held no emotion when he heard the insult and fired a single round into the old man's chest.

The powerful explosion sent Chello hurling to the ground. He rolled over. The envelope had fallen out of the waistline of his pants. He scooped it up and peered back at the wall of fire and smoke billowing into the night sky where the old Italian's mansion once stood.

CHAPTER SIXTY-NINE

Africa

After flying over Kilimanjaro and the Pare mountains, the Navy SEALS and Ugandans traveled to Bagamoyo, a small seaport town located seventy miles from Dar es Salam. It was the closest port to cross the short distance on the water to get to the island of Zanzibar.

The Ugandans were excellent guides. Dex and his men learned they were Muslims. The following morning, they got up to perform their Fajr prayer together. When they were done, they led them to the seaport and acquired speed boats. After everyone piled into boats, Idris steered the boat carrying Dex and his men through coral reefs. They relied on the African soldier's nautical experience to get them to the island. As they drew closer, Dex held up a pair of binoculars and saw the uneven coastline of Zanzibar coming into view. Five minutes later he was looking at bright red buildings and white minarets rising on the island's multi-faceted landscape. Once they got to the island, they found themselves pulling into the shallow, sheltered lagoon, filled with boats floating in its crowded harbor.

Danny Boy saw all the people walking around and commented, "There's a lot of people here. How do we know there aren't agents among them?"

"There are no enemies you have to worry about on this island," Idris said. "That I can assure you."

When they got off the boats, a pair of coastguard officials came to meet them. The men began speaking with the Ugandans in Swahili as though they were expecting their arrival. The only thing Dex and his men knew about the island was what Idris told them. Zanzibar was part of the Tanzanian mainland but existed as an independent state with its own government and security force.

Why Carlos Tagola chose this island as his sanctuary, Dex couldn't imagine. It was a tiny speck in the corner of the planet. Tanzania was made up of some twenty-five million people and more than one hundred tribal groups coexisting with different cultures, traditions, and religions. The island was a small ethnic mix of Arabians, Comorian, Shirazi, Bantu, and migrants that had flowed in from the Mediterranean, Middle East, Asia, and Europe with various languages and religions. But from what they saw of the women covered in veils and men dressed in long white robes, it appeared that Islamic culture was the island's primary's tradition.

The view of the metropolitan districts faded when they drove into the rural countryside. When they arrived at the destination the Ugandans drove to, Dex was consumed by the thought that they were finally about to meet the one man who could help them.

Two armed young men walked up to the vans when they arrived at the checkpoint. The men exchanged only a few words before they waved them through. They continued along the road until they came to a modest home with a manicured lawn and courtyard on the right side. A man clad in an embroidered shirt was standing in front when the car drove up and parked at the curb.

Everyone got out of the vans. "As-salamu Alaikum, Peace be you," the young man said, as he approached the Ugandans.

Idris promptly returned his greeting. "Wa alaykum. And peace be on you."

Dex, Sergi, Danny Boy, and Hawk were quietly surveying the surroundings when Hector Colon suddenly came hobbling out the front entrance of the home on crutches. On his head was a white turban. And the muscular looking Latino guy and an African gentlemen walked out with him also wore turbans coiled around their heads.

"Hector, you're alive!" Dex uttered.

"Yes, we made it here safely. But I was informed before you got here that Carlita is no longer among you. Where is she?" Hector inquired.

Dex answered, "She and her partner have been missing since we stayed overnight at a hotel in Uganda. We searched the property. We looked for her in Kampala. But there was no sign of them anywhere."

Disappointment etched into Hector's face. "Come inside," he muttered.

The Ugandan soldiers remained behind when Hector led the SEALS inside the home. It was modest, pristine, and clean. But Dex saw no extravagance of luxury here like he'd seen inside the kingpin's mansion back Colombia.

Hector was escorting them towards the home's courtyard. On the way there they passed a room where Dex noticed saw an old man performing prayer on a rug. He bowed and prostrated towards the east. The two men behind him then bowed and prostrated. The old woman and young woman he saw in the back row bowed and prostrated when the two men in front them did.

Hector opened the sliding glass door to the courtyard. "Wait here," he said. The SEALS settled into the chairs he directed them to and waited patiently for his return. Five minutes later, when he walked out, he was joined by the people Dex saw praying inside the room they passed by.

One of the men he saw in the room with the old man walked over to Dex with Hector.

Hector introduced him. "Lieutenant Jones, this is my cousin Carlos. The man you've been looking for," he stated.

Dex immediately stuck out his hand. "It's a pleasure to meet you, Mr. Tagola."

Carlos shook it and replied, "I've been expecting you, Lieutenant."

Dex glanced at the old man standing at the entrance to the courtyard before he went back inside.

"I saw you praying behind that older gentleman," he said.

"Yes. He's my father Hannibal Abaas.

Dex looked at him curiously. The Colombian, Carlos Tagola, was standing in from of him clad in a long white Muslim robe that hung loosely above the brown sandals he wore. On his head was Kafiyah headdress held in place by an aiglet like those worn by many men in Saudi Arabia.

Was this really the kingpin of South America? The notorious drug trafficker and his cousin Hector were marked men. Out of her frustrations his own sister described them as a plague to Colombia. But as he stood there, he looked more the part of a praying devout Muslim who'd undergone some kind of moral aptitude.

"Why would Carlita leave in the middle of the night without informing you and your men, Lieutenant?" he inquired.

"I wish I knew," said Dex.

"Do you suspect any foul play?"

"I can't say for sure. No one knew they were helping us. But I do have my concerns."

"My cousin says you came here because of the information you discovered in La aldea de los leonés."

"My platoon was conducting a covert mission when we went into your village. We were conducting a search of the residence when I stumbled across your message about the CROP and the file you processed onto the microchips."

"You took the file?"

"Unfortunately, yes. But I believe this information can help us. That it can give us the answers to the things we don't know."

Carlos retorted, "You have traveled all this way after infiltrating my village to assassinate me. Now you're asking for the answers to your dilemma and my help to remove you from it."

"You must understand, Mr. Tagola, we were deployed to Colombia under mysterious circumstances. We were brainwashed by officials from the government. Carlita and her partner Adolfo explained to us that when we arrived in South America, we were there working the Colombian task force agency. I didn't know anything about this until I saw those strange letters on your computer. I snapped me out of some kind of trance. Parts of my memory are still missing. Your sister told us Carlito, and his brother's partner Manuel, were working with us too. When they were killed in that warehouse, I promised Carlita I would do whatever I could to help her hunt down that FBI agent who set them up—Alex Weiss."

Carlos looked at Hector when he said the FBI agent's name.

"This man you mentioned, agent Weiss. He has other enemies besides us now. The Chinese syndicate society of Triads in Asia are angered by the cargo they lost in the Black Sea."

"His name was in the documents you left in the bunker. That's why I came here. I need to know everything you can tell me about the CROP."

Carlos looked at him thoughtfully again, then spoke. "What do you know about the Knights Templar, Lieutenant?"

"I've heard of them."

"What about The Order of the Quest, Knights Matta, Skull and Bones, the Jason Society, the Illuminati, the Bilderberg Group, the Council on Foreign Relations?"

Dex replied, "I've heard rumors about all of them. Back in the U.S. There was this one episode I saw on the History channel about how some of them supposedly gather in Bohemian Grove to meet in secret."

"Ever hear any rumors about the CROP, or see them on this History channel of which you speak?"

"No."

"That's because unlike the other orders, they have never been exposed. To the rest of the world, they are unknown, except by the people closely aligned within their ranks."

"You left a message on your computer that said something about the protocol," Dex inquired.

"Yes, it is perhaps the only factor those other fraternities have in common with the CROP. The idea of it has existed for centuries. Its effect is only determined by certain elements within their succeeding generations. They conjure up designed agendas which can change form depending on the era of the time. What their aiming for in this century is to crush western democracy and all of humanity's ties to religion, family, and nation. Whether you chose to acknowledge the examples by the old regimes of the Third Reich and the communist Soviet Union or not. What they want is the implementation of a one world government with one dictator surrounded by other wealthy elites they will put in key positions to help him maintain governorship over the rest of the nations and the billions of inhabitants they consider lower class citizens."

"They want to take over the world!" Dex stated.

"The notation of it certainly isn't the first of its kind, Lieutenant. During the reign of Julius Cesar, the Romans succeeded in bringing almost the entire world under their rule when they set out on this conquest centuries ago. The only dictator who came close to that feat in modern times was Hitler. He initiated that attempt on the flawed premises that Germany was the supreme Arian nation. Five years from now they are going to unleash in the U.S. what they took from the playbook of both men."

"Why the U.S.?" Dex asked.

"It is considered the most powerful nation in the world. They also see white privilege there. So, they figure they can utilize that same propaganda Hitler started in Germany, preaching a white nationalistic movement to seduce the minds of the citizens to topple the political parties as he did, before he replaced them with his own. Surely, you must have seen that documentary on your History Channel . . ."

"I have," said Dex.

"Then perhaps you should pay closer attention to the current events unfolding in your country. The divide between the two major parties is steadily widening. There are segments of the conservative society and congressional congress being targeted right now, because the CROP sees them as the perfect platform to launch the propaganda of their protocol."

"You're talking about what happened in Europe in the 1940's. This is the twenty-first century. That won't happen again."

"Don't be dismissive, Lieutenant. You know as well as I do that wars between men are fought for land and women and wealth. Humans have this tendency to be selfish. The desire for some men to divide and conquer to dominate other men has always existed. We live in this brutally violent world with generational changes. And when one generation changes from the former. New ideologies and laws that may rise with them to create new times."

"You said the protocol went back centuries. Can you be more specific about that?" asked Dex.

"The CROP's protocol is merely a state of mind born out of ancient western philosophies. In the 14th, 15th, 16th renaissance period, philosophers like Socrates, Plato, Machiavelli contributed greatly to the rebirth of learning in Europe. They were brilliant thinkers. But there are some people who find their writings questionable, and others distorted by segments of people who chose to pick out certain paragraphs to discriminate against and oppress others. For instance, Aristotle reportedly once articulated, 'It can be more certain that every man in slavery is born in slavery, and that men are by no means equal naturally, but some are born for slavery, and others dominion.'"

"Aristotle said that?" Dex muttered.

Carlos replied, "Words have a profound effect, Lieutenant. On the other hand, philosophers like Thomas Hobbs and British philosopher John Locke who succeeded those earlier thinkers, introduced theories to the contrary. Locke wrote that people were indeed equal and had a right to life, liberty, and possession of property. In fact, his theory was considered the forerunner to the U.S. constitution. But that means nothing to the CROP. They will continue the trend of conjuring up any distortions they can utilize to convince targeted segments of society that they are more socially entitled than the rest of the world."

"Surely you must know the identities of the people behind this order?" Dex asked.

"Yes. They go by the names of Eleanor Queensberry, Edward Kingstone, Julian Bishoppontiz, Arthur Knighthood, and Heinrich Rookvaunklaff. Remove those prefixes Queen, King, Bishop, Knight, and Rook from their last names. And their actual names become Eleanor Berry, Edward Stone, Julian Pontiz, Arthur Wood, and Heinrich Vaunklaff."

"Why do they choose to use those chess prefixes?" asked Dex.

"Because it's a game they've played since they were youths. They are very skillful at it. Only they no longer take their play seriously with board games. For them, the entire world is a global chess match. They are the major royal pieces. And everyone beneath them they see as nothing more than pawns to be governed and exploited."

"If this is really some sick global game to them, they won't win!" Dex exclaimed.

"In some respects, they already have," Carlos replied.

"How is that?"

"Just look at what's happening in the U.S. and other nations. Chaos! You said you were brainwashed. I'm not surprised by that. There are millions of people who don't understand this type of cognitive training of the human mental faculties. They go about their lives never really knowing just how much they are being brainwashed by their governments, political campaign officials, even commercials that often get them to think and buy into whatever they want them to. The CROP's agenda is clear. They know how to play the race card to maintain the status quo for the rich and keep the privileged in fear of possibly having to give up their lifestyle of luxuries. This ensures them the races stay divided, accustomed to their sperate unequal worlds—unable to identify, unite, even understand each other. Right now, there are nationalist movements being pushed throughout Europe by their followers. They are hoping this populace will gain momentum and spill over into the United States. Because they have chosen a candidate named Henry Tilkerson to replace your president . . ."

"Henry Tilkerson! You mean the billionaire CEO of Tilkerson Tech Enterprise?"

"You've heard of him."

"Who hasn't? His face is always on TV, in magazines, newspapers."

"Should he ever become elected president, Lieutenant, there's no doubt he will do their bidding. And he will add to the seeds of discourse that are currently being planted in your country as we speak."

Carlos's cell phone went off when he finished talking. He dug it out and answered it.

"Yes, this is Carlos," he said to the party of the line. "What can I do for you?" He paused for a moment, then said, "I'm sorry to hear about your brother, Mr. Razzoli. Yes, I gave your brother Augustine my word I would deliver the item. Just tell me where you want it shipped." Carlos waited until the party replied, then said, "No problem. I will arrange it right away. Good day, Señor Razzoli."

Carlos hung up and looked at Dex. The quiet African guy standing behind them with Hector approached him in haste.

"Carlos, I just got a call from one of the intel contacts. It was about your sister Carlita Perez. The agents of the CROP have her in their custody," he stated.

Dex muttered, "They took them from the hotel!"

Carlos's face tightened; his eyes turned like razors. "Where she is?" he demanded.

The man in the white turban responded, "She's somewhere in England. But they have not tracked the specific location."

"Tell them to keep trying," Carlos ordered. Then he looked at his cousin. "Hector, gather the men. Prepared the planes. We're going to England!"

Part Thirteen
Let Freedom Ring

CHAPTER SEVENTY

Washington, DC

The audience of protestors who showed up at the Lincoln Memorial numbered in the thousands. They were there to support the People's March.

Rashida Underwood wasted no time when she stepped up to the podium. The civil rights activist was a guest speaker. She waved to the multitudes as they cheered heroically. Then she made a quick adjustment to the mic and shouted at the top of her lungs.

"What do we want, people?"

The crowd chanted, "JUSTICE! JUSTICE! JUSTICE!"

"When do we want it?"

"NOW!"

"That's right!" she shouted. Then began her speech. "I know all of you are tired of asking yourselves that same age-old question of how we keep ending up in the Capital talking about the same old issues of discrimination, police misconduct, racism, especially in the wake of the many rallies and marches our nation have witness through the decades. But this is the twenty-first century, people. And there is no doubt in my mind that many of us already know the answer to why we must keep on coming back here. It's because of the inability of our leaders to produce real laws that will produce real change. Haven't we expressed to them what want? We have given them proposals for laws we feel will protect all citizens across this country from unjustified shootings by bad police officers and put an end to the domestic terrorism often initiated by hate groups. We have demanded the kind of prison reform bills that we know will help shrink the high rates of mass incarceration and sentencing disparities between the races. But instead of the people seeing legislative action. What we see in Washington now days are more scandals being put on the table than bills. These are bad times. What this country needs are collective resistance and healing. We can no longer be complacent with political talking points. When these changes in policies are prolonged and pushed aside. What we see is a green light for zero tolerance policing tactics and mandatory sentencing laws to continue wreaking havoc on deprived communities of color across the nation. There are fathers and mothers disappearing off the streets of their neighborhoods. They see their children being charged as adults. Think of the men, women, and children who have been hauled off in the back of police cars and separated from their families. Tomorrow they will wake up inside some jail cells and detention centers and prisons where their voices go unheard. But as we stand here today their voices will be heard. We will be their voices for tomorrow and beyond. And we will continue our demands for change. What is time for, people?"

"CHANGE! CHANGE! CHANGE!"

"I have read the report released by the CCA, the Corrections Corporation of America, in 2000, people."

"BOOOOOOOO!"

"Yeah, I know. You feel just like I did when I read the blueprint in this report. It was born out of the wide range of laws passed in the 1990's. Many states who saw their big-name auto factories going overseas began to replace them with an industrial buildup of penal housing facilities across the country which has ultimately become the hallmark of new industries in the western hemisphere. Now isn't that a pimp game being played? You're probably asking what Rashida Underwood means by that. Let me start with our very government, who went after young, African American, low-level drug dealers in the 90's, and called it a war on drugs. Except the objective all along was creating a pimp game. A pimp game disguise in the form of drug forfeiture laws that authorized police departments and task force agencies to increase their rates of arrests and collect the properties and hard-earned cash of these low-level drug dealers pretty much in the same fashion as prostitute who gives up her earnings to a street pimp! The only real difference is that our legislator calls it repossession through the forfeiture act. A street pimp calls it checking it in! And what happens to all the bling and tricked luxury cars and finances of the big drug dealer checks in after his arrest? Most of his property is sold off at auctions. The profits and any confiscated cash combined are used to buy more police cars, equipment, to more academies, more jails, detention centers, and prisons for him and other drug dealers. The drug dealer is essentially paying the bill for his own demise when he's getting pimped!"

"We love you, Rashida!" someone shouted from the audience.

She smiled and shouted back, "And I love you! The time has come for us to reevaluate our circumstances. And we must continue to stand up for what we want. Now, what do want!"

The crowd replied, "JUSTICE! JUSTICE! JUSTICE!"

Part Fourteen
The End Games

CHAPTER SEVENTY-ONE

New York

"**W**inston, I told you to call me when your flight landed back in the U.S. Now, where are you?"

Bedford replied, "Sorry about the delay. I'm on my way to the hotel right now, Mr. Knightwood."

"You better be. We will be waiting for you in the parking lot across the street."

"What's up with the change?" Bedford asked. "I thought we were meeting at the hotel."

"Just meet us in the parking garage on tier two, parking space T-25."

Winston Bedford disconnected. As his driver passed through Times Square, he glanced out the window of the limousine observing the construction workers, commuters, joggers, cyclists, and businesspeople going about their daily routines with no idea how often their lives and movements were being tracked. If they only knew how much the technological advances of their computers, flat screens, audio systems, smart phones, smart cars, smart homes, Facebook, Instagram, made it accessible for the alphabet agencies like his and others to not only to surveil but program whole populations over wider geographical locations around the globe.

The secret was well kept. But when the driver pulled into the parking garage across from the Golden Hotel. He put his thoughts back on the meeting. The driver took him to the second level. Arthur Knightwood and Henry Tilkerson were waiting inside of Lincoln Continental that was parked in an obscure corner of the parking garage. When he pulled up, the chauffeur of the Lincoln got out to open the rear door for him. Soon as he climbed into the back seat, Arthur started with his first question.

"Got any updates for on what Pitrakov plans to do to help us with the election campaign?"

"They're working on it. They have their people in place," said Bedford.

Henry Tilkerson chimed in, "My conversation with Mr. Pitrakov ended better than I expected. I'm going to do some really big things working with this guy!"

"Surely, he must feel the same. Your confidence is good. Don't lose it," muttered Bedford. Then he coughed hard.

"Thought you were going to get that checked out," said Arthur. He passed him his own handkerchief.

"It's nothing. I'm fine."

Arthur went silent as he stared at him. Bedford was blowing his nose. But he could feel his eyes on him. He prepared himself for what he expected to confront him with next.

"Sebastain Korkov's is dead, Winston," he muttered finally. "We lost a good knight."

"But we took care of Augustine Razzoli. He's no longer a problem for you. Right?"

"Yes. You got rid of one problem, but you created another one. The council is not happy that the chameleon left that home alive. He must be found and eliminated."

"I understand," said Bedford. "But I had to do some checking to find out just how much he posed a threat to you," Bedford stated. "You should have informed me Mr. knightwood. Because I remember when the chameleon entered the training camp. In those years you never told me he was the son of the Corsican. Not once did you ever mention that he'd survived the Knight's attack. So that's why you wanted Sebastain to go to Italy with him."

Arthur rebuked harshly, "It wasn't your place to know about this matter! The only matter you need to be concerned about is getting rid of him. We no longer need his service. Now get it done!"

Bedford saw the veins in his forehead and neck. A fury burned into the old man's face. He backed off. Arthur never went anywhere without armed security. And they were probably poised for action inside the pair of SUVs parked a couple of lanes over.

"I will get it done, Mr. Knightwood," he conceded. Then switched the subject. "We've picked up a trail on the three Navy SEALS from a source who came to us with the sister of Carlos Tagola. We have her in custody. I'm almost certain he will surface now."

"Good to hear. There must be no negotiation for her release unless it includes the file."

"I understand, Mr. Knightwood," said Bedford.

"I hope you do this time, Winston. Because the others will accept nothing other than a successful result. You can go now."

Bedford glanced at Henry Tilkerson's as he stepped out the back seat and shut the door back.

"Think he'll really get it done this time Arthur?" asked Henry.

Arthur replied, "Doesn't matter. He's done, Henry. There is nothing further I can do to protect him."

"He is American, like us," said Henry.

"Yes. But the others have no use for him. And they have issued the royal order."

CHAPTER SEVENTY-TWO

Colombia

The driver guided the Lexus through the streets of Cali's metropolitan district, while Ortega sat in the back seat discussing business as usual with agent Alex Weiss.

"I need another shipment. You must set it up," Weiss said to him.

Ortega heard the desperation in his voice. In fact, he was feeling his own anxiety.

"Why would I do that, señor?" he replied. "You lost the cargo in Medellin. This business is big time. The triads had a lot of investment wrapped up in that supply."

"Hey, that's nothing to worry about. Let me handle the Chinese," said Weiss.

"You said Colonel Burke had everything under control. You said nothing would go wrong. But I lost billions when that freighter went down in Medellin."

"We'll make up for it. We can always use another shipping port."

"That's easy for you to say. But the colonel sent more American troops to back to La aldea de los leonés. Hector Colon was cornered. How could they let him get away!"

"Ortega, several America helicopters were shot down over that village. We had to pull our soldiers out. We had no choice. It was a covert effort to apprehend him. This was the second time we went in without authorization from the president or congress. They are already asking a lot of questions about Operation Lion's Den. Should any more word of this get back to the states, a probe would surely be the result. We can't risk any link being drawn between us. If that happens, I will have to cut off all the aid you are receiving from us. And that would mean I can no longer guarantee your protection. Now, I need you to do this shipment."

Agent Weiss removed some papers from the pocket of his suitcoat. "See this?"

"What is it?"

"It's the legal binding document that details the moratorium on the warrant the United States District Attorney has issued for your arrest on international drug trafficking charges."

"I see. So, you're going to hold that over my head," said Ortega, giving him a contemptuous glare.

"Hey, you agree to these concessions. We really need that dope. If you decline, I'm certain you know that other people besides myself will be just as disappointed. I advise you to make the right choice today. The D.A. has been quite anxious to execute that warrant."

Weiss stuffed the papers back into his pocket. Ortega came to his senses. "Okay, I'll arrange it. How much do you need?"

"The same load as before. Perhaps a port won't be sufficient this time. I think we'll use submarines," Weiss said.

"Wait a minute," Ortega cut in. "We're not neighbors to the south of the U.S. border. I'm not going to use make-shift submarines to move this shipment like they do in Mexico. This is South America compadre!"

"Who said anything about using makeshift subs? I'm talking about using some of the finest American submarines our military have to offer!"

Ortega's expression changed. And so did his tune. "Now that's a bit better. I'll make sure you get what you want. But the deal must come with the assurance that the warrant goes away. And I want a full guarantee that you will help me take over all Tagola's territory."

Agent Weiss reached and shook hands with Ortega. As the Lexus glided down a wide avenue, he peered out the window at the pedestrians walking down the sidewalks and standing outside the storefronts. It was a sunny day. Nothing appeared to be out of the ordinary, he heard motorcycle engines and glanced into the rearview window.

He saw two men on motorcycles speeding up behind them. The Uzi's he noticed hanging off their shoulder straps alarmed immediately.

He whipped his head around to look at Ortega. "I think we got a tail," he muttered.

Ortega glanced into the mirror. The men on the bikes suddenly roared up on the side of the car and started shooting into the vehicle. The driver took a bullet in the back of the head and lost control of the car. Soon he slumped over with his feet on the accelerator and the car sped up and crashed into a streetlamp.

The bikes zoomed up the street. Ortega opened the door and staggered bleeding out of the back seat.

He was clutching a Heckler MP5. When he glanced back at agent Weiss, his head was resting against the window with splattered blood and brain dripping down the glass. The helmeted men on the motorbikes came roaring back. One of them skidded and stopped directly in front of him as he lay gurgling. He tried to lift the Heckler but was too weak by the loss of blood.

"No me Mata's! Don't kill me! he pleaded. No me matas!"

The man on the motorcycle raised the shield on his helmet. Ortega stared into the beady looking slanted eyes of the Asian assassin he saw staring back at him. A second later the man put him out his misery with one last rapid burst from his Uzi.

CHAPTER SEVENTY-THREE

Germany

Heinrich returned home to Germany. He thought it might help unclog his mind from the mounting problems he and the others were faced with. The Colombian still demanded more money from their banks. The amount increased. His last demand called for five billion. And the Stasis still had no idea to where all the money was being rerouted.

At 7:30 am he was awake, sitting inside his study when his butler walked in with a breakfast tray for him. The house was quiet. He liked it that way whenever got up to read the morning's paper. But the sound of the doorbell ringing interrupted him. He got up to answer it.

The butler gestured for him to stay. "I'll get the door, sir. Enjoy your breakfast," he said to him in German.

The butler walked to the door and opened it. A delivery man standing outside with a FedEx box.

"Guten morg, Good morning," he stated.

The butler replied, "Guten morg."

"Is Mr. Rookvaunklaff home?" the man asked. "I have a package for him."

"Ya. But he has a personal delivery person who notifies us from the gate. He never comes to the residence. How did you get in here?" the butler inquired.

His eyes swayed past the shoulder of the man to the entrance of the security gate. He kept looking suspiciously until he saw several men from Heinrich's security staff on the ground. His heart started throbbing. Then he saw bullet holes in the windshield of the Mercedes Benz parked on the drive. Both of Heinrich's security men in the front seat were slumped over as if they were asleep.

The only thing he heard next from the delivery man was Soot! Soot! The muffled noise had come from a silencer hidden inside the FedEx box the delivery man was holding. He had buried two rounds into his midsection. The butler saw the two small holes in the box as he clutched his stomach crumpled to the floor inside the doorway.

Heinrich heard the hard thump after he hit the floor. He shouted from the study. "Ivan, is everything all right? Who's at the door?"

When he got answer he started to get up. Before he took one step, the delivery man appeared at the entrance of his study. Then he slowly walked in with the gun pointing at Heinrich in full view.

Heinrich stood motionless, eyes wide with shock by the face he saw before him.

"What do you want. How did you get in here . . .? Where's Ivan?" he asked.

The delivery man heard rustling coming from the adjacent room and pulled out another gun.

Heinrich heard it too and muttered, "It's only my wife. She's sleeping."

The delivery man moved across the floor and saw the woman in bed.

Heinrich said, "Look, if it's money you want, my safe is behind the painting there."

He gestured in the general direction of it. But the delivery man didn't look.

He retorted, "I don't want your money, Mr. Rookvaunklaff. Or should I call you Heinrich Vaunklaff?"

Stunned, Heinrich replied, "Haven't we met before?"

"Not formally, until today. But I'm sure you know me as Chello Fransis..."

"The Chameleon," mumbled Heinrich.

"Yes. The son of the Corsican you and your associates sent the four knights to murder some thirty years ago. Only, they killed my entire family. Remember?"

Heinrich didn't get the chance to answer. Chello put a round in his chest. The old German jerked and sat back down in the chair. Deceased.

CHAPTER SEVENTY-FOUR

Moscow

"**P**resident Pitrakov, the CROP's problems pose a real threat to us. The other orders agree. The situation must be handled properly. They want your full cooperation."

Pitrakov stared at the minister of foreign affairs thoughtfully. News of Heinrich Rookvaunklaff's demise had reached him within hours. Now he had a decision to make. And with CROP deemed a liability. There was not much to think about.

"They shall have my cooperation. But the American . . . Henry Tilkerson. He's a valuable asset to the federation. Make sure you convey to them that the candidate's protection is vital to our national security. Send him away for a time. To any country where he can lay low on an extended vacation."

The minister responded, "I will arrange for his departure from America right away, Mr. President. What measure shall we take with the rest of the council members?"

Pitrakov turned and looked at the General in charge of the Russian navy. "Where's the yacht?"

"We have a current satellite tracking in the north Atlantic. We're keeping a close eye on its movements, Mr. Pitrakov."

"Are we prepared for a plan of action, General?"

"We have military readiness in the area. But naval comms have reported another marine vessel within the vicinity."

"Has the traffic been identified?"

"Yes. A submarine our naval comms reported as an Italian class striker. Could be just a drill they're conducting."

"What's the sub's course and speed?"

"At last report it was at zero-one-five degrees on forty knots. It's heading further out to sea. It's heading in the general direction of the yacht's stationary location."

Pitrakov pondered the information for a moment. Then he said, "That's no drill they're conducting. Seems to me they're conducting surveillance. Send a message to your naval officer to pull our hold of our sub's stationary location. We'll keep them on standby. But if this is what I think it is, we won't have to take a course of action after all."

CHAPTER SEVENTY-FIVE

North Atlantic Ocean

"We have to go through with the plan. The Russians already have things in motion," said Julian.

Lady Eleanor retorted with skepticism. "Don't let your emotions get the best of you mate. Augustine's treachery of betrayal and Heinrich's assassination didn't look good. The others could very well see this as a problem for us that we can't get rid of. And I don't trust that bloody rascal Pitrakov."

Edward cut in, "Eleanor, I think Julian has a good point. The Russians are major players. The move we've made can't easily be taken back. Besides, Pitrakov did say he would help us."

Lady Eleanor glared scornfully at him. "I see neither of you are really considering the bloody position we're in. Pitrakov is cunning. He won't jeopardize himself by taking a different stance against his own fraternity if they feel we have been compromised. As far as they are concerned any exposure of us might affect them down the road. They will destroy us. Therefore, I say we make the first move. Because if we don't, the game is over for us!"

Lady Eleanor sat back in her chair and studied the two men's faces. They had been going back and forth about it for hours until Edward finally caved.

"What is it you have in mind, Eleanor?" he inquired.

"We take a vote right now to remove the Russian president Dominik Pitrakov from power," she answered.

"We can't. Arthur isn't here. He must take the vote with us," said Julian.

Lady Eleanor contested. "Not this time. We can't wait for his vote. Besides, I'm sure he would vote in favor of this. Given the situation we're in. Do you really expect Arthur would have any disagreement?"

Neither of the men responded. She was right. Arthur wouldn't disagree. Dominik Pitrakov had enough influence with other world leaders, syndicates, and secret fraternities, for them to consider everything she warned them about.

"We must activate the agents we have inside the Russian federation," Lady Eleanor added.

"It'll be a risky task, my Lady," Edward muttered.

"My dear, it won't be as difficult as you think. I hear Mr. Pitrakov has a taste for fine Russian cuisines . . ."

"So, what are you suggesting?" asked Julian.

Lady Eleanor responded with bitterness. "I hear he's very fond of biological agents. Perhaps a little bit of toxins mixed with his dessert. Let him taste a bloody dose!"

CHAPTER SEVENTY-SIX

Miami

Winston Bedford couldn't stop pacing the floor inside the beach front condo he checked into with a couple of agents who accompanied him on his trip to Florida for security. The men were in the living room. One of them was on the couch reading the *Miami Herald*. The other was sitting in a chair with his face in a *Reader's Digest*. Bringing them along wasn't ideal, but he had to think about the Chameleon, as well as the call he got from old man Knightwood the following day to inform him the council wanted to meet with him on the Queen Jewel two days from now.

All at once, he stopped pacing and glanced at the agent reading the newspaper. "Hey, Mason. Call up room service. Order a pizza and something to drink."

"I'm on it."

The agent pulled out his phone and made the call. Bedford stepped out to the balcony to get some fresh air. He couldn't help but to wonder why Arthur said it had to do with Heinrich Rookvaunklagff, but that he didn't want to go into the details about it. As he stood gazing out at the panoramic view of the ocean water washing up on the shoreline, his phone started thrilling.

"This is Bedford speaking," he answered.

The caller spoke through the line with urgency. "Director Bedford, I've got a development. It came late, but four hours ago, three of the knight's men were spotted debarking from a plane at an airport in Boston. A group of KGB agents flew on separate planes. But they're all working together."

"How many KGB?"

"Fifteen."

"I should have been informed the knights men were in the U.S. Why are they here?"

"This is personal. They are after the Chameleon."

"They're wasting their time. Chello wouldn't be in the U.S. hiding out. But I agree this has Russian earmarks. I suppose they want payback for what happened to Sebastian. Well, I hope they find him. It'll take the load off my plate. If you get anything further, you know what to do. I'll be in Miami for a couple of days."

"Sure thing, director."

Bedford turned and glanced over his shoulder at the two CIA agents after he finished talking. When he observed them talking with the gentlemen who showed up with the pizza and drink. His attention returned to the ocean water washing up on the sandy shoreline in the distance. Watching the waves gave him a clam feeling. But then he heard a noise coming from the living room. Before he could spin on his heels, he heard something else. A man's voice behind him.

"Turn around really slowly. Keep your hands where I can them, Mr. Bedford."

Bedford did as he was told. A harsh command like that meant there was possibly a hand clutching a gun behind him too. He turned slowly, only to see the man who was talking to the two agents a few seconds ago aiming a silencer at him. The room service guy was standing inside the doorway to the balcony dressed in a white employee uniform issued by the condo's personnel service. He was a stranger. That face he hadn't seen before. But that voice was unmistakable.

"Chello . . . it's you," he stammered nervously.

"Yes. It's me," the assassin confirmed.

Bedford gazed past his shoulders. The two agents were lying on the living room floor.

"I . . . I was expecting to get a call from you after that Razzoli assignment. Why didn't you make contact?"

Chello ignored his question as took a step towards him. Then he asked his own question.

"You have no accent. How long did it take you to perfect that American English?" he asked rhetorically.

Bedford swallowed hard. "I don't understand what you mean by that?"

"Oh, I'm certain you do. I just wonder how the director of American CIA and his president would react if they both knew you were a Russian KGB double agent planted in their intelligence agency . . ."

"I don't where you got that from, but it's nothing but lies!" Bedford retorted.

Chello patted him down and collected the 9mm he had in his shoulder holster.

"Let's see who's the liar. Get in here!" he ordered.

Bedford walked back inside.

"Put your hand on the table!"

The CIA man placed his hand flat on the surface of the table. Chello put a silent round in it. Bedford bellowed at the top of his lungs when the bullet tore through the flesh.

"You . . . You shot my *thumb* off!" he cried.

"Lie again, I take off the other one. Understand!"

"Yes."

"That means I want the truth on everything I want to know . . ."

"All right. I'll tell you what you want," said Bedford.

"Good. Let's begin with the four knights you sent to Corsica thirty years ago to murder my father. It was the CROP who issued that hit. Right?"

Bedford groaned. "Yes. I was just doing what they told me. Your father was a former member of the council. He—"

"I know all about that!" Chello interrupted. "I know about the information he had on them. I know about Eleanor Berry, Heinrich Vuanklaff, Arthur Wood, Julian Pontiz, and Edward Stone. What I want to know is why he split from them with this information."

Bedford replied, "Your father was a brilliant man. But they discovered he was making business deals behind their backs. He was also milking millions from their banks. It went on for years. Eleanor Berry's parent company lost major stock for a time. The Japanese refused to reimburse the profits they made off the company. After they removed your father from the council, the Japanese businessmen he was working with started washing up on the shorelines torn to pieces by killer whales. Your father figured they were coming for him too. He was threatening to disclose their secrets. They issued the order to silence him."

"Just like they issued the order for Sebastain Korkove to silence me. And you sent him just like you sent the knights to Corsica!"

Bedford gazed down at his hand grimacing with blood dripping everywhere.

"Let me explain . . ."

"There is no explanation you can give me. The only thing I want from you is the precise location where I can find the council."

Chello grabbed a towel draped over a chair and tossed it on the table. The CIA man quickly wrapped his hand with it, surprised he was still standing in front of the Chameleon alive. The scheduled appointment for him to meet with them in two days immediately came to mind. He was reluctant to go on that vessel alone anyway, he thought. Lady Eleanor and Arthur had threatened him. What did he care about giving up their location. If it meant saving his own life, he had no problem selling out the CROP!

He looked at the Chameleon with a grim bitterness for his employers in mind.

"I have an appointment to meet with them forty-eight hours from now," he muttered. "I can take you straight to them, Chello. We're going to need a boat, but I know the exact place they will be!"

Part Fifteen
Rise of the New Populace

CHAPTER SEVENTY-SEVEN

Japan

Right after Arthur Knightwood and Henry Tilkerson got off their flight from America, the Japanese chauffeur waiting at the limousine opened the rear door for them.

"Welcome to Tokyo," he stated.

As they climbed into the back seat Arthur replied, "Glad to be here."

"Where to, Mr. Knightwood?" the chauffeur asked.

"Take us to the penthouse," the old man stated.

Henry knew the place. Arthur's exquisite penthouse was located on the hundredth floor of one of the tallest skyscrapers in Tokyo. To the pedestrian sightseer gazing up it was dizzyingly amazing. It took almost forty minutes for them to get there from the airport. When they walked inside the penthouse the incredible views of every square inch of space hadn't changed since Henry's last visit.

Arthur was unusually quiet during the entire plane flight. But after he poured himself brandy and sat down across from his billionaire friend on the sofa, the first words he spoke came out calmly.

"Henry, how are feeling, my friend?"

"Actually fine. I thought a nice vacation would be good anyway."

"Good, good," Arthur replied. "Because we'll be here for an extended stay. It's much safer."

Henry looked at him puzzled. "Safer?"

Arthur took a drink and replied. "I invited you to come along on this trip because I had a conversation with Dominik Pitrakov a few days ago. There's going to be some changes taking place, Henry."

"Is this about Bedford?"

"Winston will be meeting with the other council members . . ."

"We should be there."

"Not this time. It's over for him, Henry. And, quite frankly, it's over for the others, too . . ."

"What?"

"Their time is up, Henry."

"Arthur, they're ranking members of our council . . ."

"There will be others to replace them. Pitrakov and other world leaders and top elites are feeling the pressure. They must go, Henry. The agreement was sealed among them. The decision can't be reversed."

"I don't understand," said the billionaire.

"How could you not? Heinrich was assassinated in a room right next to where his wife was sleeping. She never heard a thing. If someone could get to him so easily like that, it means the secrecy of the order has been compromised."

"But we're members of the council. That means we have a problem as well!" Henry exclaimed.

"Quite the contrary, my friend," Arthur said. "Pitrakov is interested in what we can do to help his country from America. They won't touch us. Without us, Henry, they have nothing to gain."

Arthur grabbed a couple of cigars from the container on the table between them. After he handed one to Henry, he lit one up in his hand and took a drag from it.

"It's just you and me now, Henry," he stated, exhaling the smoke. "Consider the Russians our allies now. We'll be working very closely with the Kremlin to continue establishing the protocol's rise of the new populace movement in America. Pitrakov and I have discussed the referendums you must begin establishing once you become president. This will be necessary to strengthen the branch of executive power. Populace leaders supporting the protocol in Germany, France, New Zealand, England, Poland, Sweden, and elsewhere will expect your alignment and total contribution to the kind of propaganda movement they are leading in Europe to tear away at the foundation of democracy until it crumbles."

"What specifically will the referendums consist of?" asked Henry.

Arthur replied, "Your aim will be to persuade your base of followers to call for changes in the structure of social institutional order. Win their support and you can start to roll back any number of domestic and international concessions. For example, fracking restrictions, the Iran nuclear agreement, the EPA protection regulations, TPP, Planned Parenthood. You'll be able to increase the tariffs on Mexico, get rid of SSI, toss out DACA, put a stop to foreign immigration with the implementation of travel bands. And what did I say will help you succeed at persuading your followers leading up to that campaign?"

Henry answered eagerly, "Propagate an Alt-Right agenda with the aim of shifting public opinion over the left's lack of solutions for the issues of the economy, law and order, migrants . . ."

"Know what else will be your breadwinner, Henry?"

"What?"

"You're going to promise to build them a great big wall at the border of the United States and Mexico!"

"Now that one I never imagined, Arthur. A wall?"

Arthur replied, "Yes, Henry. And you can build it as high as you want!"

CHAPTER SEVENTY-EIGHT

North Atlantic Ocean

From the mainland of Wexford, Ireland, Winston Bedford took off in a speedboat heading in the direction of the Queen Jewel. The Chameleon remained hidden beneath the canvas at the back of the boat. He'd cut a small hole allowing him to watch every move the CIA agent made. As they neared the vicinity the council directed him to, Beford held up his binoculars. He spotted the yacht bobbing up and down on the waves two miles away.

"We're almost there," he said to the Corsican assassin.

Chello muttered back, "You know what to do when we arrive. Try anything crazy and I will put a bullet in you!"

Bedford didn't say a word. He had no doubt the Chameleon would follow through on the threat. With nothing but a vast ocean around him, he knew it was better to follow his instructions. When they got to the yacht all he had to do was act normally in front of the CROP. The assassin would take his rage out on the boat people and spare his life for helping him.

With the binoculars she held up, Lady Eleanor spotted the speedboat slashing through waves towards them.

"It's Bedford. He's alone," she said to Edward and Julian.

"Where's Arthur?" Edward inquired suspiciously. "He said he would be coming with him."

"We will find out when he gets here," Lady Eleanor responded.

When the boat approached the side of the yacht, her son Phillip spoke to the CIA man from the main deck. "Mother and the others are down in the cabin waiting for you. Please, come aboard Mr. Bedford."

Bedford got out of the boat and scaled the ladder. The young man escorted him to the cabin. When he walked in Eleanor, Julian, and Edward were seated at the polished conference table. Lady Eleanor was the first person to address him.

"Hello, Mr. Bedford. Any reason why Arthur isn't with you?" she asked.

"Mr. Knightwood phoned me shortly after my plane landed in Wessex. He said he had a business matter that came up. That he had an important errand to run. I thought he would have informed you," the CIA man replied.

"Well, he hasn't," said Lady Eleanor.

She stared at Bedford with those cold penetrating eyes for half a minute. The atmosphere inside the cabin suddenly got warm. He loosened his tie. He thought it might be the humidity in the night air. But it wasn't. It was his nerves."

"Have a seat, Mr. Bedford. I'm interested in what you can tell us about the Colombian and the soldiers," said Lady Eleanor.

Bedford sat down and responded, "I realize the soldiers and Tagola have managed to elude us. But we know they're in Africa . . ."

Lady Eleanor cut him off. "I find it quite interesting you would say that, Mr. Bedford. A few hours before you came aboard, we received information that came to us from our agents at MI-6. It was about all the money having been transferred into the accounts of the black Colombian. He has been rerouting transfers. But our agents at MI-6 were finally able to trace where the funds are being rerouted to. Would you like to know where all our money is going, Mr. Bedford?"

Bedford replied, "Yes, I would like to know."

Lady Eleanor hissed angrily, "Africa!"

"Africa?"

"Yes. They think there are others. He's asking for a whole lot more now. Did you know about this?"

"No, I didn't."

Eleanor's face twisted into a frown. "You see, that's the reason we're having this meeting, mate. Lately you just haven't produced much for us. And we have a problem with that."

Bedford glanced at Edward and Julian. Although neither said a word, their expressions mirrored the British woman's expressions.

While the meeting was in progress, Lady Eleanor's oldest son searched the speed boat. Had he started at the back he would have easily discovered the Chameleon hiding beneath the canvas. When he began examining the boat's steering equipment, Chello crawled from under the canvas and eased up behind him. He turned at the last minute, but he felt the wind get knocked out of him after a silent bullet tore into his stomach. He dropped down on the seat. Chello rolled him over the side of the boat. Then he scaled up the side on the ladder. When he made it to the deck, he moved along the rail. Ahead of him he spotted two men talking and stopped when a third man approached and got in on the conversation. He presumed they were guards. They were clumsy, too busy laughing and joking to notice him remove his dart gun from his shoulder holster. Within seconds the men were put down with the poisonous darts he expelled from it.

With his silencer in the other hand, he tiptoed across the deck and made his way down the steps leading to the cabin below. When he got to the bottom, he eased next to the right side of the cabin's window. The partial opening in the seam of the curtain allowed him to see the CIA man sitting at the table with three of the council members he immediately recognized from the photographs the old Italian had inside the envelop he gave him. He heard heated voices inside. Bedford looked stressed. Like a small child being scolded by the old woman. Bedford inadvertently glanced at the window and saw the Chameleon peeking in. He acted normal as though he hadn't. But when Chello signaled with a hand gesture. Bedford backed up his chair from the table and stood up with the gun he pulled out.

"Anybody moves I will start shooting!" he warned.

"Put that bloody gun away. You have gone insane!" Lady Eleanor shouted back.

"Insane! You lost your mind a long time ago Eleanor Berry," Bedford said. Then he waved the gun at her two sons standing at the door. "You two, take a seat at the table next to your sick mother!"

The men looked at him as if they might charge at him.

"I'm not gonna ask you again!" Bedford barked.

"Stanley . . . Philip. Do as he said," Lady Eleanor uttered.

The men walked to the table. The minute they sat down, Chello burst inside the cabin with his eyes on the council members—and Bedford too.

"Toss the gun on the floor, Mr. Bedford," he ordered.

Bedford complied and dropped it at his feet.

"Now, back away from it," Chello ordered.

Bedford did as he said. Lady Eleanor recognized the face of the intruder and snarled at the CIA man.

"Bedford, you set us up by bringing this man here?" Eleanor uttered.

Bedford smirked. "I never liked you, Eleanor Berry. And I certainly don't like your threats. You thought I would come aboard this yacht so you could throw me overboard and watch those whales you're obsessed with devour me. Not tonight, whale lady!"

Lady Eleanor started laughing. "You're a bloody fool, Mr. Bedford!"

"Shut up! Why are you laughing. Stop laughing, you old bat!" the CIA man growled.

Eleanor replied, "You're a bloody fool! My intuition tells me that you think once Mr. Fransis there kills us. He's going spare you!"

"It's the council he wants. Not me!"

Lady Eleanor looked Chello in the eyes and continued laughing, until he walked up and let off muffled shots to her left and right. Eleanor flinched and fell silent when her sons flopped out their chairs and dropped on the floor of the cabin with large caliber holes in their heads. Edward and Julian jerked back in their chairs after Chello put holes in their skulls too. Gripped by instant rage and hatred, Eleanor sat there shocked and speechless.

The yacht's underwater sonar monitors started beeping.

Finally, she muttered, "I hope you're bloody satisfied you have avenged your family Mr. Fransis. But's not going to bring them back!"

"What are you waiting for, Chello? Shoot her!" Bedford shouted.

Lady Eleanor looked at the CIA man before her eyes shifted to the sonar monitor. See those little red dots in the monitor there, Mr. Bedford?

Those tiny dots are a pod of killer whales coming this way. You're right. They were called here for you. But it appears the poor Orcas will miss their meal tonight."

She grinned at him.

Bedford blurted, "Chello, shoot her! Shoot that old bat right now!"

Chello turned the dart gun on him. "Wait! I helped you. We had a deal, Chello. It was them who gave the order . . ."

"And you sent the knights!" Chello pulled the trigger twice.

Soot! Soot!

The CIA man dropped to the floor.

Chello turned his focus back to Lady Eleanor. The two of them locked their eyes. All at once, the voice of British navy Captain squawked out a speaker sitting to the sonar monitor.

"Come in, Queen Jewel . . . This is Captain Ryan. This is an emergency alert! I repeat this is an emergency alert!"

Chello waved the silencer at the British woman. "Get up. Answer it!"

Lady Eleanor got up and followed his instruction. "This is Eleanor Queensberry responding from the Queen Jewel. What is your alert, Captain Ryan?"

The navy Captain crackled back the transmission. "Ms. Queensberry, we have been watching the suspicious activity of an Italian Striker submarine thirty miles away from the Queen Jewel. Our intercepts reveal the striker has a military installation locked on your vessel as a target. You must evacuate the vessel immediately! Copy?"

"Affirmative, Captain. Thanks for the warning, mate."

Eleanor looked at the Chameleon and smiled crazily. "Well, lad. Looks like this ends with all of us together. Unless you're man enough to put a bullet right here!" Eleanor pointed defiantly at her forehead. "Just like you did for my sons, you bloody wolf!"

The old woman started laughing. Chello glanced at the graphic screen of the sonar monitor. The tiny red blinking dots were moving steadily towards the yacht's location.

Chello muttered, "That would be too quick for you. I got a little something better in mind for you. Let's go, old lady!"

He grabbed her by the arm and escorted her up to the main deck. When they walked to the side of the yacht, Eleanor peered down at the speed boat.

"So, we're going for a little ride in the boat," she muttered.

Chello replied, "Yeah. Only you'll be going in that one!"

Eleanor glanced at the orange inflatable life raft bobbing on the waves behind the speed boat. A couple of SEALS broke through the surface of the water splashing around it.

She snapped, "You're *not* going to put me in *that* thing!"

"You can take the ladder or fly over the rail. But you're going to get in it!"

Lady Eleanor snatched her hand back when he reached for it. "I'll take the bloody ladder!" she snapped.

Chello scaled down behind her. After she was in the life raft, he released its anchor from the yacht and jumped in the speed boat.

"Looks like the Orcas will not miss their meal after all. So long, whale lady!" he muttered.

Chello sped off quickly to put enough distance between himself and the yacht.

Lady Eleanor suddenly saw the black fins of the killer whales coming straight towards her.

A mile and a half away Chello heard the big explosion behind him. When he glanced back with his binoculars, he saw the surface of the water on fire. He could see where the yacht was blown into oblivion and blankets of burning debris flying out of a thick cloud of smoke billowing into the night sky. The whale lady was nowhere to be seen.

CHAPTER SEVENTY-NINE

Dover, England

On the flight to England, Dex clung to every word Carlos Tagola continued revealing to him about the CROP and its plans.

"You mention this populace issue in the documents," Dex said.

Carlos replied, "Yes. But it's not the first time your country has seen it. Populism rose dramatically in the 1970's out of the cold war to undermine the bases of growth and support for the U.S. government. In time the CROP's privately owned ultra conservative media networks began the full push of their anti-establishment agendas. And they have plenty of other elements they will use to propagate the rise of a new populace-right in the minds of the country's citizens that the system of democracy in your country is broken."

"What does the acronym's CROP even stand for?" Dex inquired curiously.

"CROP stans for Council of the Royal Order Protocol."

"The Royal Order," muttered Dex.

"Yes."

Dex shook his head. Carlos had a wealth of information on the Royal Order. But he also learned the Colombian built up his own secret intelligence gathering service. By the time the plane landed in England, the men and women secretly networking for him around the world already knew the exact place his sister Carlita was being held.

"I have to ask you to allow me and my men to handle the extraction alone," said Dex.

Carlos contested, "They have Carlita. I go! My men go!"

"Think about this. It's not uncommon for SEALS to carryout extraction rescues in small numbers. But if you bring in the brigade, they will easily detect us. And if you get killed in combat? Everything you have on

the CROP will be lost. That could put us all in jeopardy. They're afraid
of what you know."

Carlos went quiet a moment before he replied, "All right. Just bring
my sister back!"

Dex reached out to shake his hand. "We'll get her back. You have my
word."

Carlos and his men departed. Dex and the other SEALS knew they
were on limited time when they dressed in their fatigues, packed their
gear, and set off for the extraction site with their weapons and ammo.

Hours later they were trekking through woods in secluded countryside. When they saw buildings through a clearing ahead, they drew up
close to a fence. The signs on read: KEEP OUT - PRIVATE PROP-
ERTY. Dex and his men cut though it with wire-cutters. When they
heard voices of men exiting one of the buildings they crouched down
out of sight behind bushes and held up the night vision binoculars.

A group of four men came out the building escorting a woman. Dex
zoomed the lens. His pulse quickened, thinking how fortunate they were
to arrive at the right moment for him to see that it was Carlita they were
escorting.

"It's her," he alerted. "Everybody got the visual?"

Sergio, Danny Boy, and Hawk confirmed the visual they had on her
and the CROP agents also. The agents entered the building next door
with her. Three more came out moments later. The men were standing
at the entrance talking. The SEALS took a secure route and moved closer
to the facility. They had grease paint and headsets. The gear and weapons they brought with their M4's included grenades, oracle flares, smoke
bombs, C4. But just for safe keeping, Carlos handed Dex a beacon locator
right before they parted ways.

Dex cased the building's layout. The structure was five stories. All
the windows were tinted. The name Burmaxx Medical Research Lab
was mounted above the electric doors they saw the agents moving in
and out of. The others were waiting for his signal when he motioned
to them. When he scurried across another route, they followed him
around the back of another facility and hid while they contemplated

how they were going to get inside the research lab. They had no idea how many men were on the grounds, nor inside the building Carlita entered. Going undetected was improbable. But when he saw the huge generators behind the building next door, he had a plan.

"Danny Boy . . . Sergio, see those generators? Get some sticks of C4 on them ASAP!"

The two commandos made for the generators and planted sticks of dynamite with a transmission signal that would set off the blast from a detonator. The process only took them ten minutes.

"Everything all set?" Dex asked, upon their return.

"All set," Sergio replied.

Relying on the blast as a deflection was the only alternative. Once the agents rushed out in confusion looking for the source of the commotion. They would breach the building through the safest entrance.

After they made their way around the side of the medical research lab, they stayed there with their backs against the wall. Hawk spotted an agent making rounds when he peeked around the corner. He motioned for everyone to move back. They waited. The minute the agent rounded the corner, Hawk grabbed him by the collar and showed him the K-Bar gun in his hand to silence him.

"Stay quiet," said Dex. "We're here because your buddies have a friend of ours in this building. And you're going to get us inside so we can get her back. Now, tell me where they're holding her!"

Hawk pressed the barrel of his handgun into his forehead.

The man replied, "She's on the third floor, fourth room on the right from the staircase."

Dex pointed at the back door of the facility with his M4. "Open it. Show us the way!" he demanded.

Hawk stepped back; the gun remained aimed at his head. The agent quickly unlocked the door with a key card. When it clicked open, they entered. He led them up to the second floor and down a quite hallway. Passing by the rooms the rooms they saw medical equipment and people lying on hospital beds like they were coma-induced experimental specimens out of a medical horror movie. Dex had no idea how many people knew about these secluded facilities hidden deep in this remote part of England. When they climbed the flight of steps to the third floor, they found themselves walking down another empty silent hallway like the one below.

After they followed the CROP agent to the room where Carlita was being held, Dex motioned for the other SEALS to take up their position. When they were prepared to breach the door, he gave a curt nod to the agent to open it. The hard barrel of Hawk's assault rifle pressed against his back motivated him. When he inserted the key card into the locking mechanism it clicked open. The SEALS burst in with their weapons locked. The men inside—two doctors clad in white sterile lab coats and a pair of CROP agents posted on the other side of the room—were caught off guard by their sudden entry. Carlita was lying on a hospital bed, dazed. One of the doctors standing bedside had a hypodermic needle in her hand.

Dex snapped, "Step away from the bed!"

The doctors backed up. At the sound of his voice Carlita lifted her head and saw him and then other soldiers in the room.

"Lieutenant Jones, get me out of here!" she muttered weakly.

Dex hurried to her side. He glanced at the neurol head brace they put on her. He noticed the wires on it were connected to some kind of neurology machine that monitored brain activity.

"What have they done? Are you all right?" he inquired.

"I will be, once you get me out of here!" she responded.

Hawk, Danny Boy, and Sergio had their eyes fixed on the two CROP agents, when one of the doctors eased back against a table and subtly pressed a silent alarm button.

Dex took the head brace off Carlita and helped her off the bed.

"I promised your brother Carlos I would bring you back!" said Dex. "Don't worry. I'm getting you out of here right now!"

The alarm went off. The hallway started flashing with strobe lights. The two CROP agents went for their guns. They were waiting for the moment. But Sergio and Danny Boy let out a spurt of rounds, dropping both men where they stood.

"Danny Boy, the C4 . . . Do it now!" Dex said.

Danny pulled out the detonator and pressed the button that sent the signal to the transmitters taped to the sticks of dynamite they mounted on the generators outside. The explosions that went off rocked the foundations of the other Burmaxx facilities. By the time they fled the medical research and ran into the woods, the thunderous blast set off a chain reaction. Two out of the four Burmaxx facilities went up in flames as CROP agents poured out the front entrance. Dozens of men started shooting at them. They chased them into the woods. The SEALS and Carlita ran as fast they could, with the agents' bullets biting into the dirt around their feet, chinking, whizzing past their heads.

Carlita felt weak from the drugs the doctors had given her. She was hanging on to Dex's shoulder when another onslaught of rounds came flying at them.

Dex shouted, "Get down!"

Sergio and Danny Boy got caught in a line of fire and had to break off from them in the chaos. Dex pulled a hand grenade and flung it. He heard the blast behind them as he helped Carlita to her feet. He and Hawk started returning fire. The severed leg of a CROP agent—torn off by the grenade—landed at their feet. Carlita almost tripped over it. She screamed at the sight of it.

More CROP agents swarmed into the woods. They were everywhere. They flung themselves behind a pile of logs. The ammo was getting low. The logs were the only barricade they had to shield themselves. They heard another explosion that went off at the extraction point. Through the trees they saw that the chain reaction caused by the dynamite had blown up the remaining two Burmaxx facilities. But the agents were gaining on them. A moment later helicopters showed up with spotlights searching through the trees.

Dex held up his NVs. The agents were preparing to close in on them. There was nowhere to run. They were surrounded. The reality of the situation inexplicably hit Dex and Hawk at the same time. The two of them turned and looked at each other.

Dex snapped the last clip into his M4 and muttered to his fellow commando. "Are you ready, my Indian brother?"

Hawk snapped in his last clip with a valiant smile. "As ready as you are my African brother!"

Carlita saw the look in their eyes and realized the two soldiers were about to do something she could not accept.

"Lieutenant, you can't. You can't do this!" she cried.

Dex looked at her. "Carlita, we're going to provide you with cover. When we start shooting, I want you to take off that way." Dex pointed in a southward direction, that was her only escape route.

"Do as he said, Carlita," said Hawk.

But Carlita didn't budge.

Danny Boy was bogged down behind a thicket bush about a hundred and fifty yards away. The had their NVs searching for the others when they saw Dex and Hawk suddenly rise from behind the pile of logs with their M4's blazing in the face of the onslaught of bullets flying at them. Dex and Hawk were discharging their weapons at the same time. Carlita went to the ground with her face buried in the dirt.

"Lieutenant, get down!" she shouted. She grabbed his leg and tried to pull him down.

Dex yanked his leg from her grip and shouted, "I told you to get out of here!"

A second later he heard Danny Boy's voice in his earpiece. "Dex, there's too many! We must pull back! Pull back, Dex!"

Dex and Hawk kept firing. Danny Boy and Sergio saw the agents moving in. Desperate to keep them from bearing down on them, they emerged from their position firing their weapons to draw the agents to themselves as they charged headlong into their barrage of gunfire.

Dex saw them running towards the agents, saw Sergio's body jerking backwards from the flurry of bullets that ate into him, saw him dropped to the ground and fall over sideways, saw Danny Boy fall a few feet away from him seconds later. All at once everything that sped up into overdrive in Dex's mind was suddenly moving in slow motion the moment he saw the two commandos lying motionless. Stunned, he stopped shooting. Carlita was still calling out to him as he stood there with his eyes fixed on the two fallen Navy SEALS. Seconds ago he heard Hawk's rifle ringing in his ears. That went silent too. When turned he expected to see him standing beside him. But he wasn't. He was lying on the ground sideways with half his face blown off.

"Hawk's gone!" Carlita cried.

Dex felt paralyzed. He couldn't move until she grabbed hold of his arm and pulled him out of harm's way.

"Stay down, Lieutenant!" she pleaded.

Dex checked the clip in his M4 and saw that it was empty. Then he picked up Hawk's gun and rose from behind the pile of logs again. He started firing at as many as the agents he could until his knees buckled from the impact of the enemy projectiles that found him. He fell headfirst into the logs, and rolled onto the ground, sweating, bleeding, and breathing heavily.

Carlita peeled off his jacket and tore open his shirt to check the wounds he sustained. "Why, Lieutenant . . .? Why didn't you listen to me? I told you not to do this, Lieutenant!"

Dex gazed into her eyes and answered, "I'm a soldier. Now, do me a favor. Call me Dex . . . That's an order!"

A slight smile materialized at the corner of his mouth.

Carlita smiled back. "You're a brave man. But you're stubborn . . . Dex!" she muttered.

Barely conscious, guilt began to percolate inside his head. If something happened to her it would mean he failed to deliver on his promise to Carlos that he would bring her out alive. She was examining his wounds when a spotlight from a helicopter suddenly put them under its bright beam. A few seconds later it shifted and lit up the CROP agents running towards them. The agents were less than two hundred yards away when a flurry of hot red flashes started streaking out of the sky straight at them. The helicopters they heard earlier started raining down missiles and fifty caliber rounds through the trees.

Carlita heard blood curdling screams coming from the agents. When she peeked over the log pile, she saw them fleeing in the opposite direction.

Surprised, she blurted, "Dex, I think those helicopters are shooting at the CROP agents!"

Dex used what strength he had left to push himself up enough to see the agents retreating.

"It's Carlos!" he muttered. "He's here. You'll be fine now . . ."

Carlita looked at him. "But . . . But how could he have known where to find us?"

Dex pointed at the ground and the emergency beacon locator he left lying activated beside Hawk when after he grabbed his assault rifle. Carlita turned and saw the small blinking red light. Then she slid next to Dex and cradled him in her arms while the helicopters continued lighting up the night. All they could hear was shelling and explosions. Twenty minutes later the deafening noise stopped. The woods went quiet, except for the wind howling in the treetops, twigs and branches snapping beneath the boots they heard approaching them. Carlita had the M4 ready to fire when a voice called out to her.

"Carlita Perez, put the gun down. You're safe now."

When she craned around, she saw nothing but shadows walking towards them. Wary, she blurted back, "Identify yourself!"

The voice of a man walking towards them replied. "I am the son of Hannibal and Mariana Colon/Tagola. Your brother Carlos."

Dex took hold of Carlita's hand, and uttered weakly. "I told you he was coming for you."

Carlita laid the rifle on the ground. She grabbed the small flashlight Dex's belt. As the shadows drew closer, she shined its beamed of light on the small army of men until the face of her brother appeared before her.

Astonished, she blurted, "Carlos!"

"Go with him, Carlita," said Dex.

Carlita noticed the Lieutenant's voice sounded weaker. He was fading in and out of consciousness.

"You're going with me," she muttered.

"No, I can't leave my men behind. I won't . . ."

Dex's eyes closed. Carlita shook him. "Dex . . . Dex, open your eyes. Dex, open your eyes!" she repeated.

Carlos bent towards her. "He's gone, Carlita. We must leave at once. The agents will be back with greater numbers in no time. We must hurry, my sister."

Carlita grabbed Dex's shoulder. "No! He can't be gone. You're not going to die on me now, Dex. Now, wake up!"

When he didn't' respond, Carlita began shouting at the top of her lungs. "Dex, come back! Come back! Come back! . . .

Part Sixteen
Total Recall

CHAPTER EIGHTY

San Diego, California

The words grew louder and louder. "Come back! Come back, Dex!" Dex still wasn't responding. Not until he felt that sharp sting to the side of his face from a good, hard, open hand slap. He flinched. And when he looked up from his favorite easy chair recliner, he found his cousin Chopper standing over him with his hand drawn back.

As soon as he saw his wife Gina standing behind him, he shouted, "Get out of the woods! You're both in danger!"

Chopper slapped him across the face again. "Come back, man," he repeated. "You trippin'?"

Dex shook his head. He looked at his wife like he'd snapped out of a deep sleep. "Gina . . . what are you doing here in L.A.? You're supposed to be in Philadelphia." He paused, glancing around the living room strangely. "Wait a minute . . . This isn't the apartment in South Central. Chopper, where am I? Where's my cat Boots?"

Gina placed her hand on her hip and rolled her big brown almond shaped eyes at him and frowned.

"You worried about a *cat*? You ought to be worried about telling me who is this Ms. Carlita chick I heard you spit out your mouth!" she snapped.

Chopper cut in. "Easy, Gina. Maybe he just had one of his flash-backs. Let me handle him. First of all, Cuz, you're not in L.A. anymore. We haven't been back to South Central since you got me out of the gang life. Remember? We have been living in San Diego for almost five years now."

"Why'd you slap me, bro?"

"How else was I supposed to bring you back. I told you I had to step out for a couple of hours to handle some business. But when I got back, I found you sitting there in that chair spaced out in some kind of deep state rambling on about secrets agents and assassins and so forth. You were hav-ing a conversation with yourself bro! I think you're losing it, bro!"

"Must have been a dream," Dex stated.

Gina interrupted, "A dream! Dex, I came home earlier than I expected. When I walked in a couple minutes after Chopper did, your eyes were wide open. And you were sitting in that recliner staring google-eyed at that magazine in your hands."

"What?"

Dex glanced down at the *Luxury Cruz* magazine. He hadn't realized he was still holding it. The picture of the glistening white yacht on the cover and its name *Magnificent Jewel* on the stern gave him a strange feeling. It was the same eerie feeling he got when he saw the two books on the stand beside the recliner and read the titles: *Chronicles of the Colombian Cartel* and *Assassin's Creed*. Even the face of the billionaire owner of Tilkerson Tech Enterprise he saw gracing the cover of Time magazine lying beside them jarred something inside his mind Chopper and Gina would never believe.

Not even he was certain about all the things he'd seen in his head. After he took a few seconds to backtrack the two hours he lost, he remem-bered he was watching the USC vs. UCLA football game with Chopper. Alfred the mail man pulled up and delivered the books and magazines to him. Gina called and left a message that she would be home after work.

The last thing he remembered was Chopper leaving. But he came back like he said he would. Now he was standing in front of him clutch-ing the TV remote he picked up off the end table. When he aimed it at flat screen and switched it from the Sports channel to CNN, Dex glanced at the screen and saw the face of the billionaire owner of Tilkerson Tech Enterprise pop on the screen with a breaking news alert.

"Turn that up!" he blurted.

Chopper looked at him like he lost his mind, but he turned the volume up anyway. The news woman's report in progress became the only vocal sound in the room:

"There are only two months remaining before this year's 2015 election polls close. The gap in votes between candidate Henry Tilkerson and his opponents appear to be steadily shrinking to his advantage down the last stretch of his campaign. He's only a few votes out from the front runner. No one took him seriously. No one thought he would get past the primaries. But the latest projections we see coming in now indicate that Henry Tilkerson's path to a campaign victory may very well come down to the following key swing states of Michigan, Ohio, Wisconsin, Texas, and Florida. . ."

"It couldn't be real," Dex mumbled to himself. His heart started beating like a drum. His mind suddenly filled with new questions. He needed answers now. A confirmation. Gina and Chopper would never be able to provide that. But he knew the exact place he had to go to speak with the one person he felt could.

CHAPTER EIGHTY-ONE

Burmaxx Veteran's Rehab Center
San Diego, California

Dex drove his Dodge Charger into the parking lot of the rehab center at 9:00 am Monday morning. With no explanation for the experience, he had the day before yesterday. Just before he walked through the imposing doors into the building, he cast a wary glance over his shoulder. The pretty dark brunette sitting behind the counter at the reception station looked up as he walked past.

"Good morning, Major Jones. I will let Dr. Petro know you're on your way."

Dex waved as he continued down the hall. When he approached the office door of Doctor Rubin Petro. He stopped and stared at that gold name plate like he usually did. Then he walked inside.

Dr. Petro looked up from behind his desk when he entered. "Hello, Major. Please, have a seat."

Dex took a seat. Except this time, he settled into a chair in front of the shrink's desk.

Petro smiled. "I wasn't expecting to see you back this soon. What's this serious matter you called and wanted to talk about?"

Dex responded, "I had a strange experience. Saturday, I was at home sitting on my recliner when I picked up this magazine to read it. I think I blanked out. It was like I left the living room. Except I didn't. I was right there in my chair the whole time. It was the weirdest episode I ever had."

"Really." Doctor Puerto sat up straight with interest. "When you said you felt like you left, where did you think you went to?"

Dex replied, "It felt like I went to Colombia."

Dr. Petro arched an eyebrow. "Colombia?"

"Yes. I know this might be a stretch, but I think it's where I was on my last mission!"

The psychiatrist looked at him dismissively.

"Look, Doc. I know it sounds strange. But I believe I was deployed there to carry out a mission code named Operation Lion's Den. We were there to recover a file when we were set up. It seemed real . . ."

"It wasn't," the psychiatrist interrupted.

"How do you know?" Dex shot back.

Dr. Petro hesitated, then replied, "Major Jones, you must understand that flashbacks and dreams can be delusional."

"This was no dream or flashback. No, this was different!"

"Major, there is no indication whatsoever in your military record about a mission in Colombia. But I do have your medical record of that serious head injury you suffered. It's not uncommon for a person to experience delusion after something like that . . ."

"Is that want you think? That this was just some delusional episode?"

"Major, you were in a coma for almost a week. I'm simply saying there are instances when people wake up from a comatose state experiencing memory loss. Others can wake up with false memories altogether."

Dex didn't like the logic of his assessment. The head shrink's demeanor seemed odd to him too. He thought he could play it off. But he couldn't.

"Perhaps you are right, Doc. But I saw a lot of things in my head Saturday. I remembered a lot of faces. And two of those faces belonged to you and Dr. Stephanic Castree."

The office went silent. Dr. Petro stared at him with a straight face to hide the nervous tension that seized him like an ill wind. He opened the drawer of his desk and quickly took out a bottle of Hc3 he grabbed.

"Have you taken any of the Hc3 Dr. Castree gave you last Thursday, Major? I think it'll help if you take a couple right now." He popped the cap and held the bottle out for him.

Dex noticed his hand trembling when he rebuffed it.

"You take 'em. I told you the pills do nothing for me. I know there is something going on with me. If I can't get the answer to what that is here, I will get it somewhere else!"

The minute Dex stood up to leave, Dr. Petro discreetly moved his hand beneath his desk and pressed a button there.

"You're not thinking logically about this, Major. Please, sit back down. Let's discuss this matter further," he stated.

"We've discussed it. There's nothing more to talk about."

Dex headed for the door. As soon as he stormed out and shut it behind him, Dr. Petro scooped up his cell phone from the desk and placed a call. On the second ring a man's voice came on the line.

"Hello, Dr. Petro. Everything going well at the center?"

"Not exactly. I'm calling about Major Jones. We have an emergency on our hands!"

CHAPTER EIGHTY-TWO

San Diego, California

Dex exited through the front door of the rehab center and headed for the parking lot. But he stopped in mid stride the moment he saw a Sedan roll up in front of his Dodge Charger. Two men in dark suits jump out. They peered through the car's window shield. Then they saw him. They started walking towards him. Dex bolted for the parking lot's exit.

"Major, stop! We want to talk to you," one of them shouted.

Dex kept going. He ran down the sidewalk and encountered two more men when they jumped out a black Cadillac. When they attempted to cut him off. He ran out into the traffic, dodging between vehicles. It was daring. The traffic was thick. But once he got to the other side of the street he ran to the far end of the block and stood with the small crowd of commuters he saw waiting at a transit stop for the city bus that turned the corner.

He was thinking about hopping the bus to elude the men. But then Deja vu crept into him. When turned to look over his shoulder as though he was certain he would an old white guy with a cane behind him. Instead, he saw a bright eyed little white kid staring up at him. The boy was holding his mother's hand when a grey BMW suddenly roared up to the transit and screeched to a stop.

When he spun back around, he locked eyes with the black man he saw behind the wheel. The gentleman bellowed through the car's window, "Major Jones, get in. The men coming after you are CROP agents!"

Dex watched him open the passenger side door.

Then he glanced at the men chasing him. He saw all four of them running up the sidewalk towards the transit stop. When he jumped in and shut the door, the car sped away from transit like a rocket.

"If those men are CROP agents, I must not be losing my mind," Dex stated.

"You're not, Major. It's only your memory slowly coming back to you," the gentleman replied.

Perplexed, Dex muttered, "What are you talking about?"

"Your memory was erased, Major. Everything Dr. Petro told you this morning was a lie to cover up the truth about that mission you went on back in 2011. Burmaxx's pharmaceutical developed the mind-altering drug Hyrophine Colybezentol . . . Hc1, Hc2, and Hc3. Dr. Stephani Castree used them with other techniques to place you under mind control. Dr. Rubin Petro was assigned to help keep you in the dark about your deployment. But once you stopped taking the Hc2, something happened they didn't expect would happen. The effect it had on you started to wear off."

Dex glanced at the review mirror and saw that CROP agents were no longer in sight. The driver made several turns before he pulled into a narrow alley where he stopped and got out. He went to the car's trunk and opened it. Dex didn't see what he took out. But when he walked around the side of car to the passenger door, he rapped on the window.

"Get out, Major."

Dex jumped out. "Why did we stop here?"

"So I could check to see if they tagged you," the man answered.

"Tagged me!"

"Yeah. Take off your jacket and shirt. Hurry!"

Dex took off the attire and let the man wave a device over the front of him that resembled a small metal detector. The moment he waved it over his back it began ticking.

"Why is it ticking?"

"That ticking sound means you have been implanted with a radio frequency identification tracking chip that has a GPS satellite signal."

The man placed a smaller device on his right shouldered blade to remove the foreign object from under the skin. Then he tossed it chip on the ground.

"Let's go. They might have already zeroed in on this location," he stated.

"I would have never known it was there," Dex muttered. "Maybe they were using that to control me too!"

"Not this time. Maybe when the military gave you that first discharge after your brother passed."

"How did you know about that?" Dex asked.

The man answered, "My source has lots of connections. You went to your brother's funeral in 2009 thinking it was some drug dealer on a corner in Cincinnati who shot and killed him. Not long after that, you became a soldier of fortune just so could get back at those you deemed responsible. Except you were singled out and primed to take out top drug traffickers for people in high places whenever they needed you to. You got all those contracts from that lawyer. But every one of them he passed onto you he came from the CIA."

Dex cut in, "If you're saying I was set up, but it wasn't the Hyrophine Colybezentol they used on me back then, then what . . .?"

"Ever hear anything about remote influencing, Major? Many scientists have delved into this study for years. Many populations around the world use data chips in appliances and devices. They think they are controlling them, never realizing it could be the other way around."

Dex took a closer look at the man's face like he'd seen him before.

"You look familiar to me," he stated abruptly. He pondered a long moment, trying to put a finger on it. Then he remembered. "You were on the island of Zanzibar. You were the African I saw wearing the white turban. You and Hector were in the garden with me and Carlos. The two of you followed us as we talked. I remember you came to Carlos to inform him Carlita had been taken into custody by CROP agents. But you spoke in fluent English."

"Yes. It was me you saw with Hector in the garden that day. My English is fluent because I am an African American, like you, Major. My name is Kenny Daws. The fact that you remembered this after nearly five years lets me know Carlos's plan worked out well after all . . ."

"What do you mean by his plan worked out?" Dex inquired.

Kenny replied, "Carlos already had plans for me to return. But it included keeping an eye on you when you came back to the U.S. from overseas. He wanted me to assemble a surveillance team. So, I did. We have been keeping close tabs on you from the day moved to San Diego with your wife and cousin. The mailman who delivered those books and magazines to you Saturday was keeping watch on you . . ."

"Alfred?"

"Alfred was his cover name."

"You said the drugs effect wore off when I quit taking it . . ."

"With a little help . . . yes. Carlos had his team of scientists in Africa to develop an anti-serum that would aid the depletion of the drug's potency. Once they did, we had to determine how to administer the serum into your system."

"How did you do it?"

"Oh, it's relatively easy. You drink a lot of Maxwell House. Alfred's job wasn't just delivering your mail, Major. Whenever you left home, on occasion he would go in and spike the coffee pot you left sitting on the stove."

Dex shook his head, surprised. "Alfred was inside my home . . ."

"It had to be done, Major. It was the only way you were going to regain your memory. You were so badly wounded during that gun battle with the Brits, Carlos thought you died. After you fell unconscious, Carla kept on pleading for Carlos to carry you and your men back with them. She convinced him. But when they heard the agents and British special forces returning. They had no other choice but to retreat, otherwise none of them would have made it to safety. They hid you and your men in the woods with a plan to come back for you. But when they came back, they discovered British forces found the hiding place and got to you first. When they checked your vitals, they discovered you still had a pulse. After they took you into custody you were later transferred to Great Britain."

"What happen to my team members?"

"No one knows."

"Why didn't they just kill me?"

"Carlos was still at large. You were kept alive so they could interrogate you. They figured they could extract information out of you that would lead them to him. What they didn't know was that Carlos had moles of his own planted in the British intelligence service who told him you were still alive. When he found this out, he sent a swift message to the surviving members of the Royal Order. He told them that if any further harm came to you, he would make sure the file he still possesses on them would go viral. They were still not willing to risk that kind of exposure. So, their only option was to accept the agreement of his new set of demands. He demanded that you be immediately released from the custody of the authorities in Great Britain and returned to America. And that the trillions of dollars they have hoarded continues to be divided between third world countries in Africa and other geographical locations. They had to begin a buildup of brand-new homes to provide shelter for the thousands of homeless people living in tent cities across America. They had to establish a timeline to start cutting million-dollar checks and mailing them out to the descendant of former slaves in the U.S. and elsewhere. Reparations, Carlos calls it. A back payment he said was long overdue!"

"What about their candidate, Henry Tilkerson? I saw him on the news. The election is almost over. The polls show he's running a very close race."

Kenny replied, "Tilkerson has his own personal objectives. If he wins, he will certainly push the kind of protocol the Royal Order wants to implement. His co-conspirators are in place. And they are pumping millions of dark untraceable dollars into his campaign to make sure he will be the one to replace president D'kembi. They are pampering a new wave of propaganda to recruit new followers of the protocol. And it includes targeting those blue voters they feel voted the wrong way when they helped to elect president D'kembi."

Kenny paused before his next words came out with emphasis.

"Major, if this candidate wins, he will add to mayhem. He will embrace violence and hate speech by domestic terrorist groups, turn neighbors against neighbors, whip up false flags to launch wars with other countries. The CROP's political representatives aligning themselves with him will stand before TV cameras and talk of ending poverty, inequality, crime, and providing healthcare to all, yet remain complicit as loyal agents to the CROP's protocol, a protocol which calls on them to prefer their own and to act in accordance with upholding of appears to be a systemic unequal practice of double standards. The fact is this, Major, people at the highest levels of the federal government right on down to the state and local municipal communities are complaining about the disparities and discrimination that still exists in housing, education, employment, criminal justice, healthcare, and many other areas. With the emergence of the red media, Tilkerson will rely on him and his followers to continue painting foreigners, immigration, and the left as the problem. He views them as deplorable anti-nationalists. Only because the madness of the CROP's cognitive training is designed to displace the public's focus away from the Royal Order's ultimate objective of taking control of the country's entire government using the principal rule of the hidden fraternities, Ordo ab chao, they call it."

"What's it mean?" Dex asked.

"It means order out of chaos. And this particular principal of stoking up fear, grief, and other intense emotions in people will not cease until they have tricked the people into surrendering their rights, religious beliefs, and other freedoms to the handpicked government officials they have acting in concert to get them one step closer to bringing the entire nation under the banner of authoritarianism."

"There has to be a way to stop them!" Dex asserted.

"Unity, Major. And that would take people from all racial and ethnic backgrounds coming together to resist the spectrum of discontent and division the CROP and their agents want to spread around the world."

Dex glanced at the crescent pendant hanging from Kenny's necklace. "I noticed Carlos wearing a silver crescent pedant like that when we talked in Zanzibar. I'm curious how you wound up in Africa with him and Hector Colon?"

"Hector and I are close friends. When he told me about this job Carlos was offering, I took it. For a man who hasn't seen much of the world, flying around the globe was indeed an opportunity of lifetime. In Africa my thinking changed. I learned about the culture and real history of our African ancestors. I learned that many of them were Muslims. And I said to myself that when I return to Africa my daughter would be at my side. It's about time for you to consider returning too, Major."

Dex looked at him quizzically. "That sounds like an invitation you're offering me."

Kenny turned to face him. "It is. But a warning also."

"For what?"

"You see, you were safe in America while you were under that mind control. But you snapped out of it and learned the truth. Learning the truth makes you a threat to the Royal Order all over again, Major. The way I see it, you don't have much of an option. Right now, I am heading to a private airstrip. There's a plane waiting to fly us back to Africa. I advise you to accompany me."

Dex peered out the windshield thinking about all the dangers he faced on that last mission with a total recollection of every event that occurred. It took only a few seconds to make his decision.

"Before we get on that plane there's a couple of people we must pick up. I won't leave without them," he stated.

Kenny glanced at his watch. Then he pulled out his cell phone and made a call. Someone picked up on the first ring.

"Hello, Mr. Daws. What can I do for you?" a man muttered.

Kenny replied, "Tell the pilot Major Jones and I will be a little late. We have one more stop to make."

CHAPTER EIGHTY-THREE

Rayburn House Office Building
Washington, DC
Tuesday July 11, 2016

(R) Chairman: "Lieutenant Colonel James Burke. I understand you are here today to provide testimony for this committee's inquiry into the military operation that reportedly took place in South America in the year 2011. Correct?"

Colonel Burke: "Yes."

(R) Chairman: "And we are referring to a mission code named Operation Lion's Den."

Colonel Burke: "Correct, sir."

(R) Chairman: "And you are here to also testify under oath about the extent of you and CIA deputy director Winston Bedford's roles in regard to this operation."

Colonel Burke: "To the best of my recollection Mr. Chairman. Yes."

(R) Chairman: "Let me just say Colonel that your presence at this hearing is very much appreciated. And that I hope my colleagues on the other side of the isle will share that same sentiment. With that, I now recognize the gentleman from Illinois."

(D) Illinois: "Thank you Mr. Chairman. Colonel let me start by saying I do appreciate you showing up today. And I would also appreciate it if you helped us get to the bottom of what exactly occurred. I have a report in front of me prepared by the special council assigned to handle the investigation into Operation Lion's Den in 2011. It refers to the American platoon of Navy SEALS and Army Rangers who stormed into a village outside of Medellin to infiltrate the compound of a cartel drug boss name Ortega Diez. It states unequivocally that the action of those soldiers was authorized by you and deputy director Bedford. Is that an accurate statement?"

Lt. Colonel: "Yes, Senator."

(D) Illinois: "You admitted in the deposition you gave back in 2011 that you shared this information with the CIA director Charles Eastlake and FBI director Harland McCurry."

Lt. Colonel: "Senator first, I believe my authorization was for the good of the United States. Yes, I did speak with director Eastlake about the mission. He then relayed this to the president. I also revisited the subject during a conference call with the president, director Eastlake, and director McCurry."

(D) Illinois: "Did deputy director Bedford also convey this information to the president?"

Lt. Colonel: "That I don't know."

(D) Illinois: "In 2013, you met with members of the House Select Committee to answer questions regarding confidential information they received about deputy director Bedford's alleged management of a secret team of assassins. Why did you refuse to answer the questions regarding this information when you were asked about it?"

Lt. Colonel: "It sounded far-fetched. And I felt it was more appropriate for the committee to address that issue with the deputy director of operations himself. Not me!"

(D) Illinois: Colonel I read the entire report of the House Select Committee. And there is conflict in what your testimony. In 2013, you testified deputy director Winston Bedford knew nothing about Operation Lion's Den. But today you have admitted before this committee that you and him both authorized it. Is it that you have changed your tune because new information has surfaced?"

Lt. Colonel: "I didn't recall. I think I just misspoke, Senator . . ."

(D) Illinois: "Is that something you do often, Colonel?"

Lt. Colonel: "No."

(D) Illinois: "Okay, so did deputy director Bedford manage a hit team?"

Lt. Colonel: Senator, information like that is considered classified. I couldn't answer that."

(D) Illinois: "Then I respectfully motion for the chairman to direct this witness to answer the question!"

(R) Missouri: "The witness has already answered it. It's a question he feels should be taken up with the deputy director!"

(R) Chairman: "The motion is denied. The gentleman from Illinois's time has expired. I now recognize the gentleman from Iowa. You have five minutes, Senator."

(R) Iowa: "Thank you, Mr. Chairman. Colonel, you are a decorated official of the U.S. Navy. Your record is impeccable. My democratic colleague is a bit over the line. Furthermore, it is my opinion that the independent special counsel's investigation is a witch hunt and waste of taxpayers' dollars. And there is no doubt in my mind that your authorization of that operation was given for the greater benefit of the country!"

(D) Illinois: "Mr. Chairman, I motion for point of order. The Senator's false assertions are not in precedence with the rules of these proceedings . . ."

(R) Chairman: "Motion denied. The Senator from Iowa will proceed."

(R) Iowa: "I have only one more question for you, Colonel. Have you ever been served with any indictment by the DOJ for the frivolous circus my Democratic colleagues are trying to make out of this?"

Lt. Colonel: "No, sir."

(R) Iowa: "I yield the rest of my time, Mr. Chairman."

(R) Chairman: "The chair recognizes the gentlewoman from California for five minutes."

(D) California: "Thank you, Mr. Chairman. Colonel Burke, in May of 2014 officials from the Miami Dade County DEA Division said several informants came forward to provide information on the charges that narcotics and weapons were being exchanged between American military officials and members of a cartel faction in Cali, Colombia. This report was provided by State Department officials who said they took statements from those same informants. We later learned one of the informants was identified as Ms. Adriana Diez. Does that name ring a bell with you?"

Lt. Colonel: "No it doesn't Senator."

(D) California: "Ms. Diez is the sister of Ortega Diez. The very man they discovered killed alongside an FBI agent Alex Weiss. Ms. Diez indicated that her brother was doing business with U.S. Navy officials she knew to be involved with his smuggling activities. I'm wondering why you refused to discuss the accuracy of her claims with the State Department?"

Lt. Colonel: "I wouldn't say I refused, Senator . . ."

(D) California: "Seems that way to me! The report suggests you were stonewalling their investigation like you are doing before this committee today."

Lt. Colonel: "That's preposterous! I disagree with that notion, Senator. And quite frankly, Senator, I find it offensive!"

(D) California: "What's preposterous, Colonel, is how evasive you have been during this entire inquiry!"

(R) Virginia: "Mr. Chairman, point order. She is badgering the witness . . ."

(D) California: "He's avoiding the pertinent questions of this committee!"

Lt. Colonel: "I have been advised by counsel not to answer certain questions, Senator."

(D) California: "So that you continue stonewalling. Right?"

Lt. Colonel: "No, Senator. So that I can invoke my 5th amendment right!"

(D) California: "Because you're hiding something. But trust me. We are going to find out what that is, Colonel!"

(R) Virginia: "Mr. Chairman, point of order. The Senator has crossed the line. She is continuing to badger the witness with disparaging unsubstantiated remarks outside the committee's rules of conduct!"

(D) California: "Senator, you are being complicit to the Colonel's stonewalling . . ."

(R) Chairman: [Gavel] ". . . Regular order! Regular order! The gentlewoman has one minute left. There will be no more of this exchange."

(D) California: "Colonel Burke, were you at any time aware of the federal bureau's investigation into Ortega Diez?"

Lt. Colonel: "I don't recall."

(D) California: "Well I would certainly think a decorated official of the navy like yourself would be able to answer this next question. In 2011, there was a report of an explosion that occurred in the waters of the North Atlantic. It was later discovered that yacht was struck by a Russian torpedo. Crewmen aboard a U.S. navy vessel was said to have rescued an elderly British woman from a life raft surround by a pod of Orcas that appeared to be shielding it. Were you aware of this report, Colonel?"

Lt. Colonel: "I have no recollection of that."

(R) Chairman: "The gentlewoman's time has expired . . ."

(D) California: "One more question, if I may, Mr. Chairman . . ."

(R) Chairman: "Make it quick!"

(D) California: "Colonel Burke, yesterday the special council informed this committee they received an anonymous email alleging the abbreviated letters CROP were in some way connected to Operation Lion's Den. Can you tell this committee anything about what these letters might represent?"

Lt. Colonel: "Senator, I invoke the 5th."

Part Eighteen
DAR–AL–ISLAM

CHAPTER EIGHTY-FOUR

Cairo, Egypt
Nine Months Later

From a loudspeaker on Friday, the voice of the Muhezzin could be heard calling Muslims to their holy day prayer service across the city. Kenny, Hector, Carlos, and Dex were among the procession of Muslim men walking towards the mosque of Ahmad Ibn Tulun. Carlita, Gabriela, Dex's wife Gina, and Kenny's daughter Tia, walked separately with a procession of women wearing hijabs as a sign of modesty.

Dex didn't imagine he and Gina converting to Islam when they traveled to Africa. But he understood why the others had now. They discovered the faith wasn't like it was often portrayed in the media. Many people were often bombarded with misconceptions and had no real understanding of its true teachings. Had they, they would have known the name Allah in Arabic meant God. And that God was called Allah even by Arabic speaking Christians and millions of people who spoke the language throughout the continent of Africa. They would have known Islam meant submission to one omnipotent God. And that the Muslim man and woman performed the act of submitting to the will of Allah alone through their verbal and physical displays of worship based on the faith's five pillars; Shadadah-testifying there is no God but Allah and Muhammad (SAW) is his messenger; Salat-prayer; Zakat-Charity; Saum-Fasting in the month of Ramadan; Hajj-Pilgrimage to the Holy Kabah in Mecca.

Dex and his wife discovered that Islam wasn't just meant for the Arabian people. It applied to every single race and ethnicity of people on the face of the planet. And that anyone who uttered the Shadah; testifying there is no God but Allah, and that Muhammad was His messenger, became a part of the universal Muslim community.

Now that they were within the fold of Islam, they were required to adhere to the Six Articles of Faith 1. Belief in Allah (God's) oneness without setting up idols, intercessors, and His human creations to worship besides Him; 2. Belief in His Angels; 3. Belief in the books He revealed; the Old Testament of the Torah revealed to Musa (Moses), the Gospel revealed to Issa (Jesus), the Psalms revealed to Dawud (David), the Holy Qur'an revealed to Muhammad to convey and clarify His original message in the scriptures of the previous books which remains free of any changes; 4. Belief in His many messengers with Muhammad being the last and SEAL; 5. Belief in the Day of Judgement; 6. Belief in His Divine Decree.

On their way to the mosque, Dex found himself thinking about how far he'd come. He had undergone cognitive training, taught to kill, go into war zones, and had come home unappreciated in the aftermath of his service like so many other thousands of veterans.

Kenny was thinking about his own experience as an ex-con. He and Hector and Carlos were all deemed undesirables—labeled villains, criminalized, wrote off as though they could never be rehabilitated enough to contribute anything constructive. It seemed improbable they could change. But they discovered Islam provided a path to redemption as well as a new way of life. They were migrants in a land where people lived not by laws charted in the private chambers of men inclined to manipulate them with double standards and the constant changing ideologies that influenced them. The people were taught to adhere to the laws set forth by God which encompassed all aspects of their lives from politics, sciences, economics, legislation, family, and human rights.

Individual bad acts by members of Islamic society couldn't define the religion's teachings they learned. There were members of plenty other societies who watched awful scenes of violence and sexual immoralities playing out on televisions sets and the streets of their major cities. Some people simply see it as a freedom of entertainment to satisfy the senses and excite passions with no regard to the degenerating affects it has upon the minds and morals of populations in the long run.

What they learned was that Muslims were taught to avoid excess waste and overindulgence in material wealth by living in modesty, to not earn money to boast and squander riches on frivolities, to not overlook giving assistance to the homeless and people experiencing famine. The teachings instilled in its followers to keep this social conscious of the helping needy so that the element of charity would not be lost. So that they could safeguard the unity of family and nation in face of threats and demands by foreign governments calling on them to part with their way of life.

Carlos was no longer blind to the reality of the people on this planet whose sole interest was in possessing power and control over wealth and other human beings. Therefore, he denounced his trade. And he gave up his riches to help the needy because he came realize that the world itself was nothing more than one big round village. And the only one he believed possessed all power and control of its wealth and its inhabitants was Allah!

Then he revealed his plan for Kenny to go back home to his country. First, he told him a story about mane lions roaming the Serengeti. Then he told him he believed he possessed that same courage to be the lion of black America who would give them the truth about everything he learned in the motherland about African culture and Islam.

Kenny believed there was always hope for the present and future generations of African Americans who began the research into their African heritage and Muslim ancestry. Such vital research was a necessity to build back the bonds of unity and solidarity to pave the way of reclaiming the identity and culture tied to them. Just how many would make the migration as they did, Kenny didn't know. He just knew the mental migration had to come before the physical one. And it would require acute awareness and relinquishment of mental training towards the glorification of violence, fame, and material wealth, for the betterment of humanity.

When they reached the mosque of Ahmad Ibn Tulun, the four of them stood for a moment, gazing at the astonishingly crafted architecture and unique minaret. Once inside, they removed their shoes and went to the bathing font to wash their hands, faces, forearms, head, and feet according to ritual. From there, the joined the congregation of Muslim men seated on the musella waiting for the Imam to come out to the mimbar and deliver his kutbah (sermon). When came out the voice of muezzin chanted another call. The Imam's kutbah followed. And when he was done, he descended the mimbar to lead the congregation in prayer. A short call by the muezzin went out. Kenny, Hector, Carlos, and Dex rose with the other men on the musella to align themselves behind the Imam prayer leader.

They stood quietly, waiting for the prayer to begin. Standing there, the harsh realities of brutal conflicts, greed, hate, and divisiveness that blurred the visions of men and put at risk the future of generations to come rushed up in Kenny's mind. Standing there, he was thankful for what he learned. Standing there, he was sure what the world needed most was the Muslim prayer for guidance on the opening chapter of the Holy Qur'an. A prayer recited by every Muslim man and woman in each of their five daily prayers. A prayer the Imam was preparing to recite for everyone in attendance at the Friday prayer service.

He stood facing east towards Mecca, Arabia with the entire congregation behind him. A moment later the Imam raised both of his hands to his ears and uttered. "Allahu Ahkbar!" Allah is the Greatest!

The prayer began.

ABOUT RONENIN DUVAL

R onenin Duval is a native of Michigan. He's working toward his business-admin degree and hopes to continue with writing. He studies languages, reads, and works out. *Village Boss* is his first novel.

Fresh Ink Group

Independent Multi-media Publisher

Fresh Ink Group / Push Pull Press

Voice of Indie / GeezWriter

Hardcovers
Softcovers
All Ebook Formats
Audiobooks
Podcasts
Worldwide Distribution

Indie Author Services
Book Development, Editing, Proofing
Graphic/Cover Design
Video/Trailer Production
Website Creation
Social Media Marketing
Writing Contests
Writers' Blogs

Authors
Editors
Artists
Experts
Professionals

FreshInkGroup.com
info@FreshInkGroup.com
Twitter: @FreshInkGroup
Facebook.com/FreshInkGroup
LinkedIn: Fresh Ink Group

Fresh Ink Group
FreshInkGroup.com